American Dream

1620-1765

4 Stories in 1

BARBOUR
PUBLISHING

Sarah's New World © 2004 by Barbour Publishing, Inc.
Rebekah in Danger © 2004 by Barbour Publishing, Inc.
Maggie's Dare © 2005 by Barbour Publishing, Inc.
Lizzie and the Redcoat © 2006 by Barbour Publishing, Inc.

ISBN 978-1-61626-462-8

All scripture quotations are taken from the King James Version of the Bible.

Cover design: Greg Jackson, Thinkpen Design

Published by Barbour Publishing, Inc., P.O. Box 719, Uhrichsville, Ohio 44683, www.barbourbooks.com

Our mission is to publish and distribute inspirational products offering exceptional value and biblical encouragement to the masses.

 Member of the
Evangelical Christian
Publishers Association

Printed in the United States of America.
Bethany Press International, Bloomington, MN 55438; July 2011; D10002871

Sarah's New World

Colleen L. Reece

A Note to Readers

You won't find ten-year-old Sarah Smythe and her twelve-year-old brother John in history books or on the passenger list of the sailing ship, the *Mayflower*. Yet they are real in the sense that they represent the brave children and teens who fled with their parents from England and Holland almost four hundred years ago. In America, the "New World," the Pilgrims could worship God according to their own beliefs and without persecution.

The events are real or based on real happenings. Also real are persons such as John Carver, William Brewster, William Bradford, Captain Myles Standish, and many others who sacrificed much to make a country where people could be free.

Contents

CHAPTER 1

Spies

Twelve-year-old John Smythe lay flat on the floor of the dark hallway. His right ear was pressed against the crack under the door to the parlor. He strained to make out what his parents' low voices were saying.

Just then, John heard footsteps running down the hall, and before he could move, hard wooden shoes ran into his side.

"Oomph!" John quickly covered his mouth to muffle the groan he couldn't hold back. Rubbing his bruised body, he shifted position and looked up at his ten-year-old sister, Sarah.

"Shh," he hissed.

Sarah clasped her hands against the long, white apron that covered her dark work dress and demanded, "John Smythe, what are you doing? If Father and Mother catch you, they'll—"

"They won't if you keep your voice down," he warned in a whisper. "I want to know what they're saying."

"You're spying!" Sarah accused. "Aren't you ever going to grow up? You're twelve years old—almost a man—not a three-year-old child to be listening at doors!"

"Can't you be quiet?" John hissed. He reached up a strong, wiry arm and pulled her down next to him. "You need to hear this, Sarah. It concerns us." Excitement filled his voice.

"I don't care," she whispered back. "It's wrong to listen in on others." Sarah started to scramble up, but her father's raised voice pinned her to the floor beside John.

"I see no help for it, Abigail. If we are to remain strong and true, we cannot stay longer in Holland."

"But William," Mother protested. "Is there no other way?"

Father spoke again. "Holland offered us a place of refuge and peace when we needed it. But now it is time to move on. Holland can never be our real home." He sounded sad.

"Was it not enough that we fled England before John and Sarah were born?" Mother cried.

John and Sarah looked at each other with concern. They rarely heard their parents disagree with each other like this.

"We've been here twelve years, William. Now you wish to uproot us again."

"We must find a country where we can worship freely, a place where our church will be safe from bad influences," Father replied.

A long silence followed. John edged closer to the door, not wanting to miss a single word. *Move? When? Where?* Surely they would not return to England, where they had been persecuted for worshiping God in their own way. News from across the water said things were no better in England now than when the first of their people had fled to Holland.

"I wonder if there is such a place this side of heaven." Mother sounded like she wanted to cry. "Where do you and the other men have in mind for us to go?"

John felt Sarah grab his arm. They both held their breath, waiting for Father's answer.

Father's deep voice rolled out like thunder. "The New World. America."

"America!" John forgot all about the need for silence and let out a whoop of delight. He rose to his knees and grabbed Sarah's hand. "Did you hear that?"

"Shh!" Sarah ordered, but it was too late. Quick footsteps sounded from the parlor, and the door was flung open wide.

Off balance, John clutched harder at his sister's hand, but he couldn't save himself from falling. He sprawled inside the parlor, dragging Sarah with him and landing on one elbow.

"Ow!" He released his sister, blinked in the more brightly lit room, and rubbed his elbow.

Mother gasped in dismay.

"What is the meaning of this?" Father's stern voice brought John to his feet.

Glancing at his sister, John could see Sarah's face was red with shame and that she was blinking hard to keep back the tears that filled her green eyes.

"It's not her fault," John confessed. His straight, cropped, brown hair shone in the candlelight. The big brown eyes that sometimes looked innocent and at other times sparkled with mischief looked enormous. "Sarah came in and stumbled over me. I told her to stay."

He swallowed hard, stopped rubbing his sore el and mumbled, "You always say Sarah is her brother's tried to make me stop spying, but I wanted to h

John's heart warmed a little as he caught Sarah's grateful look, but Father's answer took away the good feeling. "I don't find in the Bible that being a brother's keeper means joining in his mischief if he doesn't stop when warned."

Sarah stumbled to her feet and stood behind John. Together they awaited judgment. While Father and Mother loved their children, they also expected John and Sarah to obey.

"I'm disappointed in you both," Mother told them.

Sarah dug her toe into the woven rug and avoided looking at her mother's eyes that were so much like her own.

"So am I." Father sounded disapproving. "Sit down, please." He waited until they sat, facing each other. "I am particularly disappointed in you because of what lies ahead." He sighed and a shadow crossed his face. "In a short time, many of our people will be leaving Holland."

"For America," John eagerly said.

Father looked at him sternly.

John bit his lip and looked miserable.

"Most of the other families will be leaving all but their oldest children in Holland, but if your mother and I decide to go, we will want to keep our family together."

"You mean we would leave Holland forever?" Sarah twisted her hands beneath her apron and stared at her parents. "But what about all our friends? I've never lived anywhere but here in Leiden, and I don't want to leave Gretchen behind."

Father closed his eyes for a moment. "Leaving friends is never easy. When your mother and I left England and moved Holland, we, too, had to leave the village we had grown up You've heard us tell you the story many times. But maybe telling you more of the details will help you understand why we may have to leave Leiden now."

"You lived in Scrooby, didn't you, Father?" John asked eagerly.

"Yes," Father replied, looking out the darkened window as if he could see his childhood home. "It was a poor English village on the Great North Road between London and Edinburgh, Scotland. The road had a big name, but it was actually a narrow dirt lane used by rich people who came to hunt red deer in Sherwood Forest."

"We lived in a simple cottage," Mother continued, "but nearby was a great manor house, surrounded by a moat. The house was so large it contained everything anyone needed, including a bakery and even a chapel. But only the people from the manor house and their guests could hunt the deer. Those of us in the village lived on porridge and bread. As a special treat, sometimes we'd get a bit of fish or meat."

"That doesn't seem fair," John interrupted. "God made the deer, didn't He? So why couldn't everyone hunt them?"

"The deer were claimed by the king, and it was against the law for poor people who needed food to hunt them," explained his father. "Anyone caught hunting or eating the king's deer was punished—some were even hanged."

"How awful!" Sarah's green eyes flashed, and she tossed her head so hard that her long brown braids bounced against her back.

"But that wasn't the worst problem we faced," her mother added. "Because we wouldn't worship God the way King James wanted us to, we couldn't go to church. We had to meet in barns like criminals."

"Why did King James tell you how to worship God?" Sarah wanted to know.

"He said that 'kings are God's lieutenants and sit on God's throne,'" Father explained. "Everyone else had to do just what he said. We couldn't even ask questions! The king was afraid. If common people like us were allowed to choose their own church leaders and worship the way they believed God wanted them to, King James worried that they'd want to do the same thing in government. Then he wouldn't be so powerful.

"Our leaders became concerned about how we would survive. Elder Brewster, Edward Winslow, and William Bradford met secretly in a barn to discuss possible solutions."

"Didn't William Bradford become part of our group when he was only seventeen?" John asked.

"Yes, he did," Father answered. "That action angered the aunts and uncles who had brought him up—William's parents died when he was about nine. William's uncles ordered him, 'Give up this path to destruction. If you join that treasonous, despised group, the king's tax collectors will surely seize your land. You will be penniless, scorned, and driven out of the country.'

"William proudly said, 'I accept the king as ruler of the country. I pay my taxes but kneel to no man. I also choose my own way to worship God.'"

John's face glowed with pride as he thought of what courage it had taken for seventeen-year-old William Bradford to take such a stand.

"So what happened at the meeting?" Sarah asked.

"The meeting in the barn started with prayer," Father

answered. "Then Elder Brewster's voice rang out: 'Our people must suffer at the hands of the king's men no more! We have been taxed unmercifully. How can we go on living in a country where desperate persons are hanged for stealing a loaf of bread to keep their little ones from starving? We here this day are in danger of being thrown into jail for the rest of our lives. Or hanged on the gallows for daring to worship God in our own way! Thousands of the poor can find no work. They—'

"A horse neighed, and Elder Brewster stopped talking," Father said. "Heavy footsteps thudded on the hard ground outside the barn. William Bradford held up a warning hand. The wooden door slowly creaked open."

CHAPTER 2

Troublesome Times

"What happened?" John asked breathlessly.

"The door opened just enough to let in John Carver and our preacher, John Robinson," Father answered.

John and Sarah sighed with relief.

"John Robinson looked very stern," Father continued.

"But he is always kind to us," Sarah protested.

"Yes, but our leaders were facing a dangerous situation. Even being discovered meeting together could have landed them in prison for life, and John Robinson had just learned that two more of their followers had been sent to the dungeons. They were turned in by their own neighbors."

John gasped. "Couldn't you even trust the people you'd grown up with to keep you safe?"

"No," Mother said. "Girls and boys I had grown up playing with were willing to tell the king's men about our meetings."

"Our leaders decided it was too dangerous to stay in England any longer," Father said. "But even that decision brought problems. The law said that anyone leaving the country had to have permission. Because of our religious beliefs, we were considered traitors. The king would never agree to our leaving.

"But William Brewster reminded us that King James is not the final power on earth. 'The King of heaven and earth knows our needs,' he told us."

"It must have been hard to plan your escape without someone finding out about it and letting the king's men know," John observed.

"It was not only hard," Father replied, "it was impossible. On a dark night late in 1607, our group of men, women, and children slipped out of town and walked silently to a seaport called Boston on the east coast of England. At last we reached the small creek where a captain had promised to meet us. We waited for two days. Nothing happened, and we were afraid that someone would find us. Finally, on the second night, the captain appeared, let us aboard his ship, and collected his fee.

"Just when we thought that at last we were safe, someone bellowed, 'Stop where you are!'"

"I don't understand," Sarah said. "What happened?"

"The captain had betrayed us," Father told his family. "The officials loaded us all into smaller boats and took us ashore. We were robbed of everything we had and marched through the streets. Then we were locked up for a month before we were ordered back to our homes. Even time in prison, however, didn't change our minds. We were determined to be free."

"But everyone must have been watching you," John said.

"They were," Mother said. "And it wasn't until the next spring that we tried again to escape. This time it was even harder. All of us women and children were loaded on a small boat to sail down the River Ryton.

"Saying good-bye to our husbands and fathers was the hardest thing we'd ever done. The men and older boys disappeared into the dark and began the forty-mile walk to our secret meeting place. Then disaster struck. Our boat stuck in the mud at low tide. As day broke and people from a nearby village discovered us, they armed themselves with guns and clubs and came running toward us."

Father continued the story. "The Dutch skipper of the boat we had hired sent a dinghy to bring some of the men aboard. When he saw the mob of villagers heading toward the women and children, he panicked. He hoisted the sails, raised anchor, and sailed away!

"Those of us men who were still on shore ran to help the trapped women and children. We were arrested and hauled from place to place. The authorities didn't know what to do with us. We hadn't committed a crime, but we couldn't be sent back to our old villages because our homes had been sold."

Sarah blinked to keep back her tears. She had no idea that her parents had gone through so many hard times in England.

"Finally," Father said, "that summer we were released and sailed to Amsterdam."

"Why didn't you stay there?" Sarah asked.

"Amsterdam is a noisy city that didn't have much in common with quiet little Scrooby," answered Mother.

"And some of our group had serious arguments with each other," admitted Father. "After about a year, we moved the forty miles here to Leiden, and until recently we've been content. But our reasons for leaving Holland will have to wait for another day. It's late, so let's say our prayers and get to bed."

John opened his eyes and stared around his tiny room. He slid farther down in bed. The small amount of light in his room told him how early it was, too early even for Father and Mother to be up getting ready for the new day. Yet he felt so wide awake he knew he couldn't go back to sleep. He wondered what he could do that wouldn't wake up his parents. Father worked hard in the factory, and Mother worked at the loom. They both needed their rest.

"John, are you awake?" Sarah's voice whispered from the doorway of his room.

"Of course," he said, peering out at her over his coverlet. "Who can sleep when we may be going to America? Oh, Sarah, it's going to be wonderful!"

Sarah perched on a stool by his bed and pulled her shawl closer around her. "I just don't want to leave Leiden. It's so beautiful, and our friends are all here."

John's brown hair stood straight up from sleeping. "I'm sorry everyone won't be going, but think of what fun those who do go will have."

"I still don't understand why any of us have to leave Holland."

John awkwardly patted her hand, the way he used to do when they were both small. "There are a lot of reasons. I heard Father say—"

"You've been listening again," Sarah accused.

"Do you want me to answer your question or not?" he demanded.

"Yes, please."

"Pastor Robinson and our elders are concerned because we are getting more like the Dutch every day. We dress like them. We talk like them. I like the Dutch ways." His brown gaze bored into her green eyes. "The Dutch are fun! They laugh and dance and sing, even on the Sabbath. What is wrong with dancing and singing? God wants us to be happy, doesn't He?"

John didn't wait for an answer. "Sometimes I wish our church weren't so strict, don't you? Sarah, we aren't even allowed to smile in church, and the sermons are so long!"

Sarah's hands flew to her ears. A few weeks earlier, the deaconess had boxed them because Sarah had whispered to John. "It's no fun having your ears boxed," she admitted.

John made an awful face. "It's worse being whipped with a birch rod. All I did was smile when Elder Brewster told about poor old Jonah sitting in the hot sun and grumbling because a worm had eaten the plant that had given him shade."

John stretched and yawned. "It just seems like Jonah would have learned his lesson after the big fish spit him out and he was safe."

"It just seems like you would learn *your* lesson after you got us in trouble," Sarah teased.

He only grinned. "Run back to bed, little sister. It's almost time for Father and Mother to get up."

"I may be a whole lot shorter, but I'm only two years younger than you are," Sarah reminded him. "And say what you will, life in Leiden is never going to be the same." She scooted out the door and tiptoed to her own room, and a few minutes later John heard her clatter to breakfast in the wooden shoes she liked so well.

As the day continued, John had to admit that Sarah was right about life in Leiden changing. Gossip and rumors ran wild in every home, in factories, and in fields. His neighbor Hans, who was six months older than John, was full of news about war.

"It's feared that Spain will attack Holland," the tall, blond boy told John as they walked along the canal. "If Spain wins, Holland will become a Catholic country instead of a Protestant one, and Spain's royal family will rule over us. I only wish I were older and could sign up on a Dutch ship. Then I'd be able to protect my country."

"Some of the older boys from our group already have," John said. "What an adventure that would be."

"Almost as much of an adventure as that wild tale I've heard about some of your people going to the New World," Hans said, his long legs easily keeping pace with John. "Do you know anything about it?"

"There's been a lot of talk," John answered, careful not to reveal what his parents had told him, "but no one's made any final decision that I've heard of. Of course, people are worried that we wouldn't be able to worship freely if Holland lost the war."

"No need to worry about that," Hans argued. "We've got a navy that's more than ready to defend us. Besides," he added, his blue eyes lighting up with mischief, "if you left Leiden, who'd be able to challenge me in those skating races every winter?"

"Good point," John agreed, "although this winter *you'd* better be ready to be the challenger. I'm planning on winning those races." He glanced regretfully up at the sun. "It's getting late. I'd better run home and get my chores done."

"That's the problem with you English," Hans teased. "You don't know how to have fun."

John simply waved in reply as he dashed toward home, but his thoughts were troubled. Eager as he was for his family to leave for America, he would miss his fun-loving friends in Holland. *And for all I know, we may not leave at all,* he admitted to himself. All he could do was wait and pray that God would let Father and the others know the best thing to do. A decision must and would be made soon.

Maybe even tomorrow.

CHAPTER 3

A Startling Announcement

Two days later, John Smythe ran down the cobblestoned street toward home as fast as his long legs could carry him. Head back, elbows bent, arms swinging, he panted from running so hard but refused to slow his pace.

John's heart pounded. Only this morning he had by chance heard of a secret meeting between Elder William Brewster and other leaders of their group. Elder Brewster was in hiding because he and Edward Winslow had smuggled pamphlets to Scotland and England condemning the king! King James had ordered their arrest, but so far the Dutch government had not been able to find them.

When John raced past the University of Leiden, he nearly ran into his pastor, John Robinson. Even though he was a pastor, John Robinson also studied and taught at the university.

"What's the hurry?" Robinson laughed, dropping a friendly arm around the boy's shoulder.

"I have to get home," John said, breathing heavily. He usually enjoyed talking with his minister, but not today. News burned on his tongue, but Father and Mother frowned on talebearing. Unless something was absolutely true, their children were not to repeat it. Even if it was true, they were to discuss it only within their own family. That way no one would be hurt by idle gossip.

"Then Godspeed, lad." John Robinson lifted his arm, and the lanky boy shot off faster than an arrow from a strong bow.

When he reached his home, John burst into the house. Taking precautions to keep his voice low, he called, "We are going! Father, Mother, Sarah, we are going to America!"

"Calm yourself, John," his mother quietly said. She patted a low stool next to the loom where she sat weaving. "Father isn't home from the factory yet, and I sent Sarah with food baskets for the poor." She sighed. "Our people are sick from working too hard, especially the children. They look like little old men and women. Perhaps it is selfish, but I cannot help thanking God that you and Sarah are spared the long hours so many must work to keep food on the table. It also allows us to help others in need."

"Things will be better in America," John promised. He half closed his eyes, dreaming of the New World. "There are no kings to say we cannot take game from the forest. There are no kings to tax us and persecute us. Mother, we will be free."

Not until that moment had John realized how much he desired freedom. He had thought only of the adventures they would surely have, the excitement of crossing an ocean and living in a new country.

Just then Sarah came in, carrying her now-empty baskets. "Sarah, we will be free," John repeated.

"What are you talking about?" Sarah asked.

"We are going to America to be free. I will tell you the rest when Father comes home."

Sarah stared silently at John. Her lips drooped, and her eyes looked enormous in her pale face.

"Sarah, dear, would you please bring me a cup of water?" Mother asked. As soon as Sarah left the room, Mother told John, "Deal gently with her, my son. She is young and also fearful, as am I."

"You aren't afraid, are you, Mother?" John's mouth fell open in astonishment. "Why, you came from England and—"

"I came because we had no choice if we were to remain true to our teachings and our God." Mother's hands lay idle in her aproned lap, and her green eyes so like Sarah's held shadows. "If we go to the New World, it will be for the same reason. Our group here is growing smaller and smaller."

John thought of the small cottages near Green Gate, their meetinghouse. The poorest of their group lived in them. The Smythes were a little better off. They lived near a few other members on a narrow street. John had once shocked Sarah by declaring, "I am glad we don't live in *Stincksteeg*, as the Brewsters do. Imagine, having a home in a place that means 'Smelly Alley'!"

Now he soberly asked, "Is Father ever afraid?" It seemed impossible for tall, strong William Smythe to be afraid of anything.

"Many times." Mother smiled. "He is also one of the bravest men I know."

"How can he be brave and frightened at the same time?" John demanded.

Sarah spoke from the doorway, her hand holding a cup of water for Mother. "He's brave because he goes ahead and does what he must, even though he's afraid. That's really being brave, isn't it, Mother? A lot braver than if a person isn't frightened."

"I never thought of that, but you're right." John leaped up from the stool. He thought of what his mother had asked him to do and added, "Sarah, you're a lot braver than you think you are."

His sister blushed with pleasure. "Thank you." A cheerful whistle came from outside the door. "Father's home. Now you can tell us what you know, John."

The moment William Smythe set foot inside the door, John spoke. "Our leaders had a meeting last night," he announced, feeling important to be the bearer of such news, but speaking in a quiet voice that would not carry beyond the walls and into the street. "It is as you said, Father. We cannot go back to England. Most of our friends there have been put in prison. Our leaders speak of a colony in the New World called Virginia. They say we can also go there and start a colony, one where we can live and worship as we choose."

"How do you know these things?" his father wanted to know. "I hope you have not been guilty of spying again."

John felt his face warm at the word *again*, but he proudly said, "No, sir. I overheard John Carver talking with some men on the street, but I wasn't spying. I didn't act like I heard him, for fear he'd be upset." He took a deep breath and dropped his voice to a whisper. "The best news is that some English merchants may lend us money for the trip!"

"Are you speaking truth or jest, son?" Father sharply asked.

"Truth," John boldly stated. "John Carver said that if we agree to repay the English merchants with fish and furs and lumber from the New World, the merchants will lend us money to hire a ship, a crew, and supplies enough to take us to America."

"What about King James?" Sarah looked frightened. "He will never let us go."

"John Carver said the king will be more than happy to give permission. That way we will be farther away from him than ever, and he won't be troubled by us!"

Father laughed, and Mother joined in. Even Sarah smiled a bit.

"What will we do, Father?" John asked. "Will our family go to America?"

Father and Mother exchanged a look, and Sarah's face grew even more pale.

"We will listen to the advice of our leaders and pray for God's wisdom. Then your mother and I will decide," Father said firmly. "You and Sarah can help by praying for all of our families as we make this decision."

The news John had overheard soon ran through Leiden. John Carver and the other leaders urged their followers to leave. Yet when the final vote was taken, less than half wanted to leave Holland immediately. John and Sarah's parents were among those who had decided to leave. To their great disappointment, Pastor John Robinson quietly said he would stay behind.

"I will come later," he promised those who planned to sail. "For now, I must remain with the part of my flock who are not going to America at this time." Sadness over the coming separation lined his kind face. "Pray that it will not be long."

As they left the meeting, Sarah was very quiet. John dropped back next to her and whispered, "What's wrong?"

She looked up at him, and a tear slid down her freckled cheek. "I'm just thinking of all the friends we'll have to leave behind. There's good Pastor Robinson and the families who are staying here. Then there are my Dutch friends like Gretchen. No one our age is leaving for America."

"Would you rather we stayed behind and watched Mother and Father leave on the ship?" John asked. "Our friends who are staying won't see their parents for at least a year, probably longer."

"No," Sarah admitted. She sighed. "Leaving people you love is hard to do."

"Yes, it is," agreed Mother, turning to join their conversation. "But we won't be leaving for weeks, maybe even months. There are many arrangements to make. Why, we don't even have a ship to sail on yet. You and I will be extra busy packing things for our trip, Sarah, but you can invite Gretchen to visit us while we work as often as her parents will allow."

For the first time since they'd left the meeting, a faint smile crossed Sarah's face.

As the weeks passed, John realized the truth of Mother's words. Nothing was happening, or so it seemed. Dutch and English companies offered to finance the trip, but only if the travelers worked for them like slaves. The only good thing that happened took place in England. When King James heard about the proposed trip and that the group expected to support itself by fishing, he supposedly said, "So God have my soul! 'Tis an honest trade! It was the apostles' own calling."

"Good news," Father finally announced one evening as he arrived home from work. "A man named Thomas Weston says that seventy men called 'Adventurers' are ready and waiting to supply money for the ships, crew, and supplies. Of course, there are certain conditions."

"Is the offer any better than the earlier ones?" Mother asked.

For once, John was able to bite his tongue and stand quietly to one side. He wanted to hear what his father had to say, and he knew that if he interrupted he might be sent out of the room.

"We'll work for the investors for seven years," Father said. "That's not good, but it's the best offer we've had, and our leaders don't think we'll get one that's better." Father sighed. "We not only need money to charter a ship to take us from England to America, with crew and supplies enough for many weeks, but we must also purchase a ship to carry us from Holland to Southampton. Both ships will cross the Atlantic once we meet in England."

The Adventurers' offer created a lot of debate among those who would be traveling. John sometimes felt like he would burst with impatience. Why must everything take so long? Why couldn't people see how important it was to leave Holland? He listened to the ringing words of William Bradford.

"Great difficulties always go with great and honorable actions. They must be faced with courage. Granted, the dangers are great. They are not desperate. The difficulties will be many, but some of the things we fear may never come to pass! Others can be prevented by using wisdom. Through the help of God and patience, we can bear them or overcome them.

"We should neither make attempts that are rash nor undertake things lightly or out of curiosity and hope for gain. Our reasons are good and honorable. We have every right to expect the blessing of God."

John squirmed uncomfortably when William Bradford spoke of curiosity, but his heart raced. Would he one day be a man like this? Or would he be like Father—quieter, but equally determined to take his family to a place that offered freedom and the chance to prosper?

A secret prayer slipped from John's heart. *Make me strong. There will be much to do. I know You will go with us to America.* He longed with all his excited young heart to add *And please, make it soon* but decided against it. God might not think it polite for a twelve-year-old boy to tell Him to hurry.

In spite of John's unfinished prayer, the "soon" he longed for came before he expected it. The very next day, exciting news reached Leiden. A sixty-ton ship named the *Speedwell* had been bought and was already on her way!

CHAPTER 4

Only the Brave

"The *Speedwell* will carry us to England," John told Sarah for at least the fiftieth time. "Even now the *Mayflower* is being loaded with supplies and getting ready to meet us at Southampton. Just think. Soon we will be on our way." He searched her face for the excitement that flamed higher and higher inside him.

Sarah didn't answer. Neither did she catch fire from his promise. "If only things had been better here." She looked at her brother curiously. "Aren't you going to miss Holland at all? What about your friend Hans? And aren't you even a little bit afraid?"

"Of course." John remembered Mother's words about dealing gently with Sarah. "It's really scary knowing we're going so far away. I'll miss my races with Hans. I'll miss the young men who have married Dutch girls and won't be going with us, and those who are too old or sick to sail. It will be hard to be separated for even a little while from friends who are our own age."

He patted Sarah's hand. "After we get to the New World and build a colony, others will come. You'll see."

"I suppose," Sarah grumbled. "But I'd much rather stay here." Her face brightened. "At least this afternoon I'll be able to work with Gretchen."

Shortly after the noon meal, a knock sounded at the door, and Sarah opened it to greet her friend. As energetic as she was tiny, Gretchen's bubbly personality filled the kitchen where she joined Sarah and Mother in their work.

Sarah looked enviously at Gretchen's bright blue dress. Unlike Sarah's people, Dutch children dressed in beautiful colors, and Sarah sometimes wondered what it would be like to wear something other than drab browns and blacks.

"It must be so exciting for you," Gretchen enthused as she salted pork and got it ready for drying. "I wish my family would do something so adventurous."

"You should get together with my brother, John," Sarah said. "All he can talk about are the adventures we're going to have. But what about the dangers?"

"That's true," Gretchen admitted. "I've heard stories about sickness and storms at sea that would curl your hair."

"Girls, girls," Mother interrupted. "Let's not get carried away by wild tales. We have work to do."

The two friends turned back to their tasks, but Sarah grew sad as she thought of leaving her friend.

"I wish you could come with us," she whispered to Gretchen.

"I do, too," Gretchen confided. "But we have lots of time to spend together before you leave, and I'm planning a surprise for you before you go."

"Surprise? What surprise?" Sarah asked.

"You'll find out when it's time," Gretchen teased and then went to the pump to wash her hands before she left for home.

Just after Gretchen had left, John rushed home with a book, its cover worn from being passed hand to hand.

"Look at this book!" he shouted.

"You do not need to shout for us to hear you," his mother gently reproved. "Now what is your latest treasure, and where did you get it?"

"It's a copy of Captain John Smith's report on the New World, *A Description of New England*," John answered eagerly, but in a softer tone. "I met John Carver in the street, and he asked me to bring it home. Everyone who's going to the New World is getting a chance to read it, so we'll know what to expect."

That evening after dinner, the Smythe family eagerly studied Captain Smith's glowing descriptions of the New World. Captain Smith was not only a former governor of the colony of Jamestown, Virginia, but he was also an explorer. He had sailed the New England coast and mapped its harbors.

"America is wonderful," the captain promised. "A land where those willing to work can prosper. I urge people to leave their homes across the water and settle in this untouched, unspoiled country."

As they read each page, Father and John grew more enthusiastic about their trip. "You've heard what the explorers and fishermen say," Father added at one point. "They describe great forests filled with nut and fruit trees, deer, and wild boar. The soil is fertile, and they say there are so many fish along the coast, a man can drop a net and come up with a great haul! Some even say a fortune could be made from the fur trade."

Mother said little, but the next day, she and Sarah spent even more time sorting and packing. Sarah at last accepted that they were leaving and began saying good-bye to the land of her birth, spending every spare moment with Gretchen.

Days later, word came of a great tragedy. Father came home with the sad news. "One hundred and thirty of our countrymen have perished making the crossing," he told his family. "The Atlantic Ocean is dangerous, but it is not the sea that took them. They died from hunger, sickness, and lack of water."

He dropped his head into his hands. "Sometimes I wonder if our brothers and sisters who choose to remain in Holland are right."

John sprang to his feet. His eyes flashed. "No, Father!" His young voice rang in the quiet room. Mother shot him a warning look, and he quickly returned to his chair.

"Father, I apologize for speaking to you so abruptly," John quickly said.

"Your apology is accepted," Father said, lifting his head and looking at his son. "But I think you have something to say. Tell me what is on your heart."

"I was just thinking," John said, "did not God open a way by causing the wealthy merchants to give us money for the trip? Did not our own John Carver and Robert Cushman go to King James himself and get a grant of land in the New World?"

"The king did not issue approval," Father reminded him. "He only said he would not stand in our way or trouble us if we conducted ourselves peacefully."

Speaking earnestly, John leaned forward. "It is not as though we were going to America to grow rich, although our leaders say we are bound to be better off there than we are here. We are going because we need a place where we can worship God and read the Bible for ourselves. What if Moses had let tales of the wilderness fill his heart with fear? What if he had not followed God's leading but had told his people to stay in Egypt and obey the pharaoh?"

John saw his father's shoulders straighten and some of the old fire come back to his troubled face.

"You are right, son," Father said. "Elder Bradford says when we sail from Holland, we will become pilgrims, people who go on a long, long journey. We are pilgrims for the Lord, not for what we think we might gain." He took a deep breath. "Even Jesus became a pilgrim when He left His home and traveled to those who needed to hear His message."

A new thought struck John. "Jesus died for everyone. The Indians in America have a right to hear about Him, don't they? How can they hear if Christians don't go tell them?"

"Gretchen says the Indians are savages." Sarah's eyes rounded with fear. "She told me they steal children. She says we will have to go naked and be hungry and maybe get scalped."

"How does she know?" John demanded. "She hasn't been to America, has she? Do you think Gretchen is wiser than our leaders?"

"Children, children." Mother held up a hand. "Remember our family rule. Each may speak freely, but we do not argue. Besides, both of you are right! We cannot help but fear the unknown, yet the same God who saw us safely to Holland can and will go with us to America."

"Why did He not save the people who died crossing the ocean?" Sarah asked.

"Come here, child." Father held out both arms, and Sarah ran to him. He held her close and said, "We cannot always know why God does or does not do things the way we think He should. We can only trust Him. Sarah, you know that even if something should happen, we have Jesus' promise that we will go where He is and live with Him. Can we ask for more?"

She shook her head and wiped away tears with the back of her hand.

"There. Now run along and help your mother with the packing. John is right. We cannot turn back." His brown eyes so like his son's twinkled. "Abigail, I fancy this son of ours may one day become a preacher! He has certainly given us something to consider this day."

John couldn't help grinning, even though he knew his face, neck, and ears must be bright red. "I only spoke what I believe to be true."

Father slowly said, "That is what God expects us to do." He gave John a warning look. "We also need to remember one thing: Sometimes our beliefs may be wrong. It is important to study the Bible and pray. That way we can separate man's ways from God's."

"Yes, sir." John liked it when Father spoke to him man to man. He carefully tucked the bit of advice away for a future time when he would need it.

Preparations for the voyage went steadily forward, although the number of people who agreed to sail continued to drop. It took time for the Smythes and their friends to gather what they needed to take with them. When John's father got home from work, he and John carefully collected the outdoor equipment they'd need for building their new home, hunting, and growing food.

"If I were around next winter," John told his friend Hans one afternoon, "I'd be sure to skate faster than you on the frozen canals. Look at how much bigger my muscles have gotten from carrying and packing all these things."

"That's impressive," Hans agreed. "What are you taking?"

"Well, so far we've crated up axes and saws as well as lanterns and shovels. Then there are the nails, spades, and chisels, as well as the hammers."

"It's hard to imagine living in a place where you can't simply buy food and cloth and other things you need," Hans said.

"It's even harder actually packing all those things that we'll need," John said, ruefully rubbing a sore arm.

That evening when John and Father began packing again, Hans came over. "My parents said I could help you pack if you could use the help," he offered.

"Gratefully accepted," Father said, shaking Hans's hand. "Tonight we're tackling more of our tools—vises, pitchforks, and planes—and if we have time, we'll start packing some cart wheels."

"What else will you be taking?" Hans asked.

"Well, we'll need the cart, plough, and wheelbarrow for farming and transporting things. Our larger group is taking some canoes for exploring the rivers and streams. And the women and girls are busy getting all the pots, dishes, medicines, and clothing—to say nothing of looms and food—together. Sarah and her mother have been working for weeks to make sure we have enough food and clothing to survive. They've even packed a spit for cooking over a fire and a mortar for grinding grain."

"Won't the ship be providing food for the journey?" Hans asked.

"Yes, but because we're leaving in the summer, we'll need enough food for a year once we get to Virginia. We won't be able to plant seed until the spring or harvest crops until next fall."

"Let's hope you have a good harvest," Hans said.

"God will provide," Father answered, and they went to work.

After a couple hours of hard work, Father and the boys decided it was time to go in the house and have something to eat and drink. They found Sarah and Mother going over a stack of labeled provisions.

"I think we're ready for some rest, too," Mother greeted them.

"How is the work progressing?" Father asked.

"Well, we have most of the dried goods taken care of. There are thirty-two bushels of meal and eight bushels each of dried peas and oatmeal for the four of us."

Hans's eyes widened.

"Fresh fruit won't last long," Mother continued to explain, "so we're packing dried prunes, raisins, and currants. We should be able to get sugar and molasses in the New World from the West Indies, but we're packing as many spices as we can afford."

"I never thought of how much food one family could eat in a year," Hans said, unable to restrain himself.

"And that doesn't include the oil and vinegar we'll take to season and preserve food," Sarah added.

"Are you taking any lemon juice?" Hans asked. "I've heard that's the only thing they know of that can keep you from getting scurvy."

"You're right," Mother said.

"You mean we'll have to drink that sour stuff?" John protested, his face twisting up at the thought.

"Better to drink a little sour lemon juice than to have bleeding gums and become very sick," Father replied.

"I suppose," John said, "but I can't say I'm excited about the thought."

"That's probably the only thing about this trip you aren't excited about," teased Hans. "Thank you for the food, Mistress Smythe. It's getting late, so I'd better run home now."

"Thank you for your help," Father said.

After the family had said good-bye to Hans and were preparing for evening prayers, John thought about the upcoming voyage.

"We will have a good time on board ship," he said to Sarah. "Even if our friends won't be going, there will be older children on board. Love and Wrasling Brewster are going, although their parents are leaving the rest of their children behind. Bartholomew, Remember, and Mary Collins are also going. So is Resolved White and ever so many more—"

He broke off. "Sarah, more than half of the forty-one people who will sail from Leiden are children! Isn't that exciting?"

"Yes, it is," Sarah cautiously agreed. "You didn't say anything about Elder Bradford's son John. Isn't he going?"

"I don't know," John admitted, although he hated to confess that there was anything about the voyage that he didn't know. Sometimes Sarah teased him and called him the town crier, after the officers who went through English villages crying out the news to the people.

"Only in your case," she had said, "you carry the news to our family."

Each day brought the Smythes and their friends closer to departure. Each day saw those who refused to leave Holland sharpen their criticism of those who would sail.

One day, John was returning from the wharf when he came upon a group of people surrounding William Bradford. Curious about what was happening, John quietly stood on the edge of the group and listened.

"Why?" tearful members pleaded. "Do you think God wants loved ones separated for years, perhaps forever? Give up this mad scheme. You are weak in the faith to feel you must run away. War with the Spaniards may never come. Even if it does, God can care for His people. If you trust Him as He commands, why do you cross an ocean that may swallow you alive?"

"Oh ye of little faith," William Bradford thundered. "Will you cling to homes where your children daily grow more like the Dutch? Even now they rebel at having to attend meeting. Look at those around you. Women wearing breeches. Families laughing and dancing on the Sabbath."

He sternly looked around the circle of faces. "You quote Scripture to fit your purposes and forget the commandment given by the apostle Paul: 'Wherefore come out from among them, and be ye separate, saith the Lord, and touch not the unclean thing; and I will receive you.' "

Bradford proudly flung his head up. "I turned my back on my family. I left England, the country I love. God gave me strength to do so, and He has kept the promise given in the next verse: 'And [I] will be a Father unto you, and ye shall be my sons and daughters, saith the Lord Almighty.' Let the babble of those who follow the dictates of their conscience and remain in Holland cease. We also follow our conscience, and our Master."

The ringing words sank deep in John Smythe's heart. He shouted "Amen!" along with other supporters who stood nearby. John knew if he lived to be a white-haired, bent old man, he would never forget this moment when only the brave chose to sail.

CHAPTER 5

The *Speedwell* Doesn't!

"I am so glad they scrubbed down both ships," Sarah Smythe confessed to her brother, John. She made a horrible face. "I can't bear to think of the bugs and rats on ships!"

John heaved a bushel of oatmeal to one side of the great store of provisions, proud of being strong and able to do hard work. The New World needed men, not weak boys. "The *Speedwell* is being completely overhauled."

He stopped and panted, wiping away the sweat from his face. The July day was warm and sunny. "She's being repaired, too, and given taller masts and larger sails. Otherwise she could never keep up with the *Mayflower*. She should be ready to sail by the last day of this month." He felt a pang of jealousy. "I wish we were going on the *Mayflower*, like the London Strangers. She's three times bigger than the *Speedwell* and weighs one hundred eighty tons!"

He wrinkled his nose. "She smells better, too. The *Mayflower* is called a 'sweet ship,' because she doesn't have bad smells like ships that carry fish."

"Well, we can't go on the *Mayflower*," Sarah told him. "We could barely afford to buy the *Speedwell*, even with the money the English merchants lent us. It's big enough to hold what few of us are going and most of the provisions. Don't forget, the ship and crew are going to stay a year with us in America."

"You're right." John grinned at her. "The *Mayflower* will stay just long enough for us to load it with cargo then sail back to England. The London emigrants are only renting it."

"Why do we call them Strangers?"

John couldn't help tormenting his sister. "You're getting as curious as I am, always asking why."

She smirked and repeated what he always told her. "How can I learn anything if I don't ask questions?"

John joined in her laughter, glad to see the gloom of the last weeks lifting from her freckled face, at least for a time. "Remember what Father said? The London emigrants aren't going to the New World for religious reasons, but to see if they can find a better life. It's a good thing they are traveling with us, though. If there's trouble, they'll be there to help us. We'll do the same for them. We'll stay in sight of each other all the time, just in case."

"What kind of trouble?" Sarah looked suspicious.

John thought as quickly as he could. "Uh, you know. Like if there's a bad storm."

Or pirate ships that rove the sea, attack cargo ships, and seize their goods, a little voice inside whispered. John wasn't about to tell Sarah that! She was still frightened enough of the wild Atlantic Ocean they must cross, with its white-foam waves and mighty swells. The longer she went without hearing about pirates, the better. Anyway, they might not see a pirate the whole time they were sailing.

Five days. Four. Three. Two. The day before departure from Leiden arrived at last. Pastor John Robinson ordered a time of fasting and prayer. A solemn group gathered for the last time.

John tore his attention from the future long enough to realize how final this day was in the lives of everyone present. Unexpected pain poked red-hot needles into him. Why couldn't they just go without saying any good-byes?

He looked around the room. One day he would again see some of those remaining in Holland, for they had promised to come on another crossing. Others, especially the old and sick members of his congregation, he would not meet again until they all reached heaven where there were no sad farewells.

A wave of love threatened to undo his courage and eagerness to sail. So did some of the prayers and Pastor Robinson's farewell sermon.

John scrubbed at his stinging eyes and felt relieved when the meeting ended. In a short while, he and his family would take the first steps of the long journey that lay ahead.

"God, go with us," John whispered. He turned to Sarah, at last knowing how she felt. Tears streamed from her green eyes. Her chin wobbled, but she held her head high. John had never been prouder of his younger sister. Already Leiden seemed part of the past.

That afternoon, John and Hans took one last walk together along the canal. They were unusually quiet. Jokes seemed out of place, and they were uncomfortable admitting what they felt.

Finally, as they turned up their street, Hans stopped and

looked at John. "I'll miss you, John," he said, his eyes suspiciously moist. "I've never had a friend like you, and I don't know that I ever will again. I don't really understand why your family must leave, but I respect you for doing what you believe is right."

"I'll miss you, too, Hans," John said. "And I'll never forget you as long as I live. But don't forget when you win all those canal races that the only reason you're winning is because I'm not here to challenge you."

Awkwardly the boys smiled at each other. Hans held out his hand, and he and John exchanged a strong handshake before turning into their separate homes.

John paused in the dark hallway to rub his eyes and wait for his heart to stop pounding. He didn't want Sarah to know how hard it was for him to leave his friends. As he stood by the door, he heard sniffling coming from the parlor.

Curious, he peered around the partly opened parlor door and saw Sarah sitting in a corner, quietly crying into a handkerchief.

"What's wrong, Sarah?" John asked, rushing over to her.

"I. . .just said. . .good-bye. . .to Gretchen," she sobbed. "She gave me this as a surprise. . .so I wouldn't for. . .forget her." Sarah held out the damp handkerchief that Gretchen had embroidered with a tulip and their names.

"I know how you feel," John said, sitting down beside his sister and putting an arm across her shoulders.

"You do?" she asked, amazement crossing her freckled face. "But I thought you were all excited about leaving tomorrow."

"I am," John admitted. "But I just said good-bye to Hans, and I don't think I've ever had to do anything more difficult in my life."

John and Sarah sat together in companionable silence for a few minutes until they were ready to finish up the last jobs that needed to be done before their trip. John had never felt quite so close to his sister.

The next day dawned with good weather, but none of the forty-one people who were about to leave Leiden noticed. Slowly, they filed onto canal boats that would take them about twenty-four miles to Delftshaven. Friends, family members, and Pastor Robinson accompanied them. If some felt like cheering, they hid it well. Most faces were even more sober than usual.

The Smythes were one of the few families not leaving brothers and sisters, a grandfather, or grandmother behind, but the pain of the coming separation hung around them like a heavy, gray blanket.

"Come." Father took Mother's arm and helped her into a canal boat.

John roused from his thoughts, nimbly hopped in, and held out a hand to Sarah. She turned her head to glance behind her. "Don't look back, Sarah. It will make it harder. Remember Leiden and our friends the way they were."

Surprise showed in her face. "All right." Sarah stared straight ahead. So did John, Mother, and Father. Within a few minutes, John put aside the past in favor of the present. The canal boats were nothing compared with the *Speedwell* or the *Mayflower*. Eight hours later, they reached Delftshaven, a main shipping port in Holland.

"There she is!" John's shrill cry cut through the numbness

of misery surrounding everyone. They stared at the *Speedwell*, ready and waiting by the East India House. From that dock, the Pilgrims would embark the next day on their great adventure. Impressive stone, brick, and iron buildings lined both sides of the canal.

Seeing the *Speedwell* did what nothing else had been able to accomplish. Spirits soared. Hope burned brightly once more. The group stayed in a building near the Old Church on the canal their last night in Holland. They ate, drank, laughed, and filled the air with songs of praise and thanksgiving. Even Sarah perked up.

"It isn't bad so far," she admitted to her brother.

"Not bad! It's better than I expected." He hastily added, "I'm glad you're feeling better."

"So am I." Sarah yawned. "I'm tired, though."

"We all are," Mother said and shooed them off to their sleeping pallets.

The next day arrived heavy with river mist. While leaving Leiden had been hard, the final good-byes at Voorhaven Quay were even worse. Great crowds of people had come to see the Pilgrims off. Friends from Amsterdam. The curious. Families. John wished they had all stayed in Leiden!

Sarah pinched his arm. She pointed to weeping Dorothy Bradford. John swallowed hard. Dorothy clung to her little son, John, as if unable to tear herself away. He was to be left in the care of another family so she could go with her husband, William, on the *Speedwell*.

"How can she do it?" Sarah asked.

John didn't answer. He hadn't dreamed leaving would be this hard. Or that mothers would leave their children behind. What of Mistress Collins and Susanna White, both expecting additions to their families? He knew Susanna was taking a cradle for the baby who would be born in the New World. What if a baby came at sea? John squirmed and blushed. That was for the women to consider, not boys.

Mary Brewster stood close to her two daughters and son who would stay in Holland. Her husband, William, remained in hiding, still wanted by the police for printing illegal literature. Where was he?

Pastor Robinson led his flock in a final prayer. The emigrants hastily embraced loved ones a last time and boarded the *Speedwell*. Muskets fired. The ship's cannons boomed. People waved from deck and land. White sails billowed. The *Speedwell*, clearly identified as Dutch by the colorful flag on her mast, began to move. The ship followed the wide Maas River into the North Sea. Down the Strait of Dover. Into the English Channel that Mother and Father had mentioned in their stories of leaving England before John and Sarah were born.

None of the Smythes looked back. They fixed their gaze straight ahead and trusted God. Surely He would see them through whatever hardships or heartache they might face in order to worship Him in a free country.

Living space on the *Speedwell* proved to be far worse than expected. Even though the ship had been cleaned, the lower decks were horrible. People crowded together in damp rooms with little air and less light. Cooking could only be done when the sea stayed calm, for fear that sparks in the fire boxes might be carried by the wind and start a fire on the ship. Buckets served as toilets.

One day Sarah and John stood by the ship's rail, faces turned westward. "Can we live this way all across the Atlantic Ocean?" Sarah asked John in a troubled voice. "Why aren't things any better?"

John shrugged. "The more room passengers take, the less cargo the ship will hold. I wonder if Father would let me sleep on deck with the sailors."

"You know he wouldn't!" Sarah turned pale. "I heard John Carver say the sailors hate us. I don't know why. You might not be safe on deck."

John reluctantly gave up the idea. Sometimes the smell of so many people crowded together in such a small space made him feel sick. It would be so much better to sleep topside where at least the air was fresh. "Sarah, do you want to hear a riddle?"

"Is it funny?"

"Yes."

"Tell me quickly, please. There hasn't been a lot to laugh about since we left Delftshaven."

Her quick reply showed John how miserable she was. He felt sorry for her. Boys were allowed more freedom on the ship than girls. It couldn't be much fun for Sarah. She didn't like to poke into things and explore as he did, for fear of being caught and getting into trouble.

"Cheer up," he told her. "The voyage won't last forever."

"I hope not! What's the riddle?"

"The *Speedwell* doesn't."

"Doesn't what?" Sarah stared at him blankly.

"Doesn't *speed well*." He chuckled. "Understand? The ship doesn't speed well. It lumbers along like a sick cow!"

Sarah rolled her eyes at her brother's poor attempt at humor. "It's not that slow. We'll be in Southampton tomorrow, and it's only been a few days." She turned toward John. A strong breeze filled the sails and ruffled her brown braids.

"I know, and then we will really, truly get started on our journey."

"Hey, you two, get away from that rail!" someone shouted.

John and Sarah whirled around. An angry-looking sailor came charging down the deck straight toward them!

CHAPTER 6

"I'll Feed You to the Fishes!"

The angry sailor came straight at John and Sarah, running down the deck at top speed. "Get away from that rail!" he bellowed again. He added a string of foreign words that sounded like they might be curses.

Sarah clapped her hands over her ears and stepped back from the charging man.

Not John. He stepped in front of Sarah and planted himself with feet apart and hands on his hips. His eyes darkened from clear brown to storm-cloud black. "We aren't doing anything wrong."

"I'll teach you to talk back to me, you disrespectful whelp!" The sailor raised his brawny arm. He shook a hamlike fist and lunged closer, so close a blast of fishy breath came from between his cracked lips.

Sarah froze, unable to tear her gaze from the ugly, threatening face. She couldn't move an inch, even if her life depended on it. From the looks of the sailor, it just might!

John reached a long arm back and gave her a push. "Run!"

His order freed her feet. Sobbing, Sarah gathered her long skirts and obeyed. She kept her head turned so she could see John. Not heeding where she was going, the terrified girl crashed into something tall and solid. She let out a shriek and struggled against the strong hands that kept her from falling. "Let me go!"

"Sarah child, what is it?"

Sarah looked up into the kindly face of Dr. Samuel Fuller, physician and surgeon, who traveled alone to the New World. She sagged against him. "The sailor!" she gasped. "He's going to kill John!"

"I doubt that." The good doctor sounded amused.

Sarah twisted in Dr. Fuller's arms and looked back. She heard the sailor roar, "I'm gonna feed you to the fishes!" Several other grinning sailors had stopped their work to see the fun, yelling catcalls to the man facing John. Fear for her brother overcame Sarah's terror. She tried to break free from Dr. Fuller's arms. "I have to help John," she cried. "Let me go!"

"He doesn't need any help," Dr. Fuller chuckled. "The lout has to catch John before he can hurt him. I don't think he can. If he does, I will interfere."

Only partly reassured, Sarah stopped struggling and watched. The bulky seaman was indeed no match for John's nimble feet. The boy danced away from danger on legs made strong from running through the streets of Leiden and skating the frozen canals. He led the bellowing sailor a merry chase, up and down the deck, around great stacks of cargo. The lumbering man simply could not catch the boy who ran like lightning.

A new voice shouted above the noise, "Klaus, what is the

meaning of this?" The captain of the *Speedwell* stepped directly into the charging sailor's path and glared at him.

The seaman stumbled to a halt. "Just havin' a bit o' fun wi' the lad." He touched his hand to his cap in a rough salute, but his face turned clammy white.

Sarah's eyes opened wide with astonishment. "Why—"

Dr. Fuller placed his hand gently over her mouth. "Keep silent, child. No need to make things worse than they already are."

The captain looked suspiciously from his laughing crew to John, who had halted a short distance away and stood leaning against the rail. "Is that all it is? Answer me, boy!" His voice cut the tense air like a whip.

John hesitated. Sarah saw him look at the sailor who had lied then shrug his shoulders, a movement his sister knew could be taken as either yes or no.

"All right, then. Keep away from my sailors, you hear?"

"Yes, sir." A lock of brown hair dangled over John's forehead. He grinned and said, "That's what I was trying to do," in his most innocent voice.

"Haw haw!" All of the sailors except the one who had started the trouble burst out laughing. Klaus gave John a strange look. It still held anger, but a gleam of respect also shone in his eyes.

"Get back to work, all of you!" the captain barked.

"Aye, aye." The group broke up, still laughing.

John turned toward Sarah. His eyes sparkled with excitement and looked like twin stars, until he saw the doctor. Then his jaw dropped and he cast a quick glance around them. "What. . .did you. . .I didn't know you were here," he stuttered.

"I suspected as much." Dr. Fuller folded his arms over his

stomach. "John, John, what are we going to do with you?"

All John's boldness vanished, and he hung his head.

Sarah slipped a comforting hand in the crook of his elbow. "It wasn't his fault," she loyally defended. "All we did was stand by the rail. The sailor started yelling at us, and John told him we weren't doing anything wrong."

"Wouldn't it have been better to hold your tongue?" Dr. Fuller asked.

"Beggin' yer pardon, sir, but that's just what the lad did," a low voice said.

The doctor and the two children turned. John's pursuer stood just behind them, breathing heavily. Sarah felt the blood drain from her face. He must have sneaked back as soon as the captain left the deck. *What will happen now?* She could see the same question in John's and Dr. Fuller's eyes when she looked at them.

"The matter is settled," the doctor exclaimed. "Go about your work."

Klaus didn't budge. "Not afore I thank the lad," he stubbornly said. His hand shot out and swallowed John's. "He saved me from the cat-o'-nine-tails by holdin' his tongue." He gripped John's hand with his huge paw, and what passed for a smile twitched across his lips.

John's mouth dropped open. Sarah gulped. Dr. Fuller chuckled again. The sailor's face dropped back into its usual ferocious look. "Keep away from that rail," he warned John. "You, too." He glared at Sarah, whose eyes grew wide. "Last voyage a brat fell in the brine durin' a storm. Who fished him out? Me. Klaus. Nearly drowned. Shoulda let the fishes get him. It woulda served him right fer hangin' on the rail." The rescuer scowled and trudged away, leaving the Smythes and the doctor speechless.

"Who would have thought it?" John marveled when the sailor got out of hearing. "Klaus, of all people, a hero! No wonder he yelled at us. I guess he was trying to scare us so much we'd never go near the ship's rail again, especially during a storm."

"You just never know who may be a real hero," Dr. Fuller told them. He cocked his head to one side. "I certainly don't recommend your method, John, but you may just have made yourself a friend." A shadow crept into his eyes. "Being whipped with a cat-o'-nine-tails is a terrible punishment. Some men die from the beatings."

Sarah thought of the cruel whip made of nine knotted cords fastened to a handle and used to keep crew members in line. She shivered. "No wonder Klaus was glad John didn't tell on him!"

John just looked thoughtful, but Dr. Fuller added, "Evidently somewhere beneath that crusty, bluffing, don't-care attitude lies a tender heart. Otherwise Klaus wouldn't have risked his own life by diving into a stormy ocean to save a child."

"It's hard to believe such a mean-looking person could do a good thing," protested Sarah.

"We cannot judge what is in a man's heart by what is on his face," Dr. Fuller said. "Remember what the Lord told Samuel about judging by what we see? He told Samuel, 'The Lord seeth not as man seeth; for man looketh on the outward appearance, but the Lord looketh on the heart.'"

❧

John and Sarah kept their distance from the crew, just as the captain ordered. But every time they saw Klaus, they smiled at him.

Klaus either ignored them or grunted. He continued to scowl. He bellowed if he thought they were getting too close to the rail. Yet never again did Klaus double his fist and shake it at them. Neither did he challenge John to a footrace, as a few of the others did! Word sped through the ship that young John Smythe could outrun all of the boys and most of the men aboard.

When the *Speedwell* sailed into Southampton and dropped anchor next to the *Mayflower*, the larger ship loomed over her like a giant above a child. The *Mayflower* had come a week earlier with the sixty-one London Strangers who would sail on her to the New World. The two groups met at the West Quay, eager to meet their fellow travelers.

John and Sarah's parents and many other adults simply stood and looked. Twelve long years had passed since they had stood on English soil. The emotion of the moment would stay with them a long time.

"Look at the holes in the fortress wall," John said.

Sarah was more interested in the comfortable cottages up and down the streets of Southampton. If only King James would allow her family freedom to worship in their own way, they could stay in England. How wonderful it would be to live right in one of the neat cottages in Southampton instead of being forced to sail thousands of miles to a new land.

"Come on, Sarah." John tugged at her hand. "Father says we may talk with the children." He pointed at a group running and calling to one another between the many crates and trunks piled on the dock.

"Are you sure it's all right?" She glanced at her parents and their friends, then back to the Strangers. What a difference! Sarah's people dressed plainly. The men wore tall, broad-brimmed hats, heavy clothing, warm stockings, and sturdy leather shoes. Women dressed in dark cloaks with hoods that tied under the chin over plain dresses with white collars and cuffs.

Not so the Strangers! Sarah gasped at the rainbow-bright colors, the feathers and trimmings and buttons and lace on their clothing. One young lady in particular dazzled Sarah. Sweet-faced and stylish, Priscilla Mullins smiled at the children from her place next to her shopkeeper father, William, her mother, and her brother, Joseph. Sarah felt glad they would be sailing on the *Mayflower*.

She also liked the large Hopkins family who came to greet her parents.

"I tried to get to America once before," Stephen Hopkins boomed. "The ship wrecked in the Bermudas. This time we'll have better luck. This is my wife, Elizabeth." The woman, obviously expecting a child, smiled at them. So did the Hopkins children: Giles, Constanta, and Damaris.

A young man named John Alden joined the group. Sarah liked his pleasant face and good manners. She laughed with the others when he confessed, "I've been working here in Southampton as a cooper, making tubs and casks. I've heard so much about this exciting voyage, I just signed up for a year with the company and will be sailing to America." John Alden glanced at pretty Priscilla Mullins, who blushed and looked down. Sarah thought it very romantic.

The one person neither Sarah nor John liked on first sight was a very short man named Myles Standish. He stood with his wife, Rose, and wore a sword to remind people he was a professional soldier and had fought many wars in Europe. He had flaming red hair and a face to match.

"He looks mean," John whispered.

"I know. I don't want to be around him," Sarah agreed.

"We don't have to worry until we reach the New World," John told her. "He'll be on the *Mayflower*, and we'll be on the *Speedwell*." The corners of his mouth turned down. "At least we will be if they ever get the leaks in our ship fixed."

A few hours later, more bad news reached the travelers. Thomas Weston, the man who had arranged financing, arrived with a new contract that included harsher rules. The group from Holland refused to sign it. Would this be the end of their dream?

CHAPTER 7

Discouraging Days

How dare Thomas Weston bring such a contract?" John demanded of Father.

Father's eyes shot sparks the same way his son's often did when he was angry. "The sponsors have added two unbearable terms. They are ordering us to work for them seven days a week, but we must have two days to do our own work, or we cannot survive." He spread his hands wide. "The second demand is even worse. They want the homes we build to become company property!"

"Are they mad?" Mother cried. "We owned our homes even in Scrooby and Leiden. We'll be no better than slaves if our leaders agree to abide by the new rules!"

"We cannot and shall not agree to their demands," Father replied.

His prediction came true. The leaders flatly refused to even consider signing away the freedom they had struggled so hard to find and hoped to enjoy in the New World.

With his usual ability to be on the spot when anything

important took place, John smuggled himself into the meeting with Thomas Weston where the amended contract was to be signed.

"We shall not labor seven days for the company. Our homes must be our own," the leaders stubbornly insisted.

Weston grew furious. He angrily reminded them of how hard he'd worked to get the money they needed for the voyage.

It did nothing to change the men's minds. At last Weston shouted, "You may look to stand on your own legs!" Although the businessmen remained financially responsible for the expedition, Weston got even with the Pilgrims for not signing the new contract. He refused to pay the port fees still owing on the *Mayflower* and left for London immediately.

"What shall we do?" the travelers asked. "If the bill is not paid, we will be in trouble with the authorities. King James may cancel our land grant in the New World and take back his permission for us to go."

John shuddered at the thought. They must go or be homeless.

"We don't have any money," someone pointed out. "How can we pay what we don't have?"

After much discussion, the people agreed to sell enough of the precious tubs of butter they had brought in their provisions to meet the debt. John slipped away from the meeting and told Sarah all about it. "We will have to go without butter because of Thomas Weston," he said glumly.

"I 'spect we'll have to go without a lot of things," Sarah said. Her freckled face looked solemn. "Father and Mother said Jesus probably didn't have butter when He was a pilgrim either, so we shouldn't complain."

John felt ashamed. "They're right." He cheered up and tweaked one of her braids. "The good news is, we're sailing as soon as the *Speedwell*'s seams are recaulked. Hooray!" He turned a handspring.

At last they sailed. How the passengers celebrated! Not just because at long last they were on their way to America. Oh, no, they had another and far more wonderful reason.

William Brewster, still wanted as a prisoner by the English officials, was on the *Speedwell*.

Not even keen-eyed John Smythe knew how or when their favorite elder had come aboard. Somehow he had sneaked past the very persons looking for him and hidden himself. Once on the seas, he would be safe, at least for a time.

The celebration ended all too soon. Weather in the English Channel was so stormy, the *Speedwell* began to leak again. Pounding waves and high winds sent the ship reeling until the passengers wondered if she could ever right herself. The captain signaled the *Mayflower*, and the two ships sailed into Dartmouth, the nearest port, for repairs. Skilled carpenters spent ten days working on the *Speedwell* and said she was safe for the voyage.

During all this time, Elder Brewster was forced to remain in hiding. If he was discovered on English shores, he would be sent to a dungeon or maybe even hanged. Every man, woman, and child on board feared for his safety.

Not until early September could the expedition set out again. The weather was calm, and passengers prayed for more good weather. They passed Land's End, the last part of England they could see, and sailed on.

"This is more like it," John told Sarah, watching the sun set in a fiery splash on the ocean horizon. "America, get ready. We're on our way!"

Their joy didn't last long. Three hundred miles westward, the *Speedwell*'s leaking worsened and could not be stopped. The captain said they simply could not go on. They returned to Plymouth, accompanied by the *Mayflower*. There, the *Speedwell* was pronounced unfit for ocean travel.

"What will we do?" Mother asked.

"Go on the *Mayflower*," Father replied.

John and Sarah stared at each other. How long ago it seemed since John had longed to sail on the larger ship. Now it would happen. He could hardly wait! Then a disturbing thought entered his mind. "I heard the captain say she isn't built for so many people," he said.

"We have no choice," Father sternly told them. "It is already mid-September." Worry clouded his face. "If we had gone when we were supposed to, there would have been time to plant and harvest some winter crops. Instead, we've spent seven weeks on board ship so far, longer than the crossing itself should be.

"We've been forced to live in miserable conditions, cold and hungry and thirsty. Our food and fresh water supply have run low. People are sick. The crew is threatening to walk off. They say the emigrants interfere with their work, and in truth, some of them do."

"William, I have never seen you so discouraged." Mother placed her hand on Father's arm. Her forehead wrinkled with concern.

"I know. These are discouraging days." He sighed, his face

troubled. "Decisions must be made. Now. Some of our people are turning back. Abigail, shall we go back to Leiden with them? Only about thirty of our group plan to continue."

"John and Sarah?" Mother turned to them.

John spoke first. "What you say is true, Father. There will be little or no chance of harvest in the New World. Yet suppose we stay? If we remain in England, Elder Brewster will be thrown into the dungeon, perhaps hanged for treason. So will others—perhaps even you." He fought the fear that rose inside him. "Life was not easy in Holland, and it isn't safe there anymore. I believe we should go on, but I will abide by whatever you and Mother decide."

"Sarah?"

She looked thin and small in her plain dress. Lack of proper food had left its mark on her childish face. John desperately wished he had money to buy Sarah all she needed. He saw her struggle with the question. Her green eyes changed expressions a dozen times before she said, "I miss Leiden and Gretchen and our home." She looked down at her fingers.

John held his breath, waiting for her to continue. Father and Mother would decide, but he wanted his sister to be happy.

"I miss them," Sarah repeated in a low voice. "But there isn't any home to go back to. We sold our house and most of our things. We have to go on. As long as we have each other. . ."

"That's right, Sarah. I'm proud of you. And you, too, John." Mother drew herself up to her full height, looking far taller than she really was. "William, for better or worse, we sail with the *Mayflower*."

Father bowed his head and thanked God for his family, but

not before John saw the look in his face and the shine of tears in his eyes.

Strangely enough, once those who'd decided to continue the journey moved to their cramped quarters aboard the *Mayflower*, their hopes rose.

Slowly, then with gathering speed, the *Mayflower* sailed away from England. John and Sarah watched England grow smaller and smaller, until it became only a speck in the distance. Even though they had never lived in England, their parents' stories had sunk deep into their hearts. John couldn't hold in his feelings when he saw slow tears spill from his parents' eyes.

"Good-bye, King James, you miserable wretch," he cried, loud enough so only Mother, Father, and Sarah could hear. Such talk was treason, and some of the London Strangers loyally followed the king and the Church of England. "I hope God punishes you for persecuting us just because we want to worship God in our own way!" He shook his fist at the retreating English shore.

"John!" Sarah's horrified gasp made him realize what he'd done.

"That is quite enough." Father's arms shot out. His hands fastened on John's shoulders, and he sternly looked at his son. "Never call down God's punishment on anyone. It is a terrible thing to do."

"Not even when they deserve it?"

The hint of a smile came to Father's lips but disappeared so quickly John wondered if it had been there at all. "Nay, lad. God deals with all of us in His own time, in His own way."

"I didn't mean to say it out loud," John explained. "The words just came."

"It's just as bad to think wicked things as to speak them," Mother quietly said. "Remember the Scripture, 'For as he thinketh in his heart, so is he.' John, you *must* learn to hold that tongue of yours! It will get you into trouble again and again." She shook her head. "Soon you will be a man. I fear for you. If you do not put away childish habits and learn to control your temper, how can you be a witness for the Master?" She sadly shook her head.

John bit his lip. He hated himself when he did something wrong and made Mother look like that. He glanced at Sarah. She stood with arms crossed and a worried expression on her face much like Mother's, except it also held sympathy. John knew how tenderhearted she was. Sarah hurt as much as John when Father or Mother had to correct or punish him. She had also kept him out of trouble many times by not telling their parents of his mischief—including the incident with Klaus. Dr. Fuller also had remained silent after getting John's promise that he would be more careful of what he said and did in the future.

Now John had failed again. "I'm sorry," he mumbled. "I'll try to do better."

"You are forgiven." Father's hold on John tightened before his strong arms fell to his sides. The twinkle John thought he had seen a moment before returned and grew. "I confess, there have been times when I have felt the same way about King James and his men!"

"You?" John rocked back on his heels. His mouth dropped open.

"Aye. Then I remember that we are to forgive our enemies as our Father in heaven forgives us." He smiled at the children, took Mother's arm, and led her away, leaving John and Sarah to stare after them in wonder.

Shocked by Father's confession, John unthinkingly leaned against the ship's rail. He failed to hear heavy steps pounding down the deck until Sarah gave a small warning cry of alarm. John turned, straight into two powerful, hairy arms!

CHAPTER 8

Pilgrims, Strangers, and Sailors

How many times d' you gotta be told to stay away from that rail?" the sailor hissed. He yanked John back from the rail with such force the boy spun across the deck and landed on a pile of coiled rope! John lay still for a moment, unhurt but stunned by the unexpected attack. Sarah ran to him on flying feet. "Are you hurt?"

"No." Good intentions to stay out of trouble vanished. John leaped up, brushed his sister aside, and sprang to face the cowardly attacker who had jumped him from behind. The next instant, astonishment filled him.

"Why, it's—" His jaw dropped.

Sarah had recovered her wits enough to join her brother. "Mr. Klaus, whatever are you doing on the *Mayflower*?" she asked, pleasure lighting up her face.

Klaus grimly folded his arms across his brawny chest and continued to glower. "My name ain't Mister an' 'tis a good thing fer you that I be aboard," he sourly stated. "What'd I tell you about leanin' on that rail?"

"I forgot." John's delight at seeing the sailor again overcame fear.

Klaus rudely snorted. "Better not be fergettin' when I'm around. I ain't fishin' no more brats outta the drink, y' hear me?" He scowled even more.

"How did you get here?" John persisted. "Sarah and I looked for you before the *Speedwell* left for London. William Bradford said it would be sold and go back to being a cargo ship, instead of trying to carry passengers."

"Aye," Klaus grunted. He heaved his wide shoulders into a shrug. "I've sailed the seven seas but ain't seen the New World. All the jaw-flappin' about it gave me a hankerin' t' see wi' my own eyes." He raised a shaggy eyebrow. "Got released from the *Speedwell* an' signed on this'un." Klaus threw out his chest with pride. "Ain't no better sailor on board. Cap'n was glad t' get me."

A gleam in his eyes showed how proud Klaus was of being a good sailor. John also suspected he and Sarah had something to do with the big seaman's decision to change ships.

He wisely held his tongue. Such a remark would surely bring back the scowl Klaus usually wore that had slipped away during their conversation.

"We're glad you're going with us," Sarah politely said.

Klaus reached out a calloused hand, as if to touch her hair, then snatched it back. The scowl returned. "Some'un's gotta look atter the pair o' you," he muttered. "Ain't gonna be me, though." He wheeled and strode away without a backward glance.

"Well, I never!" Sarah indignantly said. "Why can't he be friendly?" She tilted her freckled nose and said in an exact imitation of the newcomer to the *Mayflower*, " 'Some'un's gotta look atter the pair o' you. Ain't gonna be me, though!' Who asked him to look after us is what I want to know," she added in her normal voice.

John cocked his head. His eyes sparkled. "I'm glad he's here. Besides, remember what Dr. Fuller said. You just never know. I have a feeling that before we reach America, we may be mighty glad Klaus is on board." He made a face. "At least we have one friend among the crew. Most of the sailors hate us."

"You never did tell me why." Sarah trotted down the deck to keep up with her brother's longer stride. Her dark braids bounced.

"They don't like our prayers and hymns," John explained. "Also, some of the Pilgrims treat the sailors as if they are so ignorant they aren't worth anything except to keep the ship going. I wouldn't like to be treated that way."

"Perhaps that's why I overheard a sailor say he'd like to throw half of us into the sea," Sarah said. "Klaus said that to you, too, but I don't think he meant it."

"I don't, either." Suddenly John felt gloriously happy. Having Klaus with them made everything that much better. "If he got mad and threw me in, I'll wager he'd jump right in and fish me out, in spite of everything he says!"

"I do, too," Sarah giggled.

John went back to the subject of the sailors. "Do you know what they call us? 'Glib-gabbety puke stockings!' Just because our people get seasick. Isn't that awful?"

Sarah stopped and put her hands on her hips. "It's terrible. What right do they have to call us names? The sailors curse and use bad language, even in front of our women!"

"Once they get us safely to the New World, they'll load the *Mayflower* with cargo and sail back to England," John told her. "I wish Klaus would stay with us, but he probably wouldn't make a very good landlubber."

Sarah gave a peal of laughter. "Landlubber! You're beginning to sound like a sailor, John Smythe." She danced around in front of him, grinning. "Avast, me hearties, 'tis a sail I see."

"If Mother hears you talking like that, she'll wash your mouth out with soap," John warned, but he couldn't help laughing. It was good to see Sarah happy. Most of the time Mother kept Sarah close beside her, unwilling for her daughter to be around the rough sailors.

John and Sarah soon made friends with the other children aboard, not only with the older children from Leiden, but also with the servants and children of the Strangers. They had to make their own fun. Sometimes it was watching the sailors, making sure to keep out of their way. At other times, they played with the few dogs aboard or with the ship's cat.

Sarah liked to read the books William Brewster had brought, even if they were grown-up books.

John didn't. "Why spend time reading when there is so much to learn?" he demanded. He explored all of the ship he could without getting into trouble. Anything to keep out of the damp, unpleasant sleeping quarters that held most of the passengers!

Captain Christopher Jones had moved to a small cabin so that about twenty of the persons he considered most important could sleep in his quarters. A few slept in a small shallop that would be used to explore the rivers of the New World. The rest of the passengers were crammed into the space below the main deck. The room was dim and nearly airless. Everyone slept on the floor. John longed to sleep topside with the sailors, but he had to stay with his family.

People wore the same clothes day after day. They put on everything they owned to keep from freezing in their unheated quarters. With only the salty seawater to wash themselves in, it was impossible to keep clean. Soon the smell of unwashed bodies and unwashed clothes became overpowering. When people became sick, the smell grew even worse. Could anyone stand it for two long months? The Pilgrims gritted their teeth and held on. So did the Strangers.

John amused himself by learning as much as he could about his fellow travelers and passing his new knowledge on to his family. "Myles Standish is going to be our captain when we reach America," he reported. "He is to lead us in defending ourselves against unfriendly Indians."

"Why him?" Sarah wanted to know. She gave a little shiver. "I know it's wrong not to like people, but he looks so mean! I wonder if his wife, Rose, is happy."

"Would you be if you were married to him?" John teased.

"No, sir!" Sarah shook her head. "Why can't Mr. Alden be our captain? I like him a lot. He's always so polite and calls me Mistress Smythe." She held both sides of her skirt wide and curtsied.

"John Alden is a cooper, not a soldier," Father reminded the children. "He will be kept busy making and repairing barrels, as he has done here on the *Mayflower*."

"We must be fair," Mother put in. "I've heard Mr. Standish is brave and fearless. If there is trouble with the Indians—and I pray to God there will be none—we will need an experienced soldier."

John laughed. "Do you want to hear something funny? I heard a man say of him, 'A little chimney is soon fired.'"

"What does that mean?" Sarah eagerly leaned forward.

"Whoever made the unkind remark means Myles Standish is not only short but has a bad temper that flares up quickly," Father said. "I hope, son, you will repeat it to no one else."

"I won't," John promised.

Another day he announced, "I think John Alden admires Priscilla Mullins."

"I knew that before we left England," Sarah boasted. "I can see why, too. She is friendly and nice."

"Miss Mullins is indeed a good girl," Mother agreed. "Although she is only eighteen, she has proved to be a hard worker. She helps the mothers who have small children and also does more than her share of the cooking." A smile tipped her lips upward. "That is, when we are allowed to cook. It is so discouraging to have rain and waves splash water into our living space! Hard biscuits and salted beef or pork are not proper food."

"The sailors call the biscuits hardtack and the salted meat salt horse," John said. "I like hot food better."

"I hate picking bugs out of my food worst of all," Sarah complained.

"Better than leaving them in and eating them!" John laughed

at the expression on his sister's face.

Sometimes even John found the wide Atlantic Ocean a lonely place. Questions raced through his busy mind. It was dangerous for a ship to make the crossing by herself. Suppose they were shipwrecked. No one would ever know. What if they ran out of food? They could starve, just as others had done before them.

So far, there had been no sign of pirates. John felt thankful. He hadn't repeated to Sarah the bloodcurdling stories he had teased Klaus into telling him when the sailor was off duty and not sleeping. Names like buccaneers, freebooters, and sea rovers danced in John's head. He suspected Klaus stretched his stories. Still, the wicked-looking scar on the sailor's shoulder supported his tales.

Klaus still scowled, but John knew the rough sailor liked him. "All because I didn't tell the captain of the *Speedwell* what happened that day," John muttered to himself. "I'm glad I didn't." He shivered, thinking of the dreaded cat-o'-nine-tails. Just thinking of those cords lashing a man's back made John feel sick.

Fortunately, there had been no whippings aboard the *May-flower*, at least so far.

John prayed there never would be.

❧ CHAPTER 9 ❧

Storm at Sea

Raging winds moaned and howled like screaming, hungry beasts. Day and night the roaring sea battered the *Mayflower* without letting up. She rolled and pitched. Her timbers creaked and groaned like someone in pain. With each new attack, it seemed the gallant ship must burst apart at the seams. Captain Jones and his crew fought the storm with all their might, as they had fought many others. Yet in spite of their best efforts, they could barely keep the ship from going down with all her passengers.

Mothers hugged their small children, trying to protect them from the wind and waves. People clung to whatever was fastened down in order to keep from being swept into the sea.

John was greatly disappointed that Father would not allow him to go topside during the worst of the storm.

"It's too dangerous," Father said. "If someone doesn't fall overboard before this storm ends, it will only be by the grace of God."

His words planted a seed of fear in John's heart. It was bad enough being cooped up with so many people. What must it be like on deck? "What about Klaus and the other sailors?" he anxiously asked.

"They have sailed stormy seas many times," Father reassured him. "They know what to do and how to protect themselves."

That made John feel better. Surely a seaman such as his rough friend who had faced pirates and escaped with only a badly cut shoulder could beat a storm.

John swallowed his fear and tried to comfort Sarah, pale-faced and sick from the heaving ship. "Don't worry. The ballast in the bottom of the *Mayflower* will keep her upright when the strong winds hit the sails. So will the cargo below the passenger deck."

A wild cry arose, loud enough to be heard even above the storm. "The seams! The winds have forced open the deck seams!" The next moment, a wave of icy seawater poured down onto the sick and frightened travelers, drenching them from head to foot. It soaked blankets and food. The terrified little band huddled together, seeking comfort as much as warmth.

Just when everyone felt they would surely die in the storm, William Brewster's voice rolled out. "Brethren, be of good cheer! Have we not been told the same God we worship and for whom we have abandoned our homes is the God of the sea? Remember the words of the Psalmist: 'The Lord said, I will bring my people again from the depths of the sea.' Did God not part the waters of the Red Sea long ago and bring His children safely through?"

Dripping wet, teeth chattering from his freezing bath, Elder Brewster stood among his flock and offered encouragement in the very face of death!

Elder Brewster went on. "Let us pray. Almighty Father, God of land and sea and sky, have mercy on us. If it be Thy will for us to reach America, build a colony, and worship Thee, deliver us from this raging storm. If it be Thy will to take us even unto Thyself, so be it. We are Thy children, and Thou art our Father. We are in Thy hands. Forgive our trespasses and make us—"

C-r-a-c-k. The sound of something breaking cut off Elder Brewster's prayer.

"What was *that*?" Sarah cried.

"I don't know." Father staggered to his feet, hung onto whatever he could, and prepared to investigate.

John sprang up. "May I come?"

"No!" Father's voice sharpened with fear. "Stay with Mother and Sarah!"

John dropped back to the pile of soaked blankets, wishing Father would realize he was man enough to go along at such times. *Perhaps he would, if you didn't get into mischief and acted more like a man,* a little voice inside reminded him.

Father returned in a very few minutes. "I have bad news. The main beam has cracked. The deck is in splinters."

"How could such a huge beam crack?" John demanded, not believing what his ears had just heard.

"A beam can stand only so much strain," Father replied.

"Is the *Mayflower* going to sink?" Sarah whispered. She scooted closer to her mother.

"We hope not." Father's calm voice made his daughter feel better. "We are in God's hands, as Elder Brewster said."

A cold, wet hand crept into John's. Sarah's lips trembled.

Her face was so white freckles stood out like thick stars on a cloudless night.

If only he could do something to make her feel better! John quickly thought how his sister cheered up when he said something funny. He shook his head. Nothing was funny about either the storm or having the main beam of their ship cracked.

Maybe a verse of Scripture would help. John frantically ran through some of those he'd learned in meeting until he came to one that brought a grin to his cold, blue lips. "Sarah, remember how Elder Brewster is always saying all things work together for good to them that love God?"

A spark of interest crept into her frightened eyes. "Yes, but I don't see any good now."

"There is, though. You know our clothes are dirty from all this time we've worn them. Well, the sea just washed them for us, didn't it?" John knew how weak his joke was, but he couldn't think of anything else, and he couldn't bear to see Sarah so miserable. He felt warmth steal into his chilled body when Father sent him a grateful look.

"That's right, John! Thank you for reminding us," Father said.

"Can they fix the beam?" Mother asked anxiously.

"I'm not sure. It may mean we will have to turn back to England." Father sounded sad.

"Turn back! When we're already halfway there?" John felt his old spirit return. "There must be a way to fix the beam." He raised his head. "Listen. The howl of the storm is not quite so strong."

"Thank God for that." Father started back topside. Before John could ask permission, Father said, "You may come along, son, but hang on to me at all times. The storm still rages."

When they reached the deck, John's mouth fell open. Shivers chased up and down his spine—and not just from his wet clothing. The deck had been splintered. A great crack in the main beam clearly showed how badly it had been damaged.

Captain Jones stood nearby, talking with a few men, including John Howland. The Smythes liked the hearty young man, a servant to John Carver.

"Recaulking the seams is no problem," Captain Jones stated. "But we must repair the buckled main beam."

"We cannot do that unless we go back to England," a man said.

Jones crossed his arms over his chest and stubbornly replied, "My ship is strong and firm beneath the water line. Once we get the main beam fixed, there is no need to turn back."

The arguing went on. Suddenly a great gust of wind rocked the *Mayflower.* Father wrapped his arms around John, braced himself, and shouted in John's ear, "We must go below again!" Before they could move, a great wave swept John Howland across the deck, over the rail, and into the churning sea!

"Man overboard!" The cry burst from a dozen throats.

John's heart missed a beat then pounded with the same fury as the increasing storm. No one could live in those waves!

A great cheer rose above the roaring of the storm.

"What is it?" John yelled.

"The lad's grabbed ahold o' a topsail halyard!" Klaus bellowed. Carrying a boat hook, the sailor headed toward the ship's rail at a dead run. He leaped obstacles and swept aside two of his fellow seamen when the pitch of the ship threw them into his path.

"It's a miracle!" a Pilgrim shouted.

"A miracle?" John cried, gazing on the line that hung overboard and ran out at length. There was no sign of John Howland. "He must be deep under the water!"

"He's holding on," Klaus bellowed. A few moments later, the big sailor used his boat hook and hauled Howland to safety, brawny arms straining. For the second time the seaman had cheated the angry waters of a victim.

Scared and soaked, Howland wordlessly gripped his rescuer's hand. Another cheer rose.

The winds died down a little. Or perhaps they were only gathering for another assault on the shaken, leaky *Mayflower*. The near-tragedy had taken attention away from the crippled ship, but now discussions began again.

"A great iron screw was loaded wi' the Pilgrims' goods," a sailor volunteered.

"Why would they be taking an iron screw to America?" Captain Jones barked. "It ain't a normal piece of baggage!"

"Aye, aye, sir. Mebbe that God o' their'n knew we'd need it." The sailor slapped his leg and laughed. Others joined in.

"Silence!" Jones roared. "Klaus, get that screw, if there is such a thing. With a post under it, the job can be done."

At Father's insistence, John unwillingly went below again. He wanted to see the crew raise the great screw and mend the beam. He wanted to tell Klaus how proud he was of him. Instead he had to content himself with reporting the excitement to Mother and Sarah.

"Klaus could have been washed into the sea, just like John Howland," he said breathlessly. "He is so brave. Klaus hauled

John in the same way he'd haul in a huge fish. The sea tugged and pulled, as if it didn't want to give Howland up. I saw it with my own eyes, Sarah!"

Once the main beam was repaired, the *Mayflower* sailed on. John's curiosity burned brighter than ever. One day he asked William Bradford, "Did God really cause us to bring the great iron screw? Did He know the beam would crack? And that if there hadn't been a screw, we would have had to go back?"

Bradford shook his head. "Perhaps." Deep trouble showed in his eyes. John knew why and felt sorry for him. William's frail wife, Dorothy, had not been able to bear the miserable living conditions on shipboard as well as the others. She grew paler and sadder each day. The Smythes feared she would never live to reach the New World. Would the grieving woman die at sea, without ever seeing her little son, John, who had been left behind?

John wished he hadn't bothered William Bradford. He slipped away by himself, needing time to think. Why was life so hard? Why did God allow terrible storms to come, when the Pilgrims only wanted to get to America where they could serve Him? John looked out across the water, peaceful for a change. "You treacherous sea," he cried. "You look so smooth, but all the time you're getting ready to beat against us again and again. Well, you're not going to win! You hear? God's going to help us get to America, in spite of you."

John shook his fist at the calm ocean, but shivered. What would happen next?

CHAPTER 10

Where Did Everyone Go?

One of the children's favorite things to do when weather permitted them to be on the top deck was to watch the barefoot crew at work. John would have given anything to be able to climb up and down the rigging like monkeys scrambling up and down trees in a forest. Time after time he considered it, but the threatening looks he got from the sailors dampened his enthusiasm. Besides, after his experiences during the storm, John was trying harder than ever to stay out of trouble.

"I don't have to worry about you so much now," Sarah observed one day. "I'm glad." She sighed. "John, everyone talks about whether we should go on or turn back."

"What do you want to do?" he asked her.

She stared at him from dark-circled eyes. "I'm too tired to care. I just wish we'd get somewhere. Anywhere. I'm so tired of the winds. Tired of the ship rising and falling and making so many people ill. Most of all, I'm tired of helping Mother care for the sick. I know I shouldn't feel that way, but all I want to do is drop down in a heap and sleep."

"Poor Sarah." John gently pulled one of her braids. "Lie down and rest for a little while. I'll take your place."

"You can't help the women, and more of them are sick than the men."

"If you don't rest, you'll be sick yourself," he argued.

Sarah gave in and curled up on the damp deck. John heaped blankets around her until only her green eyes and the top of her head showed. "There. Rest now."

"John, I feel so strange. It's like we left Holland years ago— not just a few weeks. Sometimes I can't even remember what it was like there. All I can think of is the ocean and the storms." Tears came. "I wonder if Gretchen ever thinks of me. I wonder if—" Her voice trailed off.

John stayed with Sarah until she drifted into a restless sleep. "I'm glad I'm not a girl," he whispered to himself. "It is so much harder for her." He searched his brain for a way to make his sister feel better. At last he came up with a plan and put it into action a few days later.

The pitching ship had steadied, at least for a time. People began to feel better. They gathered in the weak, late autumn sunshine, well wrapped against the cold air. The Pilgrims prayed, sang hymns, and talked about America.

"Tell us more about the New World," John begged a weathered traveler known for his interesting stories. All the children on board liked hearing them whenever time allowed them to gather around the old man.

"Shall I tell you about the Lost Colony?" the old man asked.

"Yes! Yes!" the children cried.

Sarah perked up enough to ask, "How could a colony get

lost?" A bit of color came to her thin cheeks and spread beneath her freckles. Her eyes sparkled.

John gave a sigh of relief. His plan was working!

"It's a curious story, and it happened way back in 1585," the storyteller began in a mysterious voice. "Sir Walter Raleigh, you all know who he is?"

"Oh, yes," they chorused. John added, "A soldier, writer, and explorer."

Priscilla Mullins, who stood a little way from the children, called, "There's a story about him meeting Queen Elizabeth. It may not be true, but people say she was out walking and stopped by a huge mud puddle. According to the story, Sir Walter Raleigh took off his coat, threw it in the mud puddle, and made a dry place for her to walk across."

"That's funny!" the children shouted.

"It's silly," eight-year-old Francis Billington announced. He and his brother, sons of Strangers John and Eleanor Billington, were troublemakers. Any mischief on board the *Mayflower* found them in the middle of it, and the Smythe children tried to stay as far away from them as possible.

"I wouldn't put my coat in the mud, even for the queen," John Billington said.

"It may never have happened," the old man laughed. "What did happen was that Raleigh became Queen Elizabeth's favorite. She gave him a twelve-thousand-acre estate in Ireland, where he planted the first potatoes. British explorers brought potatoes to England and Ireland from South America."

"What about the Lost Colony?" Francis demanded.

"I'm getting to that, young 'un. Raleigh sent a band of about one hundred men to settle in America in a place called Virginia. They dug themselves in offshore on an island called Roanoke, but they had a mighty thin time of it.

" 'Bout a year later, they sailed back to England. More colonists came, bringing supplies and stuff to trade with the Indians. All but fifteen of them also went back, according to the story. Then another bunch came. This time there were women and children among them. The sailors dumped them on Roanoke Island, but you know what?" The old man's eyes glistened.

"What?"

John looked at Sarah. She leaned forward, as eager to hear as the others.

"When the next batch came, there wasn't hide nor hair of those who had stayed in America!"

"Where did they go?" a half-dozen voices cried, Sarah's among them.

The old man shook his head. "No one knows."

"Someone has to know," John Billington scoffed.

"They don't, and the story gets even curiouser. About a month after the group that had women and children came to Roanoke, the first English child was born in America. She was John White's granddaughter, and they called her Virginia Dare." John suspected the storyteller was enjoying his tale as much or more than those who listened!

"White didn't want to leave, but the colony badly needed supplies. He sailed to England." Excitement lighted the old man's face. "War came with Spain. England couldn't and wouldn't give White supplies or a ship. He had to wait before he could sail back to America."

"And he didn't find anyone? Not even his granddaughter?" Sarah burst out.

"Right you are, little lady. All he and those with him found were the letters *CRO* carved on one tree and the word *Croatan* on another."

"But that's impossible! How could they just vanish?" John asked.

"I said it was curious, didn't I?" The storyteller's eyes twinkled, but a look of awe lurked in their depths. "Some say they must have been captured and carried off by unfriendly Indians. Others say that ain't so at all. They hold that when the colonists ran out of food, they joined a friendly tribe called *Croatans* and left the name on the tree to show folks where they were. Still others said they must have gone away to find food.

"Like I said, there wasn't hide nor hair of any of them, not even little Virginia Dare. No one knows and no one ever will know where those folks disappeared to after the ship sailed back to England."

"That is so sad." Sarah's eyes looked like saucers.

Maybe the story hadn't been such a good idea after all, John miserably thought. He knew as long as he lived, he'd remember the Lost Colony and little Virginia Dare. He'd just bet Sarah would, too. His mouth felt dry. His eyes burned. What kind of country were they going to, that swallowed people and left no trace but a few letters and a mysterious word carved on a tree?

CHAPTER 11

What Happened to All the Food?

Sarah Smythe wearily trudged down the deck of the *May-flower*. Her stomach growled. She quickly looked both ways. No one was close enough to hear except the ship's cat. Thank goodness for that. It was so embarrassing when her complaining stomach got so loud others could hear!

"I don't know why it should bother me," Sarah told the cat, who lay curled on top of a coil of heavy rope. "Everyone else's stomach is growling, too."

The cat yawned, looking bored.

"A lot you care." Sarah resentfully eyed the animal's well-fed body. "You can catch your dinner. The rest of us have to put up with moldy cheese, hardtack so dried out it has to be soaked before anyone can eat it, and bad butter!" Her stomach grew queasy at the thought of the unappetizing meals.

"What's wrong, little sister?" John said from behind her.

"I'm so hungry, I'm about ready to start in on him!" Sarah pointed at the cat and took a step toward him.

The sudden movement sent the cat into the air, fur standing

straight up. He came down on all four feet, gave Sarah a baleful look, and streaked down the deck. His angry *meowrrr* split the calm air and brought peals of laughter from the Smythes.

"Do you think he understood me?" Sarah said, when she could get her breath.

John let out a whoop. "I don't know, but he was taking no chances!"

"That he wasn't," a new voice agreed. A broadly grinning Klaus paused for a moment on his way aft. "That ol' cat lit out 's if a banshee were atter him."

"What's a banshee?" Sarah wanted to know.

John wiped tears from his eyes. "A make-believe creature that wails and howls, right, Klaus?"

"Aye, lad. But I dunno 'bout the make-b'lieve part." His shaggy eyebrows met over his eyes.

"Have you ever seen a banshee?"

Klaus shook his head. "Naw, but I kin hear 'em howlin' in the wind." He went on his way, leaving John and Sarah staring after him, then at each other.

"There aren't really banshees, are there?" Sarah pulled her warm cloak closer around her shivering body.

"No. They're something somebody made up, perhaps to frighten children." John grinned at her.

Sarah's stomach growled again, louder this time.

John's eyes opened wide. He threw one hand against his heart in mock fear. "Is that a banshee I hear? Maybe Klaus is right, after all!"

John's laughter brought stinging tears to Sarah's eyes. Her usual good nature disappeared. "Can't you ever be serious about anything?" she cried. Red flags of color waved in her thin cheeks. "John Smythe, your own sister is so hungry she's jealous of a ship's cat, and you stand there laughing!"

"I can't help it," John choked out. "You don't want rats or mice for dinner, do you? They wouldn't be cooked, of course—"

Sarah's already churning stomach couldn't stand the thought of eating rodents. In spite of Klaus and his warnings, she headed for the ship's rail.

"Sarah, I'm sorry!" John sounded miserable. He hung onto his sister until what little food she had in her came up then led her to a deserted spot that was sheltered a bit from the wind. "I was only trying to make you laugh."

Sarah ducked her head and stared at the deck. "I know." She wiped tears from her face with the back of her none-too-clean hand. "It's just that we go on and on and seem to get nowhere. The food is almost gone. What will we do if we run out of things to eat before we get to America?"

The question hung heavy in the air. John finally said without much conviction, "Well, God sent manna to the children of Israel. He could do it again, I s'pose."

His weak attempt to make Sarah feel better brought a half-smile. She closed her eyes and said, "Remember all the food that got loaded into the hold of the *Mayflower*?"

"How could I forget?" John snorted. "We laughed and told each other there was enough food to take us all around the world, not just to America."

"Where did it all go?" Sarah wondered. She opened her eyes. "I can still see the crates and crates of vegetables, lemons, and limes." Her mouth watered. "How I'd like to have some of them now!"

"So would I." John joined in the game. "It seems impossible we could eat so many sacks of flour, potatoes, dried beans, and peas. Or that all the barrels of salted-down pork and beef, the slabs of bacon, and jars of oil are nearly used up.

"Too bad we don't have a barrel of grain and a small bottle of oil like the widow who fed Elijah." Sarah sighed and fell silent, thinking of the story from the Bible. "John, if you were like the widow and only had enough meal and oil to make one little cake for us, would you give it to a stranger who asked for food? Even though it meant we would starve?"

John cocked his head to one side. Sarah could see how seriously he took her question. After a few moments he said, "It would depend on the stranger. Elijah was so close to God, it must have shown in the way he acted. Remember, Elijah told the woman not to be afraid. He also promised if she would make him a little cake, the food would never run out until the Lord sent rain and the crops would grow."

Sarah felt her heart beat faster. "Do you think the widow knew Elijah was a prophet of God?"

"She must have had faith in him, or she wouldn't have given away the food her son needed. I might give away my own food, but I'm not sure I'd give away yours or Father's or Mother's."

"It's a good thing the widow believed what Elijah said," Sarah soberly told her brother. "She always had enough to feed her son, herself, and the prophet." Sarah's empty stomach grumbled again. "Oh, dear! How can I wait until it's time for the next meal?"

John leaped up the same way the ship's cat had done earlier. "Stay here. I'll see if I can get you something."

Sarah watched him head aft, racing along at top speed. What did he have in mind? With the food supply almost gone, how could he find anything for her poor stomach? There simply was not enough food on board for people to eat between meals.

A dull ache settled in her middle. She watched the rolling waves. "Father, thank You they aren't so high now," she prayed in a whisper. She mustn't get sick again. Mother had enough to do caring for those who were already sick. Shame filled Sarah's heart. "I'm sorry to complain, God. Please, help us get to America safely."

She thought of the wonderful stories of the New World. Fruit and nut trees. Deer in the forests and no king to say hungry people must not kill and eat them. Fish—so many all one had to do was put in a net and bring in a great haul.

Still thinking of the good things to eat they would have in America, Sarah grew drowsy. A hand shaking her shoulder roused her from the daydream that had changed into a dream of summer skies, ripe fruit, and laughing children.

"Wake up, Sarah," someone whispered.

She opened her eyes.

John huddled on the deck before her, his back to some passengers who had come topside to take advantage of the calmer weather. "Shh. Don't let anyone see," he warned.

Sarah stared at the small piece of dried beef in her brother's hand. Her mind whirled. Alarm rose inside her. "John, where did you get this? You didn't *steal* it, did you?"

"Don't be a goose," he scornfully told her. "Besides being wrong, stealing food when supplies are so low would bring a terrible punishment."

He handed the meat to Sarah. She saw the hunger in his eyes

but knew he hadn't taken one morsel. "Do you have a knife?"

John licked his lips but shook his head. "You need it worse than I do." No amount of persuasion could talk him into sharing the meat.

Her mouth filled with the hard stuff, Sarah said between chewing, "You still haven't told me how and where you got it."

John shrugged, but his eyes sparkled. "What would you say if I said I told Klaus you were so hungry you'd considered eating the ship's cat?"

"You didn't!" Sarah gasped. A little stream of juice trickled from her lips. "You know I wasn't serious. What will he think of me? John, how could you?"

"Shh," John warned again. He quickly wiped the telltale drops away. "I didn't say I told him." His mischievous brown eyes glowed with the excitement of fooling his sister. "I just asked—"

"I know what you asked." She clutched the tiny remaining piece of beef in one hand and glared at him. "Did you or did you not tell him?"

"I didn't." When Sarah drooped with relief, John added, "I only said you were most awf'ly hungry."

Curiosity overcame even hunger. "What did he do?"

"He ordered me to stay on deck." John's eyes flashed with admiration. "A few minutes later he came back with the dried beef."

"What did he say?" Visions of the punishment John had mentioned danced in Sarah's head. "Oh dear, I hope Klaus didn't steal it!"

John hunched closer. His eyes darkened to the color of the

ocean when storm clouds raced above. "He didn't. He has been hoarding the piece of meat for himself. But don't try to thank him. I already told him you would be grateful, and it's best to make sure no one knows about this."

"Even Father and Mother?" Sarah felt guilty already. Yet was it wrong to protect someone who had been kind?

"The more persons who know about it, the greater the chance that Klaus will get into trouble. People might assume that he'd stolen the meat," John reminded her.

Sarah swallowed the last salty bite. "At least my stomach has stopped growling."

"Good thing." John became his usual self. "There for a while I was afraid Captain Jones might think someone set off a cannon!"

This time his teasing didn't bother her. Sarah giggled. "Or that a thunderstorm is coming close." She saw by John's grin how relieved he felt that her own storm had passed, at least for now.

"I know something fun to do." John sprang to his feet. "Let's go look at the chests of things going to the New World. It will help us forget being hungry."

"Why?" Sarah asked. "What's the fun of looking at chests so tightly closed we can't open them—and wouldn't dare, if we could!"

"We can thump on them," John suggested. "We can try to guess all the things inside of them." His hair blew in the wind that had started to rise.

"All right." Sarah got up and followed him to where the

chests holding everything imaginable sat fastened down so securely that not even the wildest waves could snatch and hurl them into the stormy ocean depths.

CHAPTER 12

Mischief on the *Mayflower*

John, Sarah, and a few other children, including the trouble-making Billington boys, daringly thumped on the top of the chests.

"This one sounds empty," Francis Billington complained, thumping away on the top.

"It prob'ly just had blankets and clothes. People took 'em out to keep from freezing," his brother John said.

John Billington thumped on another chest. "Wonder which ones have the trinkets?" He tried to shake the heavy trunk but couldn't budge it. "We hadta haul all this stuff from England just to trade with the stupid Indians."

"How do you know Indians are stupid?" John Smythe demanded.

"They must be, to want a bunch of glass beads, mirrors, cloth, and junk like that." Francis Billington stuck out his tongue and made an awful face.

"You can trade an iron pot for furs," John reminded him.

"I'll bet I could get a lot more furs from trading a musket

than an old iron pot," Francis bragged. "All they have are bows and arrows. Bang. Bang, bang!" He raised an imaginary gun to his shoulder and pretended to squint along its barrel. "I'm gonna kill me a hundred Indians, maybe a thousand. I'm gonna be the greatest Indian-killer in the world."

"No, you aren't. I am!" John Billington pitched into Francis and they fell to the deck.

"Are not!" Francis squealed, arms waving wildly.

"Am, too!" John howled when his brother's fist hit his eye.

"Stop that fighting this instant," a stern voice commanded. Captain Jones yanked the Billingtons up by the scruff of their necks and shook them hard. "Now get below, all of you!"

Sarah saw her brother's mouth open to protest. She grabbed his arm and hurried him away. The glint in the captain's steely eyes meant trouble.

"We weren't doing anything wrong," John protested.

"The Billingtons were, and we were with them," Sarah answered.

"They are always doing something wrong," John grumbled.

"I know." She felt a smile creep over her face. "At least they got caught this time and couldn't put the blame on someone else, the way they usually do."

"I can tell you what will happen," John said. "One of these times the Billingtons are going to do something so bad the captain will whale the living daylights out of them. They deserve it."

"John Smythe, watch what you say. Father will punish you if he hears you talking like that!" Sarah cried.

John stubbornly planted his feet on the deck and declared in imitation of Klaus, "Mark my words. You'll see what happens."

"You act like you want them to get in trouble." Sarah stared at her brother. "Would you like for people to feel that way about you?"

John didn't give an inch. "I only do funny things and play tricks. I don't do things that are dangerous or could hurt people."

"I know, but you worry Father and Mother and me. Not so much anymore," she loyally added. "It's probably because you're almost a man. You must have grown an inch since we left Leiden."

"You think so?" John looked pleased, and the subject of the Billingtons was dropped—but not for long. Within a few days, a terrible thing happened.

John and Sarah had just come on deck when they saw Francis Billington standing near some barrels of gunpowder.

"What's he doing?" Sarah whispered, craning her neck to see better.

"Probably nothing good." John's complaint turned to horror. "He has a musket. Sarah, get down!"

She fell to the deck, her terrified gaze fastened on Francis Billington.

"Stop that right now!" John roared, racing toward the eight-year-old boy.

Francis glanced around. A stubborn look settled on his face. "You can't tell me what to do." He pulled the trigger of the musket.

Boom!

The bitter smell of powder hung in the air. Men, women, and children came running. Sarah scrambled to her feet and raced toward the haze of smoke. "John, are you all right?" she asked.

"Yes, but—"

Klaus reached Francis Billington first. He caught him up in a grip of iron. "What were you thinking!" he roared. "Shootin' off a musket wi' kegs o' gunpowder near? Ain't there a brain in yer head? One spark coulda blown us t' bits! You should be fed t' the fishes, an' that brother o' yourn, too!" He dangled Francis above the deck and made as if to throw him overboard.

Francis, who had grinned broadly when the musket fired and people came running, tried to escape. His kicking legs only hit empty air. He tried to squirm free, fear written all over his dirty face—not for nearly blowing up the ship and all aboard including himself, but because of Klaus's scowling face and strong grip. Klaus marched closer and closer to the ship's rail.

A thrill of fear went through Sarah. "Don't let him do it," she begged John.

"He won't. He just wants to give Francis the scare of a lifetime," John whispered.

"Unhand my son, you miserable lout!" John Billington Sr. ran forward. "How dare you lay hands on an innocent child?" He faced Klaus. His fists were doubled, and his face was black with anger.

At his words, the watching crowd broke into cries of protest.

"Innocent, indeed!" a woman's voice rang out. "That 'innocent' child of yours shot off a musket next to the barrels of gunpowder and nearly sent us to the bottom of the sea!"

Billington's jaw dropped. "Is this true?" he demanded.

Francis, who still dangled like a puppet from Klaus's strong hand, couldn't say a word.

"He did, Papa! He did!" Young John Billington danced up and down in glee and clapped his hands over his brother's prank. "He made the gun go boom, and everyone came."

"Wait till I get my hands on you," Billington threatened Francis. "As for you, John Billington, get out of my sight, you sniveling talebearer!" He began to curse.

"That is quite enough of that language. There are ladies present," John Alden sternly reminded Mr. Billington. A murmur of agreement went through the crowd, and pretty Priscilla Mullins sent the young cooper a grateful look that made his eyes sparkle.

"Put the boy down, Klaus," Captain Jones ordered. "Not but what we'd all like to throw him overboard. It's what he deserves. Sir," he said, turning to Mr. Billington, "Never in all my sailing have I had the misfortune to have two such troublemakers on board as your sons. From now on, they are not to be on deck or anywhere else without you. I am holding you accountable for any further trouble," he added for good measure. "Is that clear?"

"There will be no more trouble," Mr. Billington promised. He made a grab for Francis, who managed to stay out of reach for a few moments. Mr. Billington soon caught his son. He carried the kicking, screaming boy below. Loud wails soon showed that the culprit was being punished for the latest of his sins.

"It is only by the grace and mercy of God that we have been saved this day," the Pilgrims said. They knelt on deck and thanked their heavenly Father for protecting them from an event that could so easily have ended in tragedy.

Sarah felt as limp as if she had fought a long, hard battle.

"My goodness," she breathed to John after the crew returned to their duties and most of the passengers broke into little groups to discuss the latest near-disaster. "I would have thought even Francis Billington would know better than to do something like that."

"And he thinks the Indians are stupid!" John rolled his eyes.

"You were so brave, trying to stop him." Sarah felt proud of her big brother.

Instead of answering, John hung his head. His face turned white.

"John, are you sick?" Sarah asked, concern puckering her forehead.

He shook his head. After a moment, he said hoarsely, "Sarah, if I tell you something, will you promise not to repeat it to Father or Mother or anyone?"

"Do I ever repeat things you ask me not to tell?" she indignantly asked.

"No. You're a good secret-keeper." He cleared his throat. "It could have been me today instead of Francis."

"What do you mean?"

"I long to shoot a musket," John confessed. "Sometimes my fingers itch to take Father's out and try it." He stuffed his hands in his pocket. "Only the fear of Father's anger has kept me from doing so. Besides, we will need the powder when we get to America."

Fear worse than what she had felt when the musket had been fired so close to those barrels of gunpowder dried Sarah's throat to a crisp. "Will we really, truly have to fight Indians?" she croaked.

John looked around to make sure no one could hear what he said. "I am afraid so. It all depends. Some Indians are friendly. Some are not."

"God says it is wrong to kill," Sarah whispered. Visions of terrible battles rose in her mind.

"I know." John stared out at the ocean. Sarah had the feeling he wasn't seeing water but instead was looking at a strange and unfriendly land peopled with natives who wanted no strangers among them.

He went on. "I know we must defend ourselves, but I don't think I could kill anyone." He brightened up. "Maybe if we trade with the Indians and treat them fairly, they will become our friends. Then we won't have to fight at all."

"I pray that will happen," Sarah softly told him. Her cold little hand touched his. "I don't want you to ever have to fight Indians."

"Let's talk about something else," John suggested. He got to his feet from where they'd been sitting on the deck. "We've had enough trouble for one day."

"All right." Sarah stood. "I know. Let's talk about the Hopkins family. I really like Constanta, Giles, and Damaris, don't you?" She anxiously added, "I'm afraid Mistress Hopkins can't wait until we reach America to have her new baby."

She laughed, and the joyous sound brought an answering smile to her brother's lips. "Mistress Hopkins told Mother that her husband, Stephen, says if the baby should be a boy and born on the *Mayflower*, they will name him Oceanus. Isn't that funny? Whoever heard of a baby named Oceanus?"

John chuckled and walked faster. Sarah pattered along beside him. "What if it's a girl?" he asked.

"I don't know." Sarah thought about it. "I suppose they could call her Oceana or maybe Atlanta for the sea. I still think they are funny names. Maybe they will change their minds." She slowed her steps. "John, it's been so hard on the women who are going to have babies. The storms, I mean. It's bad enough when you're feeling good, but Elizabeth Hopkins and Susanna White and Mary Collins must suffer so much more. They aren't getting the proper food."

Her heart ached with sympathy for the courageous mothers who had taken the chance of having to give birth at sea. "I hope their babies will be all right."

"I do, too," John mumbled. He scuffed his feet on the deck.

Sarah suspected he was just as worried about the women as she was but wouldn't say so.

A few days later, long after everyone had been asleep one night, Sarah roused to hear Dr. Fuller say, "Abigail, I need your help. Elizabeth's baby won't wait any longer to be born."

Wide-eyed and anxious, Sarah waited and prayed during the long night hours, heart thumping with fear. Would Mistress Hopkins and her new baby be all right?

⌒ CHAPTER 13 ⌒

A Sad Day at Sea

Just before dawn, Sarah fell into a troubled sleep. In her dreams, it seemed she was back in Holland, running through the tulip fields with Gretchen. How bright and beautiful the flowers were: red and yellow, purple and white and pink. Thick green grass grew beneath a cloudless blue sky. Sarah's heart sang. The long voyage on the *Mayflower* must have been only a nightmare. It was so wonderful to be surrounded with color after all the gray ocean and sky and air.

The scene changed. "Hurry, Sarah," John called. "The canals are frozen deeply. Father says we may skate." The jingle of skates on his arm sang in her ears. She hastily put on heavy clothing, glad for the warmth. She had been cold for so long.

Her dream again changed. A small group sat around a long table on the large main floor of their meetinghouse, the Green Gate. Great quantities of steaming hot food covered the table—enough for everyone to eat their fill and some left to carry home. Sarah's mouth watered. Why had she never appreciated what she had? Pastor John Robinson offered a blessing for the meal.

His wife, Bridget, and their three children sat next to him.

"Come, daughter. We must go to America," Father said. "Abigail. John. Come." He rose from his place at the table.

Sarah stared at him in horror. "America? Father, must we go? We haven't eaten, and I am so hungry! The ocean is wide and stormy and cold." She shivered and crossed her arms over her chest. "Please let us stay long enough to eat."

"There is no food," her father sadly told her.

She turned her gaze from him to the table. The feast had vanished. All that remained were scraps of moldy bread and cheese. A bright-eyed mouse leaped to the table and began to nibble on the unappetizing food. Sarah's stomach churned. She stood and backed away from the table.

"Come, Sarah." Mother gently shook her daughter's shoulder. "There is good news."

Good news! How could there be anything good when she was so hungry and cold?

"Sarah, open your eyes." This time John spoke.

She slowly obeyed. Father and Mother sat near her. John knelt beside her pallet on the damp floor. Understanding slowly dawned on her. Life on shipboard had not been the nightmare. She'd only dreamed of Holland with its tulips and skating, the feast that turned to crumbs. She was on the *Mayflower* and must have fallen asleep while praying for Elizabeth Hopkins.

Fear washed away her disappointment. She sat up and rubbed sleep from her eyes. "Is Mistress Hopkins all right?" she asked, almost afraid to hear the answer. "Did the baby come? Is it well?"

John interrupted her flow of questions. "That's the good

news," he cried. "Mistress Hopkins and her brand new baby son are just fine!" Mischief danced in his eyes. He dropped his voice so others outside the family wouldn't hear. "They did name him Oceanus."

Sarah giggled. "He will probably be the only person in the whole world who is named that. I'm glad they are all right." A lump came to her throat. "I was afraid for them, so I prayed."

"As did we all," Father told her. His kind eyes smiled. "There will be a great deal of celebrating today."

Father was right. The baby's arrival renewed hope in the weary travelers with hungry stomachs and misery in their bones from the damp and cold.

"Just as Jesus was born in troublesome times, so has this baby been sent to us," Elder Brewster said. His thin, worn face glowed with happiness. "Oceanus Hopkins is a symbol of the new life we shall find in America. He will grow up in a land far from religious persecution. He shall be taught to worship God and read the Bible according to God's commands, not man's. No king shall dictate and demand obedience to what the child's conscience says is wrong."

Brewster's eyes glistened. Sarah felt mist rise to her own eyes. Her heart thrilled to the picture the elder painted.

Elder Brewster continued. "This child shall be free of fear. Think of it!" His voice rang with the old fire. "Oceanus will never be haunted by shadows of the dungeon and gallows. Praise God, he shall be free, even as we, who fled from England then sailed from Holland, are free!"

"Hurrah for Oceanus Hopkins!" John burst out, unable to keep still any longer.

"Hurrah!" Many took up the cry. For the first time in weeks, the fire that had filled hearts and souls before the Pilgrims left Holland spread over the faces of the weary Pilgrims. They burst into a spontaneous song of praise, thanking God for bringing them this far and asking His help for the rest of the voyage.

Yet just as the *Mayflower* itself went up and down with the force of the waves, so life on the ship had its ups and downs. One young sailor persecuted the Pilgrims. He never missed an opportunity to make fun of the sick people. He used as much bad language as possible, even in front of the women and children. Strong and conceited, he strode the deck, prancing over and around the sick and miserable Pilgrims.

"Fine lot ye are," he taunted. "Half of ye'll never make it." He grinned an evil grin. "Soon as yer bodies're heaved into the sea, I'll help meself to all ye brung with ye. I'd as soon throw half of ye in now."

When a few of the Pilgrims tried to reason with him, the sailor only bragged and blew, cursed and ridiculed them more. His ugly grinning face haunted the sick and made everyone feel worse. Only by the grace of God did the Pilgrims resist the temptation to throw their tormentor overboard.

Sarah knew how hard it was for John to hold his tongue. "He is no Klaus, grouchy outside and caring in his heart," she told her brother. "If you answer him back, that sailor might fling you into the sea." She shuddered at the thought. "Promise me you will stay away from him."

"I promise." John smiled at her. "I believe he's nothing but a dirty-mouthed braggart, but I wouldn't put it past him to carry out his threat—if he thought he could get away with it and hide what he did."

About halfway through the voyage, the sailor fell ill and died. William Bradford said, "Thus his curses light on his own head, and it is an astonishment to all his fellows for they note it to be the just hand of God upon him."

Other passengers agreed, and the superstitious crew wondered if such a fate might come to them if they persecuted the Pilgrims! The sailors kept as far away from the Pilgrims as possible for the rest of the journey, so the tired travelers didn't have to put up with as many insults.

"Do you *really* believe God made the sailor die because of what he did?" Sarah asked John. "What Mr. Bradford said makes me feel funny in here." She put her hand over her heart. "All of us do bad things. That's why Jesus came, so we could be forgiven for our sins. I don't like to think the God we pray to would kill someone just for being mean."

"William Bradford didn't say for sure that God killed the sailor," John explained. "He just said the man brought curses on his own head and that the rest of the crew believed God made it happen." He squirmed and admitted, "It makes me feel funny, too. Let's go ask Father and Mother."

Father considered their questions carefully. "It is not for us to know God's ways. Some see the tragedy as God's punishment. Others say the sailor would have become sick anyway." He looked deep into his children's troubled eyes. "The important thing is to live every day in a way that is pleasing to our Master. That way, we will be ready to meet God when we die."

"You have to be sorry before your sins can be forgiven, don't you, Father?" Sarah asked. She leaned her head against his shoulder and looked into his face. John stood nearby.

"Yes, child." His hand smoothed her tangled braids and rested on her head for a moment. Shadows darkened Father's dark eyes.

"Do you think perhaps when the sailor got sick, he was sorry and asked God to forgive him?" John put in.

Father sadly shook his head. "I pray that he did. Sometimes people do call on God and ask for mercy just before they die. I fear the young sailor may not have been one of them, but only God knows for sure."

"I wish Klaus knew Jesus." John sighed. "I've tried to tell him, but he just says a God as great as ours wouldn't care about poor, miserable sailors."

To the children's surprise, Mother laughed. Her whole face lit up. "Son, the next time you have the chance to speak of the Lord to Klaus, ask him if he's ever heard of Peter, Andrew, James, and John."

"From the Bible?" Sarah wrinkled her forehead.

"That's it!" John shouted. "They were fishermen, too. Why didn't I think of that?" He disgustedly flopped down on the floor beside Sarah. "Jesus loved those men like brothers. He called them away from their fishing nets and made them His disciples. Wait till I tell Klaus!"

"Be careful that you don't rush at your sailor friend, sounding as if you know everything and he knows nothing," Father warned. "Pray for God to give you a chance to speak of His Son. In the meantime, Klaus will be watching to see if knowing Jesus has made any difference in your lives."

"How can we show that?" Sarah wanted to know.

"Be honest. Stay out of trouble. Keep the Sabbath holy." Father stopped to take a breath.

John's face turned red. He glanced at his sister, as if asking whether Father knew he had played games with John and Francis Billington in a corner on a recent Sabbath when there was nothing to do between the long meetings. Sarah shrugged. She certainly hadn't told, but Father and Mother had a way of knowing things without being told!

"I know God rested on the seventh day," John said. "But Jesus said if a man's sheep falls into a pit on the Sabbath, there is no sin in getting it out."

"This is true." Father's eyes twinkled. "Remember this, though. If the sheep falls into the pit *every* Sabbath, you should either sell the sheep or fill up the pit!"

Sarah and her family laughed at Father's joke.

A short while later, their laughter stopped. William Butten, a young manservant to Dr. Fuller, died. The passengers gathered on deck for a short service. Sarah huddled between her parents, with John on Father's other side.

This second burial at sea was far different than the first. Few people had mourned the loss of the sailor who had been an enemy of the Pilgrims. Most watched with dry eyes when the man's body was committed to the watery depths. Now a pleasant young man's dream of one day living in the New World had been cut short.

Sarah took a deep breath and listened to Elder Brewster. "It is so sad," she whispered to John after the service. "We don't know if he has any family. William Bradford said he didn't think so." Her voice trembled.

"I know." John looked solemn. Sarah had the feeling he was remembering, as she did, what Father had told them about being ready to die by living right.

The very next day, pieces of driftwood appeared on the water. Birds slowly circled above the ship. Captain Jones cautiously announced, "Smell the change in the air? Notice how the wind has lessened? We must be getting close to land!"

CHAPTER 14

"Land, Ho!"

With the change in the weather, hope again returned to the travelers. All day Wednesday and Thursday the winds decreased. The ship inched forward. Weary passengers slept uneasily, waking now and then to wonder if the storms would come again. So many times when they thought the wind moved on, even worse gales had attacked the *Mayflower*. Would it happen once more?

Daylight came slowly that Friday morning, sixty-six days after the gallant ship had sailed from England. What would the new day bring? Would they really see land, or would Captain Jones's cautious predictions prove to be a false alarm? Sarah and her family roused to a long-awaited call from the lookout, the call even John had begun to think might never come.

"Land, ho!" the lookout bellowed.

Scrambling from every corner of the ship, the passengers raced to the top deck. They peered over the ocean to the western horizon. A low, dim mass showed dark in the chilly November morning. People rubbed their eyes to make sure the thin hump was real.

They sailed closer. A bleak and sandy shore with a few trees appeared.

"Land!" Sarah screamed.

"Land!" a hundred throats echoed her grateful cry.

Elder Brewster's voice rose above the rest. "Praise be to Almighty God! We have reached the New World!"

After her first glimpse of America, Sarah looked away and let her gaze travel over her fellow passengers. Father and Mother stood silently, not cheering like many of the others. John's eyes gleamed, but he kept silent. Tears streamed down worn faces. All turned toward the dim outline that meant the end of their journey. Men as well as women wept and were not ashamed. Many fell on their knees and blessed the God of heaven who had brought them safely to their new home.

Sarah's tender heart filled with sympathy for frail Dorothy Bradford, who lay in her husband's arms, too weak to stand. Stephen and Elizabeth Hopkins were nearby—Oceanus in his mother's arms, their other three children pressed close to their sides. Myles Standish touched his sword. Was he thinking of possible trouble with the Indians? Sarah pulled her shawl closer and shuddered.

Even the Billington boys stood motionless. Sarah grinned. The strong clutch of John Billington's hands on his sons' shoulders showed he had taken to heart Captain Jones's orders concerning Francis and John Jr.

"We are here," John Alden said.

Sarah smiled when Priscilla Mullins raised her head and repeated, "Yes. We are here." A crystal tear slid from one eye, and the look she gave the young cooper said far more than words.

Sarah turned her face back toward land. Bitter disappointment shot through her. Where were the fertile fields in which crops so miraculously grew? Where were the forests that held deer and wild boar for the taking? Most of all, where were the buildings, the homes of those who had come before and sent back such glowing reports?

A little distance away, Klaus leaned against the rail. Now that the *Mayflower* no longer pitched and rolled, Sarah dared go over to him. "Are you glad we are here?" she asked.

"Aye, lass." For once, Klaus made no attempt to scowl and act unfriendly. "I be thinkin' 'tis been a hard journey." His face settled into its usual frown.

Sarah realized how much she was going to miss the crusty seaman. "I suppose you'll be going back soon. To England, I mean. Father said the *Mayflower* would sail back as soon as she was loaded with cargo."

Klaus snorted. "An' where'll we be gettin' cargo?"

Sarah's eyes widened. "Why, from the Virginia colonists, of course."

John's voice cut in. "This isn't Virginia, Sarah." He sounded strange.

"Where are we, then?" She strained her eyes again, hoping against hope to discover all the wonderful things the New World was supposed to have. Her spirits dropped even farther. Not a ray of light came from shore. No ships lay between them and the land toward which they sailed. No activity hinted there were signs of life in the lonely stretch of earth ahead.

"New England," Klaus grunted. "The winds o' fate blew us off course."

"That's right," John said. "Shoals and winds have forced us away from the Virginia Colony where we agreed to settle."

"Oh, dear!" Sarah had counted on warm greetings, perhaps a feast, from those already in the New World. Surely they would be glad to see new settlers, even those who planned to start their own colony. "Now what will we do?"

Captain Jones, John Carver, and others were already discussing the issue. "We have a fine day ahead of us. The wind is slight and from the northeast," Captain Jones said. "We must tack about and sail southward. Agreed?"

"Agreed," the leaders answered. At the captain's command, the *Mayflower* turned and started south. Within a few hours, she reached Pollock Rip, below Monomoy Island, known for heavy breakers and dangerous shoals. Captain Jones eyed it with alarm. Did he dare try to navigate the churning sea, now that the wind had died down?

"We will turn back," he decided. "Nightfall must not catch us here."

"Good thing," John whispered to Sarah. "Klaus says this must be one of the most dangerous areas on the whole coast."

The *Mayflower* finally pulled free of the rip. She slowly sailed north, following the low and wooded shoreline. Before dawn on Saturday, she had reached Cape Cod. The sun rose. The ocean calmed, and the ship sailed into the wonderful, open Provincetown harbor Edward Winslow described as "large enough for a thousand sails to ride in safety."

John and Sarah quietly watched the sails lower. They heard

the splash of the anchors drop. The journey had ended. Yet it had taken a terrible toll. Every person showed the strain of hunger and sickness. Even the children had aged in the two endless months at sea.

Behind them lay persecution. Behind lay their friends and loved ones. Were they even at this moment anxiously wondering what had happened to the *Mayflower* and her passengers? Praying, perhaps, that the same God who watched over those in Holland and England might continue His loving care to the Pilgrims?

Ahead lay—what? Winter, cruel and harsh. Fierce storms, too intense for the Pilgrims to search the unknown coast. No friends to welcome them. No towns, houses, or inns to provide comfort. They must continue living on the *Mayflower* until some kind of shelter could be built, and that shelter must be built immediately.

The ship needed to start back to England as soon as possible. Captain Jones must make sure they carried enough food and drink for those on board, but he could decide to leave at any time. If he did, those remaining in America would be stranded—on their own until another ship arrived.

"Who knows when that might be?" many asked.

"The New World is hideous and empty," Sarah cried. She gazed into the wilderness, wondering about the people and beasts that lived there. Would they attack the colonists who tried to take over their land?

"Summer being done, all things stand upon them with a weather-beaten face," William Bradford murmured. "The whole country, full of woods and thickets, represents a wild and savage hue."

Sarah didn't understand everything he said, but the part about the New World greeting them with a weather-beaten face sank into her mind.

She turned away from the forbidding coast, fancying that it shouted, "Go home, Pilgrims. Go home, Strangers. You don't belong here."

Did John sense how she felt? Perhaps. His rough hand squeezed hers. "It isn't home yet, Sarah, but it will be."

"I just feel like we don't belong anywhere." She sighed. "Not in Holland or England or on the *Mayflower* or here."

"I know, but at least we crossed the ocean safely." He ran one hand through his brown hair until it stood straight up and waved in the breeze. "Don't you think God can take care of us on land as well as at sea? He brought us through some pretty terrible storms!"

William Bradford said much the same thing in a meeting of the Pilgrims and any others who chose to attend. "We shall be sustained by the Spirit of God and His grace," he told the assembled group. "Let us give thanks."

One by one, the Pilgrim leaders prayed. Many voices rose loud and strong, John Carver's and William Brewster's among them. Some spoke in hushed tones, as if the men could not believe they had actually defied wind and wave and come safely into harbor.

"Now that we have thanked God, what shall we do first?" someone asked.

"Wash our clothing!"

The reply brought a storm of laughter, but everyone agreed. Long weeks of wearing the same clothing with no way to keep clean had made the living quarters stink. Everyone looked forward eagerly to when they could go ashore and scrub away the dirt and stench of travel.

Just before dusk that evening, Sarah stole away from the other children who were amusing themselves at a game. She needed to think. Besides, she was tired, so tired her bones hurt. "My heart hurts, too," she whispered.

"Are you all right, Sarah?" John came up to where she stood huddled in her warm cloak, gazing at the unfriendly land that would be their new home.

Instead of answering him directly, she said, "Nothing is like we thought it would be, is it?" She hated the little tremble in her voice but couldn't seem to keep it from coming out along with her question.

"I guess not." John shoved his hands in the pockets of his rough coat. "Of course, this isn't Virginia, but maybe it will be even better." He cocked his head to one side and whistled a lively tune.

"How can it be?" Sarah wanted to know.

"For one thing, there's no one here to tell us what to do. If we had landed in Virginia—"

"I wish we had. At least there are other people there," Sarah protested. "And food. I'm not the only one who is worried. I heard Father tell Mother he didn't know how we could survive. It's far too late to plant and harvest any crops."

"Thanks to the *Speedwell* that didn't!" John laughed.

Sarah knew he was trying to cheer her up and managed a weak smile. "I know. It didn't speed well at all." She glanced over her shoulder, facing east.

"We won't starve," John promised, although how he could say such a thing, Sarah didn't know. "Now, what else is bothering you, little sister?"

"Klaus is going to leave us, and I don't want him to go."

"Not as soon as we might think," John whispered mysteriously. "There is a chance the *Mayflower* won't be able to return to England until spring."

"Did Captain Jones say so?" Sarah demanded.

"No, but Klaus told me the year is getting on so fast it may be too dangerous for the ship to start back. It was a stormy enough crossing, and the weather is getting worse and the gales heavier all the time." John sighed, and his usually laughing mouth set in a straight line. "I wish Klaus would stay here. One or two of the crew have agreed to stay and help with the building, but he just laughed and said he was no landlubber. Oh well. No sense worrying about it until it happens. Anything else bothering you?"

"Yes!" A lump rose to Sarah's throat, making it hard for words to get past. "Being hungry and frightened is bad enough, but. . .but, John, it just isn't fair!"

∽ CHAPTER 15 ∽

Spying Again!

John Smythe stared at his sister. "Fair? What isn't fair?"

"William Butten," Sarah said in a small voice. Her freckles stood out more clearly than ever, and her green eyes blinked back tears. "Why did he have to die before he even saw the New World? He was so close!"

"It makes me sad, too." John felt the same way he had when Dr. Fuller's young servant had been lowered into the waves. He stared at the shore. "Elder Brewster says we should give thanks that others of us didn't die. Many crossings lose a lot more than one crew member and one passenger. The storms we went through could have torn the *Mayflower* apart."

"I am thankful." Sarah dashed away tears with the back of her hand. "I just wish it hadn't happened."

John continued to gaze at the wooded area ahead of them. "So do I, but it doesn't help to look back. We're going to be plenty busy getting settled before winter gets any worse." He leaned on the ship's rail, then jerked back. "Even with the ship anchored in calm waters, Klaus still keeps an eye on me," John complained. "He has a way of mysteriously appearing just when I'm thinking about doing something!"

"Good for him," spunky Sarah said. "You need someone who can read your mind and stop you from getting into trouble before it happens."

The corners of John's mouth turned down. "I thought you said I'm better than when we left Holland."

"You are, but that doesn't mean you're perfect," she teased.

"What good does it do to try and be good if people just keep thinking you haven't changed?" He knew he wasn't being fair, but he didn't care. It hurt to think Sarah couldn't see how hard he was trying to be the boy Father and Mother and God wanted. Well, all he could do was work harder.

John's good intentions flew away on the breeze all too soon. It began when the leaders called a meeting in the crowded main room to discuss plans. When the men began to gather, John boldly marched in with them.

"What are you doing here?" someone sneered.

John folded his arms across his chest and drew himself to his full height. "I am very close to being a man. I have a right to be here," he haughtily told them. He then showed the irresistible smile that often got him what he wanted.

This time it didn't work. Loud laughter echoed through the crowd, especially from some of the London Strangers. John saw a sympathetic look on John Alden's face, but Myles Standish and others just scowled. In spite of all John's protests, he was ordered away from the meeting.

Anger filled his heart. How dare they treat him like a child? John flexed his wiry arm and proudly noted a swelling muscle.

Had he not been one of the few who remained well for most of the journey? Only the worst storms had laid him low, and then only for a short time.

"I can't bear to miss what they say," he told Sarah. "I won't, either." Hot color flew to his cheeks. "I'm going to find a place to hide so I can see and hear what goes on. Come with me, Sarah. You need to know about our future, too."

His sister shook her head until her dark brown braids flopped up and down. "John Smythe, don't you remember the last time I spied with you? Father and Mother were disappointed in us. I felt terrible."

"This is different," he tried to explain. "I went into the meeting openly and honestly. Is it my fault the men wouldn't let me stay?"

"That doesn't excuse your spying," Sarah flared up. She put her hands on her hips the way she did when most upset with him. "Think what will happen if those same men catch you listening!"

"Father won't let them do anything to me, although *he* might!" John said. "Besides, I'm not going to get caught. Neither will you. Please, Sarah?"

To his amazement, Sarah flatly refused. Sneaking admiration crept into John's heart, along with a little feeling of regret. Way down inside, he had to admit how much he'd always liked being able to lead Sarah—even when it was into little paths of temptation! John quickly pushed away the thought and pleaded with her again to join him. Sarah only shook her head and stood her ground.

"If you haven't learned anything on the voyage, I have,"

she told him. "I can't stop you from spying, but I don't have to join in. Remember what Father said the other time? Brothers' keepers shouldn't go along with other people when they do things that are wrong." She stuck her freckled nose in the air and marched off.

For a moment John was tempted to give up his spying idea. Then he thought of the rumors about all the exciting things to be discussed. No! He had to be there, to learn for himself what lay ahead.

"Curiosity can't be a sin," he told himself. "Otherwise God wouldn't have made me always wanting to know why."

Perhaps not, but sneaking into a meeting where you aren't wanted and shouldn't be is wrong, his conscience argued.

John let out a great breath of air and half turned to follow his sister. The sound of angry voices stopped him in his tracks. Forgetting all about his conscience, he tiptoed toward the meeting room. The door stood open. The men gathered there were so intent on their argument that no one saw John slide inside.

A quick survey of the crowded room showed a pile of torn sails in the corner, waiting to be mended. A single quick dive put John under them. He held his breath and waited, but no one came to challenge him. Heart pounding like waves against the *Mayflower*'s hull, the boy lifted a sail. To his disappointment, all he could see was the backs of men waving their arms as they argued.

John dropped the sail. At least he could hear. He bit his lip when laughter bubbled up and almost out. He hadn't really needed to sneak in and hide. The men's voices were loud enough to be heard halfway back to England!

Snug under the sails, John listened hard. He burned with anger when William Brewster, William Bradford, John Carver, and others spoke of the sponsors' demands. "You remember how they demanded ownership of the homes we build?" they said. "And how we must work for them seven days every week, with no time to attend to our own needs?"

A rumble of agreement went through the assembly. "I remember how we sold tubs of our precious butter to pay the port fees," someone called out. John thought it was Myles Standish.

The arguing went on. "We aren't at our grant and have no legal right here."

"We owe nothing to King James! This is the New World, America, a free country. We shall go where we please and do as we choose!"

"Nay," a strong voice protested. "That leads to lawlessness. We must have laws and obey them. We must also stay together. There are few enough of us, God knows. Even with His help, it will take all of us working together to make it through the winter." Someone cheered.

A voice John recognized as belonging to one of the Strangers disagreed. "We who are not of your faith know what will happen. You Pilgrims will take over and force us to obey whatever you decide."

"We shall never do that!" Elder Brewster's clear tones brought a hush to the noisy crowd. "Did we not come to America to get away from the absolute rule of a king? We must make laws and choose the leaders who rule this new land in the same way we choose our church leaders. Every man who is the head of a household shall vote, in order to have a say in the government. What affects one affects our common good."

A little wave of approval sounded from the listening men.

"Write down all our ideas, that we may agree or disagree with them," came the suggestion. "Here is paper. Put on it those things needed to make us a strong colony, one that rules itself."

It took time to list the ideas, to agree even on what would be put down. John grew restless. He wished they would hurry and finish so he could tell Sarah everything he had heard. Even though she would not join his spying, he knew she wanted to hear what had happened.

At last the agreement was reached and signed. It began by saying, "In the name of God, Amen. We whose names are underwritten, the loyal subjects of our dread sovereign King James, by the grace of God, of Great Britain, France, and Ireland, king, defender of the faith. . ."

Questions filled John's mind. Why must they declare loyalty to someone who had treated them so badly?

The agreement went on to state that the travelers had undertaken their voyage to plant the first colony in northern Virginia for the glory of God, the advancement of the Christian faith, and the honor of the king and country.

Again John was confused. How could one honor a man, even a king, so wicked that he executed those who worshiped according to their consciences? John liked the final part of the agreement better. Those who signed it bound themselves to become a body to make fair laws and choose their own leaders as needed for the general good of the new colony. They agreed to obey the will of the majority and vote for rules and leaders.

Make their own laws? Not wait for King James to tell them what to do? Crouched beneath the sails, John covered his mouth with his hands to hold back a cry of excitement. Never before had English colonists broken free from their king's rule! King James always appointed a governor, made rules, and forced the colonists to obey without question, just as they had done in England.

Now the people were free. For the first time in the history of the world, English men, women, and children would live under rules of their own making, rather than the king's.

John could not bear to miss seeing the men sign the paper. He crawled from his hiding place, taking advantage of the excitement in the room, and cautiously worked his way to just inside the door. Should anyone notice him, they would think he'd been drawn in by curiosity. John grinned mischievously. So he had!

The cheering had long since given way to the seriousness of the moment. On tiptoe, neck craned, John watched the men sign, forty-one in all. Though young, they looked old from the hardships they'd faced during the ocean crossing. First to sign the paper was highly respected, godly John Carver, who had been given authority over the trip when the *Mayflower* sailed from Southampton. William Bradford, Edward Winslow, William Brewster, and Isaac Collins followed. Then Myles Standish strode forward, sword hanging at his side. Next came John Alden. One by one the men signed, heads up, shoulders back.

The colonists took their first action by voting John Carver to continue as governor for a year. If he did not do a good job, someone else would be elected to replace him.

John slipped out. His eyes burned. His mouth felt dry—more from the thrilling events he had seen than from thirst. He raced down the deck and waved to Klaus, who gave his usual grunt, followed by a twitch of his lips.

"Sarah?" Words spilled out like beads from a broken string when John found her. He poured into her eager ears everything he could remember and triumphantly ended, "And our own John Carver will continue to be our governor!"

She clapped her hands. The kindly man never failed to stop and talk with the children, no matter how busy he might be with the affairs of the colonists. When John repeated, "We are truly free, Sarah," her face broke into a wide smile.

Later that day, the Smythe family drew apart from the others. Father looked straight at John. "I fear I should punish you severely for spying again."

John's heart leaped to his throat. He felt glad for the early evening shadows that partly hid his face. How had Father known? John cast a quick glance at Sarah, but she shook her head. Good old Sarah! She hadn't told. Thankfulness ran over him. She never would, even though she no longer would let him lead her into mischief.

"What do you have to say for yourself?" Father sternly demanded.

A hundred thoughts chased through John's mind. He would not lie. God surely hated a coward, who refused to accept punishment when he sinned. John looked into his father's face.

"I know I did wrong. I deserve whatever punishment you give me."

He spread his hands wide, unable to put what being there at the signing of the agreement meant to him. "I am sorry to have troubled you, but I cannot say I am sorry for hiding and listening." He looked down.

"For this time *and this time only,*" Father quietly said, "I am glad you followed curiosity's leading. I would not have had you miss those moments. They will affect life in America for as long as the world stands!"

John's mouth fell open in astonishment. Sarah gave a surprised squeak. Mother sturdily said, "As am I. None present on the *Mayflower* will forget this day." She laid one hand on her son's rough hair. "My son, your father and I have seen how hard you struggle to be obedient. So has your heavenly Father. Continue trying, John. A man who cannot control himself is only half a man." She and Father moved away together, leaving the children alone.

Two Pilgrims slowly walked by. Their voices sounded hushed in the growing dusk. "Our new colony is to be called Plymouth," one said.

"Aye, and we are pioneers. Along with crops, we plant the light of God's truth in this land to which He has brought us." They passed on.

"Pioneers." John thrilled at the word. "Mother was right. If we live to be older than Methuselah, we will never forget this day. Soon we will go ashore." He fell to dreaming of forests and Indians, wild game and tall grass.

A small hand slipped inside John's larger one. He looked at his sister's troubled face. Sarah had grown braver and more independent during the hard journey, but she was still the little sister who loved and needed him.

Mother's words from what felt like a lifetime ago came back to John. *Deal gently with her.* He freed his hand and dropped an arm around her shoulder. "Don't worry, Sarah. God helped us escape to a free country. He will take care of you." He added, "So will I."

Sarah relaxed. "I know."

John squeezed her shoulder and proudly raised his head. He gazed at the unexplored shores of the New World and silently vowed, *God, no matter what happens, I will keep that promise.* Then he gently led his sister from the dark deck toward the flicker of light below. Father and Mother would be waiting. He grinned. A glint of mischief came to his eyes. So was the New World. He could hardly wait for tomorrow!

Rebekah
in Danger

Colleen L. Reece

A Note to Readers

Rebekah Cunningham and her brother are fictional characters, but they represent real children who came to America from England and Holland. The hardships they faced, both on board ship and in their new home, helped make our country a place where all can worship God in whatever way they choose.

Although the main characters are fictional, this book is filled with incidents that actually happened. Many of the minor characters are true as well: Governor William Bradford, Captain Myles Standish, John Alden, and others. If not for Samoset, Squanto, and Chief Massasoit, the real-life American Indians who helped the Pilgrims, the colony at Plymouth would never have survived their first long and tragic year in the New World.

Contents

CHAPTER 1

A New Land

The New World, November 1620

I'm tired of working," eleven-year-old Rebekah Cunningham muttered to herself as she crawled into her familiar hiding place under the chicken coops on the *Mayflower*'s deck. On the long trip across the Atlantic, this cramped little corner had been her refuge when she needed a few minutes alone. Now she heaved a sigh of relief as she crept back into the tight nook.

Mend this stocking, Rebekah. . . . Stir the pot. . .milk the goats . . .sweep the floor, Rebekah. . . . Mend this mattress. . . . Don't forget to keep an eye on your brother, Rebekah. . . . Have you done your sewing yet, Rebekah? . . . The list of chores never seemed to end. By the time she had one day's worth of work done, it was nighttime—and then the next morning, she had to start all over again. She had been so excited about reaching land, thinking that once they were no longer at sea, life would be easier. Instead, things were just the same. If only they could all move off the *Mayflower*. Rebekah was tired of the stinky old ship. She wanted room to run. She was tired of tripping over someone every time she moved.

When they had first set sail from Holland, it had all seemed like such a grand adventure. Rebekah knew that her parents had lived most of their lives in England, but she had been born in Holland, and she was both excited and terrified at the thought of seeing somewhere new. Her parents and the other Separatists had come to Holland so they could worship God the way they wanted, without the king forcing them to meet secretly.

Rebekah had been happy in Holland. It was the only home she had ever known, and she had hated to leave all her friends. She worried about what it would be like to live somewhere ruled only by the strict Separatist leaders. The Dutch had sung and danced and laughed, and Rebekah had enjoyed visiting her friends' homes, where everyone seemed to always be having a good time.

But she knew this was the very thing that had worried the church leaders. The Separatists' children were no longer separate. They were beginning to dress like the Dutch and act like the Dutch. They even talked like the Dutch. Meanwhile, the Separatist adults had such a hard time fitting in with the Dutch that it was difficult for them to find jobs and earn a living. The church elders also worried that Spain might conquer Holland, turning it into a Catholic nation. If that happened, the Protestant Separatists might face the same persecution they had endured in England.

And so the Separatists had found English merchants who were willing to take them on board their ship to the New World. First, they had to travel to England, though. The whole thing had involved lots of complicated, grown-up arrangements that seemed to take forever.

When they finally set sail from England, Rebekah and her brother, Will, could hardly keep still. They had run from one side of the *Mayflower*'s deck to the other, trying to see everything at once. The rise and fall of the deck beneath their feet, the sight of fish leaping from the waves, the way the moon looked sinking into the sea—each new experience filled them with wonder.

But as their journey went on week after week, the wonder wore off. Their sleeping quarters were so cramped that there was never any room to move around below deck. Many people became sick, and the dark quarters smelled of vomit, diarrhea, and too many unwashed human beings packed into too small a space. The children grew tired of the meager meals, and their stomachs hurt. The exciting adventure had turned into long, dreary weeks that seemed as though they would never end.

But now at last they were here in the New World. The *May-flower* was anchored off the shore, and soon they would have a chance to go on land. But first they had to hear the news from Captain Standish, who had gone with a few other men to see what the land was like. Rebekah could hardly wait until she could finally go on shore. She longed to feel solid land beneath her feet. When she thought about eating fresh food again, her stomach growled with anticipation.

She moved deeper into the shadows beneath the old coops. The chickens that had survived their journey clucked gently, eyeing Rebekah sideways from their beady eyes. She knew that soon one of the men would move the coops onto the land. But in the meantime, Rebekah was going to take refuge here one more time. She pushed back the curly wisps from her dark brown braids that poked out from her hood and tickled her nose. Then she snuggled her wool cloak more tightly around her shoulders and wrapped her arms around her knees. With a sigh, she let her mind drift into a daydream.

"Captain Standish!" She recognized her ten-year-old brother Will's voice, and she heard his feet race across the deck. Rebekah peeked out from a crack between the coops and saw the red-faced, mean-looking man who had been chosen chief military officer for the new colony in America. Her brother saluted smartly as he skidded to a stop in front of the captain. Rebekah pressed back deeper into the shadowy recess. She would be in big trouble if Captain Standish caught her shirking her duties.

"What do you want, Cunningham?" Standish gruffly demanded. "Can't you see I'm busy? The people are waiting to hear what our scouting party discovered. Step out of my way. I have to enlist volunteers for a longer exploration." The corners of the captain's mouth turned down. "I suppose it will have to be after the Sabbath. Anyway, we have to find a place for our permanent settlement. I don't have time to waste standing here talking to you." Standish waved his hand, as if to brush Will aside like a troublesome insect, and Rebekah's blood boiled.

Rebekah leaned forward to glimpse the pale November sunlight shining on Will's short dark hair.

"I know, sir. That's why I stopped you. I want to go with the exploring party," announced Will.

Rebekah was proud to hear Will keep his voice steady.

"You?" Standish laughed unpleasantly. "I need men, not lads. Try again in a few years, if we survive that long in this godforsaken land." The corners of his mouth turned down. "We'll be lucky if any of us are alive by the end of next year."

"Sir, I am almost eleven," Will persisted. "I'm strong. I can also outrun every boy and most of the men on board ship." Rebekah saw her brother flex his right arm and grin.

Captain Standish planted his feet apart, his hands on his hips. He gave Will a sour, unconvinced look. "You're a cocky one, aren't you? I thought you Separatists were taught it's a sin to boast."

"Is it boasting if you know you can do something well?" Will asked. "I only told you because I thought you might need a swift runner to carry messages."

Reluctance crossed the captain's hard face. He looked Will over from the top of his head to the tips of his worn boots. "Hmm. You are tall for your age. Wiry, too." He hesitated and tilted his head to one side. "I might be able to use you, at that." Standish drew his brows together in a ferocious scowl. "Very well. You may go if your father agrees and—"

"He plans to volunteer."

"Quiet, whelp!" Standish roared. "If you go, you are under my command. You will obey my orders, keep your mouth shut, and stay close to your father. Understand me?"

"Yes, sir," Will mumbled.

"Dismissed." The captain marched across the ship's deck, his boots thumping loudly on the wood.

Captain Standish barked, "I know you're all waiting to hear what those of us who first stepped foot on the New World discovered in the brief time we were ashore. We saw no signs of habitation. The sand hills here are similar to the downs in Holland but better and wooded. We suspect there are miles of forests. We saw an abundance of oak and sassafras, pine and juniper. We saw birch and holly, some walnut and ash. Near the swamps are cedar and red maple." His dour voice brightened. "Although we didn't find any good water, we dug into the earth. It is rich, black, and good for planting."

A murmur of approval swept through the people on board. The first sight of the rocky coast had been less than promising. Rebekah knew that rich, black earth meant abundant crops.

"I suppose it is too much to ask that any of you Separatists will consent to be part of an exploring party until Monday," Standish continued, and Rebekah heard the sneer in his voice.

"Monday will be time enough," Governor John Carver quietly told him. "Tomorrow will be given over to preaching, praise, and prayer, as is our custom. Monday we will begin our work." He cleared his throat gently. "My wife, Katherine, and the other women are eager to wash clothes. Did you find a place suitable for such a long-postponed purpose?"

"Yes. There is a small pond not far away. The water isn't good for drinking, but it will serve well for washing."

"Good. While the women and girls are scrubbing the stink of the voyage from our clothing, we men will separate into groups." Governor Carver looked over their number. "I suggest that those who are too sick to be among the exploring party use the time searching for food."

"I agree." Captain Standish took charge once more. "Cunningham," he said, "if you consent to go with me, bring your son. He may prove useful, if he can live up to his boasting as to speed!" Loud laughter came from the group of people; then several men stepped forward to volunteer, Rebekah and Will's father among them.

Rebekah knew that she had best leave her hiding place now, while everyone was distracted. She quickly crawled out and stood up, smoothing her skirts. When she turned, she caught her mother's eye, but Mother only smiled, and Rebekah hoped her mother hadn't been watching her daughter creeping on her hands and knees from under the chickens.

Lucky Will, Rebekah thought. *He will get to go exploring, while I have to scrub mountains of laundry.* Then her envy turned to worry. Would her brother and father be safe out in the wilderness? What if they were attacked by wild animals? What if something dreadful happened and they never came back?

Rebekah always worried about her brother's safety. Although he was only a year younger than she was, she had always been the more sensible of the two. Will had a habit of flying off the handle—and then he ended up in trouble. She knew their parents counted on her to watch over him and do her best to keep him out of trouble. Sometimes the responsibility seemed like a heavy load to carry.

"Please, may I go?" she heard her brother ask their father, and she knew Will felt not even a tinge of fear.

Father looked him over, much as Myles Standish had done earlier. "I see no reason why not, especially as Captain Standish has requested it." Rebekah saw that a twinkle lurked in their father's eyes, though his mouth stayed solemn. "How is it that he knows so much of your running skills? And what is this about boasting?"

Will's face turned dark red from embarrassment. "Uh, I didn't know whether he knew I could run fast, so I told him. I didn't think it was wrong to do so, when God has given me long legs that have learned to travel swiftly."

"I see." Father folded his arms across his chest and grinned. In that moment, his expression was almost identical to Will's. Father turned to Mother. "Well, shall we let this son of ours go?"

Perfect trust showed in Mother's eyes. "So long as he promises to stay close beside you," she agreed.

Before Will could holler with delight, Rebekah asked, "Why must you go? There are plenty of men. I know you're almost a man, but you don't know how to fire a musket. What would happen if you crossed paths with a bear or wolf? What good would you be to the scouting party?"

"If Captain Standish thinks I am man enough to go, I am, Rebekah Cunningham. Oh, what's the use? You're a girl, and girls are always afraid!"

"That is enough, Will." Father's smile vanished. "Your mother was a girl herself not long ago, and I don't know any man braver than she. Did you not see how she cared for the sick and weathered the hardest storms on the Atlantic without a word of complaint?"

Father's hand lightly touched Mother's shoulder, then came to rest on Rebekah's head. "This one is just like her. There is no fear for herself in your sister. Only for you, and with just cause. In the past, there have been occasions when you were careless and fell into trouble. Rebekah has truly been her brother's keeper. It is well for you to remember this and show her more respect."

Father's stinging criticism made Will hang his head. "I'm sorry," he told his sister. "Forgive me?" He grinned. "If I find any curious or pretty things ashore, I will fill my pockets for you."

Rebekah rewarded him with a smile. "Thank you, but be careful, please."

"I will," Will added with a sigh. "I only wish we could go tomorrow and not have to wait until Monday."

"Explore on the Sabbath?" Rebekah frowned at him. "You sound like a heathen." She proudly raised her chin. "Elder Brewster says we must always set a good example for the crew, the London Strangers, and the Indians. What kind of example would it be to have you go tearing off on the Lord's Day?"

"She is right," Mother put in. "It is God's own commandment. 'Remember the Sabbath day, to keep it holy. Six days shalt thou labour, and do all thy work: but the seventh day is the sabbath of the Lord thy God. . . . For in six days the Lord made heaven and earth, the sea, and all that in them is, and rested the seventh day.'"

"Mother, why did God need to rest?" Rebekah asked. Her forehead wrinkled. "I wouldn't think God would ever get tired."

"I have always felt God set aside that time to simply appreciate and enjoy all the beautiful things He created," Mother said. A little smile played about her lips. "Perhaps He felt a little like you do when you slip into your hiding place beneath the coops—as though He needed some quiet time." Mother laughed at the expression of embarrassment on Rebekah's face, and then she continued, "God also set an example for us. So did Jesus. Setting aside one day out of every seven to remember Him and spend time being glad for all He has given us is not too much to ask, is it?"

"No, Mother."

But Rebekah couldn't help but squirm a little, thinking of the endless services they held each week. If God was trying to be nice to them, surely He could have thought of a better way for people to spend their quiet time than sitting in stuffy, boring services. Many times in Holland, she and Will had envied the Dutch children, especially on Sunday. The Dutch boys and girls laughed and sang and played games just outside the church door. The deaconess who sat with the Separatist children in a special section watched them with a sharp eye. She made sure they never whispered, and they certainly never laughed. If they did, they were sorry.

Rebekah made a face as she remembered. A few times she and Will had forgotten the strict rules against talking and laughing. The deaconess promptly boxed their ears. One time she whipped Will with a birch rod. When they weren't listening to sermons or singing hymns on Sundays, Will and Rebekah were expected to sit quietly. Sabbath days seemed to never end.

"I don't understand how it can be wrong to be joyful," Rebekah had complained to Will more than once. "God must have been happy when He finished His world." Now Rebekah secretly sighed. She loved God. Yet how could she live through another long, long Sunday knowing that on Monday they would finally step onto the shores of the New World, land of freedom? Even if she had to do laundry all day, it would be better than being on board the ship.

CHAPTER 2

Laundry

To Rebekah's joy and Will's dismay, the scouting party from the *Mayflower* did not go on Monday, after all. While the women and girls waded, small children ran on the sands. How good it felt to be out in the fresh air after the long days and nights huddled in their smelly quarters!

Some of the men walked the beach. Excitement spread when they found mussels and clams. For nine weeks, the travelers had been without fresh food. The Pilgrims had never seen clams or mussels before and didn't know anything about eating them. Many of them stuffed themselves and ended up sick. Fortunately, Father and Mother cautioned Will and Rebekah not to be greedy. They escaped the stomach upsets that followed.

Meanwhile, carpenters examined pieces of the damaged shallop. "Sorry," they told Governor Carver and Captain Standish. "The boat has been battered so badly by the crossing it will take us some time to get it ready for use."

Standish scowled. Rebekah knew the captain hated for

things to come up and make him change his plans. Rebekah suspected that Will secretly sympathized with the captain. Surely Will was as eager as the new military leader to explore the New World!

Tuesday passed with Will so impatient he worked off his extra energy by racing up and down the deck. A cold Wednesday morning dawned. Standish, privately called "Captain Shrimp" by some, announced, "We will go on foot." He glanced south toward what appeared to be the mouth of a river, then shook his head. "That can come later. For now, we will go northeast." He strutted to the head of the scouting party. "Muskets ready?"

"Ready," came the answer.

Rebekah looked at the gun her father carried. She hoped he would know how to use it correctly. Only this morning she had watched Captain Standish demonstrate how to use a musket for the benefit of those who didn't know. It took time to load. First, Standish poured black powder down the muzzle and then tamped and wadded it. Next, he dropped in a lead ball and shoved it down with a thick pad. When the captain completed his preparations and released the trigger, Rebekah nearly jumped in the air at the yard-long burst of flame, a deafening roar, and a cloud of smoke.

If it takes all that time to get ready, she wondered, *won't the Indians or bears or deer already be gone by the time anyone gets around to shooting?*

Rebekah watched as her brother fell into step at the end of the line, close behind his father. She hoped he could manage to stay out of trouble. If there was one false move on his part, she knew the captain would order the youngest member of the party to return to the *Mayflower*.

A gruff voice said in her ear, "Your brother best step lively, lass. 'Cause I plan on being right b'hind him."

Rebekah turned and a grin spread over her face as she looked up at Jake, the big sailor she and Will had made friends with on their voyage. "You're going, too?" she asked him.

"Came t' see the New World, didn't I?" Jake snapped, face grim as ever. Only a flicker of light in his small dark eyes showed the friendship he felt for Rebekah and her brother. "I best be catchin' up or I'll be left behind."

Rebekah gave the sailor a smile. "I'm glad you will be going along." She eyed the wicked knife stuck in Jake's belt and the way the seaman rested one hand on its hilt. He had fought pirates and had a long scar on his shoulder to prove it. If the explorers ran into danger, Jake would be a good man to have with them.

She waved until her father, Will, and Jake had at last disappeared between the thick trees. With a sigh, she turned away.

"There's work to be done," her mother reminded, her voice gentle.

Rebekah heaved yet another long sigh, this one even louder and wearier than the last. "Mother, don't you ever wish you could go off with the men sometimes instead of doing women's work?"

Her mother shook her head. "Nay, Rebekah, I can't say I do. I have to confess, I would like to go along just to keep an eye on my menfolk. But otherwise, I'm content to stay behind. In fact, I'm eager to be scrubbing all that dirty laundry. It will be good to have everything clean again." She put her hand under

Rebekah's chin and lifted her face so she could look into her daughter's eyes. "You'll see. It will be fun to be up to our elbows in sudsy water. And it will be good to be on solid land for a change. There may even be time for you and your friends to play hopscotch and tag in the evenings."

Comforted, Rebekah returned her mother's smile.

In the days that followed, Rebekah followed her mother's example, while her father and brother roamed the beach and forests. Always a good helper, Rebekah worked alongside Mother, scrubbing clothes and dirty blankets. She won approving looks and high praise from the other women for her hard work.

"Mercy, she is as good as a full-grown woman," some said. Mother only smiled, but the pride in her face made Rebekah feel good. She thanked God that she was strong, in spite of being short and petite. She flew from task to task, green eyes shining and curly dark brown braids tossing. Mother was right. The work was hard—but it was also fun. It felt good just to be off the ship, with room to run and breathe.

During the days of hard work, Rebekah had a precious memory she kept treasured in her heart, like a rare jewel in a box. It helped a lot during the anxious time of waiting for Father and Will to return. Each time fear for their safety sneaked up and grabbed at her, Rebekah whispered what Father had told Will: "There is no fear for herself in your sister. Only for you. . ."

Once Rebekah asked her mother, "Do you think Father was

right? About me, I mean. That I don't really worry about me. Just about Will."

"You are a loving sister," Mother said. "Any boy would be proud to have you care for him as you do Will. Even though he teases you, always know how much he cares about you. You are also a joy to your father and me."

Rebekah blushed until the red dimmed her freckles.

As the days went by, though, Rebekah's back began to ache from bending over to scrub the dirty clothing. Her arms ached from carrying the heavy wet blankets and stretching up on tiptoe to hang them to dry. By evening, she was too tired to play with her friends. She wondered what the men were doing.

"Mother," she said with a sigh, "I'm starting to wish again that I were Will so I could go exploring, too. I want to see more of the New World than what we can from here, and I'm getting tired of cleaning these smelly old blankets." She looked with loathing at a pile of blankets waiting to be washed. They were stiff from dried saltwater and the vomit of sick passengers.

Mother's eyebrows raised, and Rebekah hurried on. "I know it's silly. Goodness, Will barely got to go, and he's a boy." She giggled. "Can you imagine what Captain Standish would look like if I begged to go scouting? I can just see him." Rebekah placed her feet apart, squared her shoulders, and made fists of her hands. She put them on her hips, tucked her chin into her neck, and said in a deep, unnatural voice, "Be gone with you! Girls are made for tea parties, not exploring parties!"

Mother's green eyes sparkled with laughter. "Respect your elders, Rebekah."

"I do. It's just that Captain Standish acts like he is more

important than anyone else." Rebekah dropped her imitation. A troubled look crossed her face. "He isn't a believer, is he?"

"Nay, but we pray he may become one of us." Mother sighed. "We must also appreciate what he is doing for us. Father says he feels Captain Standish will be faithful to his duties, no matter what happens."

"I'm sorry I made fun of him."

"As am I sorry for laughing at your nonsense," Mother admitted.

Boom! Boom, boom, boom!

"The signal!" Rebekah joyfully shouted. "The men are back!" She ran, shading her eyes with one hand. "Will promised to bring me whatever he found," she cried. "I wonder what it will be!"

She caught sight of Jake, marching near the front of the company this time, and she moved back. Friend he might be, but the sailor's scowl sent shivers through Rebekah sometimes.

"Jake is not a believer, either, is he, Mother?"

Her mother shook her head. "I doubt it. But he has been a good friend to you children. I was grateful for his watchful eye while we were on board ship."

Rebekah nodded, but her green eyes were cloudy. She knew the church leaders preached that not everyone was chosen by God to go to heaven. But she hated to think that God might not love Jake. Surely God would see past the sailor's ferocious exterior to the kindness she knew lived inside him.

"Does God love Jake, do you think?" she asked her mother. "Is he one of the elect?" She bit her lip, looking troubled. "He won't send Jake to hell, will he?"

Her mother glanced down at her daughter's face. "I believe

God loves everyone," she said softly but firmly. "The Bible says that God is not willing that anyone should perish. He wants us all to have eternal life." She smiled. "We must pray that Jake will come to know how much God loves him."

Rebekah puzzled over her mother's words for a moment. Was her mother saying she did not agree with the teachings of the church?

Then Rebekah recognized her father's hat, and she forgot about her worries. Father and Will were walking toward her and Mother, their eyes bright with eagerness. Rebekah dashed forward and flung herself at them.

"You're home!"

CHAPTER 3

Joy and Tragedy

Rebekah danced around Will. "I am so glad you are safe!"

He grinned at her. "Aren't you glad to see Father, too?"

"Of course I am," Rebekah replied indignantly.

"You worry more about me, though, don't you?" Will teased.

Her freckled nose went into the air. "With good reason." When he started to protest, she laughed and said, "Never mind. What did you bring me?"

"Just you wait and see!" Will's eyes sparkled, and his hands crept toward his pockets. "Hold out your hands and make a cup of them."

Rebekah started to obey, then put her hands behind her back and demanded, "You won't give me something squishy, like a worm, will you?"

"Where would I get a worm this time of year? C'mon, Rebekah. You can trust me. Honest. Put your hands out and close your eyes."

Rebekah slowly did as her brother asked. All the time he had been gone, she'd tried to think what he might bring her.

Cones from the evergreen trees? Pretty shells? She felt a shower of small objects pour into her cupped palms, then something long and rough. Her eyes popped open.

She looked at what she held. Dried seeds. They were hard yellow kernels and an ear that was bigger than any grain she had ever seen. "Oh, Will!" she whispered. "It's the best present in the whole world. What is it?"

Will laughed. "It's the Indians' grain. We've been calling it corn, though it's not like anything we've seen at home. We're going to plant it come spring. And in the meantime, we will eat it."

"Where did you get it?"

"We got it from the Indians."

"Real Indians? What were they like? Were they frightening?"

A shadow passed over Will's face. "We never saw them. We found the corn near a grave. There was an abandoned house there, as well."

Rebekah frowned. "How did you know the Indians wouldn't come back for their corn?"

Will shrugged. "Captain Standish commanded us to take it all."

Rebekah's eyebrows pulled together. "Isn't that stealing? What if the Indians come back for their corn and find it gone?"

Will looked unhappy. "I know. That's what I said. But Captain Standish wouldn't listen to me."

Rebekah shook her head. "Well, of course not, Will. You're just a boy. What did Father say?"

"He said we had to obey the captain's orders. We need the food desperately, after all. Father said we will pray that God will show us how to make things right with the Indians."

Rebekah let go of her worries and closed her fingers around the corn. "What will it taste like, do you suppose?" Suddenly, she wanted to hug her brother and dance, even though the Separatists permitted no such foolishness. Real Indian corn, here, in her hands! And her brother and her father had returned to them safely.

"Mother, just see what Will has brought!" Rebekah said when she could finally tear her gaze away from her gift.

"I know. Isn't it wonderful? William, how glad we are to have more food," Mother said to Father with a grateful look. "Our stores were perilously low."

"I want to hear every single thing that happened," Rebekah told Will. "But first, we have some news for you. While you were gone, we had a visitor."

Will, who had wearily dropped to a pallet on the floor, sat up straight. His eyes opened wide enough to satisfy even Rebekah. "A visitor? Don't tell me an Indian came when we didn't see any!" Disappointment spread over his face.

Rebekah laughed. "I didn't say it was an Indian."

"There's no other ship in the harbor, and we're miles from any other white people." Will looked puzzled. "Who else could it be? Did he come in a canoe?"

"No." Rebekah giggled again. For once she had news before Will. It was fun to keep him guessing.

"Then he must have walked," Will figured out. "Is he still here?"

"He's still here, but he didn't walk." Rebekah burst into laughter. So did Mother.

"Go ahead and tell him," Mother finally said.

"Susanna White had her baby," Rebekah explained. "The first white child born in New England. Susanna and William named their new son Peregrine."

"Peregrine! I thought the Hopkins family had already chosen the worst possible name when they called their son Oceanus," Will protested.

"Peregrine means *pilgrim* or *wanderer,*" Mother put in.

Will grinned. "You were right, Rebekah. He isn't an Indian. He didn't come in a canoe, he didn't walk, and he's still here. Now will you listen to what happened to us?"

"Of course." She scooted closer to Will, propped her elbows on her knees and her chin in her hands, and prepared to hear Will's and Father's adventures.

An hour later, Will finally finished his exciting stories of everything that had happened on the trip. Rebekah solemnly said, "I want to see the New World, but I don't want to be so thirsty I don't know what to do like you were. Or have to fight my way out of thorn thickets. You and Father will be in danger whenever you go on one of those expeditions."

"God will protect us," Will told her.

Rebekah shook her head. "Not if you do foolish things. You'd better stay close to Father."

"I have to." Will made an awful face. "Captain Standish will have my hide if I don't. So will Jake." He grinned. "That is, if Father doesn't get to me first!"

Rebekah wasn't satisfied with the answer but didn't want to nag. She touched a torn place on her brother's jacket. "Tomorrow when it's lighter, I'll mend that for you."

"Thank you." Will yawned. "I don't know when the next scouting party is going out. I hope I get to go along."

"Don't plan on it," Father warned. "I heard Captain Jones say he planned to lead the next party. I suspect it will be after the shallop is ready. Captain Jones wants to explore the river we saw close to where we found the corn. The river's mouth is swampy, but it's wide enough for the shallop."

"Do you think Captain Standish might speak a good word for me?" Will asked. Rebekah noticed how round and anxious his eyes looked.

"Perhaps." Father's brown eyes twinkled. He yawned. "It's been a long trip. Time to say good night."

Rebekah lay wide-eyed and sleepless long after her family fell asleep. When she did close her eyes, visions of Indian graves, Indian corn, and angry Indians ran through her head.

"Lord," she prayed, "You know I wish Will would be happy just to stay here with me. He isn't, though. He will be terribly disappointed if he can't go again. Please keep him safe, and help me to be brave."

Comforted at last, Rebekah fell into a deep and restful sleep.

Ten days later, the shallop was repaired enough for use, although more work needed to be done on it. Thirty men climbed aboard, but not Will. Captain Jones chose those he wanted and scoffed at the idea a mere lad could be useful to him. "Stay here and protect the ship," Jones said.

Rebekah knew he was mocking her brother. She was glad Will was wise enough to realize that showing disappointment or arguing with the captain would merely strengthen the older man's opinion that Will was too young to go.

"Aye, aye, sir." Will put on as cheerful a grin as he could and saluted. The surprise in Captain Jones's face made Rebekah proud of her brother.

"Good fer ye, lad," Jake hissed before ambling down the deck in the rolling sailor's walk the crew used in order to stay upright during storms.

Father echoed the words. "Taking disappointment like a man is important," he told Will. "Each time we do this, it makes us stronger for the next time." He glanced at the sky. "It may be well you were left behind, son. I don't like the looks of those clouds."

Father's fears proved correct. The scouting party ran into terrible weather. The shallop had to turn back. Some of the Pilgrims refused to do so. They waded through icy, waist-deep water to get to shore. Up hills and down valleys through six inches of snow they went. The wind blew. It snowed all that day and night. When they finally returned to the ship, many of them were so sick that they never recovered.

When the weather improved, the scouting party tried again and found a few deserted wigwams, built of bent sapling trees with the ends stuck in the ground. Thick mats covered the wigwams both inside and out. A mat also covered the wide hole used as a chimney. Another mat made a low door. Even more mats served as beds.

The scouting party found wooden bowls, earthenware

pots, many baskets, deer feet and heads, eagle claws, and other curious things.

At Corn Hill, where they had first discovered the corn, they dug in the frozen earth and discovered more corn to eat as well as some beans. Again, the settlers vowed to pay the Indians for what they took. They triumphantly carried their treasures back to the *Mayflower*.

"This is a real find," the leaders told the people when they returned to the ship. "Indian corn is well known by the explorers from the Caribbean and the Carolinas, as well as here. It gives two harvests a year and makes into good bread. We are fortunate, indeed, to have found it."

Rebekah wasn't sure how she felt about the corn. They needed the food desperately, but if they took the Indians' corn, what would the brown-skinned people do for food? She put the worry out of her mind when the scouts reported they'd seen a plentiful supply of game: deer, partridges, wild geese, and ducks. Will would be happy to go hunting with the men, and the fresh meat would be a welcome addition to their diet. And it would be their own food, fairly earned, not stolen.

Edward Winslow described seeing whales in the bay. "One lay above water. We thought she was dead. One of the men shot, to see if she would stir. His musket flew into pieces, both stock and barrel! Thanks be to God, no one was hurt, although many stood nearby. The whale gave a sniff and swam away."

Rebekah was glad the whale had not been hurt. But Captain Jones and others more experienced in fishing decided they would try whaling the next winter. They could make three thousand to four thousand pounds in whale oil, a fortune indeed!

To Will's delight, as soon as the shallop was completely repaired, another expedition set out. This time Captain Standish was in charge. He took the same group that had gone with him on his earlier expedition. Will waved good-bye to Mother and Rebekah, then huddled between Father and Jake. Later he told Rebekah that the cold was so intense that the spray froze on their coats. Two men fainted from the cold.

While Will and Father were away, Rebekah kept busy helping Mother and the other women. They were still sleeping at night on the *Mayflower* and spending most of their time during the day there, too, and Rebekah was heartily sick of the cramped quarters. She longed for the day when their family could once more live alone in their own home, rather than sharing every moment with many other families. She yearned for the freedom to run and run, without tripping over the belongings and stretched-out legs of the others in their group. Once more, she could not keep herself from envying Will and the freedom he had simply because he was a boy.

One night she lay awake, listening to the familiar sounds of snores, fussy babies, and soft murmurings all around her in the crowded sleeping quarters. The air was thick with the odor of many unwashed bodies, but Rebekah barely noticed, being used to breathing the heavy air. But she was tired of listening to so many other families settling down for the night. Two women were arguing nearby, their whispers hissing like angry wasps. Someone else was crying softly, long shuddering sobs that Rebekah knew belonged to a grown woman rather than a child.

The sound made her uneasy, and she held her hands over her ears, trying to shut out the noise. If only she could fall asleep so that she could wake up and it would be morning, time to get up and go up on the deck in the fresh air.

"Hush now, Dorothy." Rebekah recognized her mother's voice, speaking softly to William Bradford's wife. Rebekah took her hands away from her ears so that she could hear better. "I know it's hard to be so far from your little son," Mother was saying, "but you must trust him to our Lord. God is with your son across the ocean in Holland, just as He is here with us in this new world. In God, you and your son are not separated at all. Think of it like that."

"I cannot." The words sounded more like a moan, as though Dorothy Bradford were in pain. "My little son. My baby. . ." Her voice dissolved into sobs. "I should never have left him."

"Little John will be safe there in Holland, Dorothy," Mother answered quietly. "You know that's what you and William decided. Think of how hard the voyage was. So many of us fell ill, including you yourself. You know it's hardest on the children. And now with winter coming, we know hard times may lie ahead, as well. Your little boy is safe and warm and well fed, and you shall see him again by and by, when you and William have built a good home here."

"I should never have come to this terrible place," Dorothy choked out.

"But you are here now, Dorothy, and William needs you by his side."

"I am no use to William," Dorothy sobbed. "I am too ill. I will never be well again."

"Of course you shall be well. You are already far better than you were."

But Rebekah could tell that Dorothy Bradford was crying too hard to listen to the reason in her mother's voice. "I cannot bear it," she wept. "I cannot bear to live without him. I will never see him again. I hate this place. I shall die here, I know, and never see my little John again."

"Hush, Dorothy." Mother's voice was gentle but firm. "You must have faith. You will make yourself more ill if you continue crying like this. Our men need us to be strong."

"I cannot be strong," Dorothy Bradford wailed.

"Rely on God," Rebekah's mother replied, "and He will be your strength."

But Dorothy Bradford would not listen. She was still crying when Rebekah finally fell asleep.

The next day, the early morning hush was split by the sound of a scream. Rebekah sprang up from her mattress, her heart pounding. "What is it?"

Mother pushed the hair back from her face as she scrambled to her feet. "I don't know. I'll go see."

She disappeared up the ladder to the upper deck. Rebekah waited, her blanket clutched around her against the morning chill, her heart pounding with a terrible foreboding.

From the deck above, she heard the sounds of agitated voices. A man shouted something. Rebekah thought she heard the word "overboard," and then there was the *thump-thump-thump* of running feet, followed by a *splash*. Rebekah dropped the blanket and yanked on her skirt and waistcoat. Not bothering with her stockings, she ran barefoot up the ladder.

Mother and several other women were leaning over the ship railing. "What happened?" Rebekah asked.

Her mother glanced at her, but she seemed to barely see Rebekah. "A woman has fallen overboard," she said, her voice trembling. Her face was very white.

The women huddled together, waiting while one of the sailors climbed back on board the *Mayflower*, the limp and dripping body of a woman clutched in his arms. As he threw his leg over the railing, Rebekah saw it was Jake. His face was grim as he gently laid the woman down on the deck.

"Oh, Dorothy," Mother whispered.

Rebekah stared down at the pale, quiet face of Dorothy Bradford. She looked more peaceful than Rebekah had ever seen her since they left Holland.

She was too quiet, though. With a gasp of fear, Rebekah looked up at her mother's face. The look in Mother's eyes told Rebekah the truth.

Dorothy Bradford was dead.

CHAPTER 4

More Trouble

All day, Rebekah huddled in her spot between the chicken coops. No one called her name, bidding her to do some chore. An awful hush hung over the *Mayflower*. Even the sailors went about their business quietly. The sound of weeping floated up from the sleeping quarters below. Rebekah had cried, too, but now she had no more tears left to cry.

She watched the hens shift their silly heads from side to side. Their soft, gossipy voices comforted her a little, but her heart felt heavy and strange inside her. She kept remembering the conversation she had overheard the night before between her mother and Dorothy Bradford. Dorothy had been right: She would never see her son again. Why had God let her die?

The question went around and around inside her mind, until at last, tired from lack of sleep, her head slipped sideways against the chicken coop. With a shuddering sigh, she slid into a shallow sleep.

"I wonder where our womenfolk are." The sound of Father's puzzled voice made Rebekah raise her head.

"Why would they all be below deck in the middle of the day?" That was Will's voice now. "Mother? Rebekah?"

"Here." Rebekah scrambled out from between the chicken coops and lifted her woebegone face to her brother. "Oh, Will, the awfulest thing has happened!"

Will's face turned white. "Not Mother!" The terror in his voice drove the fog from Rebekah's mind.

"No," she reassured her brother. "It's not Mother."

"I am fine, son." Their mother's muffled voice came from the hatchway.

Father ran to put his arms around Mother. "What is it, Abigail?"

Mother's words fell as heavy as hailstones. "Dorothy Bradford has drowned."

"It can't be true!" Will looked more astonished than distressed, and Rebekah knew he truly couldn't believe what had happened.

Rebekah remembered the way William Bradford had looked when he said good-bye to his young wife. She had seen the tenderness in his eyes, and the memory made her choke with fresh tears.

"How did it happen?" asked Father.

"A tragic accident." Mother sounded as if she had wept so many tears there were no more left in her. "Apparently, she fell overboard when no one was around to hear her cries and save her." She took a deep breath. "Will, stay here with your sister on deck and tell her about your journey. I wish to speak with your father below."

"Of course." Will put his hand on Rebekah's shoulder. He

peered into her tearstained face and asked, "Why is Mother acting so strange? She isn't like herself at all."

Rebekah looked down at the deck. She gulped and twisted her apron front into ugly wrinkled knots, but she could not find the words to answer her brother's question.

"What's the big secret?" he demanded.

She looked at him, afraid to put into words the awful thing she had heard earlier. "Promise you won't tell?" she said at last. "Mother doesn't know I heard her talking with some of the other women. I don't believe it, anyway!"

"Don't believe what?" She could hear that Will's patience was slipping, and for a moment she could not understand how he could sound so annoyed in the midst of such sorrow. Then she realized that he still did not truly believe that Dorothy Bradford could be dead.

Rebekah stood on tiptoe and whispered in his ear. "Some people are saying Dorothy Bradford's drowning wasn't an accident!"

Will jerked back from his sister so quickly she nearly lost her balance. "Rebekah Cunningham, what did you say?"

"Shh!" She placed a finger over her lips and leaned close again. "Some of the people say Dorothy Bradford did not drown from an accident."

"You don't mean somebody pushed her?" Will looked sick. "That's impossible!"

"No, but it's just as bad." Fresh tears came to Rebekah's eyes. "They say she leaped into the sea, that she hates it here and went crazy because she won't ever see her little son in Holland, and—"

"It's wicked gossip, and I don't believe a word of it!" Will cried, keeping his voice low. "She was only twenty-three years old. I know she's been sick, but so have a lot of others."

Rebekah's stomach churned, and it felt like a heavy rock lay in the bottom of it.

"Mother doesn't think it's true, does she?" Will asked.

"Nay, son." Father had come up to them so quietly that neither had heard him. "Neither do I. This is a sad thing, and the least said about it, the better. William Bradford will need all our friendship. Don't mention his wife to him. He has already shown he prefers silence in the matter." Father put an arm around each of them. "Mother and I are counting on you to be loyal."

"What if people talk to us about it?" Rebekah asked.

"Simply tell them you have been asked not to speak of it." He sighed and looked across the bay. "Only ninety-nine of our number will sail to our new home. God grant that we do not lose many more."

Long after Father went below, the children stayed on deck. Will quietly told Rebekah that there had been a storm and the explorers had seen some Indians. He quickly described the area where they would settle. Rebekah asked a few questions, and then they fell silent. Neither made any attempt to seek out friends, even Jake. They had known Dorothy Bradford since they were small. They still found it hard to believe the frail, white-faced woman had drowned.

"It will be many months before the news travels across the ocean," Will said at last.

Rebekah thought of Holland where a small boy waited

for a mother who would never come back to him. Her eyes stung. *Please, God,* Rebekah silently prayed, *take care of William Bradford and his son. Keep little John safe.* She wondered if Dorothy Bradford would be able to see her son from heaven.

"Will?" Rebekah asked quietly. "How can people who don't believe in God stand it when someone they care about dies?"

"I don't know." Her brother stared out into the growing darkness. "We feel sad enough even though we know we will see them again in heaven." He fiercely added, "It will be a lot better place than this! Just think of it, Rebekah. God and Jesus will be there, and no one will ever get sick or die again. Or be hungry. Or sad."

Rebekah pulled her cloak closer around her. "If Father or Mother die, how will we find them when we go to heaven?"

"Don't worry about it. They aren't going to die for a long, long time," Will told her.

"They're lots older than we are, so they probably will die first," Rebekah said.

"I never thought much about it." Will paused. "I guess Jesus will make sure we find each other. It's like Mother and Father are always saying: We just have to trust Him. No matter what happens—even if we die—we'll be all right."

He shrugged, as though he were trying to shake such serious thoughts off his shoulders. "It's getting dark, and we have to go below," he said, changing the subject.

"I wonder how long it will be until we set sail."

That Friday, four days after the return of the explorers, the ship hauled up its anchor and sailed into the bay. Neither Will nor Rebekah looked back at Provincetown Harbor. The spot held too much sadness. Strong headwinds slowed the *Mayflower*'s progress. It took until Saturday to cover roughly thirty miles across the bay. The ship anchored about a mile and a half from shore because the water was shallow.

A foot of snow lay on the ground. Women shivered and stood close to their husbands and children. Children stared round-eyed. "We shall continue to live on board ship until we build shelters," Governor Carver announced. "It will be necessary to take people and cargo ashore in the smaller boats."

Captain Jones looked sour. Jake had told Will and Rebekah that Jones wanted to get the Pilgrims off his ship as soon as possible. "Tired of yer company, he is, and wants to save his vittles," Jake said.

Now the children exchanged delighted glances. Their friend Jake would remain with them, at least for a time.

The Sabbath passed in the usual manner, with prayers, psalms, and songs of praise. On Monday a band of armed men marched away to explore. Will wasn't included this time, but he and Rebekah listened eagerly to their report when they returned.

"It's a good land," one said. "The soil looks promising. Great sections are already cleared. There are signs that huge cornfields once existed, although they don't appear to have been planted for at least a year. It looks like the Indians just up and abandoned them for no reason at all."

Rebekah couldn't help asking, "Why would they do that?" She was glad when her father repeated her question loud enough for everyone to hear.

A puzzled look crossed the speaker's face, and he rubbed his bearded chin. "Your guess is as good as mine."

Another man eagerly put in, "We discovered berry bushes, timber, clay, and gravel. There is a high hill well suited to the building of a fort. From it, we can see the harbor and the country all around. It's ideal for defense, with a place for our cannon. We also found a clear, running stream of good water."

Governor Carver looked around the assembly. "What more can we ask for than already-cleared land, sweet water, and a fine view of the surrounding area?" He hesitated and spread his arms wide. "We are ill prepared to meet the many challenges of this land. Yet we have all that is needed."

His voice rang out, and he counted on his fingers. "First, we have faith: in Almighty God and in ourselves. Second, we have courage. Did we not cross an ocean known for claiming ships and passengers? Third, we have good sense. Fourth, we have determination. Here, by the grace of God, we will build our colony, our home—and we shall call it New Plymouth."

Mighty cheers rose from the company, Will's and Rebekah's among them.

Governor Carver immediately ordered twenty of the strongest men to go ashore in the shallop and begin cutting wood. When a wild storm blew in, Rebekah knew that this time Will wasn't at all disappointed that he had to stay on ship. The anchored *Mayflower* tossed violently. The waves were so high the shallop could not get back. Those in the woodcutting party found themselves marooned and miserable for a few days.

One day, as Rebekah and Mother were mending clothes with the other women, Mary Allerton gasped.

Mother gave her a knowing look. "Is it time?" she asked.

"Aye," said Mary.

"Quick, Rebekah," Mother instructed. "Clear out a corner for us in the sleeping quarters. Tell anyone who asks that it's time for Mary's baby to be born. Then get a bucket of water and some clean rags." Without waiting for an answer, Mother quickly turned to one of the other women, asking her to help get Mary safely down the ship's ladder.

Rebekah hurried to obey Mother. As soon as the other passengers understood what was happening, they created a private corner for Mary. One of the men went off to let Isaac Allerton know his wife was about to give birth.

When Rebekah returned with the water and rags, she could see that Mother was worried. Something wasn't right. Rebekah stood beside Mary and wiped the young woman's face with a cool cloth. The birth seemed to be taking forever.

Finally, a beautiful baby was born—but it never opened its eyes or took a breath.

As Mary hugged her lifeless baby and cried, Rebekah quietly stroked Mary's back, trying to comfort her. Everyone had been looking forward to the birth of another baby. But instead of feeling joy, they were now full of sorrow.

Soon, Christmas Day came. The Pilgrims considered Christmas a pagan holiday and did not celebrate it, but the others on ship had a small feast. They invited the Pilgrims to join them.

Knowing the weather would soon become even colder, people worked harder than ever. Some cut trees. Others split the logs. The first thing to be built was a twenty-foot-square "common house" to store tools and house the workmen, as well as serve as a shelter for the sick and a church.

Rebekah again felt as though all she did was work, work, work. From before daylight until long after dark, there were jobs to be done. Will was as busy as she was. Everyone needed food and shelter. Muscles that had gotten little exercise during the months on the *Mayflower* quickly grew sore from the hard work.

"At least everyone being so busy keeps them from arguing and quarreling with each other," Rebekah whispered to Will one night.

He moved his sore shoulders and yawned. "That's 'cause if everyone doesn't work together, none of us will survive," he told her. "There are a few who complain about our leaders. They say they were better off under the king of England's rule than starving in America."

He sighed and patted his growling stomach. "I know we need to finish the common house, but how I wish some of us could go hunting or fishing! We'll have to wait until next year for ripe berries and fruit and nuts, but scouts say there's a lot of seafood and waterfowl." He licked his lips. "I'd give anything for the leg of a roasted duck."

"So would I." Rebekah shifted position and rubbed her aching back. "I am tired, tired, tired. Sometimes I think if I have to carry another bucket of water for cooking, bathing, or washing clothes, I'll scream! I won't, though. Mother stays so cheerful and always has such a sweet smile, I can't complain to her. Just to you."

"That's good." Will yawned again, opening his mouth so wide Rebekah wondered if he'd dislocated his jaw. "Father and Mother are working even harder than we are. Besides, what good would complaining do? The work still has to be done."

"It never ends." Rebekah drooped against her brother's shoulder. "When Mother and I aren't cooking and washing and mending clothing for our own family, we help those who are too sick from scurvy and pneumonia to take care of their families. There's no time to spin and weave cloth for more clothing."

She put a rough hand to her mouth to nurse a sore finger. "Ow! Making torches from pine logs leaves my hands full of splinters. We have to have something to see by, though. I can hardly wait for spring, so we can dip wicks into melted fat and make candles. We're also running low on soap." She made a face. "I hate making soap. It's so hot stirring the lye and fat in the big kettles over the fire."

"Poor Rebekah. I'm tired, too."

Rebekah looked at the dark circles under her brother's eyes and knew he was speaking the truth. If only they didn't have to work so hard! Yet if everyone didn't do all that they could, their small group would never survive the winter.

Once the common house was built, families built their own homes. Father built a simple thatched hut that looked like an Indian lodge. Some of the settlers made dugout caves in the hillside. Single men lived with families to cut down on the need for houses, and plot sizes were determined by family sizes. New

Plymouth was laid out in the shape of a cross to make it easier to defend. A sturdy stockade surrounded it.

Will and Rebekah soon learned how unforgiving their new home could be. Peter Browne and Will Goodman took their dogs when they went to collect reeds for thatching. They didn't return that afternoon, so Myles Standish sent out a search party. No trace of the two men could be found.

That night, everyone in New Plymouth wondered where the two men were. The next day, the men returned and told their story. Their dogs had scared up a deer. Eager to bring in fresh meat, the two men followed. They got lost in the woods. Noises like the howling of wolves terrified them, and they wandered all night in the forest. Will Goodman's shoes had to be cut off his frostbitten feet. He died a few days later.

When Rebekah learned what had happened, she tried to be brave. Yet her heart filled with fear every time Father or Will left New Plymouth. The only way she could bear their leaving was to remind herself how much God loved them. Rebekah tried to hide her worries, but she felt sure Will suspected her secret. He never said anything, but almost every time he returned, he brought her a pinecone, a curious shell, or a funny story. They made her feel a little better.

But it was hard to be brave when so many in their company were falling sick. . .and many were dying. Sometimes, Rebekah wondered if this new world was trying to punish them for invading its shores. When she looked at the cold, rocky ground, she felt as though it were an enemy. Thoughts like that made her shiver. Her only comfort was to whisper a prayer, knowing that God understood her fears.

Will never seemed to be afraid. He loved to go out with the men. All the strangeness, all the adventures, still excited him. But the day came that Captain Standish said Will had to stay behind when the men went out hunting. "It is growing too cold," Captain Standish said, "and we do not know what dangers the weather will bring. Too many of you are sick, and we cannot risk losing more of our company. Only the strongest men can accompany me."

Rebekah was relieved. She did not like knowing both her brother and father were facing unknown dangers. She would sleep better if at least Will were home with her and Mother.

But Will was furious. "I am not a child," he said between his teeth. "I am as strong as any of those men."

Rebekah giggled. "No, you're not, Will. You're only a boy."

Will's face grew red, and his eyes were bright with anger. Rebekah's heart sank. She knew that look. It was the look Will always wore when he was filled with rebellion.

Right before he got in trouble.

CHAPTER 5

Where Is Will?

I'm going to follow the men," Will told Rebekah when they were alone. "I'll catch up with them, and then they'll have to let me go along with them. I'll show them I'm strong enough to be one of them."

"Don't, Will," Rebekah begged.

But her brother would not listen. "Promise me you won't tell Mother," he said. "Not until I'm gone."

Reluctantly, Rebekah nodded. With a curious feeling of foreboding, she watched Will march away. She already regretted her promise not to tell Mother where he was headed.

He's been good, she tried to tell herself. *This is the first time in ages he's done something he knows he shouldn't.* She sighed. *But I would feel better if I knew for sure that Will found the hunting party. Then even if he got in trouble, I'd know he was safe.*

Rebekah stared into space, deciding what to do. With Mother, Father, and Will busy around the new settlement, she was responsible for most of the home chores. She had more than enough work to get done that afternoon without worrying about Will. Suddenly, a smile crossed her face. She reached for her cloak that was hanging on a peg by the door and quickly stepped outside. With hurried steps, she headed toward the sentry.

"Where be ye off to in such a hurry, little Miss Rebekah?" asked the guard.

"I was wondering if you saw my brother, Will," Rebekah said.

"Aye, he left a few minutes ago to catch up with the hunting party. With those long legs of his, he's probably with them right now. Did you need to get a message to him?"

"Oh, no," Rebekah said, a relieved smile crossing her face. "I just wasn't sure if he had left yet. Thank you for your help."

With a nod of her head, she turned back to the small hut Father had built for their family. Removing her cloak, she quickly began catching up on her work.

Rebekah and Will slept in a loft above the one main room where the family cooked and lived. Each night, the children climbed a ladder and slept on beds made from straw mattresses on the floor. Now Rebekah climbed up to the loft to shake the mattresses and smooth them out. She also tidied the sheets, blankets, and rugs they had brought from Holland. They never put the rugs on the earth floor. Instead, they kept them on the beds for added warmth.

Scrambling down the ladder again, Rebekah shook out Father and Mother's straw mattress. As soon as he had time, Father would make rope springs so they could have better beds, but Rebekah wished they could someday have featherbeds. The linen bags filled with goose feathers made soft mattresses in summer and warm coverlets in winter.

"I should be thankful for what we have," she told the warm room. Father had laid wooden boards across two wooden sawhorses for their table. At night, he put the boards against the wall to make room for the mattress. They had no chairs. Father always said, "When there is only one chair in a household, the man sits in it while his wife and children stand. I cannot be like them. Nay. Will and I shall make a bench, and we will all sit together. One day we shall have enough chairs for all."

A quick glance at the fireplace that provided light, warmth, and a place to cook showed it needed wood. The corners of Rebekah's mouth turned down. It always needed wood. Sometimes she felt the fireplace was a greedy beast that sulked when she didn't feed it enough.

The thought made her laugh, a pleasant sound in the small room. How hard they had worked to gather their wood! She and Mother picked up fallen branches. Will and Father split and sawed. The whole family had carried the split wood to their home and built a great mound just outside the rough wooden door.

After Rebekah had added wood to the fire, she straightened the everyday clothing hanging on wooden pegs on the wall. Their Sabbath clothing lay in a chest, along with extra bedclothes. Mother often warned them about being careful of their clothes. What they had brought with them would have to last for a long, long time.

Rebekah was so involved in her work that she didn't notice how late it was getting. A sharp gust of wind at the corner of the hut reminded her. She ran outside.

An army of storm clouds played tag across the sky. Rebekah shivered from the cold. "At least Will had sense enough not to go off hunting by himself," she whispered. "Surely the hunting party will start for home when they see the dark sky." But in the deep woods, would the men notice how dark it was getting?

Rebekah shook her head and went back inside. She stood by the fireplace to get warm and wondered if Father and Will would return before the storm hit. Memories of Will Goodman dying so soon after he got lost in the woods troubled Rebekah. But what could she do?

"I can pray," Rebekah told the crackling fire. She plopped down on her knees before the blazing fire.

"Dear God, please be with Will and Father and the other men. Will did wrong to run after the hunting party, but You know how he gets sometimes. You understand him even better than I do." Rebekah stayed on her knees for a long time, and when she got up, she felt better. Now if only Will and Father would come home soon!

"We may have venison stew for supper," Will had promised her before he left. Rebekah's mouth watered. Yet as each minute passed, a cold knot of fear grew in the pit of her stomach. Three times she wrapped up in her cloak, went outdoors, and peered into the worsening storm. But she saw no sign of Will or the hunting party.

Again and again, she wondered what to do. Another hour went by. Rebekah's smile had long since vanished. She continued to wait for her father and brother, a prayer on her lips, fear in her heart.

At last, Mother arrived, rosy-faced and chilled. "Ah, that

is good, child!" She hung her wet cloak on the peg closest to the fireplace and held her hands out to warm them. Then she looked around the little room. "Where is Will?"

Rebekah hesitated. She would not lie, but the faint hope that Will would come soon made her say, "I don't know. He went out." *All true,* she told herself.

"Where can he be? I didn't see him." Mother looked worried.

"Do you think Father will come home soon?" Rebekah ventured to ask. "I hate it when he is gone. Especially after what happened to Will Goodman." Her voice sank to a whisper. "So many people have died since we left Holland. . . ."

"I know, dear." Her mother held out her arms, and Rebekah ran into their warm circle. "But we shall all meet again—and then we will be together forever."

Rebekah's arms tightened around her mother. If only she could hold her close and keep her safe from sickness and death. She longed to tell Mother that each time someone died, the fear of losing her or Father got worse.

Be brave, she told herself. *Don't make Mother more worried than she already is.*

Mother sat down on the bench Will and Father had made, pulling Rebekah down beside her. Shadows from the fire flickered on her tired face. "Life is hard here, harder than any of us imagined." Her eyes glistened, and Rebekah knew she was close to tears. "I do all I can, knowing the next time I go to the common house, one or more will be missing."

Rebekah had never felt closer to Mother. "Why do our men bury the dead at night?" she asked in a low voice.

Mother held Rebekah so close the girl could hear the steady

beat of her mother's heart. "We dare not let the Indians know how many of our people have died," Mother said huskily. "Once they realize our numbers are small and that we are so weak, they may become bold enough to attack."

Rebekah and Mother silently huddled together on the bench until a sound came above the storm. "It's Will!" Rebekah felt weak with relief. She sprang up and flung wide the door. Father entered, empty-handed and with a set look on his face, but there was no sign of Will. A furious blast of wind sent a cloud of smoke from the fire through the hut.

Father slammed the door shut. "We found no game, but at least we got home before the worst of the storm." He smiled at his wife and daughter but only with his lips. His eyes held no hint of their usual sparkle. "I'll change into dry clothing." He shrugged out of his wet coat and looked around. "Where's Will?"

"Isn't he with you?" Rebekah asked, fear filling her heart.

"With me? Why would he be with me? You know Captain Standish didn't want Will in our hunting party today."

"But Will left, and the sentry said he was headed toward the hunting party," Rebekah explained.

"Left?" Father's eyebrows met in a frown. "When?"

"He went a long time ago."

"You mean Will is somewhere out in this storm?" Father's face turned whiter than snow. "Abigail, did you know about this?"

"Nay." Mother turned to Rebekah. "How could you let him go?"

"I tried to stop him!" Rebekah cried. She covered her face

with her apron and burst into sobs. "I'm so tired of trying to be a brother's keeper! Will won't listen to me, and I get blamed for what he does!"

Shocked silence filled the hut. Rebekah cried harder. She knew the church elders taught that children should always speak to their elders, especially their parents, with respect. It truly wasn't fair for her to have to always bear the burden of Will's mischief—but now she feared she would be in more trouble than ever.

"Daughter, I spoke too hastily," Mother said.

"As did I." Father picked up Rebekah and hugged her. "We know your brother can be a trial, and you are to be praised for your love and patience. We also appreciate how much you have grown up. It is not your fault he is rebellious. You cannot change Will. All you can do is continue to set a good example. Will must decide for himself how he will behave. Forgive us, Rebekah."

The humbleness in Father's voice surprised Rebekah. "I. . . it's all right. I know you are worried. So am I." She buried her face in her father's shoulder. "I've waited and prayed and waited and prayed all afternoon."

Father set her down. "I'll get a few neighbors and see if I can find him." He put his wet coat back on and slipped outside.

The waiting went on, and Mother tried to help time pass quickly by having Rebekah eat some food. Less than an hour later, Father returned. "The storm has increased. We can do nothing until morning," he said heavily. "Rebekah, go on up to bed."

She reluctantly obeyed, feeling Father had things to say to Mother he didn't want her to hear. For once, her curiosity matched Will's. When she reached the loft, she crouched near the top of the ladder. Spying it might be, but she could never sleep without knowing what Father had to say. She had to listen hard, but she did manage to catch his words.

"I pray to God the rain doesn't wash out Will's tracks. I also pray Will is wise enough to remember what he's been taught, which is to find cover and stay there. If he wanders around, it will make our search a lot harder."

Rebekah crept to her bed and buried herself in her blankets under the rug. She lay sleepless, praying for her brother until the first rays of light crept into the sky.

Just as she slipped into sleep, a loud pounding on the door startled her awake. She sat up on her mattress and listened, her heart pounding. After a moment, she recognized Jake's loud, gruff voice. . .and then Will's. With a glad cry, Rebekah leapt to her feet and tumbled down the ladder.

"Look what I found," Jake was saying.

Mother and Father wrapped their arms around Will. They looked as though they might never let go.

"He's all right," Jake said. "Just a mite hungry and cold. I'll leave ye to yer breakfast now."

He ducked out of the low doorway. Mother and Father stepped back from Will, and the joy and gratitude on their faces faded into something sterner. "I'll let your mother get you something to eat," Father said. "And then, son, you and I shall have a talk."

That was one talk Rebekah had no desire to hear. She did not envy her brother one bit today.

In the days that followed, Will was unusually quiet and obedient. Rebekah knew he was trying hard to prove to Father and the other men that he had learned from his mistake. She also knew how embarrassed and ashamed he always felt once his rebellious feelings died down. Rebekah felt sorry for Will—but she was relieved to have him safe inside the stockade.

The days slipped past, one after another. More and more people fell ill, but Mother, Father, Will, and Rebekah stayed well. Rebekah began to feel more comfortable in their new home.

Then one cold night in the middle of January, the cry, "Fire! Fire!" echoed throughout New Plymouth. The Cunningham family jumped up from their sleeping mats and snatched more clothes. Even in the dim light of a pine torch, Rebekah could see the terror on her parents' faces.

❦ CHAPTER 6 ❧

Fire!

A dozen voices took up the cry. "Fire! The common house is on fire!"

Rebekah and Will raced toward the common house. Rebekah was more frightened than she had ever been in her life. She knew that the common house was filled with the sick, including William Bradford, who had collapsed while working, Governor Carver, and many others. "Please, God, help them!" Rebekah prayed under her breath.

Someone shouted words as she dashed past, but she could not make out their meaning. Cries of terror came from the gathering crowd.

Rebekah put on a burst of speed and caught up with a man running in front of her. Frantically, she snatched at the man's rough sleeve. "What is it?" she gasped.

"Gunpowder," the man panted. Sweat and fear covered his face. "Barrels of it. Some open. Stored in the common house!"

"No!" Rebekah's hand fell away. The new danger threatened not only those who lay ill, but all of New Plymouth. It was far more deadly than the flames that burned the common house's thatched roof and spread to its walls. If the fire ignited the gunpowder, it would explode. Rebekah and Will exchanged terrified glances.

"Here! You, boy! And you, lass." A man coming toward them from the common house thrust wooden buckets into their hands. "Fetch water, and be quick about it!"

Rebekah had felt as though she were frozen stiff with fear, but the man's order released her from her horror. She turned and raced after Will toward the water. Would the spark that set the common house on fire destroy everything they had worked so hard to build? Would it claim victims from the rows of sick inside the burning building?

"God, save them!" she heard Will yell, never slowing his pace. He filled his bucket and dashed back to the burning building. Rebekah did the same, being careful not to spill the precious water. When she got there and passed the bucket to eager, waiting hands, a great sob of relief tore from her throat.

The barrels of gunpowder sat away from the common house, safe from harm.

"Who got the powder out?" Will demanded of a breathless, soot-streaked man standing nearby.

The man slapped at stray sparks on his clothing. "God, I reckon." He coughed. A river of tears poured down his grimy face. "I never saw such a thing." He coughed again. "Even the weakest among us somehow managed to help! They tottered up from their sickbeds, grabbed those barrels as if they were feathers, and hauled them out." He mopped at his face and put out a spark greedily burning yet another hole in his already-tattered garment. "We lost a lot of clothing we can ill afford to spare, but praise be to God, no one was killed, at least so far." A shadow darkened the speaker's face. As if suddenly aware of his own weakness, he slumped to the ground and lay there panting.

Rebekah bit her lip, understanding only too well what the man meant. The fire and gunpowder had been cheated of their victims. But from the looks of those who had staggered from the common house and stood shaking with chills, their efforts could bring more death to the settlers. She had nursed enough patients on the voyage across the Atlantic to know how people looked when they were seriously ill.

All through the night, Rebekah and Will continued hauling buckets of water to the common house. Everyone was fighting the fire, but the people who were sick eventually collapsed in the snow. Rebekah noticed that Mother was busy helping them get up and leading them to small homes where at least they could stay dry. Father was pouring water on the roofs of nearby homes to keep them from catching fire.

Finally, the fire was put out. As the tired group looked at the steaming roof, they knew even more work lay ahead. The roof needed to be repaired and the common house cleaned before the sick could return to their shelter.

Will and Rebekah looked at each other. As she wiped her nose with the handkerchief a Dutch friend had given her so long ago, Rebekah said, "Will, don't you sometimes long to be back in Holland where at least we had time to play with friends?"

"Do I ever," Will said. "And we weren't so tired or hungry, either."

Rebekah let go of her gloom with a determined shake of her head. "Well," she said, "we certainly can't go back now. And if we're going to survive, we need to keep working. I'd best go help Mother cook up some porridge for everyone."

Sickness and death continued to haunt the colony. Sometimes, Rebekah hated the New World, with its cold and hunger. What good was it to be free to worship as they pleased when so many people in the colony lay sick and helpless? How many more would they lose in this harsh land?

Rebekah was especially sad when Captain Standish's wife, Rose, died. She had grown to admire the gruff captain as she saw him work among the sick with Elder Brewster. "After what I've seen him do," Will confided to Rebekah one day, "I'll never call him Captain Shrimp again."

The Cunningham family was alarmed one morning when Will woke up flushed with fever. Having seen so many people die, Rebekah was terrified her brother would be next. For days, she did everything she could to help Mother take care of Will. She helped with the cooking and washing, and she stayed by Will's side every chance she had, wiping his forehead with a cold wet rag. "God, please help my brother get better," she prayed over and over beneath her breath. She did not think she could bear to lose Will.

When Father, Mother, and Rebekah were so tired they could no longer keep their eyes open, Jake stayed at Will's side. The sailor's big hands proved surprisingly gentle as he wiped Will's hot face with the cloth dipped in cool water. Jake also managed to secretly bring Will small portions of food. The family never asked, but they suspected Jake saved it from his own rations.

Finally, Will was able to get up, although he was so weak he could barely walk across the room. His eyes looked enormous in his thin face, and his freckles stood out as if painted on his nose and cheeks.

The first afternoon he was able to sit up, Will peppered Rebekah with questions about what had been happening. "At least there hasn't been any trouble with the Indians," he said.

Rebekah sniffed. "Depends on what you call trouble. No one can leave any kind of tool lying around or it mysteriously disappears. One of our men went out for ducks and saw Indians coming this way. The men working in the forest left their tools and came back after their guns. When they got back, both the Indians and the tools had vanished." The corners of Rebekah's mouth turned down. "Now the Indians are getting bolder. One day they stole tools from some of our people who left them just long enough for the midday meal!"

"We need our tools or we can't cut wood and make crops," Will protested.

"Don't judge them too harshly," Mother told the children. "This was their land before we came."

"It's ours now. The king gave it to us," Will protested.

Mother sighed. "I wonder how we would have felt if someone came to our house in Holland and told us it no longer belonged to us. The king means nothing to the people who were born here across the ocean."

"Elder Brewster said it's for their own good," Father spoke

quietly. "He says when we tell the Indians about God and Jesus they will be happier."

Rebekah was glad the Indians would have a chance to learn about Jesus. But she wondered if the Pilgrims were using that as an excuse to make them feel better about stealing what rightfully belonged to the Indians. The thoughts that filled her head were strange, uneasy ones, and she tried to push them away.

When the Pilgrims who were still living aboard the *Mayflower* fell ill, Captain Jones insisted most of them be taken ashore. "I can't risk having my men take your sickness," he barked. "It's bad enough we couldn't leave and go back to England as we planned. We don't intend to get your consumption and pneumonia."

Some of those who had been passengers on the *Mayflower* weren't much kinder.

"One man fixed meat a few times for a friend who said he would leave him everything," Rebekah whispered to Will. She knew Father and Mother didn't approve of telling tales, but she was so angry she just couldn't keep it to herself. "The man didn't die right away, and you know what?" Rebekah clenched her hands into fists. "The man who was supposed to be his friend called the sick man an ungrateful cheat! He said he wouldn't fix him anything more. The sick man died that very night."

Rebekah's mouth turned down at the corners. "Why are some of our own people acting this way? How can they, when we so badly need to help each other?"

"From fear." Will sadly shook his head. "The crew on the

Mayflower is said to be even worse. They snarl at one another like dogs. Jake says they think they're all good fellows when they're well. But once sickness strikes, the healthy crew members absolutely refuse to help those who are ill. They are afraid to go in the cabins and risk infection."

"That's terrible!" Rebekah exclaimed.

"Well," Will said, "at least one good thing happened. Remember the boatswain who never missed a chance to curse us and tell us how worthless we are?"

"How could I forget him?" Rebekah rolled her eyes. "He was awful! He never said anything nice about any of us."

"He has now." Will took in a deep breath. "The few people from our group who were allowed to remain on board the *Mayflower* are pitching in to help the sick crew members. Our people refuse to just let the sailors die. Hard as it is to believe, the same boatswain who couldn't stand us told our people before he died, 'You, I now see, show your love like Christians one to another, but we let one another lie and die like dogs.' Can you imagine that?"

Rebekah blinked hard. "I'm glad, but I wish he hadn't died. I hope he knew Jesus."

"I do, too."

Rebekah felt sadness shoot through her like an arrow. "Not just him, but all the others. More than half the crew is dead. I don't know if any of them knew Jesus." A great lump came to her throat. "I hope so." Rebekah took in a deep breath, held it, then slowly let it out. "Will, do you know what I want almost more than anything in the whole world?"

"Enough food to feel really full?" her brother asked and

patted his flat stomach.

"More than that. More than anything except for you and Father and Mother not to die." Rebekah swallowed hard at the thought. There had already been too many deaths. Some whole families were wiped out, although no girls and only a few boys had died.

"What do you want?" Will asked.

"To have Jake know Jesus. I think maybe he's starting to. The last time I talked to him, he said, 'Somethin' fer a man to think about, how ye Pilgrims are kind to everyone.'"

"What did you say?" Will leaned forward eagerly.

Rebekah shrugged. "I told him it was 'cause that's what Jesus would do if He were here and folks were sick, even folks who cursed Him."

Will's face glowed with pride. "Good for you! I don't think I'd have had the courage to say that, but, oh, I'm glad you did!"

"So am I." Rebekah grinned, the first real smile that had settled on her face since before Will got sick and worried them half to death.

"What did Jake say then?"

"Nothing." The disappointment she had felt when she talked with Jake came back. "He just cocked his head to one side and raised a shaggy eyebrow like he does when he's tired of talking, and then he mumbled that he had to get back to work."

"Maybe he will think about it," Will comforted. "I love telling people about Jesus. He's the best thing in the world. I wish everyone could understand about how much He loves us. If they did, people wouldn't be so crabby and scared and mean to each other. They would know that God would keep them safe, no matter what—so then they wouldn't feel as though they had to fight and snatch for the things they want."

Rebekah liked the way her brother put her own thoughts into words. She looked into Will's face. "Will, someday when you grow up, you might be a preacher, like Elder Brewster. You could, you know."

Will shook his head. "I can't imagine being a preacher. A carpenter, maybe, or a fisherman, or explorer. Besides, you know you don't have to be a preacher to tell people about Jesus."

"Perhaps not, but you'd make a good one." Rebekah's faith in her brother remained unshaken.

"Well, you were the one who told Jake, not me."

Rebekah giggled. "Silly, girls can't be preachers. And I just wish I had said more."

The next day she wished it even harder. Father brought terrible news. Jake was violently ill and lay burning with fever and freezing with chills aboard the *Mayflower*.

"I feel it's only fair to warn you he will probably die," Father added sadly, "although our people are doing everything they can for him."

"No!" Rebekah cried. Tears burned behind her eyes, but she shut her lips tight to keep back her sobs. She ran away to the new hideaway she had found, between two stacks of firewood. Curled up tight, with her chin resting on her knees and her cloak snugged around her elbows, she began to pray harder than she had prayed in her whole life.

CHAPTER 7

The Promise

For a full week, Jake hung onto life with every ounce of his strength. Those who cared for him shook their heads and said he should have died days before. They marveled that a man so sick still lived.

For a full week, Rebekah, Will, and their parents prayed for the seaman. Rough and without polish though he was, Jake had proven himself to be their friend again and again. Rebekah couldn't think of him without crying. When she remembered the food he had brought them so many times, she wept bitter tears. "If he had eaten it instead of giving it to us, he might not be sick."

"Hush, child." Mother's stern command shocked Rebekah. Their mother sometimes scolded Will, but she seldom raised her voice to her obedient, even-tempered daughter. "Jake chose to give you the food. Don't spoil his gift by feeling guilty. You know he would not want it so."

Rebekah sniffled, and Will sent her a weak smile. She knew her brother wanted to think of something to cheer her up, but he couldn't. How could anyone laugh or think of funny stories when Jake and so many others lay close to death?

"Father, may I go see him?" Rebekah pleaded.

"You mustn't!" Will cried. "You could become sick and die!" For once, Will was the fearful one.

Rebekah looked into Will's face and read there the terrible fear that haunted her as well: Who else would they lose to death's dark grip? She smiled at him, trying to chase away her own terror as much as his.

"Jake didn't let that stop him from coming when you were so sick," she reminded her brother.

Fresh horror sprang to Will's eyes. "Did Jake catch his illness from me?" He ducked his head and tears ran down his cheeks. "It's my fault. It's all my fault!"

"William Cunningham, stop that this minute!" Father thundered. "I will not have you carrying on in this manner. It is unbecoming to a child of God. We have put Jake in our heavenly Father's hands. It is not for us to place blame on ourselves or on others." His white, set face showed no trace of his usual kindly expression.

The children gasped. Father had never spoken to them in that tone. Will raised his tear-streaked face and stared at their father.

"It hurts me to have to speak to you this way, but I must." Father looked weary. "God has blessed you both with loving, tender hearts. He sees and is pleased that you care when others are sick or in trouble. However, you need to remember something. God does not expect you to carry the burden of all the sins and hurts of the world on your small shoulders." A gentler look crept into Father's face, and he stroked Rebekah's tousled braids. "That's why Jesus came. To carry all the hurt for us."

"Father is right," Mother said in a low tone. "Jesus took those burdens to the cross. Our part is simply to trust and serve Him. Don't fret, Will. Nor you, Rebekah. It has taken your father and me many years to learn this." Mother smiled at Father. "Many times, we still feel like we need to take a hand in whatever life brings—to control it—instead of waiting for God to do His perfect work, as He has commanded."

"We must learn to be patient," Father added. "The Bible tells us this over and over. The prophet Isaiah said, 'But they that wait upon the Lord shall renew their strength; they shall mount up with wings as eagles; they shall run, and not be weary; and they shall walk, and not faint.'"

"It's hard," Will muttered.

Father lowered his voice and whispered, "That's where the promise comes in."

"The promise?" The children's ears perked up. For a moment, the excitement of a possible mystery took their thoughts away from death and dying.

"The Bible is filled with promises, such as in Psalm 23," Father told them.

"I know that one," Rebekah cried. "David said the Lord was his Shepherd and would take care of him—"

"Even in the valley of the shadow of death," Will quickly finished. "Is that the promise you meant?" He looked at Father.

"It's a good one but not the one I was thinking about." A faraway look came into Father's eyes. "When your mother and I fled from England to Holland, we didn't know what would happen. What if we were stopped by the authorities, beaten, or put in jail? I could bear it for myself, but I felt I could not stand it if your mother suffered at the hands of King James's men."

A look of gratitude came to his dark eyes when he looked at Mother. "I finally shared my struggles with your mother. She reminded me of the promise, a single verse. We claimed it as our own. It has kept us going all through the years. Each time life becomes unbearable, we repeat the scripture."

"What is it?" Rebekah and Will asked at the same time.

"In Paul's first letter to the Corinthians," Father said quietly, "the great apostle promises we shall never be given more than we can bear, and that God will make a way for us to escape."

"Always?" Rebekah left her mother and crept into her father's welcoming arms.

"Always, Rebekah." His face shadowed. "This doesn't mean God answers every prayer the way we think He should or that He gives us all the things we ask for. It does mean He answers in the best way."

Rebekah felt her heart pound with fear. Her throat felt dry. Surely the best way wasn't for Jake to die without knowing Jesus! Her nails dug into his hands. "Father, I just have to see Jake," she choked out.

Father looked down into Rebekah's face. She felt as though she were being carefully weighed. "Are you strong enough to see your friend close to death, perhaps dying? To smell the poison that is taking lives? The stink of sickness that clings in spite of what all those who are able to help can do?"

"I am." Rebekah raised her head and looked her father straight in the eye. "Haven't I already carried slops for those in the common house and helped clean up when they have been sick?"

She saw Father look at Mother, and Rebekah's heart leapt when she saw her mother's nod.

"Aye, lass," Father said with a sigh. "So be it."

"May I come, too?" Will asked. His face was pale but determined. "Jake is my friend, too."

"Very well," Father said. He gently put Rebckah aside. "Come with me, but mind what you say." He paused. "Let the Spirit of God guard and guide your tongues."

Rebekah didn't fully understand what Father said, but she nodded, anyway. They boarded the *Mayflower* and walked toward where Jake lay. She tried not to gag. The stench of sickness and death on the ship made her want to head for the rail.

Oh, God, she prayed, *help me.* Taking small breaths in the hopes of keeping from heaving, she followed her father's sure steps down the deck she and Will had so often walked with Jake. Would they ever stride that deck together again?

"Jake, it's William Cunningham," Father said in a loud, clear voice when they reached the tossing, turning man. "I have young Will and his sister Rebekah with me."

The seaman's restless fingers picked at the blanket on which they lay. He opened his eyes, but Rebekah knew he didn't recognize them.

Could this gray-faced man really be Jake? It seemed to be impossible. Where had all his magnificent strength gone, his way of showing without a word he could control any situation?

But it was Jake, for the sick man turned eagerly toward the sound of Father's voice. A broken whisper came from between his parched lips. "Tell th' lass. . ."

"The lass? Do you mean Rebekah? Tell her what, Jake?" Father asked.

Jake stared straight ahead, and Rebekah knew the sailor could not see Father, though Father was leaning close to him. Jake lifted a trembling hand to his mouth. "Tell th' lass. . ." He made a mighty effort to raise himself but fell back to his pallet, breathing heavily, moving his body as if seeking a comfortable spot to rest. Sweat clouded his face.

"Is he dying?" Will whispered.

Rebekah's heart gave a mighty lurch.

"He's very close to it." Father put a hand on Jake's shoulder, then turned to the children. "Stay with him, and I'll fetch water."

One of the hardest things Rebekah ever had to do was sit with their friend while the seconds limped into minutes. She tried twice to speak, but she could not find her voice. At last, she managed to say, "Jake, we're here. It's Rebekah. And Will is here, too." She hesitated, and then she added, "So is Jesus. He's here with you, as well."

A slight change came over Jake's still figure. His breathing slowed, and his thrashing body grew quiet. Rebekah pressed her lips tight together. Was this the end?

"Keep talking to him, Rebekah," Father instructed as he placed a bucket on the floor and dipped a cloth into the cool water to bathe the seaman's face. "One of the workers just told me that ever since Jake fell ill, he has been repeating, 'Tell th' lass' over and over. Let him know you hear him."

Rebekah leaned closer, being careful not to get in Father's way. "I'm here, Jake. It's Rebekah. Remember all the things we did together? Remember the long voyage we had together and all the stories you told Will and me?"

Rebekah searched her mind for things that might help her reach their friend. Or had Jake already gone so far down into the deep, dark valley of death that only God could help him?

"That's it!" Rebekah whispered. "Listen to me, Jake." She placed her hands on the big man's shoulders and gently shook him. " 'Yea, though I walk through the valley of the shadow of death, I will fear no evil.' David said that. He knew God was with him and he didn't have to be afraid. You don't have to be scared, either."

Jake didn't open his eyes, but something in the way he turned his head toward Rebekah's direction gave her hope. Again and again she repeated Psalm 23. Each time she came to the part about the valley of the shadow of death, Jake quieted, until he lay like one dead.

At last, Rebekah grew so hoarse, she could barely whisper. Father laid a hand on her shoulder. "Come, lass. We have done all we can. Now he is in the Father's hands."

Despair filled Rebekah. Why hadn't God heard her prayer? If only they had come sooner! Perhaps Jake would have asked Jesus to forgive and save him. She slowly stood, feeling like someone had kicked her in the stomach. "He's dead."

"No, Rebekah. Just sleeping."

A stubborn hope sprang up inside her heart. "Will he live?"

Father shook his head. "I cannot say. I do know your words reached him and stilled his tossing and turning. Now all we can do is wait."

"Let me stay with him," Rebekah begged. "Mother needs

you, but Will and I could stay here. It may be the last thing we can do for him."

"You know the risks." Father's keen gaze studied Rebekah's face. "You, too, may fall ill."

Rebekah thought of those who had died, many who had fallen ill after caring for others. "Father, Jake would do it for us. You know he would."

Tears sprang to Father's eyes. "Aye. Stay then," he said in a low voice. "And don't forget that when we serve others, we serve our Master." He touched Rebekah's cheek and then Will's uncombed hair. Rebekah felt they had been given a blessing.

One of the strangest nights Rebekah would ever know began when Father left. Neither she nor Will spoke, and Jake was silent except for his heavy breathing. For the first time in many days, Rebekah had time to think. Midnight came, followed by the early morning hours.

"Our bodies are at our lowest point after the midnight hour, before the dawn," Father had warned before he wearily trudged away. "Then also comes the greatest danger of loved ones slipping from this world into the next."

Would that happen to Jake? What had the sailor wanted to tell Rebekah so badly that even in his fever he continued to call out for her? Perhaps he had only wanted to say good-bye.

But maybe. . . Another possibility occurred to her, and it was so wonderful that she felt fresh strength flow through her as she silently kept watch. What if during the time of sickness Jake had remembered what she had told him about Jesus? What if he had cried out to the Lord in his heart, asking to be forgiven and saved? Wouldn't he want the one who had told him about Jesus to know?

Rebekah scrunched up her knees, rested her elbows on them, and laid her head on her folded arms. *Please, God, I have to know.* It took all her courage to add, *If it be Your will.* She prayed the words again. And again.

Only this time she couldn't finish the prayer. Her eyes closed. Her breathing slowed. Her head still resting on her arms, Rebekah slept.

A slight sound roused her. She opened her still-tired eyes and saw that Will was sleeping, too. And it was daylight.

Oh, no! Some guards they were, sleeping the hours away instead of keeping watch. If they were sentries posted outside the stockade, they would be severely punished.

Rebekah was afraid to look at the pallet on the floor beside her. With a deep breath, she gritted her teeth and looked down at Jake.

ᖡ CHAPTER 8 ᖢ

You Can't Stop Me!

When Rebekah looked down at Jake, she expected to see a corpse. Instead, the sailor's small eyes twinkled. The shadow of a grin touched his lips. He licked them and croaked in a hoarse, unnatural voice, "Ye stayed with me?"

"Yes."

Their voices made Will raise a sleepy face, and his face exploded into a grin when he saw that Jake was still alive.

"I be thinkin' yer a brave lass." Jake laid one big paw on Rebekah's hand, then turned to Will. "And you, too, lad." His grin grew a bit wider before his mouth settled into its familiar stern expression. "Now git, afore ye catches the fever."

Rebekah knew better than to argue. "I'll come back later. You'll be better then." She and Will stood and turned to go.

Jake's low voice stopped her where she stood. "Mayhap I will be better by and by. But no need to fret if I ain't. That Friend of yers, Jesus. . . He fergive me." A look of wonder came into the sailor's face. "Me, who's sailed the seven seas and done black things! And all I had to do was ask."

Rebekah ran back to Jake's pallet and knelt next to him. She grabbed Jake's hand and squeezed it tight. "This is the best present anyone ever gave me!" she cried.

"Aye, mate." Jake smiled again. It softened his face until he looked like a different man. "I be chartin' a new course now." Some of his old fierceness came back. "But didn't I tell ye to run along? Now git, the two of ye!"

Rebekah and Will laughed at the scowl that no longer hid Jake's tender heart. Jake's eyes shone steady and true, showing how much he had already changed in the short time since he signed on with a new Master.

Proud to be the bearers of such good news, Rebekah and Will raced back to their parents.

"Now all he needs is rest and good food," Rebekah announced. A frown chased away her joy. "Where are we going to get food for him?"

Father smiled. "Captain Standish is sending a few men for game." He laughed at Will's obvious excitement. "A good meat broth will help Jake and the others."

"May I go?"

Rebekah knew Will was holding his breath. Ever since the time Will had tried to catch up with the men by himself, Captain Standish had ordered the boy to stay behind.

To Will's disgust, Captain Standish did not relent. Rebekah watched while Will bit his tongue to hold back hasty words that might mean he'd be left out of future hunting parties. She knew disappointment burned inside him when Father and two other men left with Captain Standish.

"I'm needed at the common house," Mother told Will and

Rebekah. She put on her warm cloak and bonnet and told Will, "Cheer up. I know it's hard being left behind, but next time you will probably get to go. Besides, after staying with Jake last night, you two need some rest." A moment later she was on her way, leaving the two children alone. Father had forbidden them to go back to the *Mayflower*.

"Jake sent word that you were to stay away," Father said. "When I get back, I'll go see that all is well. I want to tell him how glad we all are over his decision to accept Jesus."

Will sat and glared at Rebekah, who had done nothing to deserve his ill will. "It's our duty to help Jake," he said. "Besides, I'm tired of people thinking I'm only a child."

His expression changed. Rebekah watched his face uneasily, wondering what thoughts were taking shape in his mind. "Rebekah," he burst out, "I'm going to show them I'm not a child. All of them!" He hastily collected the warmest clothing he owned.

"Where are you going?" she gasped. "Father told you to stay off the *Mayflower*. And if you try to follow the hunting party again, you'll end up in trouble just like last time. If you do something silly, you won't be proving how grown-up you are. Just the opposite!"

But her brother's lips were set as though he had made up his mind.

"Will, you're going to get in trouble." She stamped her foot. "Well, I won't let you do it." Sparks flew from her eyes. "You're tired from being up all night, and you need to rest. Besides, you're still weak from being sick. I'm going right to the common house and tell Mother you're planning something you know you aren't supposed to do!"

Will whirled around to face her. "If you do, I'll never forgive you!" A black scowl appeared on his face, but then he smiled at her, his eyes full of pleading. "C'mon, Rebekah. You never tell on me, and I've been good for weeks now!"

"All the more reason you shouldn't disobey now," she told him. But some of the anger left her eyes.

Will added layers of clothing. He carefully took down a musket from the rough wall of their home and went through the slow process of loading it. Rebekah watched with anxious eyes. She heaved a sigh of relief when he finished. "Be careful," she warned.

"I will. I just want to be ready when I see a deer."

"Then you are going after the hunting party! Will Cunningham, you know what's going to happen. Father will be so upset with you, and what if you get lost? Remember what happened last time? I'm not going to let you go!"

"I'm going, and you can't stop me," he told her. "We don't know that Father and the hunting party will find game. I might. I'll head a different direction from the one they take. That way, if they don't find deer, I may. Jake needs broth, and later, he'll need the meat. So do we. You're so thin that when you stand sideways, you hardly cast a shadow!"

Rebekah couldn't keep back a small giggle.

Will went on. "Do you think Jake would stay home with the women and children if we needed food? Don't be a goose, Rebekah, and don't tell anyone."

Rebekah's giggle changed, and she sounded hurt. "You don't have to be so cross."

Will looked ashamed. "I'm sorry. But I need to get out of this place."

Rebekah searched his face. "Why, Will? Why are you so eager to run off all alone in the woods?"

Will looked down at the ground. "I'm not sure," he said slowly. "I just have to." He lifted his head and looked at his sister. Then he said in a rush of words, "Last night when we were sitting beside Jake, I felt so helpless. Jake could have died while we were sitting there with him—and there was absolutely nothing I could do to stop it from happening."

He flung his hands out wide, and Rebekah heard the frustration and fear in his voice. "I still feel helpless. As though I'm just sitting here waiting for death to sneak up and take someone I love. I can't just sit here doing nothing. It's driving me mad. I have to do something."

Rebekah studied her brother's face. She understood his feelings. But their long night at Jake's side had made her feel calmer somehow, more sure that God was in control of their lives. It seemed to have had just the opposite effect on Will. His eyes were wild, and she could see he was breathing fast.

This was apparently another one of those moments when Will seemed bound and determined to get in trouble. And this time, there would be no Jake to find him and bring him home. All too often, when Will was determined to have his own way, someone got hurt—usually Will himself. Rebekah had learned that if she could keep him from going off on his own when he was in one of his moods, she could usually curb his more foolish impulses.

"All right," she said suddenly. "But I'm going with you."

Will looked startled. "You can't."

"Oh, yes, I can. If you're going, then so am I."

Will hesitated. Then he shrugged. "Put some warm clothes on, then. And let's get going."

Rebekah and Will had a bad moment at the gate. The sentry challenged them. "Who goes there?" he shouted.

"We'll never get past him," Rebekah whispered, feeling relieved.

But then the sentry recognized them, and his face relaxed into a smile. "Where are you two children going?"

"I saw some rabbits on the hillside by the woods," Will said. "We thought we'd try to snare some for our supper. Some rabbit stew would taste awfully good."

"That it would," the sentry agreed. He raised an eyebrow at the musket Will carried. "And if you should see a deer, you're all ready, I see."

Will grinned and nodded. He shifted the weight of the musket and stood straight and tall.

"Well, don't go far, children," the sentry said. "You don't want to get lost."

Rebekah nodded, and she and Will hurried on their way. "Children!" Will hissed under his breath. "I'm sick to death of being called a child."

"You shouldn't have lied to him about the rabbits," Rebekah said, her voice laced with disapproval.

"I couldn't very well tell him we were hunting deer, could I?"

"He suspected it, anyway."

A faint trail led off into the woods, and the children followed it, bickering all the way. A half mile down the trail, though, Will found deer tracks and droppings. "These look no more than a few hours old." His voice was full of excitement. "Father and the others will be happy to see us when we come back with all the meat we can carry. We'll have to figure out a way to hide it so animals and Indians don't find it before someone comes for the rest of the meat."

Rebekah gave him a skeptical glance. Will was already planning what they would do with meat they hadn't even found yet.

But Rebekah, too, soon became caught up in the excitement of tracking the deer. The children stopped arguing and instead discussed how much the fresh meat would help Jake and the others. They were so intent on watching the ground that they failed to notice the storm swooping toward them. Huge clouds joined others, but not until they hid the pale winter sun did Rebekah notice and look up at the sky.

"There's going to be a storm!"

Will shifted his gaze between the tracks and the sky a half-dozen times. "Deer seek shelter from bad weather," he said slowly. "The one we're tracking might be just ahead. It might be hunched down in a bed beneath the trees to protect itself from the storm." Will plunged ahead, scanning both sides of the trail. No deer.

"Might as well turn back," he muttered in disgust. "It's getting so dark I couldn't see a deer unless it jumped up in front of me, and then I probably couldn't kill it. Of all the days for a storm, it would have to be this one. Let's go home."

The children turned around and strode back down the trail

the way they had come. Their feet felt heavier now, almost as heavy as their spirits. Going home with meat was one thing. Neither of them looked forward to arriving empty-handed!

"How far did we come, anyway?" Will asked. He came to an abrupt stop and stared around at the gathering darkness. Rebekah also peered at the path, trying to recognize some landmark that would tell her how far from the stockade they were.

"That's funny," she said after a moment. "I don't remember stepping over a fallen tree in the trail before." She pointed to the downed log that blocked their path ahead.

Will suddenly looked uneasy. "Maybe we took the wrong fork back where the trail branched."

Rebekah nodded. "That must be it."

They turned, retraced their footsteps, and tried the other path. It led directly to a huge, uprooted tree and ended.

Thoroughly confused, Rebekah and Will went from one promising trail to another, only to become more hopelessly lost than ever. Worse, Will stumbled and fell. The musket flew out of his hands. They searched on their hands and knees in the darkness, but they could not find it.

Rebekah felt sweaty and cold by turns. The growing gloom soon hid any landmarks she might have recognized. All she could see in every direction was endless forest. The only way they could keep on the faint trail was to kick out with their legs as they walked. When they hit brush, they knew they had strayed from the path.

Rebekah's stomach growled loudly, reminding her that the last time she had eaten was too long ago. "Why didn't we bring some food?" she complained.

Will didn't answer. The rising wind bit through their clothing. Rebekah stamped her feet to get them warm.

"I guess I thought I could get a deer and be home before anyone knew we were gone," Will said at last. "If we only had a fire! No chance of that without the musket." He waved his arms to warm himself. "I wonder what Father would do if he were caught out like this?"

Plop. A large wet drop fell onto Rebekah's face. *Plop, plop, plop.* Others followed. From the look of the angry clouds, an icy downpour had overtaken the children.

Rebekah and Will dove beneath a tree with thick drooping limbs. Its overlapping branches grew so close together they protected the children from the rain, but Rebekah knew their problem wasn't solved. Huddled against the rough tree trunk, she tried to think. "We should pray," she said. "We should ask God to help us."

"Why would God want to help us?" Will's voice sounded sullen, but Rebekah knew he was feeling guilty. Will always felt guilty after one of his rebellious moods was over. "If I were God, I might want to help you. It's not your fault you're out here, not really. It's all my fault. I knew you were right. I knew it was wrong to go. And now that we're here, it doesn't seem like there's much point in asking God to get us out of a mess that I created all by myself."

"You might as well ask why God would want to send Jesus to die for us," Rebekah said. "I don't think God only helps people who never make mistakes. The Bible always sounds as though God is willing to help whenever someone asks Him. Besides, I don't think we have a choice." She looked around at the thick darkness, and her voice wavered. "No one knows where we are. We can't just stumble around in the dark all night. We'd better pray."

Will still didn't seem convinced that God would want to listen to him. After a moment, though, he sighed. "All right, then. I'll pray." He hesitated for a long moment. Then he bowed his head and said softly, "God, you helped Daniel in the lions' den, but he got thrown in. He didn't just walk in by himself." Will sighed again. "I should have listened to Rebekah. Forgive me, please, God. We sure can't help ourselves, and no one knows we're here but You."

"Please help us, God," Rebekah added. Then they both said together, "Amen."

Rebekah felt a little better now that they had asked God for help, but Will still seemed discouraged and angry with himself. "Why am I so foolish?" he asked, hitting his forehead with his palm. "No wonder Captain Standish and Father don't believe I'm a man."

Will and Rebekah huddled together beneath the tree's meager shelter. Exhausted from the long night at Jake's side, Rebekah finally fell into an uneasy sleep.

Later, she awoke stiff and half frozen. The slight warmth the branches offered could not keep back the increasing cold. She sat shivering, thinking about her brother, who still slept at her side.

Even the tossing storms of the wild Atlantic Ocean had not been able to drown Will's spirit of adventure. She had never seen him as shaken as he was now. She knew he bitterly regretted leaving the settlement without permission.

When she was shivering so hard that her teeth rattled, she poked Will awake. "We can't stay under here. I'm freezing."

Will jumped up and hit his head on a branch. "Ow!" Rubbing the sore spot, he turned back toward Rebekah. "If we walk to keep warm, we may be getting farther from the settlement. But what else can we do? We're in an awful mess."

"God," Rebekah whispered, "please help us."

Suddenly, she grinned at her brother.

"I know what to do."

CHAPTER 9

Left. Right. Left. Right.

Left. Right. Left. Right. Rebekah and Will swung their arms and marched. Cold, hungry, and miserable, they wanted to run, but they dared not. Rebekah knew that Will's head was throbbing, a painful reminder to him to keep a steady pace. If they crashed into a low-hanging branch, they could be knocked senseless. They might freeze to death before they recovered.

Left. Right. It was getting harder now. How could a person keep going when her legs felt weaker than water? Could she starve to death in just one night? *Don't be a goose,* she ordered herself.

"Have to keep moving," Will mumbled. "Jake needs broth. Meat."

But Rebekah was so tired. Perhaps they should stop this endless marching and rest.

"No!" The sound of her own sharp cry alerted her to the dangerous state into which she had fallen. She scrubbed at her eyes.

"We can't stop," Will muttered.

Rebekah remembered every horrible story she had heard of those who rested in the freezing cold and never woke up again. The stories also kept her walking long after she felt she could not keep on.

Left. Right. Left. Right. Was she going mad? Rebekah giggled wildly. Dangerous or not, she had to stop.

"I won't sit down," she panted. She leaned against a tree trunk to catch her breath, and after a moment, Will joined her. If she closed her eyes for just a moment, would sleep keep them shut? Will might fall asleep, too. She couldn't chance it.

Left. Right. On and on and on. Was this how a beast of burden who walked in a circle turning a mill wheel felt? She and Will leaned against a tree again. *What are Father and Mother doing right now?* Rebekah wondered. *Will we ever see them again?*

Left. Right. Left. Right. Her feet felt like two anchors, weighing her down when she must keep moving.

"God, forgive me," she heard Will whisper. She reached for his hand with her numb fingers. Their hands clung together, warming each other.

After what felt like a lifetime, Rebekah knew she couldn't walk another step. She leaned against a tree, as she had been forced to do so many times throughout the long dark night. Her eyes closed. She felt the rough bark of the tree on her hands when she slid to the ground, but she was too tired to care. Beside her, Will slumped to the ground, as well. They leaned against each other, too exhausted to go on. Dimly, Rebekah realized they dared not sleep, or death would take them, as it had taken so many others. But she was too tired to fight the sleepiness that swept over her.

"Will? Rebekah?"

Rebekah stirred. "God, is that You?" she asked sleepily. Had she and Will died and gone to heaven?

"Will! Rebekah!" The cry came again. Strange. It sounded like Father. What was he doing in heaven? Or were they all back in Holland? Had everything been a dream: the *Mayflower*, Jake, the terrible night of walking? Rebekah struggled to understand.

When a third cry came, she felt Will struggle to his feet. He shouted, "Here! We're here."

His shout was so weak that Rebekah feared Father would never hear it.

"Son, where are you?"

Rebekah forced her eyes open, got to her feet, and called, "Father?" Her voice was barely more than a whisper. She swallowed, licked her lips, then screamed at the top of her lungs, "Father, we're here!"

A crashing of brush and heavy, thudding footsteps told her she had been heard. She sagged with relief against the tree. A heartbeat later, Father burst into view. He raced toward them and gathered them both in his arms.

The others of the rescue party followed close behind. "How'd you manage to keep from freezing?" one wanted to know.

"We prayed," Will said. He looked at his sister and grinned. "Then Rebekah remembered a story Jake told us once about a man who got trapped by a blizzard and didn't have any food or a way to make a fire. He knew he had to keep walking, or he'd freeze, but he couldn't see where he was going. Neither could we, so we did what he did." Will stopped for breath.

"What was that, son?" Father asked. His arms tightened, sending warmth through the children's shivering bodies.

"We walked around the same tree all night. It kept us warm, and we didn't wander any farther from the settlement." Will yawned.

After a moment of stunned silence, relieved laughter came from the rescue party. One man slapped his leg, chuckled, and said, "Well, I never! Cunningham, those are mighty clever young ones you have."

Rebekah's heart thumped with pride. "It wasn't me," she said. "God made me think of the story." She looked at the men's faces. Some looked convinced. Others did not.

"I still say it's mighty clever," the man said again.

Father quietly added, "If Will had done as he was told, he and his sister wouldn't have been in trouble at all."

"That's right, lad. Listen to your father from now on."

"I will." Will looked at the ground. "I guess this is my last hunting expedition for a long time."

"It could have been your last forever," Father reminded him. "Now, let's get you home where you belong. There you will stay until you learn to act like a man instead of a child who goes running off when he doesn't get his own way."

Rebekah knew Will deserved everything Father said, but she also knew how much he must hurt to be corrected in front of the men. Captain Standish's judgment would be far harsher than Father's. She hoped her brother would take it like a man. Neither of them would ever forget what could have happened to them without the love of God to protect and help them.

Afterward, Rebekah didn't remember much of the trip home. At one point someone spotted Will's musket and rescued it from the snow, but Will barely noticed. One weary step after another, the children managed to keep going until just outside the settlement. Left. Right.

When the stockade gate swung open, Rebekah's knees buckled. Father slung her over his shoulder and carried her. If she hadn't been so tired, she might have been embarrassed to be hauled home like a sack of grain. As it was, she was just glad not to have to walk anymore.

"Abigail," Father called as he opened the door to their little home, "the children are safe and unharmed. They need food and rest. Bring warm, dry clothes and broth. We'll talk later."

The last thing Rebekah remembered clearly was the sensation that the ice inside her was melting as she drank her mother's broth. Then she vaguely remembered her father's strong arms helping her up the ladder to bed. After that, she remembered nothing at all.

Rebekah awakened to pitch darkness. Had she only dreamed that Father and the others had come for them? Was she still in the woods? She cautiously shifted her body. The straw in her mattress crackled, telling her she was safely home. She turned over and fell asleep again.

The next time Rebekah woke, daylight had come. She glanced sideways at her brother's sleeping shape and then slid farther under her covers. The day was likely to bring hard moments for her brother. Captain Standish would certainly kill any hope of future hunting expeditions. Others in the colony might laugh at the boy who wanted to be a man but sneaked off like a sulky child.

"Lord, help him to bear whatever scolding we get," Rebekah whispered. "Help me to be a good big sister."

"Will. Rebekah. Dress and come down quickly," Father's ragged voice called.

Something in Father's voice frightened Rebekah. She had an uneasy feeling that he was not calling them down to scold them for their adventure. Her muscles stiff and aching from their night in the forest, Rebekah managed to get into her clothes and down the ladder. She left Will still fumbling his way into his wool pants.

Rebekah ran to the fireplace and warmed her cold hands at the blaze. Its cheerful glow felt good, but even the fire could not melt the icy fear in her heart. When she looked at Mother's face, she saw that her mother's lips trembled.

Father waited until Will stood beside Rebekah before the fire. Sadness lined Father's face as he said, "Children, you must be brave."

"What is it?" Rebekah clenched her hands until she felt the nails bite deep into her palms.

"Word just came from the *Mayflower*. Our friend Jake died in the night."

Rebekah buried her face in her apron.

"No," Will said hoarsely. "No, no, no! Jake was getting better. You know he was. That's why I went for the deer. He couldn't have died. It must be another crew member." He started for the door.

Father caught him halfway there. "Running isn't going to help."

"Let me go!" Will twisted and turned. "It isn't true." He stared up into Father's face. "Did he know we were lost?" When Father looked blank, Will shouted, "That's it, isn't it? He knew and tried to come for us." He buried his face in his hand. "What have I done?"

"Stop this, Will." Father shook his son, not hard, but enough to get his attention. Father's eyes blazed. "You had nothing to do with Jake's death. Plague took him, as it has taken many others and will take more. Jake never knew you were missing." Father pulled Will to him in a big hug.

Rebekah wiped away her hot tears. Her mother's arm went around her and held her tight.

Father looked over Will's head at his daughter. "We grieve, yet we praise Almighty God that our friend met Jesus, our Savior, before it was too late. The bearer of the news said Jake died with a smile on his face and the words 'Tell th' lass' on his lips."

A great sob tore free from Will's throat. He jerked from Father's arms and bolted up the ladder. Rebekah heard the crackle of the straw as he threw himself on his bed.

After a moment, she followed him up the ladder into the dim loft. "I loved him, too," she whispered. "I thought he was going to get better. I thought God had healed him." Her voice broke. "Sometimes I don't understand God."

The two children were silent for a long moment. Finally, Rebekah sighed. "Father and Mother are so sure of their faith. Maybe someday we'll be as strong as they are."

Will sat up and looked at his sister. With a sob, he put his arms around her, and the two children clung together. Perhaps later they would have more to say to each other, and they would find a way to comfort each other's hearts. Right now, Rebekah was just glad they still had Father, Mother, and each other.

Just thinking that made Rebekah's mouth go dry with fear. All she could do was cling to the promise that God would never send more than they could stand but would always make a way of escape.

CHAPTER 10

What Is a Samoset?

Afew weeks later, as Rebekah trotted alongside her little brother, she suddenly noticed that he was no longer so little. In fact, he was taller than she was. The realization made her giggle. She clapped her hand to her mouth and quickly looked around to make sure no one had heard her laughing on the Sabbath—but it felt good to laugh again after so many days of sadness.

They had just come from Sunday meeting, and Father and Mother were walking ahead of them. Rebekah looked sideways at Will. "My, that was a good sermon." She laughed again. "Elder Brewster's scripture was about you."

Will stopped dead still. "Whatever are you talking about?"

"The scripture," Rebekah patiently repeated. Her green eyes twinkled with fun. "Weren't you listening?"

"Not very well," Will confessed. He was staring at the *Mayflower*, and Rebekah knew he still ached inside each time he saw the ship where Jake had died.

"You should have been," Rebekah told him. "It just fits the

way you are now."

Curiosity seemed to finally pull Will's attention from his sad thoughts. "Really? What scripture was it? What did it say?"

"First Corinthians, chapter 13, verse 11." She smothered another giggle, and her face lit up with fun. "You know. The one where Paul says when he was a child, he spoke and understood as a child, but when he became a man—"

"He put away childish things," Will soberly finished for her. "Do you really think I'm like that?"

"Oh, yes." Her cap-covered braids bobbed up and down. "You're ever so much more grown-up. You're kinder to me, and I heard Father tell Mother he was proud of the way you took your punishment like a man."

She slid her hand into the crook his elbow made. "Father said even when Captain Standish roared like the wind, you held your tongue and looked straight at him. Mother's awfully proud. So am I." She hesitated, then whispered, "God must be proud, too."

"I hope so." Will scuffed his boot on the hard ground. "I'm trying."

"I know," she said sympathetically.

They walked in silence. For the first time in many days, Rebekah was filled with contentment. The cold winter could not last forever. On days like this, when the sun shone, she felt spring must soon be on its way.

Then suddenly, as she looked up ahead at her parents, she gave a little cry and sprang forward. Mother had fallen to the ground. When Rebekah reached her, she saw her mother was as white and still as a dead person. Rebekah's heart pounded with terror.

Father snatched up Mother in his arms and raced toward their hut. "Will, fetch Dr. Fuller," he ordered. "Tell him she collapsed for no apparent reason. Rebekah, run ahead and spread the mattress."

Will looked up at his father's ashen face. "Shouldn't you take her to the common house?"

"Nay. Home is closer. Go, lad, and don't stop to argue!"

Will turned and ran as if pursued by a thousand howling wolves. Rebekah hurried ahead to get her mother's bed ready. Dread kept time with her flying steps. Would Mother be taken next? "Please, God, spare her. Not just for our sake, but for the sake of others who need her so much." Rebekah's prayer came out in little gasps as she ran.

Minutes felt like a lifetime before Dr. Fuller reached the Cunninghams. Will had delivered his message and flown home without waiting for the physician. The kindly, overworked doctor bustled in. "Eh, what's all this? Is my best helper giving out on me?" He quickly examined Mother. She didn't even move.

Rebekah held her breath, waiting. Will was standing more still than a mouse that suspects a cat may be nearby. Father sat on the homemade bench, head bowed. Rebekah knew he was praying. Finally, Dr. Fuller finished his examination, rose from beside the straw mattress, and smiled. His expression filled Rebekah's heart with hope.

"Now, now, nothing to worry about." The doctor's face crinkled into laugh wrinkles. "She's just plain worn out. Our bodies keep going and going when we push them. How well I know!" He yawned mightily. "But eventually they give out.

If we don't give them the rest they need, then they take it for themselves. That's why your mother collapsed."

The doctor turned to Father. "Your wife has no fever," Dr. Fuller said. "She has no signs that foretell illness. I'd say what she needs is a good night's sleep. Don't wake her, even for food. Her body needs rest." He yawned again. "In fact, that's what I'm going to do: rest. All my other patients have either died or are mending."

He shook hands with Father and Will, then tugged on a braid that showed beneath Rebekah's cap. "It's your turn to play nurse, Mistress Cunningham. See that you do a good job."

"I will," Rebekah promised.

Dr. Fuller went out, leaving the others to follow his orders.

The rest of the day, Mother lay without moving. Once when Father and Will weren't looking, Rebekah bent low to make sure she still breathed. She felt her mother's slow, steady breath against her cheek and sighed in relief. But when evening came and the Sabbath ended, Mother still slept.

"Should we ask Dr. Fuller to come again?" Rebekah anxiously asked Father.

"I hate to disturb him when he is so tired." Father knelt and touched Mother's forehead. "Her skin is cool and dry. She has no sign of fever. We will let her rest."

"Shall I stay up with her?" Rebekah volunteered.

"Should Dr. Fuller be wrong, although I have no reason to believe this is the case, you will be needed more on the morrow. Go to bed, child. I will watch."

All through the long night hours, Mother slept. Neither did she waken when morning came. Thoroughly alarmed, Rebekah coaxed Father into letting Will fetch the doctor again.

After Dr. Fuller examined Mother, he assured them again that she would be fine. "I expect her to wake before night," he told them. "If she should not, then is time enough to be concerned."

Shortly after he left, a sound from the mattress brought all three watchers to Mother's side. She opened her eyes, yawned, stretched, and looked around. "Mercy, what am I doing here at this time of day?" She looked confused, and then her face cleared. "My goodness, I fell asleep walking home, didn't I? I never heard of such a thing." She glanced around the hut. "I hope you ate without me." A frown wrinkled her forehead. "I smell something cooking. Surely you are not breaking the Sabbath by cooking food?"

"It's no longer the Sabbath!" Will shouted. A broad grin spread over his face. Matching smiles covered Rebekah's and Father's faces.

Father reached down a hand to help Mother get up. "It's Monday and time for dinner. You have slept ever since the meeting yesterday."

"Dr. Fuller said we weren't to disturb you unless you didn't wake before dark," Rebekah explained. She clasped her arms around her mother's waist. "I'm glad you're awake. It frightened me when you stayed asleep for so long."

Mother began to laugh. She laughed so hard the others joined in. "A grown woman, sleeping all the hours on the clock twice around! I do feel rested, though." She looked ashamed. "I hope no one needed me."

Father shook his head. "Not even Dr. Fuller. He says the

worst is over and his patients are mending." The laughter in his eyes died. "Almost every family but ours lost at least one person."

A lump came to Rebekah's throat. "We lost Jake."

"Indeed we did, although we haven't actually lost him. We've just parted for a time." Father looked with joy at Mother. "Let us give thanks for your mother's recovery."

Signs of spring began to appear at Plymouth Colony like a long-awaited guest. They brought a wave of relief and hope. Surely things would be better now that the harsh winter was slowly retreating. The little band of surviving settlers prayed for good weather, asking the Lord to bless the land.

Yet many of those who survived were still weak. How could the few strong ones left in the settlement take on extra duties and provide for everyone? There was also the ever-present fear of Indian attack.

One day in mid-March, Will burst into the Cunningham home as if chased by a whole tribe of unfriendly Indians. Eyes wide with excitement, he cried, "Mother, Father, Rebekah, come quick. Just come see!"

Will frightened Rebekah so badly, she dropped her knitting. "Father and Mother are at the common house. Will Cunningham, is this another of your tricks? Just when you've been good for such a long time?"

"It's not a trick," he indignantly told her. "Are you coming, or aren't you? If you don't, you'll miss all the excitement." He placed his hands on his hips and glared at Rebekah. "C'mon, will you? Father and Mother will have heard the news. They'll be there before I get back with you." He hurried out the door and started up the lane.

Rebekah quickly took care of her knitting and ran after him toward a cluster of people on the road a little way ahead. The children headed straight for Father and Mother, who stood at one side of a small, gaping crowd.

"What is it?" Rebekah stood on tiptoe, trying to see.

"Him!" Will stepped out of her way and pointed to a tall, black-haired Indian halfway across the clearing between the settlement and the woods. The Indian carried bow and arrows and steadily walked toward the nearest group of men.

"Is he going to scalp us?" Rebekah squeaked.

The men reached for their muskets. The Indian never faltered. He was close enough now so the settlers could get a good look. Rebekah knew her eyes grew large as cartwheels. She felt herself blush and quickly looked away. So did the other girls and women. The unexpected visitor wore no clothes. Just a little war paint and a leather apron that hung down from his belly! Who was this bold Indian who marched into the colony instead of skulking in the woods?

He reached the men. "Welcome." The word sounded strange on the lips of the nearly naked man. "Samoset."

"Did you hear that?" Will whispered. "He speaks English!"

"What is a samoset?" Rebekah whispered back.

Will choked back a laugh. "Not *a* samoset. Samoset. That must be his name."

Rebekah risked another look, making sure she kept her gaze on the stranger's face. "Why did he come here, and what does he want?" she wondered.

"That's what we need to find out," Father said.

CHAPTER 11

Hair-Raising Stories

The first thing Samoset did was ask for something to drink. The settlers quickly took on their roles of hosts, and once his thirst was satisfied, Samoset told his story.

He explained he wasn't from the area but came from Monhegan, an island off the coast farther north. He said in broken English that he had learned the white man's language from English fishermen there. To prove he told the truth, Samoset mentioned the names of many captains who fished there.

He'd come to Cape Cod the year before and remained eight months. He added he could reach his home with one day of good sea breeze, but it took five days to go by land.

Fascinated by the visitor, the Pilgrims brought out a long, red, horseman's coat. Samoset wrapped himself in it, grunted, and talked on. The settlers brought food: butter, cheese, a slice of duck, and pudding. He ate and ate and talked and talked. It appeared Samoset had no intention of leaving.

"What will we do with him?" Will whispered. Even in the red coat that covered his nakedness, Samoset was a frightening figure.

Others wondered the same thing. The Pilgrims decided to take Samoset to the *Mayflower*, but they ran into trouble. A headwind and low water made it impossible to get the shallop across the flats to the ship. Stephen Hopkins at last agreed to keep Samoset overnight and guard him without seeming to do so.

"I wish we could have quartered Samoset," Will grumbled to Rebekah later. "Think of all the stories he could tell us! Now we'll have to hear them from the Hopkins family."

Rebekah's mouth turned down. "I'm glad we don't have to keep him. He might tell us stories of how the Indians scalp people."

Will grinned mischievously. "I guess you could say they would be hair-raising tales, couldn't you?"

Rebekah's green eyes flashed. Her freckled nose went into the air. "Humph! You won't think it's so funny if we wake up murdered in our beds."

"If we're murdered in our beds, we won't wake up," Will answered. When his sister's face turned red, he quickly added, "Don't be mad, Rebekah. I was just joking. Besides, if Samoset were unfriendly, he would never have come right into the settlement. He'd have brought a band of warriors."

Rebekah finally agreed, and Will said no more about hair-raising tales.

The next day Samoset left, the proud possessor of a ring, knife, and bracelet. He promised to come back with some of the Wampanoag Indians, who would bring beaver furs for trade.

The next time Samoset came, he arrived on a Sunday with five tall Indians wearing deerskin clothes.

"It's too bad they came today," Rebekah said. "We can't trade on Sunday."

"It is awkward," Father admitted. "Our leaders will just have to explain we don't trade on Sunday."

Will ran up to his family, bursting with news. "Wait till you hear what's happened!" he shouted. "You'd never guess, not in a million years!" He didn't give them even a minute to answer but said, "The tools. The Indians brought back the tools they stole from us."

Mother clapped her hands, and Rebekah cried, "Then they must be honest." She stopped and wrinkled up her face. "If they are honest, why did they take our tools in the first place?" Then she remembered something, and the same funny feeling she had known weeks earlier came back. She lowered her voice so no one else could hear. "What's the difference between our taking their corn and them stealing our tools?"

"Your mother and I have never felt comfortable about that," Father quietly said. "Even though our leaders have vowed to repay the Indians when the crops are harvested."

Samoset soon brought someone else to the settlement, an Indian named Tisquantum, or Squanto. Squanto's life had been hard. Rebekah listened in wonder as Squanto told his story. Years ago, a captain named Weymouth had explored the northern New England coast. He took Squanto back to England with him. There the Indian learned to speak the white man's language.

Nine years later, Squanto sailed back across the Atlantic as interpreter to Captain John Smith. A man named Hunt commanded one of the ships. Hunt persuaded twenty Indians, including Squanto, to board his ship.

Rebekah burned with anger when she learned what happened next. Hunt kidnapped the Indians, took them to Spain, and sold them for twenty pounds each. Pride filled Squanto's face, and he drew himself up with great dignity. "No Patuxet shall be slave to a white man. I escaped to England, lived with a merchant, then sailed to Newfoundland as a guide and interpreter." Two years ago, Squanto had returned to his home of Patuxet.

A sad look came into the Indian's dark eyes. He placed one hand over his heart. "Plague had killed all but a few of my tribe. Those who yet lived had joined the Wampanoag and their mighty warrior chief, Massasoit. I found them and also stayed with the Wampanoag."

Governor Carver asked, "Squanto, will you not stay and help us? You have lost most of your people. So have we. Sickness and starvation have taken more than half our number since we came a few months ago. Our food is almost gone. We want no trouble with your people."

Squanto turned his glittering gaze on the governor and crossed his arms over his chest. His voice rolled out like a judgment. "Chief Massasoit and the Wampanoag are very angry. The white men stole their corn."

"We did that, and it was wrong," Governor Carver admitted. "Our people were starving and needed food. We will replace the corn when we harvest our fields."

Squanto grunted. Rebekah had the feeling he admired Governor Carver for being so honest. She remembered her father telling her that Indians respected courage, and it surely took courage to confess to stealing the corn and to admit it wasn't right.

"I will stay. First, I will talk with Chief Massasoit. If he will come, I will bring him to you so our tribes might have peace." He turned and marched away.

Samoset and Squanto had been bold but friendly. Chief Massasoit and his twenty scantily clad warriors, however, strode into New Plymouth as if it belonged to them! Massasoit appeared to be a few years older than Squanto and stood as tall and straight as one of the arrows he carried. Chief Massasoit kept his kingly air all through the hearty meal and gifts brought to him by the Pilgrims. At last, the time came to talk about peace. Squanto interpreted.

After a brief battle with her conscience, Rebekah followed Will. The children tucked themselves into a good place where they could see and hear without being noticed. Missing the meeting between Chief Massasoit and the governor was unthinkable, but they knew better than to ask Myles Standish for permission to be present. Every time the captain looked at Will, the captain's glare shouted he hadn't forgotten a certain Will Cunningham's disobedience.

Massasoit, king of the Indians, was indeed a fearsome sight. He sat on cushions. Sweat and grease covered his head and red-painted face. White bone beads, a knife on a string, and a tobacco pouch hung from his neck. His warriors also had painted faces: red, white, black, yellow. Rebekah was relieved that they had come on friendly terms. She would hate to have the men meet up with them in the woods otherwise!

Governor Carver and Massasoit talked for a long time. At last, they made a treaty. Rebekah listened carefully to Squanto's explanation of the agreement. Neither Massasoit nor any of his people would hurt the Pilgrims. If any of his people did hurt them, Chief Massasoit would send the guilty person to the Pilgrims for punishment. If any of the Pilgrims harmed an Indian, they would turn the person over to Chief Massasoit. If any tools were taken, the chief would see they were restored. If anyone made war unjustly against either the Pilgrims or the Indians, the other group would provide protection.

Chief Massasoit also promised to send word of the treaty to his neighboring tribes, so they would follow it, as well. The Indians would leave behind their bows and arrows when they visited the Pilgrims. The settlers would do the same with their muskets when they were in the Indians' presence. Through this treaty, King James would recognize and honor Massasoit as his ally and friend.

After the meeting, Governor Carver, with great ceremony, escorted Massasoit to the brook and bid him a courteous good-bye. Then they put their arms around each other and hugged. Rebekah watched with wide eyes, hardly believing what she was seeing.

Will threw his cap into the spring air. "At last, things are better, Rebekah. The best thing is that Squanto and Samoset have agreed to help us plant corn and will spend the summer nearby."

⌛

Soon the Pilgrims found it hard to remember when Squanto had not been among them. He knew so much! He showed them how to raise the finest corn, beans, and pumpkins by planting dead herring with the seeds. He taught them the best places to fish and how to catch eels. The children were delighted by their improved diet. Mealtimes were much more interesting now.

Everyone who could worked hard. Rebekah, Will, and Mother, along with the other women and children, spent long hours in the fields. Father and the rest of the men cleared and tilled land. What little time they had at home was gobbled up by other tasks. Furniture making, candle making, spinning, weaving, sewing, shoemaking, and a hundred other duties cried out to be done.

Father and Will stole what time they could to fish. Although they both enjoyed fishing, they needed to catch lots of fish to help make a living. Dried fish shipped to markets in Europe could be traded for cloth and other needed supplies.

Other men caught whales so they could send whale oil to Europe. John Alden continued his cooper business. A blacksmith also served as a dentist.

In early April, a silent group of settlers stood on shore watching the *Mayflower* set sail for England. Not one Pilgrim had accepted Captain Jones's offer to take anyone who wanted to sail back with him. Rebekah winked back a tear. Would she ever see Holland again? Or the Dutch friends she and Will had skated and played with? She sighed. "Father, will we ever go ho—back?"

Father watched a strong breeze fill the sails of the *Mayflower* and move her out of the harbor toward the wide Atlantic. "Nay, child. This is our home now." He placed one arm around her shoulders, his other around Mother, and smiled at Will. "God is good. He has brought us safely through the winter. We are at peace with Chief Massasoit and his tribes. We have much to be thankful for."

"We mustn't forget Squanto," Mother said. "Surely God sent him to us, that we might learn to live in this new land."

Will said nothing. Rebekah knew he wouldn't go back to Holland if he could. Seeing the *Mayflower* move toward the horizon where it would dip out of sight brought back memories. The crossing. The poor food and lack of good water. The storms that threatened to tear the ship apart at the seams. Most of all, their good friend Jake.

Rebekah hadn't been back on the *Mayflower* since their friend died. Would Captain Jones and the small crew who must battle their way across the heaving seas miss the rough seaman? Rebekah turned away to hide her tears. Better to do as Father said and be glad that life was not as hard as it had been during the winter.

But the peace of New Plymouth exploded a few days later. Will and Rebekah were working together in the fields near Governor Carver. Suddenly, he clutched his head and groaned. He staggered toward his home.

Will and Rebekah continued working, but they watched anxiously as Dr. Fuller hurried to Governor Carver's home. It seemed like the doctor stayed with the governor for an eternity. When he finally left the governor's home, Dr. Fuller's face was grim.

Rebekah and Will looked at each other. Was Governor Carver only the first? Were any in the colony strong enough to survive a second round of sickness?

CHAPTER 12

Danger for Squanto!

The Cunningham family and all the other Pilgrims prayed for Governor Carver to get well, but just a few days after he fell ill, he died. The whole colony mourned.

"Pray for me, Rebekah," Will confided as he solemnly prepared his musket. All the men and boys who had muskets were going to fire off volleys of shot in honor of Governor Carver. "I don't want to shoot at the wrong time or do something stupid," he admitted to his older sister.

Rebekah gave his arm an encouraging squeeze. "I know you'll do fine," she said, "but I'll pray for you, anyway."

Somberly, the Cunningham family joined their neighbors outside in the warm spring air. When the time came for the muskets to be fired, Will fell into line. Rebekah saw he was paying careful attention to the orders that were given. His hands must have been sweaty from nervousness, for he quickly wiped them on his pants. Rebekah knew he didn't want his finger to slip off the trigger.

Boom! Boom! The sounds of the shots echoed across the settlement.

Rebekah sighed in relief when it was over. Her brother threw her a grateful look. He'd managed to stay out of trouble ever since that terrible night in the woods, and Rebekah was glad nothing he'd done during this important event had drawn attention to her brother.

Shortly after Governor Carver was buried, the men of New Plymouth voted for a new governor. Rebekah and Will knew better than to try to sneak into that meeting, but they were glad to learn from Father that William Bradford would be their next governor.

Now that spring had arrived, Sunday meetings were more pleasant. No longer did they have to bundle up in all the clothing they possessed to keep from freezing in the unheated meetinghouse.

"I wish the tithingman would go away," Will complained to Rebekah one Sunday. He rubbed his head. The tithingman's rod had feathers on one end to tickle those who nodded, a knob on the other to whack those who fell asleep. He walked up and down checking on people and had given Will a smart *whack!* Rebekah took care to sit up straight on the hard wooden pew and concentrate on the elder in the high pulpit. Yet even she found it hard to pay attention. Sometimes the sermons lasted five hours.

"At least I didn't have my neck and heels tied together and get left without food for a whole day," Will soberly said. "That's what the governor ordered when Will Billington refused to take his turn standing guard at night. He would have carried it out, too. It's a good thing Mr. Billington said he was sorry and would keep watch for strange Indians and fire, like the rest of the men."

"Let's talk about happier things," Rebekah pleaded. She didn't like to think of people breaking the rules and being punished. "Did you know Edward Winslow and Susanna White are getting married?"

"Yes. I heard they have both been lonely since Mistress Winslow and William White died." Will squinted his eyes against the bright sun. "Rebekah, if Mother or Father died, do you think the other one would get married again?"

Rebekah thought for a moment. "Perhaps. They'd want us to still have a mother and father."

Will shrugged. "I'm not sure I like the idea. Can you imagine anyone ever taking Mother and Father's place?"

"I don't want to think about it," Rebekah said. "I'm so tired of death and dying. I hope all of us who are left live to be as old as the mountains!"

"Maybe we will." He flexed his right arm, and Rebekah knew he was proud of the muscle that popped up. "Now that Squanto has taught us how to fish and plant, we shan't go hungry." He laughed. "Do you want to hear something funny?"

"Of course."

"I asked Squanto how he knew the very best time to plant maize and the seed we brought with us," Will explained.

"What did he say?" Rebekah promptly forgot to be sad. Over time, she had learned not to be afraid of Squanto.

"He told me the time of planting must always be 'when the leaves of the white oak are as large as a mouse's ear.'"

Rebekah chuckled. "A big mouse's ear or a little mouse's ear?"

"Can you imagine Squanto's face if I asked him that?" Will demanded. He crossed his arms over his chest, planted his feet apart, and deepened his voice. "White boys ask too many questions."

"You sound just like him!"

"I know." Will went back to his normal voice. "I like Squanto. He has been so good to us. He. . .he's almost as good a storyteller as Jake." A shadow crossed his face and he quickly added, "We have to go back to hoeing. Now that the maize is growing so well, it's hoe, hoe, hoe." He bent over his work.

"I think it's pretty, all green and in rows." Rebekah looked over the large cleared space. "Father said we prepared ninety-six-thousand hillocks and trapped and carried forty tons of dead fish to make the crops grow!" She looked at her small hands. Calluses from hard work marred the pink palms. Her short nails were rimmed with earth. "I guess it will be worth it when the harvest comes."

Because friendly relations had been established with the Indians, a new problem arose. Throughout the spring and into the summer, groups of visitors came regularly, always expecting food. In desperation, two ambassadors were chosen to go see Massasoit and ask him to call a halt to the frequent visits. The Pilgrims simply didn't have food to spare. Edward Winslow and Will Hopkins served as ambassadors, with Squanto as guide and interpreter. Will wanted to go with them and longingly watched the three set out.

To the travelers' dismay, Massasoit had very little food, for he had only recently arrived at his home. What little the visitors were given and a few bits of fish on the way home barely provided strength enough for them to again reach New Plymouth.

Rebekah listened when Edward Winslow told the story.

"We had nothing to eat the first day. The next morning was used in sports and shooting. About one o'clock Massasoit brought two boiled fishes that were supposed to feed forty people!" He groaned and patted his stomach. "If we had not had a partridge, I fear we should have starved. Swarms of mosquitoes meant we could not stay outdoors. Being crammed together with Massasoit, his wife, and two other chiefs on bare planks on the floor, to say nothing of the fleas and lice, made sleep impossible. We knew Massasoit felt ashamed he could offer us nothing better. We told him we wished to keep the Sabbath at home and departed on Friday before the sun rose."

Rebekah hugged her knees, glad Father hadn't gone. Adventuring was fine. Being hungry and eaten alive by insects was not!

Another Indian came to live with the settlers. Hobomok was a member of Massasoit's council. Captain Standish made a special point of winning his friendship, but Squanto loyally served Governor Bradford.

One day Hobomok and Squanto went to Nemasket, an Indian camp about fifteen miles to the west. There they hoped to arrange for trade between the colonists and the Indians.

A few days later, Hobomok raced into the settlement. "Squanto has been murdered!" he gasped. His long hair hung in strings. Sweat beaded his frightened face. "The Nemasket chief Corbitant hates the English. He started a quarrel with us. He tried to stab me, but I escaped. It is said Corbitant has also helped the mighty Narragansetts take Massasoit." His chest rose and fell from his hard run.

Governor Bradford immediately said, "I need volunteers to go with Captain Standish. We cannot allow this thing to go unpunished. Doing so would encourage more such incidents. No Indians would ever again dare be friendly with us. Corbitant and others like him will first kill them, then massacre the colonists. Men, who will go?"

Rebekah watched her brother bite his lip to keep from shouting, "I will!" Such childish behavior would immediately bar him from the expedition. Instead, he hurried to his father, who had already stepped forward. "Take me with you," he said. "Please?"

Father hesitated. He gave Will a measuring look, then turned to Captain Standish. "The lad's wiry body and fleetness of foot might be of use."

Standish looked at Will with cold eyes. "That it might. Has he learned to obey orders, and will you be responsible for him?"

Rebekah saw Will squirm and look guilty, but Father said in a clear, ringing voice, "He has and I will." Rebekah hoped her brother would prove himself worthy of his father's faith.

"See that he stays out of the way," Standish ordered. "If I need him, I'll say so. Otherwise, he's to keep back." A somber look came to his face. He wheeled toward Will. "I do not expect that those of us who bear arms and attack shall all be killed. If we are, you must run as you have never run before and carry the news to Governor Bradford. Should the Indians kill us, they will be wild with triumph, perhaps crazy enough to launch an attack on the colony."

"Yes, sir." Although Will's face was pale with fear at Standish's words, he kept his gaze level, and he saluted.

Rebekah's heart thudded against her ribs as she watched her father and brother fall into line. It had been months since they had ventured outside the stockade, and then it had been to explore and discover food. Going into the night for the purpose of finding and destroying Indians was far different. Would any of the men, even Father, come back alive? Yet the murder of Squanto could not be ignored. *Please, God,* she silently prayed, *keep them safe.* No other words would come to her mind. Even though Corbitant and his followers were the enemy, Rebekah could not pray for their deaths.

With Hobomok as guide, the party set out for Corbitant's camp. Rebekah sighed and turned away. She took her mother's hand as they walked back to their hut. Now all they could do was pray.

Rebekah's heart leapt when the men finally returned. While the gathering of adults buzzed with news, she grabbed Will by his sleeve and pulled him aside. "Tell me everything that happened," she commanded.

Will told her how he knew he would never forget that August night. Every rustle of brush had rung in his ears. The muffled steps of his companions sounded like thunderclaps. Surely any listening Indian could hear the hard beating of his heart.

At last they reached their destination. The rescue party fired their muskets into the air. A wave of terror filled the Indian village. Men, women, and children were ordered not to stir, and Captain Standish marched into Corbitant's hut.

"Corbitant isn't here," Captain Standish called minutes later.

The next instant, some braves made a dash for the woods, straight toward the spot where Father had pushed Will down behind a log and ordered him to stay! Will flattened himself on the ground and shoved his face in his arms. Shots rang out, followed by cries. Will burrowed deeper behind the log. Then a shout brought him to his feet.

"Come, Will. The danger is past." Father reached for Will's hand and then pointed to a tall figure.

"Why, it's Squanto," Will gasped. "I thought he was dead!"

"Neither dead nor injured," Father explained. "The people here know nothing of Corbitant's wicked doings. See, they are bringing food."

"But the shots!" Will protested. "Men cried out."

"Some of the Indians were frightened by us and were afraid we had come to harm them. They tried to run away, and our men, thinking those who were fleeing were working with Corbitant, started shooting. Three of the Indians were injured by musket fire, but they will be fine," Father assured him. "Thank God, there was no more bloodshed than this. The rumor about Massasoit appears to be just that—a rumor. Captain Standish says we shall take the wounded braves back to the settlement and dress their wounds. We will keep and care for them until they are able to travel back to their own people. This will bring goodwill between us and the Indians."

Will suddenly felt weak in the knees. At last, he had been in an actual raid. But Indian braves had been injured in the attack. He decided that fighting the Indians was not as exciting as he had thought. It was terrible!

"Were you frightened?" Rebekah asked.

"Yes, I was," he confessed.

She didn't answer for a time. Finally, she asked him quietly, "Do you still want to go adventuring?"

"Yes, but not on Indian raids. I'd rather be a fisherman than an Indian fighter. Does that make you happy?"

Her green eyes shone. "More than I can say."

"All the time I was lying behind that log, I thought how awful it would be to have to run back with news of a massacre! Or how you'd feel if Father or I got killed. I still like adventuring—hunting animals for food and discovering new things. I don't like hunting people. Perhaps we have to in order to protect our settlement, but if we could just have peace, I'd be happy."

"So would I." Rebekah slipped her hand in his, then ran off to help their mother. She couldn't help but wonder what would happen next in Plymouth Colony.

CHAPTER 13

Thanksgiving and Good Fortune

For the next month, many of the Indian chiefs praised the settlers for the way they had handled the incident. Some sent messengers from many miles away to offer their tribes' friendship. Others claimed themselves to be loyal subjects of King James. To everyone's surprise, even Corbitant offered peace through King Massasoit.

Autumn brought more work: Will and Rebekah spent hours with their neighbors, preserving and drying as much food as possible from their small harvest. They had already dried berries and fruit that had ripened earlier in the year. The settlers did not intend to go hungry this winter. The men explored more of the country around them, made treaties with other tribes, and traded trinkets to the Indians for beaver skins.

Then great news came. Will burst into the Cunningham home and shouted, "Mother, Rebekah, Governor Bradford has declared a celebration, and it is to last three whole days!"

"When?" Rebekah demanded. "Why? Who is it for?"

"Soon," Will told her. "It's a time for giving thanks that

God has brought us through our first hard months in the New World. Everyone in New Plymouth will join together and. . ." Will hesitated, and then burst out, "Massasoit and his tribe are to be our honored guests!"

A broad grin spread over his face, making him look more like the mischievous boy who had boarded the *Mayflower* than the young man he was starting to become. "Squanto says we may have ninety Indians here for the feast."

"Ninety? Mercy on us," Mother gasped. "Think how much time it will take to prepare enough food for one meal, let alone three days of celebration!"

"Governor Bradford says everyone in the colony must help." Rebekah could see that Will was thoroughly enjoying himself. "The Indians have promised to bring deer and wild turkeys. Four of the men have been sent to kill wild ducks and geese. Father and I will join others in fishing, plus gathering shellfish and eels."

"I suppose the girls and women will have to cook all this." Rebekah made a face. "Well, someone else can take care of the eels, slimy old things."

"You don't have to do all the cooking," Will promised. "Governor Bradford says the younger children are to turn the great spits over the open fires where the meat roasts. They also will gather nuts and watercress."

"We will have to make great kettles of corn and beans," Mother planned. "Oh, my. Think of the baking. We will need journeycake and cornmeal bread and—"

"Be sure to make enough food," Will interrupted. "Indians are always hungry." He grinned. "Me, too." His mouth watered.

"I hope they don't eat up all the good things before I get a chance at them."

"Remember, son, they are our guests and will naturally be served first," Mother said firmly, but her eyes sparkled with fun. "However, I can't imagine there not being enough food for all."

"There isn't room in the common house or any of the other houses," Rebekah pointed out. "How can we feed so many people?"

"The men will lay planks on sawhorses," Will said. "We'll eat outside."

Rebekah peered out the open door at the warm, mid-October sunshine. "God has already decorated for our feast, hasn't He?" She smiled.

"Indeed He has," Mother agreed. "I have never seen a more beautiful sight than the colored leaves against the dark green forest. There were times when I wondered if we would all be here to see them together."

"Why, Mother! You never told us you were afraid," Rebekah said in wonder.

Mother wiped her eyes with one corner of her apron. "Every time I cared for the sick, it was as though I cared for one of you or Father."

Will and Rebekah looked at each other. How hard it had been for Mother, who had bravely kept her fears to herself for the sake of her family. Rebekah put her arm around her mother's waist and whispered, "It's all over now."

"Yes, child." Mother's beautiful smile bloomed like a flower after rain. "Now is a time for giving thanks to our heavenly Father. Come. There is much to be done."

❧

"Mother spoke well," Will told Rebekah days later when the feast began. "I never, ever saw so much food, not even in Holland."

"That's 'cause we didn't have almost a hundred hungry Indians coming for dinner!" Rebekah giggled. She nodded toward the brown-skinned people who had swarmed into the settlement. "Does Massasoit ever laugh? I'm not afraid of Squanto now, but Chief Massasoit makes me feel a little strange when he comes. He's so serious—perhaps because he is the king."

"He is serious, but look at his people. They're really having a good time."

Rebekah couldn't help staring. The tribes chattered away in their own language. They laughed and poked one another in the ribs, evidently sharing private jokes. And how they ate!

"Are you sure there will be any food left for us?" Will questioned. "You'd think the Indians hadn't eaten for months."

Rebekah rolled her eyes. "If you had helped prepare as much food as Mother and I did, you wouldn't ask such a question. If I never see a dish of succotash again, it will be all right with me."

Rebekah liked the games and contests almost as much as the food. She was pleased when Will won some of the races, while she enjoyed playing stool ball, a game in which a leather ball stuffed with feathers was driven from stool to stool. But she liked the parade best. One man blew a trumpet. Another beat a drum. Men marched and fired their guns.

Rebekah wasn't sure what she thought of the Indian dancing. Their dances were beautiful to watch, but their chants made chills race up and down her spine. After she got used to the strange noises, though, she decided they were beautiful, too.

At last, the three-day celebration ended. The great mounds of food were no more. Thanks and praise to God for His goodness still echoed throughout New Plymouth. Will patted his full stomach and watched the Indians prepare to leave. "I hope we have another feast next year," he told Rebekah.

"It was hard work, but so do I," she said. "I don't know if we will, though." She sighed. "If only all the Indians were our friends, we could eat together and have peace. They aren't. The Narragansetts hate us. Remember the snakeskin tied to the bundle of arrows they sent? Squanto said it was a challenge that meant they wanted war."

"It didn't frighten Governor Bradford and his counselors," Will proudly reminded her. "They refused to back down and returned the snakeskin with powder and shot and the message we had done no wrong. The message also said if the Narragansetts would rather have war than peace, they'd find us ready to fight. The arrow came back, but there has been no attack. Don't worry, Rebekah. A strong fence surrounds our settlement, and every night a man stands guard. Our men are ready to fight at the first cry of fire or attack." He smiled at his hardworking sister. "Besides, God has taken care of us so far. Perhaps war will never come."

Rebekah already knew all those things, but hearing Will repeat them made her feel better.

Early in November, the Pilgrims took stock of their harvest.

Their high spirits fell with a thud. The small harvest simply had not produced enough to see them through another winter. Governor Bradford called the people together. "We planned for much larger crops," he soberly said. "Since this did not happen, we must take harsh measures. The ration of meal to each person must be cut in half."

A ripple of protest swept through the assembly. "There is no other way," he told them. "Otherwise, we shall be no better off than we were last year." The people reluctantly agreed they had no choice, but many looked at one another in fear. How could they get by on a half ration of meal?

A few days later, everyone forgot their troubles for a time. Will brought the news to Mother and Rebekah. "A ship is on the horizon," he shouted. "It is coming nearer and will soon anchor in the harbor!"

"Is it the *Mayflower*?" Rebekah asked.

Will shook his head. "This looks like a much smaller ship. Mother, Rebekah, do you think any of our friends from Leiden will be aboard?" His brown eyes sparkled at the idea.

A little worry frown creased Mother's forehead. "Perhaps. I do hope the ship's hold is filled with food supplies. Even by going on half rations, we barely have enough for those already here."

When the *Fortune* anchored and its passengers came ashore, every person in New Plymouth eagerly awaited them. Fourteen long months had passed since the Pilgrims had left England. Now, new, strong people had come to help settle the colony. Supplies from the ship would give strength to continue with the task.

But joy over greeting friends from Leiden soon changed to dismay. Although young and strong, the newcomers were terribly unprepared. They didn't have any food—not even biscuits. They also didn't bring bedding and pots and pans, and most of them had very few clothes. Many of them had sold their coats and cloaks at Plymouth in order to get money for the voyage from England.

"It's not fair," Rebekah complained. "They should have brought supplies. Everyone here is tired. Now we have to take these people in and care for them!"

"Didn't God send Samoset, Squanto, and Massasoit to help us?" Father asked. "We will share what we have."

Will said, "Those on the *Fortune* felt the same way we did when we first saw Cape Cod. They were afraid we had all been killed in an Indian massacre or died of hunger. The captain said he had just enough food to take the crew on to Virginia. No provisions were sent for the settlers."

Rebekah watched her brother's face flush with anger. "Will Weston sent a letter bawling us out for not sending cargo back to England on the *Mayflower*. He said the Adventurers are furious and would never have lent us money if they'd known they wouldn't start getting some back soon." Will scowled. "More than half of us died, and all they can think of is their precious money. And Will Weston dared to sign himself our very loving friend!"

"I hope Governor Bradford sends a message back telling those people all we have gone through," Rebekah indignantly added.

"I am sure he will reply in a manner suited to a godly

man," Father quietly told his family. "Just because others are ill-mannered and judge us unfairly does not mean we are to answer in anger."

Rebekah hung her head. Would she ever be as patient and good as Father?

By mid-December the *Fortune* was ready to sail back to England. It was loaded with cargo, including many beaver and otter skins that would begin paying off the money that the Pilgrims owed. Robert Cushman also traveled on the *Fortune*, carrying a contract signed by the Pilgrims. Although the terms were harsh, the colonists had their charter and for the first time were legal owners of New Plymouth.

Will and Rebekah watched the ship until it disappeared over the horizon. "So much has happened, I wonder what is ahead," Rebekah mused.

Will gently tugged on one of her dark braids. "Whatever it is, we know God loves us and will take care of us." He proudly raised his head. "Governor Bradford says, 'As one small candle may light a thousand, so the light here kindled has shone unto many, yes, in some sense to our whole nation.'"

"As long as the world lasts," Rebekah mused, "do you think people will learn about the Pilgrims and how we came to a land where we could worship God in the way we believed right? Even more of our people will come, but I'm glad we were the first."

Will nodded. "I love the New World, don't you, Rebekah?"

Rebekah thought hard before she answered. Did she feel it had all been worth it? All the hardship and misery, sickness and death, starvation, and fear of attack? She glanced at the dark, ever-mysterious forest and shivered. She turned toward the sea. Sometimes it danced and sparkled, but it often roared with wind and storm. Last of all, she looked at her brother. He had grown up so much in the past months. She knew the day was coming when she would no longer feel so responsible for him, when she could trust him to make wise decisions for himself.

"Well?" She could see on his face that he was hoping with all his heart that in spite of everything, Rebekah shared his love for their new home.

A smile tipped her lips up and a happy laugh rang out in the cold December air. "I love our new home, too," she said. "I wouldn't want to live anywhere else in the whole wide world." Her words hung in the cold December air, and mischief came into her face. "Race you home!" She took off in a whirl of skirts, happy laughter floating back over her cloaked shoulder.

Thank You, God, she prayed while she ran. *Thank You for keeping us safe. Thank You for blessing us here in our new home.*

Maggie's Dare

Norma Jean Lutz

A Note to Readers

In 1744 and 1745, the Great Awakening, a revival that swept through the American Colonies, was at its peak, led by the Reverend Jonathan Edwards. While many of the first English settlers in New England had left their homes either because of a desire for religious freedom or because they wanted to tell Native Americans about Jesus, many of their descendants over one hundred years later did not know what it meant to have a personal relationship with Jesus. Going to church was simply something "good people" were supposed to do. Jonathan Edwards and other leaders of that time were used by God to "awaken" the people to a personal love for Jesus.

Maggie's Dare also reminds us that slavery was common in the Northern colonies, as well as in the South. Although there were always some people who fought against the evil of slavery, it took two hundred years and the Civil War before slavery was outlawed in the United States.

CONTENTS

The Launch

Maggie Baldwin struggled to restrain the excitement bubbling up inside her. Her younger brother, Caleb, at age eight, could run about the Souder shipyard with abandoned glee. But at age twelve, she was expected to use decorum befitting a lady. The moment their father, Dr. Reidan Baldwin, pulled their small black carriage to a halt, Caleb leaped down and began running and hopping about.

Maggie wished she could run right alongside him. Instead, she waited for her father to secure the harnesses and come around to help her down. Controlling her hoops while getting in and out of a carriage was a skill she'd not yet perfected.

She landed lightly, then reached up to be sure her straw bonnet was secure. Decorated with bright blue ribbons and new feathers, the made-over hat was as stylish as any in Boston. Maggie's nanny, Hannah Pierce, said so. Hannah assured Maggie that blue was the best color to go with Maggie's copper-colored hair. Hannah's opinion meant a great deal to Maggie—not only was Hannah the Baldwins' nanny, she was also the best seamstress in the city.

The launching of a new ship provided a great deal of excitement for the city of Boston. In fact, the citizens turned the event into a holiday. Even Maggie's older brother, Evan, was given the afternoon off from his accounting books at the countinghouse of the Souder Shipping Line.

"Look!" Caleb called out. "It's the governor's carriage! Zounds! What a fancy carriage. Wish ours looked like that."

"Caleb," Maggie warned, "watch your language." She glanced about, hoping no one had heard. To her father, she said, "Good thing Mother isn't here to hear him talk like that."

"If your mother were alive, Margaret," said Dr. Baldwin, "I'm sure she'd keep a tighter rein on him than you or I."

Her brother was right about Governor William Shirley's carriage. There were few carriages in all of Boston as elaborate as his. Other shipping merchants such as the Winthrops and the Chiltons also owned ornate carriages that were shipped over from England. And their uncle Reuben drove about town in the stylish carriage left to him by his late father, Josiah Souder.

Her father offered his arm, and Maggie hooked her gloved hand in the crook of it as they strolled through the bustling crowd. "It appears as though all of Boston has turned out for this launch," her father said as he gently guided her along.

Suddenly, Caleb's attention was turned in a new direction. "There's Evan!" he exclaimed, pointing down the wharf to where the new ship, *Thetis*, stood tall and proud. "And Uncle Reuben is with him." Without waiting for his father's permission, Caleb sprinted through the crowd toward his older brother and uncle.

"I hope he doesn't injure anyone," Maggie quipped.

Her father chuckled. "One would think he hadn't seen Evan at breakfast this very morning."

As they talked, Maggie glanced about to see if her friends, Adelaide Chilton and Celia Winthrop, had yet arrived. Following the launch, she would be a guest for high tea at the Chilton home, and Celia would be there, as well. Maggie was looking forward to the gaiety of the afternoon more than the launch.

The towering ship stood silently waiting, resting in its giant cradle made of wooden stocks. Workers were busy greasing the timbers that ran in back of the ship into the water. This would allow the ship to glide out easily from the stocks.

The air was filled with the aroma of fresh-cut pine. Stacks of honey-colored lumber lay about the area ready to be used to finish the interior cabinet work on this ship or to be part of Uncle Reuben's next project. Maggie's industrious uncle, who was a stepbrother to her father, was always busy in some new venture. In spite of the pockmarks on his face, caused from a bout of smallpox, he was quite handsome. He cut an imposing figure as he stood greeting the citizens of Boston and awaiting the magic moment of the launch.

"Good day, Maggie, Reidan," he called to them as they approached. "Didn't I tell you this one would be in the water before 1740 was out?"

"That you did, Reuben, that you did," Maggie's father agreed. "But it's not under sail quite yet." He wet his finger and put it up to the wind. "This cool wind tells me we'll have an early winter. Perhaps you'll be iced in before she's fully loaded."

Maggie knew her father was joking. The breeze off Boston Harbor was quite balmy for late September.

Uncle Reuben knew it was a joke, as well. "Not much you'd know about launching weather or sailing weather, either, Dr. Baldwin," he said with a smile. "A ship would be in great peril with you at the helm."

"The very reason I leave all this frivolity to you, Reuben," Father said with a wave of his hand. That wave indicated not only the Souder shipyards, but also the nearby Souder Shipping Line offices and extensive warehouses on Long Wharf. Maggie's uncle owned them all.

Caleb was leaning back, gazing up at the ship. "It's so big!" he said.

"But not my biggest," Uncle Reuben retorted.

"The biggest is the *Stamitos*, which is on a return trip from Barbados just now," fourteen-year-old Evan told them.

Uncle Reuben gave Evan a smile and slapped his shoulder playfully. "That's right, Evan." To Maggie's father, he said, "This boy's a natural as a ship merchant. I'll wager he knows where nearly every Souder ship is just now and when it's due to return."

Maggie was proud of her brother, who looked striking in his russet greatcoat with the swirls of gold braid and decorative brass buttons down the front. The same gold braid was repeated on his cocked tricorn hat. Large sleeves folded back revealed crisp ruffles at his wrists. Although Evan cared little about his fancy wardrobe, Uncle Reuben required that Evan dress like a dandy for work each day.

"He's a bright boy all right," her father was saying in agreement. "Much better in the shipping business than I."

"Most anyone would be better in the shipping business than you, Reidan," Uncle Reuben teased.

"But who calls me when they're sick?" her father retorted.

The two of them teased one another mercilessly. Hearing it so much, Maggie had grown used to it. "Where's Aunt Lucille?" Maggie wanted to know.

"Feeling poorly," her uncle replied. "We felt it was best for her to rest."

Maggie wasn't surprised. Aunt Lucille was a small, pale lady who seemed sad much of the time. Over the past few years, she'd given birth to four babies, all of whom had died. The heartbreak and grief had been too much for her.

Just then a rumble of wheels sounded from behind them. They whirled around to see a carriage coming right down the wharf. People scattered out of the way.

"Only Lucas Chilton would ride through the crowd to be seen by all," Evan quipped. "And take a look at his new calash."

Maggie admired the new low-slung carriage with low wheels and a collapsible top. Not even Governor Shirley had one like this. As the carriage came to a halt midway down the wharf, the liveried footman stepped down to open the door for the Chilton family.

"May I go see Adelaide?" Maggie asked her father.

"Of course," he answered, releasing her arm. "You go on."

Not only did the Chilton family have a new carriage, but Adelaide was arrayed in a lavish plum-colored silk dress piped in dark velvet. A stunning matching hat topped out the ensemble. Amid such finery, Maggie felt a trifle awkward. Thankfully, the feeling lasted only a moment, for Adelaide had spotted her.

"Maggie! There you are, Maggie. Isn't this all so exciting? I love celebrations, don't you?" Adelaide allowed the footman to assist her to the ground. "You are still coming to high tea this afternoon, are you not?" She smoothed her skirts with her white kid gloves as she glanced about. "Is Celia here yet? Oh, we're going to have such a delightful time together."

Maggie laughed at her friend's chatter. "In answer to all your questions: I love celebrations, I'm still coming, and Celia's not arrived."

"Good day, Margaret," Adelaide's mother said as she swept gracefully from the carriage step to the ground. "Adelaide does chatter like a little squirrel, doesn't she?" Pert Chilton carefully adjusted the full skirts of her gown, which was every bit as lovely as her daughter's. "I dare say, I wonder how you put up with her."

Before Maggie could comment, Mrs. Chilton continued, "Your uncle seems to have commandeered the attention of every citizen in Boston. I'm amazed at this crowd."

Adelaide grabbed Maggie's arm. "Come, Maggie. Let's hurry down to where your uncle and father are. We don't want to miss a thing! Oh, and there's Evan."

Maggie noticed Adelaide's voice always rose a bit when she was anywhere near Evan, which didn't happen very often. Maggie knew that Evan viewed the Chilton business as competition in the shipping industry, but it was more than that. He appeared to try to avoid Adelaide altogether.

"Come, Mother," Adelaide said over her shoulder.

Lucas Chilton was already down the wharf at the launch site involved in animated conversation with Uncle Reuben. Maggie was astonished that he would leave his wife's side, forcing her to walk alone. Her father would never have done that to her mother. Although Maggie was only four when her mother had died, she remembered many details about the red-haired, Irish immigrant, Fiona Baldwin.

The workers had finished greasing the ramp, and it was nearly time for the launch. The girls hurried to join the group clustered nearest the ship. Polite greetings were made all around; and true to form, as soon as Evan had given Adelaide a polite hello, he moved some distance away.

Just before time for the launch, petite Celia Winthrop came tripping toward them. Maggie waved. "Celia, thank goodness you've arrived. They're preparing to knock out the forms."

"I'm so glad we didn't miss anything," she told them, quite out of breath. "The new baby was fussing, and Mother couldn't decide whether to bring him along or leave him with the nurse."

Eleanor Winthrop with her husband, Andrew, soon joined the group, and Mrs. Winthrop did indeed hold the baby in her arms.

Just then, Adelaide leaned over to Maggie. "What's that in your brother's hand?" she asked.

Thinking Adelaide meant Evan, Maggie looked in his direction. "Nothing that I see."

"No, no. Your younger brother."

"Oh, Caleb? That's his garden snake, Beagan."

Adelaide released a loud gasp. "A live snake?"

"Beagan?" Celia said. "He *named* a snake?"

"It means *little one* in Irish," Maggie told them. "Caleb takes him most everywhere."

Hearing his name, Caleb skipped over to them. "You wanted to see Beagan?" He proudly held up the wriggling little creature, and Adelaide and Celia both jumped back.

"Ugh! Get that nasty thing away from me!" Adelaide protested. She spread her fan and put it to her face as though to protect herself.

"It's only a little garden snake," Caleb said, stepping closer. "If you look real close, you can see all the pretty designs."

Celia squealed and jumped behind Maggie.

"I guess you'd better put him back in your pocket for now," Maggie told him. She'd often played with garden snakes—and toads, as well—when she was younger. It had never occurred to her to be frightened.

At the sound of the commotion, Dr. Baldwin turned around. Seeing the problem, he motioned for Caleb to come back to his side.

"All safe," Maggie told them.

"Thank goodness," Adelaide said with a sigh.

Uncle Reuben provided a blessed interruption as he climbed up on a section of scaffolding and called out for the people's attention. He prayed a short prayer over the *Thetis*, asking God to watch over her and protect her while she was under sail. The governor gave a short speech, followed by another speech by one of the magistrates. At last, Reuben Souder called out, "Release the supports!"

Hammers banged as the forms were knocked out of the way. Other workers stood at the sides to push, giving the heavy bulk the boost it needed to commence sliding. Wild cheers went up as the ship picked up momentum and slid down quickly and easily, ending with a monstrous splash into Boston Harbor. Seagulls shrieked and wheeled about overhead, joining in the noisy event.

Maggie gasped and clung to her friends as the men scurried about to pull ropes and bring the now-launched ship firmly into the dock before it could float away. She felt she couldn't breathe until the vessel was secured on the far side of the dock. The Boston selectmen and magistrates formally shook Uncle Reuben's hand and congratulated him on the successful launch. There was much bustling about and what Maggie's father called "hobnobbing."

"Ships are so thrilling," Adelaide was saying. "They can take a person to exciting far-off lands. Of course, when we came over from England, I suffered terribly from seasickness, but I'm sure one would get used to it eventually. I believe the sailors call it getting your 'sea legs.' Funny saying, isn't it? Sea legs?"

The girls giggled as they walked along. The crowd began to thin out as people slowly strolled back to their carriages.

"I have an idea," Adelaide said, pulling them to a halt. "Let's ask if you two can ride back to our house in our carriage."

"That would be great fun," Maggie agreed.

Celia nodded. "Let's ask."

Maggie turned about to see her father and Caleb still talking with Evan and Uncle Reuben. She hurried back to his side. "Father!" she called out excitedly. "May I ride to the Chiltons' home in their new carriage?"

Father smiled at her. "I see no reason why not. We'll see you there."

She tiptoed to reach up and kiss her father's cheek. "Oh, thank you, Father."

"I want to go in the new carriage," Caleb piped up. "Let me go, too."

"No, Caleb," her father said. "This is just for Maggie and her friends."

"Not fair!" Caleb stuck his lower lip out in a pout.

"Come on, Caleb," Evan said, "you can ride with me and Uncle Reuben in his carriage."

While Caleb's attention was diverted, Maggie turned to rejoin her friends.

"Celia can come with us," Adelaide called out to Maggie. "Can you?"

"Yes," Maggie called back. "Father says it's fine."

As she hurried back toward her friends, a young girl emerged from the crowd. Her hair was disheveled beneath a soiled mobcap, and her drab, threadbare dress hung limply to her ankles. Maggie judged her to be a year or so older than Caleb. The girl gazed wide-eyed as though she were soaking in the beauty and finery about her. Then she spied Maggie, and Maggie could feel the girl admiring the ruffles and lace of her best Sunday dress. As Maggie drew nearer, the girl stood as though transfixed.

Suddenly, Maggie felt a yank on her arm. Adelaide had grabbed her. "Don't touch that girl," she said in a loud whisper, as she dragged Maggie out around the young girl. "Don't you know? Her mother keeps company!"

Maggie knew that meant the mother had men come into her home. But what did that have to do with this little girl? As Maggie was assisted up into the fine calash, she gave one glance back, and her eyes locked with the sad eyes of the forlorn girl.

CHAPTER 2

High Tea

There was plenty of room in the calash for all three girls and Adelaide's parents. The ride to the Chilton home at the edge of Boston Common was a delight with the open top and the breeze blowing on them. Adelaide and her mother held up face masks to protect their skin from the sun and wind. The girls chattered and giggled the entire way.

The stately three-story Chilton house was surrounded by dozens of carriages. Many guests had already arrived for high tea. Clusters of footmen, dressed in smartly tailored liveries, gathered about, visiting together beneath a large shade tree in the yard.

"You girls may have your tea served in the upstairs nursery if you like," Pert Chilton said as the carriage stopped. "I'll have the servants serve you there."

"How wonderful, Mother," said Adelaide. She turned to Maggie and Celia. "Our own private tea party. What fun!"

The double parlors of the Chilton home had been opened by pushing back moving partitions. The guests milled about, laughing and visiting, as the Chiltons' servants brought them their tea on silver trays. A servant at the door took the girls' cloaks.

Governor Shirley and all the magistrates were there, arrayed in curled, powdered wigs and brightly colored greatcoats. Lilting melodies filled the room as a gentleman played the spinet at the far end of the room.

If this were an evening party rather than a tea, Maggie was certain the guests would be dancing. She'd heard that the Chiltons entertained often with evening dances, and it made her wish she knew how to dance.

Lucas and Pert Chilton were courteous hosts and insisted that Adelaide greet as many guests as possible before going to the nursery. Maggie watched as Adelaide graciously mingled and chatted, giving little curtseys and extending her hand to the gentlemen.

Maggie wasn't sure she'd be able to do all that if it were required of her. Anyway, she couldn't imagine her father giving such a large party. First of all, their house wouldn't hold such a crowd, but second, Dr. Baldwin didn't think much of Boston's growing social scene. Even now, he was sitting off in a corner alone. Maggie realized he'd probably agreed to come only because of her. If Mother had not died, if Father had his lovely Fiona by his side, Maggie knew everything might be different.

Just then, Adelaide appeared and began ushering both Maggie and Celia up the wide curving stairs. "Hurry, before Mother thinks of something else." Adelaide giggled as she lifted her skirts and hurried up the steps with Maggie and Celia in her wake. They scurried down the long hall into an alcove, which opened into the spacious, sunny nursery.

Maggie had been in the Chilton home on one other occasion and was quite taken with its enormous size. The family often had friends from Salem—other shipping merchants—visit, and during those visits, parties occurred almost nightly. Hannah Pierce often quipped, "There was no hoity-toity in Boston until the Chiltons arrived!"

In the Baldwin house, the nursery looked like a nursery, but Adelaide's nursery looked like a sitting room. Maggie wondered what Adelaide would think of Caleb's blocks, tops, and toy soldiers being stacked on the shelves and his large rocking horse sitting right in the middle of the room.

Adelaide arranged three delicately cushioned chairs in a circle around a small Pembroke table spread with a plaid cloth. "I'm overjoyed to have my very own company today," she told them. "Now that Clark and Oliver have left for Harvard, the house is so dreadfully dull. You've not met my brothers yet, have you? They're such great fun. Here, please sit down, and I'll ring for our tea." She tugged at a tasseled bellpull near the door as Maggie and Celia sat down, arranging their hoops carefully.

Before Adelaide could be seated, a soft tapping sounded at the door. "Mercy. How could they get up here that fast? Winged feet?"

As she opened the door, there stood Caleb, leaning against the doorframe. A strangled gasp came from Adelaide. "Do you still have that—that slimy reptile?"

"Yup. But Beagan's safe in my pocket."

Maggie was mortified. "Caleb, what do you want?"

"Can I come and be with you, Maggie?" he said, looking past Adelaide. "I don't want to stay downstairs."

"How did you know where I was?" Maggie demanded.

"I'm mighty good at tracking and following. I'd make a good Indian, wouldn't I?"

"Caleb, go away. This is just for us girls," Maggie ordered, trying not to appear unkind. She didn't want the girls to think she was hateful, but she knew they didn't want a little brother bothering them.

"Oh, please, Maggie. I won't hurt anything. I promise I'll keep Beagan in my pocket. And if he crawls out, I'll put him right back in."

Celia gave a shudder. "How ghastly," she said.

Maggie rose and went to the door. "I apologize for the interruption, Adelaide. Excuse me a moment." Stepping into the alcove, she closed the door, then took her little brother by the shoulders. "Caleb, you're causing me a great deal of embarrassment," she said softly. "Now go on downstairs with Father and leave me alone."

"Father is just sitting. I don't want to just sit."

"Where's Evan?"

Caleb shrugged. "Outside somewhere. He said he didn't care to come in." He pulled Beagan out and let the little snake crawl through his fingers.

"You must put your snake away while you're here. You saw how the girls reacted—other ladies will do the same. Now go find Evan." It was just like Evan not to come in. She had one brother who wouldn't mingle socially and another who wouldn't leave her alone. What a disaster!

"But no one is serving sweetcakes outdoors." Caleb's shoulders sagged a little.

"You're being impossible," Maggie said, becoming more and more flustered. "You must go back down and leave me alone." Gently, she guided him down the hall to the open balcony overlooking the double parlors. From that vantage point, she waved to get her father's attention. It took a moment, but when she finally caught his eye, she pointed at Caleb. Dr. Baldwin quickly came to the foot of the stairs.

"Caleb, come down here this moment," he said firmly.

"Not fair," Caleb spouted, as he hurried down the curving steps to his father.

Maggie heaved a little sigh. Finally she could be with her friends. By the time she returned to the nursery, the two servants were bustling about, setting the tea things on the table. A tea service of blue and gold sat primly on a black-and-gold Chinese tea tray. The silver cake basket, full of sweetcakes, wafers, and tiny sandwiches, was placed next to the tea service.

"I'm so sorry," Maggie said as she sat at her place. "I don't know what got into him."

"I'm sure he wouldn't have hurt anything," Celia said.

"Oh, now," Adelaide said, gracefully pulling off her kid gloves, "we certainly don't need a little one pestering us." She lifted the cake basket and passed it to Maggie. "Now if it'd been your older brother, that might have been different." She gave a wink, and Maggie was shocked. This girl was quite forward.

"Shall I pour?" asked one of the servants. The girl was not many years older than Adelaide.

"Oh, mercy me, no," Adelaide said with a wave of her hand.

"None of you colonists know how to pour properly."

"Yes, ma'am." Maggie could tell the girl was not even a little embarrassed.

"Adelaide!" Celia spoke up. "Shame on you."

"Well, it's the truth. Mother and Father haven't been able to employ decent help since we left London. No one here has been trained properly."

"Will there be anything else, ma'am?" the girl asked, inching toward the door.

"No, Hayley. You may go."

When the servants had departed, Adelaide poured the tea into thin cups decorated in pink rosebud designs. "It's true what I said, girls. Mother and Daddy have searched every nook and cranny of Boston for trained help, and it simply can't be found."

Maggie wasn't sure what to say since her family didn't have a single servant. Sometimes Hannah hired girls to come in and help pluck the geese or do spring cleaning, but that was temporary.

"Our servants seem to do fine," Celia put in as she took her cup and sipped from it.

Maggie did likewise but was fearful the fragile little cup might crumble right in her fingers. When the cake basket was passed, Maggie chose a golden sponge cake, which looked soft as a cloud.

"And such odd servants we get," Adelaide went on. "Take Hayley, for instance." She leaned forward slightly, raising her eyebrows. "She's a revivalist!"

"No!" Celia said with a soft little gasp. "Is she really?"

Before Maggie could catch herself, she blurted out, "What's a revivalist?"

"You mean you don't know?" Adelaide touched her forehead. "You live here in Boston and you don't know what a revivalist is?"

Before Maggie could answer, Celia explained, "They follow the itinerant preachers, Maggie. The ones who hold wild meetings—which they say are religious—in barns."

"In a barn or right outdoors in a pasture," Adelaide added. "Can you imagine such irreverence? A dirty old barn—to hold church?"

"The people become quite agitated, I'm told." Celia wiped her fingers on the white linen napkin and reached for a slice of fruitcake.

"Very agitated," Adelaide agreed. "Like this." She set down her cup and threw back her head. Touching her forehead with her hand, she gave a loud groan. "Oh, I feel it, I feel it. . . . Ooh, I feel the Spirit."

Maggie giggled with glee at the sight of the lovely Adelaide acting out such a part.

"Or like this," Celia said. Jumping up from her chair, she knelt down and began to beat her breast, crying, "Oh, save me, save me! Please save me. I need to be saved."

"Then they jump up and down, waving their arms!" Adelaide leaped to her feet to demonstrate. As the pantomimes continued, the three girls were consumed with fits of giggles until they could barely breathe beneath their whalebone corsets.

"I shall never have to wonder what a revivalist is after that demonstration," Maggie said, dabbing at her eyes with her kerchief. She'd laughed so hard, tears filled her eyes.

"Really, it's quite vile," Celia said, as she tried to catch her breath. "My father says they are completely in error."

"And my father calls them the 'bumbling backwoodsmen,'" Adelaide said. "He feels they should be run out of any town they dare come into."

"They must be pretty bad," Maggie said thoughtfully. She helped herself to another sandwich.

"Very bad," Celia said. "They have absolutely no reverence for the church."

"I can tell you one thing," Adelaide said. "You'll never catch me going near one of their wild heathenistic meetings. Why, even Pastor Gee of North Church will have nothing to do with them. And both Clark and Oliver say all the professors at Harvard are dead set against them."

A tap on the door interrupted their little party. "Girls!" came Mrs. Chilton's voice. "Sorry to interrupt your merrymaking, but guests are leaving, and Dr. Baldwin is asking for Maggie."

"Oh, Maggie, I wish you didn't have to leave so soon." Adelaide rose to give Maggie a hug. "It was a pure pleasure having you."

"I enjoyed every minute, Adelaide," Maggie told her. "Thank you for such a charming tea party."

"It was rompish good fun," Celia agreed, also giving a hug. "Let's do it again soon."

The girls tripped down the stairs to find the parlor nearly empty. Evan was waiting at the door for Maggie. "It's about time," he said under his breath. "I'm quite ready to leave."

"Just a moment. My wrap."

Suddenly Adelaide was beside them, holding Maggie's cloak. "Evan, how good that you could come to our home. Do come again, won't you?"

"As I find opportunity," he said, bowing stiffly and replacing his tricorn hat. "Maggie, please. Father's waiting."

Maggie was attempting to tie on her hat while Evan was putting her cloak about her. "Give me a chance to tie my hat," she protested. But Evan was bundling her right out the door and down the steps to the waiting carriage.

"Really, Father," Maggie complained once she was seated beside him in the carriage, "both my brothers were impossible today. Do you know how that makes me appear to Adelaide and her parents?"

Dr. Baldwin clucked at his team of bays. "I dare say, I probably wasn't much better. I nearly fell asleep in the corner."

"There, you see?" said Evan. "Father doesn't care for the Chiltons any more than I do."

"I just wanted to eat with you," Caleb chimed in.

Maggie moaned. "I like Adelaide and Celia, and I long to be invited again, but how can I if the three of you act like awkward misfits?"

"She's right, boys. We owe her an apology."

"I'm sorry, Maggie," said Evan.

"Me, too," Caleb echoed.

Dr. Baldwin put his arm around her. "And I apologize, as well. Perhaps we should have insisted that Hannah come along. Hannah would have seen to it that the three of us behaved more gentlemanly!"

"That she would," Maggie agreed.

Even though Maggie loved Hannah with all her heart, it was times like these when she wished her own mother were still alive. As they left the area of Boston Common and drove up Hanover Street to Copp's Hill, Maggie thought back over her delightful time at the tea party. How she wished she could have tea parties every day.

If she socialized more, perhaps she would know about such things as the revivalists. She wouldn't have admitted this to the girls, but they made her a bit curious about these strange services. What could the revivalists possibly have done to cause so much anger and mistrust?

❧ CHAPTER 3 ❧

Washday Blues

Y ou're attacking that candlestick as though you were at-tempting to kill it," Hannah said with a chuckle. Her jolly face, as usual, was bright and smiling.

Maggie was sitting at the wooden kitchen table polishing the brass candlesticks. They stood in a row on the table, wait-ing their turns to be polished to a high sheen. "I thought you were tending the laundry kettle," Maggie said.

"I came in to see how near done you were. I'll need help as soon as you can come out."

"Yes, ma'am," she answered, her voice sullen.

"What a blessing that we can still do the wash outdoors. I pray the mild autumn weather lasts." Hannah stepped into the pantry off the kitchen and came back out with the soap bar in hand and a knife for grating it. "Old Man Winter will drive me inside much too soon for my liking." When Maggie didn't answer, Hannah moved toward the back door. "Hurry then, will you please?"

"Yes, ma'am." Helping with the laundry meant hauling

several buckets of water from the well to the wash pot and then wringing out the clothes, which became heavy and bulky when wet.

At the door, Hannah paused. "You seem distracted this morning. Are you coming down with something?"

"I'm fine."

"You look a bit peaked. I'll tell your father when he comes home. You may be in need of a tonic." The door closed on her last words.

Maggie wasn't sure a tonic would help. She was sound in body, but something deep inside wasn't quite right. As she polished the candlesticks, she wondered who cleaned up melted wax and polished the candlesticks at the Chilton home. But she didn't really have to wonder. She knew for a fact it wasn't Adelaide. Perhaps it was the girl named Hayley—the one who went to the wild barn meetings.

Once the brass candlesticks were shiny, Maggie firmed a candle down into each one. The burned wick of each candle was trimmed off in preparation for the evening's use. Hannah was strict about the candles being prepared first thing each morning. "You don't wait until dark to prepare for the darkness," she'd say. Then she always added, "Likewise, don't wait until you're at death's door to prepare for departure."

Hannah had a saying for everything. When Maggie was a little girl, she'd loved all Hannah's quaint sayings. Now they seemed aged and yellowed like some of the books in Father's study. She couldn't imagine the lovely Pert Chilton ever uttering such antiquated sayings.

When the candlesticks were finished, Maggie set them on

a tray and placed the tray on a pantry shelf. She shook out bits of burned wick and wax shavings from the skirt of her plain day dress. Maggie had grown so fast the past few months that the sleeves of her day dress were becoming much too short. She was now as tall as Hannah and nearly as tall as Evan.

Another thing Hannah was strict about—they didn't put on their nicer dresses until the morning work was completed. Maggie was willing to wager that neither Adelaide nor Celia even owned a day dress, let alone one with sleeves that were too short.

In the dooryard, the fire under the iron wash kettle had set the water into a rolling boil. Hannah, who was stirring the clothing vigorously with her wash stick, looked up as Maggie came out. "I'm nearly ready for rinsing, Maggie," she said. "Bring more water."

At the well, Maggie filled two buckets, but she could only carry one at a time. She poured the clean well water into a copper rinse tub that sat on a low table near the fire.

"I wish Evan were here to do this," she said.

Hannah straightened up and pushed at the small of her back with her free hand. "Now since when have you ever seen men doing a woman's work?"

"I don't mean he should do the laundry, but he could at least carry the water before he leaves."

"Your brother was up before daylight carrying water, young lady, but it wasn't for our work; it was for the horses."

Of course, Maggie knew that. She knew he had also split and stacked much of the wood that was delivered to the house. But somehow that didn't console her.

Hannah lifted the hot laundry from the wash pot with the wash stick and slung the wet clothes into the rinse water. From there, Maggie assisted as each piece was wrung out and spread out across the shrubbery to dry in the sunshine.

It was nearly time for lunch before they were finished with the laundry. If her father could get away, he was usually home for lunch, at which time he assigned her Latin lessons for the afternoon. When Evan was younger, he attended the nearby Latin School where Caleb now attended, but Dr. Baldwin taught Latin to his daughter at home. The lessons used to be fun and challenging, but recently she'd begun to wonder why she had to continue. It seemed senseless to continue studying every day.

Together, Maggie and Hannah carried the wash water, then the rinse water, to the edge of the kitchen garden, emptying the kettles on what remained of the plants. "Hannah," Maggie said as they carried the kettles back into the kitchen, "have you heard about the revivalists?"

Hannah nodded as she stirred up the fire to start the noon meal. "I've heard of them."

"If they're so terrible, why are they allowed to come into the city?" Maggie wanted to know.

"Are they so terrible?"

"They're bumbling backwoodsmen who are in error," Maggie said as she took down the pewter plates from the shelf and set the places at the table. Father enjoyed his noon meal in the kitchen, while supper was served in the dining room. "Why, I hear they've never been educated and don't even write out their sermons."

"And what do you think of these kinds of preachers, Miss Margaret?"

Maggie stopped a minute. "What do I think? Well, I don't know, since I've not heard them. But I know I wouldn't want to, since they are in error."

"Just remember, people often suspect that of which they are ignorant."

Another one of Hannah's sayings. But it failed to answer Maggie's questions and made her almost miffed. "One surely isn't ignorant if it's common knowledge that these people are irreverent enough to hold services in dirty barns or even outdoors," Maggie retorted.

Hannah cut up a cabbage and some carrots, added them to a kettle with pieces of pork, and put the pot over the fire to boil. "Holding a service out-of-doors is wrong?"

Maggie stopped what she was doing. "Well, of course it's wrong. We have our churches in which we show reverence to God. Don't you think it's wrong?"

"My opinion doesn't seem to matter here. You're the one with all the questions. And," Hannah added, "seemingly the one with all the answers, as well."

Maggie felt anger growing against Hannah. The feeling was confusing and rather frightening. She'd never been angry with Hannah before. Thankfully, Father chose that moment to show up for his noon meal.

Maggie was a trifle worried that Hannah would bring up the subject of the revivalists while they ate. She wasn't ready to discuss the subject with her father. But her worry was for nothing because Hannah didn't breathe a word of it.

After their meal, Dr. Baldwin called Maggie into his study, where he outlined her afternoon lessons. Generally, her lesson consisted of copying scripture into Latin and writing her own compositions in Latin, as well. In addition, there was assigned reading in a book from her father's library collection. Today's assignment was no exception.

As her father prepared to leave, Maggie blurted out, "Father, how much longer must I continue to work on daily lessons?"

A look of surprise registered on Dr. Baldwin's face. "Why, Maggie, I thought you enjoyed learning. I've attempted to give you the same opportunities as your brothers to expand your mind and to use the talents God has given you."

"But I've been studying much longer than Evan ever did. He left Latin school when he was only eleven, and here I'm nearly thirteen."

"Evan continues to learn daily at the countinghouse. Your uncle Reuben says he's learned not only the accounting but much of the overall management of the entire shipping lines."

"But I'm not Evan," she answered quickly. Then before she could stop the words, she said, "Adelaide doesn't work on lessons every day. Nor does Celia Winthrop."

Dr. Baldwin nodded in a knowing way. "I see. So, tell me, is it your intent to become like Adelaide Chilton?"

Once again that strange sensation of confusion swept over her as it had when she was talking with Hannah. It was as though her insides were all jumbled up like the curdled milk in the butter churn. What *did* she want? She wasn't really sure.

When she didn't answer, her father came to her and put his arm around her shoulders. "I propose a solution, Maggie. Your birthday is coming up near Thanksgiving time. I ask that you continue your studies until your birthday, and then we'll discuss the matter. Is that agreeable?"

Her father was always so kind and so fair. How could she argue with him? Part of her almost wanted him to get upset at her. "That's agreeable," she replied. But silently she wished she could rid herself of the constraints of the tedious lessons that very afternoon.

"Good," he said softly, planting a little kiss on her forehead. "You may work in here if you'd like. The light is better."

Admittedly, Maggie did love to be in her father's study with the tall windows that looked out on Hannah's flower gardens. "Thank you. I will."

"Now set right to work, for you'll be needed to help Hannah prepare for our evening guests."

"Guests? Who's coming?"

"I told you the other day that Ben and Judith and the children are invited for supper."

"Oh." Maggie fought to keep the disappointment from her voice. Only the Pierces. How she wished they could entertain *important* people.

After her father left, she changed out of her day dress and returned to her father's study to work. Sitting at his writing desk, she found herself staring out at the bright fall sunshine and the towering shade trees that were growing crimson and gold.

Actually, she didn't really mind Hannah's younger brother, Benjamin Pierce, and his wife, Judith. Ben was funny and liked to joke about the fact that he and Maggie were both redheaded.

"No one else understands us redheads," he'd say to her with a big smile on his face. "We redheads have to stick together through thick and thin."

She didn't even mind Ben's son, Jacob, who was Evan's age. But the three little boys, Adam, Burke, and Henry, all younger than Caleb, were regular little mischief-makers. And after enjoying high tea at the Chilton home, the Pierces seemed rather ordinary.

Maggie struggled to collect her thoughts and concentrate on her lessons. Midway into the afternoon, she heard voices at the front entrance to the house. Daytime callers were usually for Hannah, but they called at the rear entrance. Who could be coming to the front?

Hannah went scurrying past the study on her way to answer the knocking. Curiosity getting the best of her, Maggie replaced her quill in the inkstand and followed. When Hannah opened the door, there stood one of the Chiltons' footmen, arrayed in his bright green-and-gold livery.

"The Misses Chilton and Winthrop request your presence for an afternoon outing," the footman announced, waving his hand toward the street. At the gate were Adelaide and Celia riding sidesaddle on highbred, prancing mounts.

"I'd love to, but. . ." Maggie turned to Hannah, who was shaking her head. "I'm working on lessons." The footman gave her a blank stare. Unaccustomed to such formality, Maggie came down the steps to the front stone walk. "No matter," she said, walking past the footman, "I'll tell them myself."

"Maggie," Adelaide called out as she approached, "come riding with us. It's a perfectly lovely day. And even though

Johnson isn't nearly as much fun as my brothers, we can still have a good time."

"Johnson could even help you saddle up," Celia added.

Maggie wasn't sure whether to be proud or embarrassed, but she needed no help saddling Amaryllis. Her father had seen to it that she learned to tack her horse the same as Evan, and she'd never ridden sidesaddle. They didn't even own a sidesaddle.

"Thank you ever so much for thinking of me," she replied, "but I have Latin assignments that must be finished this afternoon."

"Assignments such as schoolchildren are given?" Adelaide asked.

Maggie flinched. "My father feels very strongly that I should never stop learning," she said in defense. Even as she said it, she wished she could toss the lesson in the fire and jump on Amaryllis and ride away with the girls. What a fun afternoon it would be, talking and laughing together as they rode in the brisk autumn air.

"I'm sorry you can't come," Celia said as she adjusted her forest green riding cloak about her. "Perhaps another time."

"Let me know in advance so I can get permission from Father." Maggie opened the front gate for Johnson, who had followed her down the walk. He remounted his horse. As he rode a few feet away, Adelaide made a silly face at him behind his back, causing both Maggie and Celia to snicker.

The girls urged their own mounts forward. "I'm not sure I could guarantee advance notice," Adelaide said over her shoulder. "Celia and I are inclined to do things on the spur of the moment."

Maggie had no answer. Her days were spent working

alongside Hannah doing many of the household chores. She couldn't imagine going for a ride on a whim. "Thanks again for the kind invitation."

The two girls waved as they rode away, their riding cloaks glowing like spring flowers against the dusky fall foliage.

With halting steps, Maggie returned to the house to finish her lessons and help prepare for the evening company.

A Splendid Idea

"I've decided I'll cut little pieces of soft flannel and stuff it in my ears," Maggie said to Evan. She watched as he poured grain for the horses. She knew Hannah probably needed her in the kitchen, but she'd escaped for a few minutes before company arrived.

"Are you saying you don't enjoy the chatter of three little boys?" Evan asked with a chuckle.

"Four, counting Caleb. And chatter is hardly the word for the noise they make."

Evan slapped one of the horses on the flank to make him move over. "Henry's but a toddler," he countered.

"He's learning to chatter quite well and will soon be taught plenty of mischief by both Adam and Burke."

Evan took the wooden hay fork from its hook on the wall and crawled up the ladder to the loft, pitching down loose hay stored there from the summer. Maggie stepped back to avoid a coating of dust on her clean dress. Their father loved fine horses and kept a stable full of them. Maggie's delight was to assist with the spring colts.

"Take care that you don't say a careless word about the boys around Hannah," Evan warned her. "She dotes upon all her nephews—Jacob included."

"Of course I wouldn't do that. That's why I'm talking to you out in the stable."

"Tell you what." Evan descended the ladder and then leaped from the halfway point, hitting the floor with a thud. "I'll suggest to Father that you and I and Jacob go for a ride following supper. How will that be?"

"But there'll be dishes to clean."

"Judith is always willing to lend Hannah a hand." He shrugged. "Do you want me to ask or not?"

Maggie wasn't sure what she wanted. What she'd really wanted was to ride with the girls that afternoon, but it wasn't to be. She walked over to Amaryllis and patted the mare's soft nose and felt the warm breath on her hand.

"Are you feeling all right?" Evan asked.

"I wish people would stop asking me that," she said sharply and regretted the outburst the moment it came out. "I'm sorry, Evan. Hannah asked me the same thing this very afternoon."

"I can well imagine why. You've been acting differently the past week or so."

"Different how?" Maggie laid her face against Amaryllis's velvety cheek. She knew she sensed strange things going on deep inside her, but she didn't know it showed.

"I can't describe it," Evan replied. "Sort of dreamy-eyed."

Just then, Hannah was calling from the dooryard. The guests had arrived, and there was work to be done. Maggie didn't take well to being called "dreamy-eyed," but there was no time to talk it over.

"A houseful of Pierces" is how Hannah described a visit from her younger brother and his family. Maggie could tell from the tone of Hannah's voice that she was proud of all of them. Since Hannah had never married, she enjoyed doting on Ben's children almost as much as she did the three Baldwins.

Hannah set a separate smaller table for Caleb and the younger Pierce boys in the sitting room. After Dr. Baldwin gave thanks, Hannah sat with the children periodically to keep order and yet served the others when needed. Maggie was thankful she'd not been asked to sit with the little ones.

Father, at the head of the table, served up generous portions of Hannah's delicious boiled beef and cabbage. Ben was placed next to Father, Judith was next to him, and then Maggie beside Judith. Evan and Jacob sat on the opposite side of the narrow dining room table.

Little Henry sat on his mother's lap to eat but kept hopping down and crawling back up. Maggie scooted her chair away so she wouldn't get in the way. She wondered how Judith would ever eat, but it never seemed to bother her. Judith gave the impression of being the perfect mother, never getting riled or speaking a cross word.

Ben, a lifelong friend of Father's, served as editor of the *Boston News Letter*. Not only did Benjamin Pierce know all the latest news, but he loved telling funny stories. Maggie never saw her father laugh much until Ben was around.

That evening, however, conversation turned to the Pierces' church—the Brattle Street Church. "You really ought to come one time to see, Reidan," Ben was saying to Father. "The changes in people's lives are truly beyond description. The fervor for God is there, and we see genuine conversions among common folk of the city."

Judith agreed with her husband that, indeed, new things were happening at their church. Maggie was all ears. Especially when the word *fervor* came up. Could this have anything to do with the revivalists she'd heard about from Adelaide and Celia?

Maggie glanced at Evan to gauge his reaction. She'd been meaning to ask him about the subject. Now she wished she had.

Evan's face told her nothing, and Father had put on his best "physician's face" as Maggie called it. Her father often had to mask his true feelings when tending someone who was seriously ill. Evan mimicked it perfectly. It was a marvel to Maggie, whose feelings seemed to be spelled out plainly to everyone.

Jacob, on the other hand, leaned forward and smiled. Maggie thought he wanted to say something, but he wouldn't interrupt the adults' conversation. As he leaned forward, he must have stretched out his long legs, for a sharp kick on her ankle made Maggie jump. Jacob immediately knew he'd kicked her. His legs were getting so long, Maggie wondered if he simply forgot how far they reached.

Their eyes met, and Jacob straightened in his chair as his cheeks turned pink. "Pardon me," he mouthed. Maggie nodded, then tried to concentrate once again on what Ben was saying about conversions. What was a conversion? Then she wondered why Jacob blushed at having kicked her ankle. She'd known him since they were small children, and he'd never blushed before.

Just as the conversation was growing increasingly interesting, Hannah motioned for Maggie to come and help cut and serve the huckleberry pies. Caleb came tripping out to the kitchen as well, followed closely by seven-year-old Adam and six-year-old Burke.

"May we have *two* pieces of pie, Hannah? May we please?" Caleb said. His voice all but drowned out the conversation at the dining room table. "We're big enough to eat two, aren't we, fellows?"

"Yes, yes, Aunt Hannah," Adam chimed in. "Two pieces."

"I can eat a whole pie," Burke said as he strutted about.

"Go back to your places and clean up your plates, or you won't get even one piece of this pie," Hannah warned.

"If we clean up our plates, then may we have two pieces?" Caleb wanted to know.

"Then may we have two?" Adam echoed.

Hannah stood with a spatula dripping lavender-blue juice poised in the air. "The best way to find out is to obey. Get to your places this minute!"

By now, toddler Henry was behind them. As they turned in their hurry to get away from the riled-up Hannah, they plowed right into him, knocking him to the floor. He set up a lusty wail, and Judith came to pick him up, cooing to him that he wasn't hurt at all. By the time the pie was served and Maggie was seated once again, the talk about the Brattle Street Church was over.

True to his word, Evan asked Father if Maggie could join

him and Jacob in an after-supper ride. Father looked first at Hannah, knowing she would need assistance. But before Hannah could speak, Judith said, "Oh, let her go. I'll help Hannah with the cleaning up. I'm sure Maggie did her share in getting supper ready."

Maggie gave Judith a smile. "Thank you very much. Father? Hannah?"

"You have my permission if Hannah agrees," her father said.

"Go ahead," Hannah said with a wave of her hand. "You missed one ride today. I wouldn't want you to miss out twice."

"Missed a ride?" her father asked. "What ride?"

Hannah bustled about, gathering the dirty plates to take to the kitchen. "That pretty young Chilton girl and the Winthrop girl came calling. With a footman, no less."

"Their footman?" said Ben with a twinkle of mischief in his eye. "What's this, young Maggie? Are you getting hoity-toity on us?" He put his fingers in front of his face as though his hand were a fan, waggling it back and forth. "Ta-ta," he said.

Maggie felt her face growing warm.

"Now, Ben," Judith said, placing her hand on his arm. "Don't be a tease. Maggie can ride with whomever she chooses."

Ben leaned over toward Maggie's father. "Better keep a close watch on her, Reidan. The next thing you know, one of those Harvard-bred Chilton boys will be getting sweet on your girl."

Now it was Jacob who spoke up. "Father," he said, rising quickly to his feet, "that's not fair. Come on, Maggie, Evan. We're supposed to be taking a ride *before* dark."

As Jacob nearly pushed her out of the dining room, she heard Ben call out, "Sorry, Maggie. It was all in jest."

After hurrying to her bedchamber to shed her hoops and grab her hooded cloak, she ran out the back door only to be greeted by Caleb, Adam, and Burke all chanting, "Maggie's a hoity-toity. Maggie's a hoity-toity."

"Quiet, all of you," she ordered as she lifted her skirts and ran past them. Thankfully, they didn't follow. Perhaps she should have stuffed her ears after all.

When she stepped into the stable, Evan was starting to tack up Amaryllis. "I'll do that," she snapped.

Evan stepped back. "Just trying to help."

Maggie's insides were churning, and her eyes burned. She wasn't sure she could talk. "I know. I'll finish."

"Come on, Jacob. She can do it herself. When the copper kettle gets steamed up, it's best to clear out of the way." With that, he led his horse out the stable door.

When she was little, Jacob and Evan had delighted in teasing her about her Irish temper. Jacob was the one who started calling her a steamed-up copper kettle because of her copper curls. She held her breath, expecting Jacob to take up the teasing, as well.

Instead, he came over and silently began to lend a hand, not giving her a chance to protest. "Father's accustomed to a houseful of rowdy boys," he said softly. "He's a wit-snapper with all of us, and we think nothing of it. Perhaps he forgets that girls are different."

He snugged up the girth while Maggie fit the bit into Amaryllis's mouth and flipped the bridle over the long, soft ears. When they were finished, they led their horses outside. "Here," Jacob said, "let me give you a hand up."

Maggie wanted to tell him she'd never needed a hand up and surely didn't need one now. But he was being so kind, she didn't resist. Evan was fairly well down the lane before they caught up with him. When he heard them cantering up behind him, he took off like a streak. The race was on!

The three rode with wild abandonment almost the entire way to Boston Common. Down tree-lined Tremont Street they galloped, laughing and gasping for breath. The common, filled with evening strollers, forced them to slow their pace as they approached. In spite of the cool evening breeze, Maggie left her hood down where it had fallen during the wild ride. She felt better now, her anger blown away in the wind.

"Let's ride the perimeter," Evan suggested. "By the time we ride all the way around and take a slow walk home, it'll be nearly dark." The other two agreed by falling in on either side of him, letting the horses lope along gently.

Maggie happened to glance over at the imposing three-story Chilton house on the hill at the far side of the common. "Evan, do you think Father would consider purchasing a sidesaddle for me?" she asked.

"Our tackroom is full of saddles," her brother answered. "Why would he want to purchase another?" Evan always seemed to think in terms of money.

"Most all ladies ride sidesaddle," Maggie said. "Perhaps it's high time I did, as well. Do you think he would?"

"Why not ask him to give one to you as a gift for your birthday?" Jacob suggested.

"What a splendid idea! I'm surprised I didn't think of it myself." For her birthday, surely Father would consider a saddle.

She wondered how long it would take to grow accustomed to riding in a different manner. One thing was certain, she'd do very little wild racing sitting sidesaddle.

As they rode along, Maggie's mind went back to the conversation at supper about the Pierces' church. How terrible it would be if Ben convinced her father to attend Brattle Street Church. What would she do then? Would Adelaide and Celia laugh at her and call her a revivalist?

At that very moment, she looked up to see Adelaide strolling with her mother through the formal gardens beside her house. Quickly, Maggie lifted the hood of her cloak and pulled it over her head and far past her face. The last thing she wanted was to be seen riding astride her mount without her hoops.

"Are you getting chilly?" Jacob asked her.

"Yes, quite. Let's hurry back."

CHAPTER 5

The Invitation

One Saturday late in October, Maggie and Hannah were busy in the kitchen with the weekly baking. Caleb had been required to carry armloads of wood until the baking oven was piping hot. While Hannah rolled out piecrusts and filled them, Maggie kneaded the bread on the wooden bread tray.

The early morning had been quite cool, but by midday the kitchen was ghastly warm and the back door was left open. Maggie's sleeves were rolled up, and her forearms were coated with flour.

Having helped get the fires going, Caleb was then sent to the garden to gather the last of the cucumbers. Hannah planned to make pickles after the baking was finished.

Suddenly, an excited Caleb came running in the back door. "There's a man riding up," he said, "dressed in fancy green-and-yellow livery."

"Oh, my," Maggie said. "That sounds like Adelaide Chilton's footman. Is he alone?"

"All alone," Caleb answered.

"Go to the door and see what he wants," Maggie told him.

"One moment, please," Hannah said as she trimmed the last bit of crust from the edge of one of her pies. "*I'll* go to the door."

If Adelaide were with the footman, Maggie knew she would die right on the spot.

Caleb was on Hannah's heels as she left the kitchen to go to the front door, where the knocker was now sounding. Maggie didn't move. She heard voices; then Caleb came sprinting back into the kitchen. "It *is* the footman, Maggie! He's asking for you. He's asked for Miss Margaret Baldwin. What do you suppose he wants?"

Maggie had no idea. She took a towel and attempted to brush off as much of the flour from her arms and dress as she could. Should she pull her ruffled mobcap off her curls or leave it? Just then, Hannah appeared at the door. "Did Caleb tell you?"

"Yes, ma'am."

"Then what's detaining you? The gentleman is waiting."

"Hannah, I look dreadful," she said. "Simply dreadful."

"My dear Maggie," Hannah said gently, "I don't think it will matter to this gentleman how you look. Come now."

Giving a sigh, Maggie followed Hannah through the house to the front door. The footman named Johnson stood there with his hat in his hands.

"Good day, Miss Margaret Baldwin," he said when Maggie had stepped out onto the front steps. "I've a message from Miss Adelaide Chilton."

"Yes?" Maggie said, smoothing the skirt of her day dress.

"Miss Chilton and her mother have retained a dance master who shall be coming to their home on Thursday afternoons precisely at three to give instruction. Both Miss Chilton and Mrs. Chilton request the pleasure of your presence."

"Oh, my! Hannah, did you hear? Dance lessons at the Chiltons'!"

"I can hear." Hannah stood in the doorway behind her.

"May I? Oh, please, Hannah?"

"We must ask your father this evening."

Maggie paused, then turned back to Johnson. "Please tell Miss Chilton and Mrs. Chilton that I thank them for the kind invitation. I'll ask my father this evening for permission, and I'll let Miss Chilton know tomorrow at church." She felt pleased that she'd thought of the answer quickly and said it so confidently, in spite of how she looked.

"Very well." He replaced his tricorn hat and added, "I shall give her the message. Good day."

"Good day to you, sir."

Maggie fell against the door as she closed it. "Oh, Hannah, I can scarcely breathe. I think I'm going to faint dead away."

"No time for swooning now," Hannah quipped. "Wait till the bread's in the oven."

But Hannah's practicality couldn't dim Maggie's ecstasy. She twirled round and round as she followed Hannah down the long hallway.

Caleb, who had run back to the kitchen ahead of them, leaped out at her, singing, "Maggie's a hoity-toity. Maggie's a hoity-toity."

Maggie was both startled and angered at his outburst. "Caleb, how dare you?" she shouted. "Hush this minute."

"We've no time for quarreling," Hannah said sternly. "There's too much work to be done. Caleb, if you can't speak kindly, don't speak at all. Now get yourself back out to that garden. As for you, Maggie, learning not to raise your voice is more important than learning to dance."

"Yes, ma'am," Maggie said meekly. She couldn't remember the last time Hannah had reprimanded her. She returned to the bread bowl and punched at the soft, swelling dough, pounding it back down. Anger boiled up inside of her at Caleb for spoiling her special moment.

"Dancing," Hannah said under her breath, shaking her head. She placed three pies on the long-handled paddle, carried it to the oven, and shoved the pies deep into the hot brick cavern. "What's this world coming to, what with young ladies dancing?"

"It's quite proper—really it is," Maggie insisted. "Many families in Boston have a dance master come in." Suddenly she had a frightening thought. "You won't talk Father out of letting me go, will you, Hannah?" If Hannah ever did such a thing, Maggie knew she could never quite forgive her.

Hannah was quiet for a moment. "I've never told your father how to raise you children. I don't plan to start now."

"I'll talk to him privately in his study after supper." Turning the dough out onto the breadboard, Maggie took the large butcher knife and swung it down hard—harder than necessary—to cut off a piece of dough to form a loaf. "Far away from Caleb!" she added.

Father was late. That happened sometimes when emergencies arose. Supper without Father was always lonely for Maggie. She wanted to wait for him, but she knew that was silly because they never knew at what time he would arrive.

And besides, Hannah was a stickler for having meals on time.

Caleb had already spoiled her secret by spilling the news to Evan the moment he arrived home. She felt like strangling him. "If you tell Father before I have a chance to speak to him," she warned, "I'll—"

"Maggie," Hannah said sternly. "Empty threats are born in an empty head."

Maggie wanted to sass back, but she bit her lip. During supper, Evan talked about the goings-on at the shipping yard, all of which was of little interest to Maggie. In her mind, she was rehearsing how she would ask Father about the dance instructions.

Caleb happily munched on the warm slices of brown bread. Maggie marveled that he should have so few problems.

Following supper, Evan said he was going out to the stable to oil the tack. Her brother enjoyed the horses almost as much as their father. As soon as the dishes were cleared away, Maggie hurried out to the stable to be with him.

She found him sitting cross-legged on the floor of the tack-room with a harness draped across his lap, rubbing in the linseed oil. Maggie loved the aroma of leather mingled with rich oil. She sat down and watched him for a time. Just being with him seemed to quiet her insides. Evan was steady and unchanging, while her own emotions were flighty and unpredictable.

"What do you think of the invitation that came for me today?" she asked.

"If it's what you want, I'm very happy for you."

"Sometimes when I hear a lively tune, my feet almost take a mind of their own. Now I'll know where to tell them to go."

She laughed at her own little joke, and Evan smiled. "The minuet, the cotillions, and contradances—I'll know each and every one."

Again, Evan was quiet.

"I'm pleased that you're happy for me," Maggie went on. "But what do you think of it? Of dancing instruction, I mean?" She knew she was fishing about, but she truly wanted to know.

He adjusted the bridle, causing the metal pieces to jingle, then looked over at her. His eyes were gentle, just like Father's. Her own green eyes, she'd been told, were like her mother's. "I guess I'm accustomed to instructions resulting in something more tangible than dance. Don't forget, Maggie, I'm a businessman."

Evan truly was becoming a man. It scared her sometimes when she saw how mature he was becoming.

"So you see it as frivolous, perhaps," she ventured. "But do you see it as wrong?"

He shook his head. "I don't see how I could be the judge of that. You must know that for yourself."

"How do you think I can know?"

"Trust your conscience."

Maggie thought on that for a moment. She wasn't sure she could agree. Could she really trust her own conscience? "What do you think Father will say?" She picked up a piece of hay straw and twisted it around her fingers.

"You'll find out soon enough. Why ask me?"

She shrugged, but she knew the answer. She wanted Evan to assure her that Father would indeed say yes. Not wanting him to clam up, as he sometimes did, she changed the subject. "Evan, can *you* trust *your* conscience?"

"Most of the time, I believe I can."

"What does your conscience tell you about the revivalists?"

After some thought, he said, "I don't know enough about the subject to have an opinion."

"You know as much or more than I do."

Evan looked up from his work. "Which isn't much."

Maggie ignored that remark. "Surely you must feel one way or another about it. Adelaide and Celia say they're unlearned, ignorant men who don't even study or write their sermons. They just jump up and speak with no forethought. I think it sounds just terrible. I don't know why they're even allowed to enter the city."

If she was hoping to egg her brother on, she could have saved her breath, for he remained quiet. Presently, there came the sound of Father's carriage, and Maggie leaped to her feet.

"You're saved for now," she told Evan.

He laughed. "There's never an end to your questions."

Together they ran out to greet Father. "I must talk to you privately in your study," Maggie said almost before he could step down. "Just as soon as you've eaten."

"Sounds important," he said, kissing her cheek.

"I'll see to the horses, Father," Evan said. "You look tired."

"I appreciate that, Evan. The Penlows' baby is quite ill. I've been there most of the evening." He put his arm about Maggie's shoulders. "As a matter of fact, I joined the family for supper, so we can have our private conference this very minute if you wish."

Hannah must have duly warned Caleb against saying a word about Maggie's news, for he greeted his father at the kitchen door in a gentlemanly fashion. Maggie sighed with relief. After the doctor had hung up his hat and coat, they went right to his study, where Hannah had already lit the lamps.

"This must not be an ominous occasion," he said as he pulled a chair nearer to his writing desk and waved her toward it. "Your face is cheery, and all the freckles seem to be glowing at one time."

"It's certainly not ominous. It's wonderful!"

"What could be so wonderful?" Dr. Baldwin asked as he sat down at his desk.

Quickly, Maggie explained Johnson's visit and the message from the Chiltons. "It's only one afternoon a week. It wouldn't take much time at all. What do you think, Father? May I go?"

Her father leaned back in his chair and gazed at her. "Dancing instructions. Mmm." He rubbed at his chin. "What was Hannah's reaction?"

"Hannah said she never interfered with how you raised us." Maggie didn't want to tell him that Hannah seemed quite negative about the whole thing.

"It's times like these that I wish your mother were here," he said thoughtfully.

Maggie wished the same thing—many times—but she didn't want to talk about Mother just now. She sat quietly waiting. It was best not to try to sway him one way or the other.

"Obviously, you're very pleased about the invitation."

"Very pleased. I feel honored to be invited."

At last he said, "I appreciate all the hard work you do along-side Hannah each day. One afternoon a week wouldn't hurt." Father stood, came over to her, and took her hand, lifting her to her feet. "I can hardly believe what a lady you've become, Margaret. Yes, tell the Chiltons you accept the invitation. Go on and have a little fun!"

She threw her arms about his neck. "Oh, thank you, Father! Thank you." Her heart felt as though it might explode.

"We have no footman," he said, grinning. "Pray tell, how will you get the message back to the Chiltons?"

"Oh, silly, I'm to talk with Adelaide at church tomorrow."

She hurried out to go tell Evan. At that moment, tomorrow seemed years away and the following Thursday even longer.

CHAPTER 6

Aunt Lucille's Problem

Maggie was grateful that her father was Reuben Souder's stepbrother. That relationship meant the Baldwins sat in the Souder pew at North Church. The spacious church with its grand tiers of galleries was the only church she'd ever known. She had warm memories of being snuggled on her mother's lap in church. Somehow, sitting in their special pew on Sunday mornings made her feel closer to Mother.

This particular Sunday, as her family entered the church, Maggie's mind was on other things. Carefully, she adjusted her hoops to maneuver down the aisle toward the front. Hannah had Caleb in tow, seeing to it that he behaved. Evan always sat on one side of Father and Maggie on the other.

Maggie craned around to see if the Chiltons had arrived, but their pew was still empty, as was the Winthrops'. Gently, she lifted her skirts, arranging the hoops in order to sit down and prevent them from flying up. Uncle Reuben and Aunt Lucille came in just then and sat toward the aisle. Aunt Lucille was still wearing her black mourning garb because of the death of her last baby.

Next came the Winthrops with Celia in the lead. She caught Maggie's eyes, gave a little wave with her fan, and smiled. Maggie nodded and smiled back. Eleanor Winthrop was carrying the baby, who was fussing and complaining loudly.

As the bells pealed for the last time, calling to all the latecomers, the Chiltons arrived. Maggie turned to give a little wave and was astonished at what she saw. Pert Chilton and Adelaide both wore powdered wigs, the curls of which were piled to a nice height. At the neck in the back hung several loose curls, some of which hung over Adelaide's shoulder. Soft tiny feather plumes were arranged fanlike at the crown of curls on top. Their full-skirted satin overdresses swished as they came down the aisle.

Maggie had never seen such luxuriant hair fashion. She was almost too shocked to wave. It was obvious everyone in church was staring at them, but Adelaide and Pert seemed to enjoy the attention. From what Hannah had told Maggie, Pert and Lucas Chilton had been titled people in England and were accustomed to being the center of attention.

Suddenly, Maggie felt overwhelmed. She marveled that Adelaide would even want to be friends with her. Maggie had one church dress, which she wore every Sunday. She would, in fact, have only one dress to wear to the Thursday dance instructions. Maybe she should ask Father if she might purchase fabric to make a new dress. But no, that would never do. She was already planning to ask him for a new saddle. There simply wasn't enough money in the Baldwin household for extravagances.

The congregation brought out their psalters as they sang

psalms together in lovely harmony. Following the singing, the Reverend Joshua Gee, dressed in flowing robes, ascended the stairs to the pulpit loft. Maggie fidgeted and toyed with her fan, unable to concentrate on the message as her worries gnawed away inside her.

Difficult though it may be, her only choice was to refuse the invitation for the dance instruction. By the time the Reverend Gee had turned the hourglass over several times, Maggie had made her decision. Better not to go at all than to go and make a fool of herself.

For the congregation of North Church, gathering in the churchyard after service was as much a social event as was launching a ship or serving high tea. Clusters of people gathered beneath the sprawling trees to visit about the week's events. As soon as Maggie was out the door and down the steps, she was grabbed by both Adelaide and Celia. Giggling, they drew her away from the crowd and toward the Chiltons' carriage.

"I was so eager all during service to hear your answer about the dance instruction," Adelaide said, laughing, "I could barely sit still. It occurred to me to use one of my brothers' slingshots and ping that hourglass, breaking it all to tiny pieces."

"Can't you just see the look on the reverend's face if you did that," Celia joined in, "with the sand flowing all down the pulpit into little piles."

In spite of herself, Maggie laughed along with them. How silly to think that breaking the hourglass would change the time or quicken the sermon. Her thoughts of refusing the invitation fled. The girls didn't seem to care what Maggie was wearing. They just wanted her to be a friend.

"Father gave his approval," Maggie told them. "I may attend the dance instructions."

Before the words were out, Adelaide and Celia gave excited squeals.

"You'll be quite impressed with our dance master," Adelaide confided when they'd quieted down. "He's just arrived from England and is greatly in demand." She spread her fan and whispered behind it. "But since Mother and Father knew him in London, we have first claim on his time."

"My mother's so pleased to think I'll be growing in the social graces," Celia put in.

"Isn't it terribly expensive?" Maggie asked. Then she wished she hadn't mentioned money.

"No matter," Adelaide said as though the brush of her fan eliminated the problem. "My mother plans to see to it that quaint old Boston grows in the ways of proper 'societal interchanges' as she calls it. Even if she must do it single-handedly and pay to do it."

Maggie glanced over at Mrs. Chilton, who was talking and laughing with those in the churchyard. Maggie could easily imagine the lady doing almost anything she put her mind to.

"The Thursday instructions may begin with just the three of us, but eventually Mother expects it to grow. One day there may be evening classes with young men in attendance." Adelaide leaned nearer to Maggie. "Perchance, Evan may even want to attend."

Maggie doubted very much that Evan would ever attend dance instruction, but she didn't want to say so. "You can always invite him and see," she said.

Adelaide giggled. "I might just do that," she said.

"Your new hair fashion is stunning," Celia told Adelaide. "I must talk to Mother about our having wigs, as well."

Adelaide touched one of the curls that hung over her shoulder. "This is how ladies are wearing their hair in all the courts of London. My aunt sends Mother sketches—we receive new ideas with nearly every ship arriving from England."

Being with these girls meant that Maggie would be up on all the latest fashions. The very thought made her heart pound in excitement.

Just then, Caleb came running up. "Father's looking for you, Maggie. It's time to go."

Quickly, she bid her friends farewell and joined her family at her father's carriage. As usual, two or three young widows had converged on Father. Different ones continually sought him out to gain his attention. Maggie was secretly pleased that he ignored them all. She wasn't interested in having a stepmother.

As was their custom each Sunday, they drove to Uncle Reuben and Aunt Lucille's home for dinner. The Souders lived just up the hill from the Baldwins in the house where Maggie's father had grown up. Father said the house didn't look much different back then, except for all the unique artifacts Uncle Reuben collected from around the world—lush rugs from the Orient, a delicate tea service from India, pink conch shells from the West Indies, and, of course, the best pieces of furniture from London. In spite of all the clutter, the house seemed hollow and empty to Maggie.

Since Hannah felt she must make her contribution toward the dinner, Father made a stop at their house. Caleb and Evan ran inside and brought out several pies to take along.

"'Twould be ever so much simpler if they would come and eat with us every week," Hannah said as they were on their way once again.

"I believe we've discussed this before," Father said in his quiet voice.

He was right. Hannah said the same thing nearly every Sunday. Maggie agreed with Hannah. She'd much rather have the Souders come to the Baldwins' bright, noisy, airy house than to go to their sad, dark, dreary one.

While the Souders could afford to hire several servants, they retained only a lady named Freegrace, who'd been with the family for years. Actually, a number of servants had come and gone in years past, but Aunt Lucille, who was sometimes difficult to please, was never happy with any of them. She trusted only dear, sweet Freegrace.

As the carriage drew to a halt in the front dooryard, Freegrace hurried out to greet them and to help carry in the pies.

In spite of the awful scars on her face and arms from a childhood accident, Freegrace always had a smile. She seemed to shine with an inner peace and beauty.

"The Souders arrived home just ahead of you," Freegrace told them, "and Mr. Reuben is putting his horses away. Mrs. Lucille went to lie down for a time."

Maggie clucked her tongue. "She's still feeling poorly? It's been nearly six months. Do you think she'll recover?"

"Her body would recover were it not being taken down by a sad spirit," Freegrace said as she held open the front door. "She grieved deeply for the loss of the third child. The loss of the fourth was more than she could bear."

"Evan and I will take the carriage around to the stable," Father said. "You ladies go on."

"I want to come with you," Caleb protested.

"Help the ladies with the pies and then come on out," his father suggested.

"Yes, sir." He took two of the pies and sped into the house ahead of all of them.

The windows of the Souder home were cloaked in heavy damask draperies, leaving the house dark and cheerless. Maggie hurried through the hallways to the bright kitchen in the back, where Freegrace would not allow curtains at the windows.

A fat black kettle of brown beans hung over the fire in the massive kitchen fireplace. The rich aroma coming from the bubbling kettle filled the entire house.

Without being told, Maggie went to the parlor closet, took down the pewter plates, and set the table. Presently, Aunt Lucille came out from the front room bedchamber.

"Hello, Maggie. How kind of you to help. Where is everyone?"

"Good afternoon, Aunt Lucille. Father and the boys are at the stable, and Hannah is in the kitchen with Freegrace."

"My, my, I really must lend a hand. I can't expect all of you to do my work." Aunt Lucille's mourning dress hung loosely on her thin frame, and her small face seemed even paler against the harshness of the black.

"No one minds helping, Aunt Lucille," Maggie said gently. "I don't believe there's much left to do."

Aunt Lucille gave a weak smile and moved slowly to the

kitchen. It had never occurred to Maggie before that a person's spirit could be sick inside. But then, she'd heard her father speak of some people who had a will to live and others who did not.

Maggie could remember her aunt in happier days. What an alive, vibrant lady she'd been. How could she be so excited over dance instructions when her aunt was in such deep misery? Surely there must be something someone could do to help poor Aunt Lucille.

CHAPTER 7

The Mystery Girl

The dance master, Mr. Helver, was tall and thin with a hook nose and shaggy brows. His long feet seemed far too big for his body. When Maggie arrived at the Chilton home and saw him for the first time, she nearly laughed out loud. How could she take seriously a man who looked so funny? She soon learned, however, that Mr. Helver was great fun. If there was anything he could do better than dance, it was make jokes about himself.

"If I can learn how to steer these big boat-feet," he'd say with a chuckle, "surely I can teach you girls where to put your dainty little slippered feet."

Pert Chilton—she encouraged the girls to call her by her first name—played the spinet with a touch as light and cheerful as she herself was. Unlike the cluttered Souder home, the Chilton parlor was set about with the perfect number of appointments and a logical arrangement of furniture pieces. The soft colors were in good taste, lending to the brightness of the large room. The rug had been rolled up and moved out of the way, and the place bubbled with music and laughter.

Maggie was sure someone had sprinkled her feet with magic dust. Like a frisky lamb skipping about the meadow, she bobbed and bounced and flounced about, with the music coursing through her. She found herself wishing it would never end.

At half past the hour, Mr. Helver called for a rest period. "You lovely young ladies need no rest, I'm sure," he said, as he caught his breath, "but most assuredly, I do." He seated himself in the overstuffed chair by the bay windows, fanning his face with his white handkerchief.

Laughing, the girls collapsed onto the nearby sofa. "I need a rest, too," Adelaide said. "I seem to be quite weak from lack of practice. Mother," she said, turning to Pert, "we may have to have dances every week so I can build up my strength."

Pert laughed. "Every week would be a terrible strain on the servants. They'll need much more training before we hold our first dance."

Hayley came into the room with a tray full of glasses of water for everyone. Maggie found her throat was quite dry.

Pert rose from where she sat at the spinet and pulled a smaller chair close to the sofa.

"Would the servants be prepared by Christmastime?" Adelaide asked.

Maggie watched Pert's hands as she reached for a glass of water. They were fine-boned, smooth as ivory, with tapered fingers that seemed especially created for playing music on the spinet. These hands had never been plunged into a tub of wash-water and lye soap; that was certain.

Pert took a sip of the water, then thought a moment. "By Christmas? Possibly."

"Then might we hold a Christmas ball?" Adelaide asked.

Her mother's face lit up. "Why, Adelaide, what a perfectly splendid notion. Why, yes, Christmas would be perfect. We could schedule it shortly after Clark and Oliver return from school for their holiday."

Adelaide leaped to her feet and spun about. "How sublime. A ball! We'll have a Christmas ball." She turned to Maggie and Celia. "Of course you're all invited—and your families, too."

"Come, ladies," Mr. Helver said, leaping to his feet like a jack-in-the-box. "If you're to be ready for a Christmas ball, we mustn't waste my valuable time. You're not paying me to sit idly about."

There were several cotillions that Mr. Helver introduced, and at first the sequences were somewhat confusing. It helped that Pert had already taught Adelaide several of the steps. After hearing the news of an upcoming ball, Maggie could hardly keep her mind on the instructions. Instead, she envisioned herself dancing about the floor at a real ball. Now she would have to have a new dress.

By the time the hour of instruction was completed, Maggie felt she had conquered most of the steps. Adelaide's mother even commented on how quickly she had learned. "You seem to be a natural at dancing, Maggie. How pleased I am that you could come and be with us."

Her words and her friendly smile gave Maggie a warm glow inside.

After Mr. Helver left, Pert sent the girls to the nursery, where they enjoyed a grand tea party. This made the day doubly pleasurable.

Later, Maggie couldn't remember how their conversation had turned to the revivalists, but as they were eating sweetcakes and sipping tea, they were once again laughing at the wild antics of these strange people.

"I heard of a mob in New York City," Celia said, "who followed their preacher through the streets, dancing and shouting and singing. They wave their hands in the air like this." Setting down her teacup, she demonstrated by closing her eyes and waving her arms back and forth above her head while the other two snickered.

"It's as though they think no one else is a Christian since we don't believe as they do," Adelaide was saying.

Maggie wanted to ask just what the revivalists did believe, but she didn't want them to know how ignorant she was about the matter.

"They call themselves the 'New Light,'" Celia said with a little sniff. "I suppose that makes us the 'Old Light.' How dare they? I don't think conversion is necessary, do you?"

Thankfully, Adelaide answered. "Of course not. I was baptized as a baby, and I've been in church all my life. I don't need anyone to tell me whether or not I'm a Christian—I already know."

Maggie agreed with that fact. No one had better try to tell her she wasn't a Christian.

By the time Father stopped by in his carriage to fetch her, she had a much better idea of what the revivalists were all about. And she didn't like them one bit.

A cold wind had whipped up while she was enjoying the warmth and laughter of the Chilton home. Stepping outside, she pulled her cloak tightly about her and put up the hood before allowing Father to assist her into the carriage.

"Your cheeks are pink," he said, "and I don't believe it's from the cold. I trust you had an enjoyable afternoon."

"The afternoon was sublime," she said, echoing Adelaide's expression.

"Sublime, was it? That's good to hear. And did you learn to dance?" He clucked at the team and the harnesses gave a delicate jingle as the horses stepped out.

"I did learn and very well, too. Pert said so."

"You mean Mrs. Chilton?"

"She wants us to call her by her first name. It's not improper when the adult requests it, is it?"

"I suppose not."

Dusk was beginning to gather. A tiny smattering of stars had appeared. The air was clear and sharp, which meant there was sure to be a hard freeze. Maggie found herself wondering if Hannah had been able to bring in all the pumpkins and squash and the last turnips. Her conscience was smitten that she'd not been there to help.

The afternoon, however, had been too wonderful to have to think about an old garden. "You should have seen the dance master," she told her father. Her description of Mr. Helver's lanky frame and large feet and the manner in which he told silly jests brought a smile to Father's face.

"Seems to be a jolly fellow," he commented absently.

"Perhaps you'll meet him."

"Not likely. Dancing's not one of my finer talents."

"But if there were a dance—say it was a grand ball—and you

were invited, you'd come, wouldn't you? Wouldn't you?"

Father looked over at Maggie. "Something tells me this is not an empty question."

"Oh, Father," she said, unable to contain her excitement, "the Chiltons are planning a Christmas ball, and we're all invited. *All* our families, Adelaide said. Celia's family, as well. Governor Shirley will no doubt be there, too. But," she concluded, dropping her folded hands into her lap, "I would have to have a new frock."

"I see no reason you couldn't make a new frock—you and Hannah together."

"But I also wanted to ask you for a sidesaddle for my birthday, and it all seems so very much to ask for. Is it terribly wrong to want two things at the same time?"

At this outburst, Father laughed out loud. She wasn't sure why he was laughing, but it sounded glorious in the still night air.

"My dear Margaret, slow down and back up. You're much too fast for this weary old doctor. What's all this about a sidesaddle? You've said nothing about it before. I had no idea you wanted to ride sidesaddle."

"I didn't when I was still a little girl, Father. But all ladies ride sidesaddle, and well. . ."

"Ah yes, we're back to this subject of your growing up, and I keep forgetting. Tell me, does your sidesaddle have to be a shiny new one right off a ship from London?"

"Oh, no." She gave a little laugh at the thought of the Baldwins ordering much of anything from London except for her father's medical equipment. "You know me better than that."

"If not, then I believe I can barter for a rather nice sidesaddle. Boston is probably full of them. In fact, I'll start with Uncle

Reuben. How will that be?"

Suddenly she felt warm, safe, and snug beside her father. She really loved him very much. "That would be. . ."

"Sublime?"

They laughed together. "Sublime," she echoed. "And then I can have the new dress?"

"You can have the new dress."

"And you'll come to the ball?"

"Now, now, let's not get carried away. For the present, let me think about it."

Just as Father turned the team to take the carriage up Hanover Street from Tremont Avenue, a man came running toward them, waving his arms. "Dr. Baldwin," he called out. "Dr. Baldwin, please come! My sister's dying! Please come!"

"Jump in," Father told him. "Show me the way." Turning to Maggie, he said, "Looks like you'll have to come along."

Father had never forced any of his children to work at his apothecary shop nor to accompany him on calls. He respected their wishes in their choice of vocation. Evan had ridden along a few times, but Maggie never had. She couldn't bear to see someone sick and suffering.

The man who jumped into the back of the carriage was of the beggarly type. As he gave directions, Father drove the carriage south of Long Wharf into an area where the buildings were crowded together. The carriage lamps cast eerie shadows on the walls of the old buildings. Here there were no rolling pastures, no leafy shade trees, no elegant flower gardens. Seldom, if ever, had Maggie been down these streets.

Presently, the man instructed Father to turn into a narrow

alleyway because, as the man said, "Me sister lives in a room in the rear." Midway through the alleyway, he directed Father to stop. "This here's it. Please wait, and I'll let her know I fetched you."

The man jumped to the ground and tapped at the wooden door. Slowly the door opened, and there stood a little girl. Maggie looked and then looked again. She could hardly believe it. It was the little girl she'd seen on the dock the day of the launch!

CHAPTER 8

Maggie's Best Birthday

As soon as Maggie recognized the girl, she remembered what Adelaide had said about her. . .how Maggie had been warned not to even touch her.

"Maggie, I can't let you stay out here. You understand, don't you?" her father was saying as he stepped down.

Under other circumstances, wild horses couldn't have dragged her into that tiny room that fronted on the filthy alleyway, but her father's expression gave her no choice.

The little girl stared as Maggie followed her father into the cramped, smelly room. In the far corner, lying on a cot with a dirty straw tick, was a woman whose ashen face told Maggie she might be nearly dead.

Father turned to the little girl and asked a few questions. Her name, she said, was Ann Cradock. The ill woman was her mother, Sarah. The mother had had little to eat since the previous day, and there was no food in the house. The doctor turned around to say something to Sarah's brother, who had directed them there, but he was gone.

"Did you see him leave?" Father asked Maggie. She had not. She was too busy staring at this horrible place. Living in such squalor was unimaginable to her.

"I was going to send him, but. . ." Her father was pulling his leather pouch from his waistcoat pocket. "Maggie, we must. . . There is a grocer's shop over on Water Street at the corner." He dropped a few shillings in her hand. "Take the lantern from the carriage and go purchase cheese, bread, and a little tea."

Fear gripped at Maggie's insides. *Go out on that street? Alone? What is Father thinking of?* Then she looked at the sick lady and the sad little girl.

"The shop may be closed," she told him, straining to steady her voice. "What should I do then?"

"I know the grocer," came Ann's quiet voice from the corner.

"Of course you do," Father said gently. "And he would recognize you. Will you show Maggie the way?"

Ann nodded.

Having the little girl along was some comfort, but not much. Maggie had heard stories of people who'd been beaten, robbed, and left for dead on these back streets. The cold wind blew down the alleyway as they went outside. Ann's shawl was thin and ragged. Carefully, Maggie stepped up on the carriage and lifted out the lantern.

"I've not had a nice light before," Ann said.

"Well, you have one now."

The shop was closed, but Ann knew the way to the back, where she knocked and knocked until the grocer's wife came to the door.

"Why, it's little Ann," the lady said in surprise.

Maggie quickly introduced herself, explained the situation, and asked if they could purchase a few items.

The woman shook her head and pursed her lips. "There's no more credit. . . ."

"No, no," Maggie said. "*I'm* making the purchase." She rattled the coins in her hand.

"Oh, mercy me, that's much different. Come along."

Maggie waited as the tea, bread, and cheese were packaged, while Ann walked about studying each and every barrel, as well as every counter. From the pennies Maggie received in change, she purchased one piece of candy and handed it to Ann. The girl's eyes fairly sparkled.

Back at the room, Father had laid a small fire in the fireplace, and water was heating in a kettle. Maggie brewed the tea and watched as her father helped Sarah Cradock take a few sips from a cup. When he was satisfied that she could swallow nourishment, he prepared to leave, giving Ann specific instructions for her mother's care through the night.

When they were back in the carriage, Maggie's father thanked her for assisting. "This certainly wasn't what I had planned, but that's the way of a doctor's life."

"Father, did you know that Sarah Cradock is not a nice lady?"

"Perhaps not, Maggie, but right now she's a very sick lady, and that's all that matters."

That night, as Maggie lay warm and cozy in her own featherbed, the entire Baldwin house seemed different to her. There were no servants such as the Chiltons had, but she had a father who cared for her and a loving nanny who doted on her. She was warm and dry, and foodstuffs overflowed in both the pantry and the cellar.

Even the next day as she went about her work, Maggie was unable to get the picture of hungry little Ann Cradock out of her mind. In her studies, she'd learned many scriptures that talked about helping the poor. She mulled over an idea of how she might help Ann.

The following Thursday, after another delightful dance lesson had left them breathless, the girls gathered in the nursery for tea. During a brief lull in the conversation, Maggie told the girls about Ann Cradock, her dying mother, and her lack of food and warm clothes. "It occurred to me," Maggie said, as she nibbled a slice of lemon cake, "that perhaps we could give her some of our old clothes."

While Maggie expected some reluctance from her friends, nothing could have prepared her for the outburst that came.

Celia stiffened instantly. "Have some street urchin wear a dress of mine right out there in the marketplace? I should say not! What if someone recognized it?"

"Besides," Adelaide joined in, "wherever would such a raga-muffin wear a fine frock of silk and satin? One doesn't put finery on a sow who goes back to wallow in the mud." Adelaide set down her teacup and placed her hand softly on Maggie's arm. "Maggie, my dear, I know you mean well, but stop a moment and think—you can't be expected to dress all the beggars in Boston."

"No, I suppose you're right," Maggie agreed. "I guess I spoke too quickly. I had not thought the situation through." How she wished she'd kept her thoughts to herself. What must the girls think of her? But no matter, for soon they were talking of other things such as plans for the upcoming Christmas ball.

As the days passed, excitement of Maggie's upcoming thirteenth birthday crowded out all thoughts of Ann Cradock. And Thanksgiving preparations almost crowded out Maggie's birthday.

Annually, the governor proclaimed a Thursday either late in November or early in December for the colony's giving of thanks, and this year it was to be the last Thursday in November, the twenty-eighth—five days after Maggie's birthday on the twenty-third.

Hannah had already set aside a good store of spices and molasses as well as a barrel of flour for when the Thanksgiving baking began in earnest. In a wooden cage in the dooryard, a fat chicken and a gobbling turkey were held until time for Hannah to lop off their heads and pluck them.

Together, Maggie and Hannah had shopped for the perfect fabric for Maggie's ball gown, but now there was precious little time to sew on it. "After all the fuss of Thanksgiving is over," Hannah promised, "we'll spend every spare moment on your dress."

The Pierces came for dinner to celebrate Maggie's birthday. Hannah had prepared simple fare, since the best of everything was being saved for Thanksgiving—and the Pierces would be with them for the holiday, as well.

Following their meal, Evan and Jacob slipped out of the house and returned from the stable with Maggie's gift of a new sidesaddle. Everyone, even Father, teased her about wanting to sit upon such a contraption, but she rubbed her fingers over the smooth leather, admired the tool work, and was extremely pleased. "Thank you, Father," she said. "I thought you were going to find one that had already been used. This looks brand-new."

"Favor was with me," Dr. Baldwin said, giving her a teasing wink.

She might never know how her father managed the fine purchase—or exchange—whichever it was. She turned to Evan and Jacob. "Let's go to the stable. I want to try it out."

"One moment, young lady," Hannah interrupted. "What about the rest of your gifts?"

"More? There's more?"

Laughter rippled around the table. "Most young ladies would be demanding more," Ben said with a chuckle, "but our Maggie is happy with just an old sidesaddle."

Of course it wasn't "just an old sidesaddle," but, as usual, Ben was teasing her.

"Here's my gift," Hannah said, handing over a small tissue package tied up with embroidery thread. Gently, Maggie pulled off the thread and unrolled the paper. There lay a piece of the most elegant lace she'd ever seen. "Oh, Hannah!"

"We'll use it for the ruffled sleeves and the inset of the bodice of your ball gown," Hannah said. "How will that be?"

"Perfect," she managed to whisper.

"And look!" Caleb said, bringing out a bigger parcel from the drawer of the sideboard. "Just look what else. We all got this for you—all of us together." He waved his hand about the table, which meant even Ben and Judith had joined in.

Maggie marveled that the talkative Caleb had been able to contain this secret.

The brown package lay lightly in her lap. Her nervous fingers picked at the tight knot in the twine until Jacob reached over with his jackknife. "Allow me."

She held the package out, he cut, and the cord fell away. There in the paper lay a pair of soft kid dancing pumps—all in white. The high square heels would make her feel even more like a lady. She could scarcely believe her good fortune. She looked at the smiling faces surrounding her.

Hugging the shoes, she said, "Thank you, all of you. Thank you for your kindness and thoughtfulness." Then she went around the table hugging everyone—everyone except Jacob, that is.

Later that evening, she and Jacob and Evan scurried out through the cold night air to the stable. It was too dark and too cold to ride, but she saddled Amaryllis with her new sidesaddle and then mounted and walked her up and down the length of the stable.

Evan took one of the lanterns and checked each of the stalls, talking softly to each of the horses as he did so. Jacob had hung the other lantern on a nail on the wall.

"It'll take some getting used to," she told the boys, "but I like it. I like it very much. This is how a lady is supposed to ride." She came back to Amaryllis's stall and stopped. Jacob reached up to help her down.

"Thinking of you dancing the night away at the Chiltons' ball will take some getting used to, as well," he said.

"You don't approve of dancing?" she asked.

Evan stepped up to rejoin them. "I don't think that's what he's getting at, Maggie," her brother said, smiling. To Jacob, he said, "I'd most gladly let you go in my place, my friend. I find the whole idea frightfully dull. But Father insists that I go."

"He does?" Maggie said. "I mean, he did? He's told you to go?" Things were moving too quickly. Her mind seemed to be swimming.

Evan laughed. "Father informed me we're all going, even Hannah. He said the whole family was invited and the whole family will go. Can you imagine Caleb eating up all the refreshments?"

This was turning out to be Maggie's best birthday ever. As much as her father disliked such social gatherings, she realized he was doing all this for her.

It wasn't until later in the evening after all the company had gone home that she was able to think more about Jacob's comment. Why wouldn't he want her dancing at the Chiltons'— unless he meant he wanted to be there dancing with her? Suddenly, her face grew very warm in spite of the chill in her unheated bedchamber.

Soon they would all move their feather ticks downstairs to be closer to the heat through the worst of the winter. She slipped into her long nightgown and buried herself beneath the warm quilts.

It seemed strange that Jacob wished he were attending the ball and Evan wished he were not. *Do people always want what they don't have?* she wondered.

And why should the Baldwins be invited to this ball anyway? It made little sense. By a strange twist of fate, her stepgrandfather had deeded this fine house to her father and also left him a tidy sum of money. In reality, Maggie was the daughter of an Irish immigrant mother and a hardworking doctor father. Her family was no different than the Pierce family, but they were invited to the ball and the Pierces were not.

The more she thought about it, the more like an imposter Maggie felt. How confusing life could be.

The Christmas Ball

The day before Thanksgiving, Maggie went to the market with Hannah to pick up a few last-minute items. As yet there hadn't been enough snowfall for the sleigh to be brought out of the carriage house. Maggie hoped they could take the sleigh to the ball. What fun that would be.

The streets around Faneuil Hall and Dock Square were elbow-to-elbow with holiday shoppers. That morning Maggie had helped Hannah butcher the chicken and turkey and dress them out. That night the fowls would be put on to boil.

"Let's buy a sugarloaf and a few candies just for the fun of it," Hannah was saying. "The little ones will enjoy a special treat."

"So would I," Maggie said with a laugh. "That is, if I can find room for candy after all those pies you've baked."

"We'll make one more stop in here, and then we will go to your father's shop to see if he's ready to drive us home."

As she turned to follow Hannah into the shop, Maggie spied a small girl dressed in thin rags walking along the street. She immediately recognized Ann Cradock. Maggie wondered how the girl didn't freeze with only her brown shawl as protection against the raw November wind.

Maggie drew her cloak more tightly about her and hurried into the warmth of the store. By the time they came out again, the girl was nowhere to be seen.

With most of the holiday meal prepared, the Baldwins set off Thanksgiving morning for a meeting at the church. Hannah and Father had successfully convinced Uncle Reuben and Aunt Lucille to come to the Baldwin home for the day. And, of course, all the Pierces would be there.

There were many guests at the church meeting since family members from out of town were home for the holiday. Fair weather and favorable travel conditions had increased the number greatly. The usual Sunday two-hour sermon was shortened because the pastor knew the parishioners had mountains of food at home waiting to be consumed.

Two extra members sat in the Chilton pew—Clark and Oliver were home from Harvard for a few days. Maggie had never met the Chilton brothers because they were gone from home much of the time. When not at school, they were usually off traveling. Both looked dapper in their elegant powdered wigs and gold-trimmed greatcoats.

In the churchyard following service, Adelaide immediately steered Maggie toward the Chilton brothers. "Maggie, come meet my brothers. This is Clark," she said, indicating the older of the two, "and this is the one who teases me mercilessly,

Oliver." The two bore little resemblance other than their nice smiles. While Clark's face was lean and chiseled, Oliver's was fuller, softer, with blue eyes that laughed in merriment.

"And this is Margaret Baldwin, daughter of Dr. Baldwin," Adelaide said to her brothers, "but we call her Maggie."

Both young men gave jaunty bows on introduction. "My pleasure, Maggie," said Clark simply. But Oliver held her hand a moment longer than Clark and said, "I understand you will be attending the Christmas ball that Mother is giving. I'd be honored if you held a place for me on your dance card." His blue eyes danced as he spoke.

Maggie swallowed quickly, trying not to choke. "I believe I could find a place. Thank you for asking."

There was no chance for further conversation, because it was time to go. At her family's carriage, Evan leaned over and whispered, "What did the Chilton boys have to say to you?"

She gave him a puzzled look. It wasn't like him to ask such a thing. "If you'd wanted to know, you could have come over and been more sociable yourself," she snapped.

He asked nothing further.

Throughout the rest of the day, Maggie's heart pounded every time she remembered Oliver's words. The excitement of his invitation greatly overshadowed the day of feasting. In fact, she almost looked forward to the day being over and all the guests leaving.

A game of "button, button, who's got the button," was of little interest to Maggie, but since Evan and Jacob were good sports to play with the little ones, she joined in as well. After several parlor games were played, Judith put her boys down for naps. Maggie seized the moment to head for the stable. Jacob and Evan followed.

"If you ride sidesaddle," Jacob warned, "we may race off and leave you."

"Go right ahead," she said coolly, firming the lovely new saddle on Amaryllis's back. "I've ridden alone before. I can do it again." The truth was, she rarely ever rode without a chaperone.

Evan looked at her over the back of his horse. "That's a fine way to talk to Jacob. Are you feeling all right?"

"I believe you asked me that same thing the other day. Of course I feel all right."

"Then why are you acting so oddly? You haven't been yourself all day."

Maggie led Amaryllis out of the stable without answering, chiding herself for wearing her feelings in broad view. She moved to the mounting block, which she needed now that she rode with hoops. A jump and a swing up just wouldn't do. She was in the saddle before the boys came out.

"I would have helped you if you'd waited a moment," Jacob said. His tone sounded hurt, but Maggie ignored it. She couldn't help how Jacob chose to feel.

In spite of Jacob's warning, the boys didn't ride off and leave her; rather, the three of them sauntered along at a slow gait. Today they chose to ride through the pastures near and around Copp's Hill. They rode along chatting about small things of little consequence. It was a relief to get out of the stuffy house. The air off the Charles River felt cool and refreshing on Maggie's face.

As they rode down the hill toward the Charlestown Ferry,

Jacob suddenly recognized someone boarding the ferry. "I believe that's Mr. Leverett down here. He accompanied the Reverend Jonathan Edwards to our church last week. Excuse me while I go extend to him a greeting."

Maggie waited with Evan as they watched Jacob ride to greet the man, talk a few moments, then ride back to rejoin them. The name *Jonathan Edwards* was one that Maggie had heard often from Adelaide and Celia.

"I fail to understand how you could associate yourself with ones who are in such a spirit of error," Maggie said to Jacob as they continued the ride.

"And how do you see it as a spirit of error?" Jacob asked.

"Unlearned men who've not been ordained, jumping up to speak before they've even written out thoughtful sermons—of course it's in error."

"How can you pass judgment when you've not even heard what they have to say?"

"The scriptures instruct us to do things decently and in order," she said stiffly. "I've heard about the disorderly tumults and indecent behavior. Wild people waving their hands and shouting—that's not how church should be conducted."

"When men like Jonathan Edwards and George Whitefield preach, thousands flock to hear them. Can all those people be wrong?"

"It's not difficult to lead weak people astray," Maggie said, which was something Celia had often remarked. "Revivalists shouldn't be allowed to come into another preacher's area. They're too dangerous."

"The Reverend Colman at Brattle Street Church *invites*

them to come," Jacob said.

Maggie shook her head. "That makes no sense. No sense at all."

"Have you ever seen a life totally changed by the power of God?"

"What do you mean? My life is different from a sinner's because I'm a Christian."

"Have you ever seen a sinner become broken and contrite in humble repentance and then turn suddenly joyful because he knows he's been redeemed?"

Maggie wasn't sure how to answer. The question confused her.

"Perhaps you should come one time and see for yourself, Maggie."

"I never would," she said flatly, closing the conversation. Later she realized that her brother had not said one word during the entire conversation, so she still didn't know how he felt on the issue.

With Thanksgiving out of the way, Maggie and Hannah spent every afternoon and evening working on the new dress. True to his word, Father allowed Maggie to decide about the Latin lessons, and she quickly and with great relief put an end to them.

The satin frock was turning out lovelier than she'd ever dreamed. Hannah could simply glance at a dress and deftly copy the design. Her skills were amazing.

One afternoon as they sat together in the sitting room, it began to snow. Their chairs and the sewing table were arranged close to the blazing fireplace. Unbidden, thoughts of Ann Cradock came to Maggie's mind. She thought of her own warm home, the new dress, and all the blessings she enjoyed. Quite without planning, she told Hannah about Ann, describing in detail the sad state of her living conditions.

"I was wondering," Maggie said, "if we might have enough fabric to make a warm cloak for the girl."

Hannah smiled. "What a generous, kind thought, Maggie. I believe we have enough in the scrap bag to make the lining. We could purchase a warm wool for the outer layer. Let's make one for the mother, as well, since they both seem to be in need."

Maggie wasn't sure about helping a mother who was living in sin, but she'd leave that to Hannah. The cloak she stitched would be for little Ann. But even as she made her decision, she wondered how her paltry efforts could ever make a difference.

Several days of snow meant it was time for Evan to bring out the sleigh, clean it up, and wax the runners. To Maggie's delight, they would ride in the sleigh to the ball.

Hannah assisted in creating a crown of copper curls high atop Maggie's head, much like the wig Adelaide now wore. They worked on her hair most of the afternoon prior to the ball. Maggie could scarcely calm herself, and bubbles floated about in her tummy most of the day. She had worn her new dance pumps to the last two dance instruction sessions in order to get used to them. They were like wearing a pair of soft gloves.

Hannah helped her lace up her whalebone stays till she could scarcely breathe. Her pink shift and quilted petticoat were draped over the pocket hoops, and the soft green brocade overskirt lay over that. The lacy sleeve ruffles hung gracefully from her elbows as she turned about so Hannah could make adjustments here and there. At last, she was ready.

Father surprised Maggie by wearing a new maroon greatcoat and new knee breeches with ribboned garters that matched his coat. He bowed low, almost sweeping the floor with his cocked hat, as Maggie descended the stairs.

"My dear Margaret," he said, gazing up at her, "you will undoubtedly be the loveliest girl at the ball."

"Thank you, Father," she said, taking his arm. "You say that only because I'm yours."

"I say that because it's true," he insisted. "How I wish your mother could see you now."

"What do you think she would say?" Maggie wanted to know.

"Why," he answered with eyes twinkling, "she'd say you'll be the loveliest girl at the ball."

"Oh, Father!"

"I expect you to save the first space on that dance card for me."

"I will," she said, "and that's a promise."

Evan agreed to drive the sleigh, and it pulled up to the dooryard with bells jingling brightly in the velvety winter night. Everyone was dressed in their finery, and Maggie was quite proud of her little family.

Lights were ablaze in the Chilton home, causing every window to shine golden against the darkness. Even the dormer windows on the third floor shone like miniature lighthouses. Beacon Street and the yard of the Chilton home were filled with sleighs as well as a few carriages that had managed to make it through the snow. Several footmen stood about seeing to the horses. Since the Baldwins had no footman, Evan would have to periodically come outside and check on the team.

The clogs strapped on Maggie's feet helped to keep her new pumps out of the wet snow. She did her best to keep her skirts lifted as her father helped both her and Hannah up the walk to the front door. Even before the butler opened the door to let them in, the lilting melodies greeted them. Tantalizing aromas of cider and eggnog floated about. Boughs of evergreen and yards of lacy ribbons decorated the front hallway, giving it a festive air. The servants had barely taken their wraps when Adelaide was there by her side, breathlessly greeting everyone.

"The house is lovely, Miss Adelaide," Hannah said politely. Maggie wondered if even Hannah felt a bit overwhelmed at such excess.

Father also made polite remarks and then was met by Lucas Chilton, who was as regal in appearance as the governor himself. Mr. Chilton shook Father's hand and then ushered him into the ballroom. The double parlors were opened and all the rugs taken up. The furniture was pushed against the walls to give the maximum space for dancing. Refreshments were being served in the Chiltons' sitting room down the hall. Here, too, the rooms had been festooned with garlands of greenery, highlighted in graceful ribboned bows.

Maggie was surprised to see an orchestra made up of several violins, a cello, a clarinet, and of course the spinet. Small wonder the music gave off such an exquisite sound.

Surely no court of London ever hosted such a group in such

grand style and elegance. The room exploded with a rainbow of color from the men's gold-trimmed greatcoats and ladies' satiny dresses.

Maggie had never received so many compliments in her entire life. One person after another told her how lovely, how "ladylike" she looked. Even Celia and Adelaide, whose dresses had been ordered from London, gave her warm compliments.

After Pert and Lucas Chilton had formally opened the ball, others quickly joined them on the dance floor. Just as her father had requested, Maggie gave him the first dance, a cotillion. She was delighted to discover that he knew the steps. Partners changed often, and the pace was lively. The white kid dance pumps barely touched the floor, for Maggie fairly floated. While she had thought she might feel out of place, she felt right at home. Dance after dance, fun and laughter, music and more music—Maggie wished it could go on forever.

Caleb was enamored with so much good food, and Hannah was obliged to keep a close eye on him. Thankfully, he'd let his beloved snake free for the winter, so that was a worry out of the way. Her father was most obviously enjoying himself, and Maggie even observed him asking a few of the widows to dance with him.

After dancing once with Maggie, Evan was absent much of the time. When asked, he said he was checking on the horses, but Maggie suspected they didn't need to be checked all that often. Whenever he was inside, Adelaide was as near to him as she could get.

Many of Boston's finest young men were signed to dance with Maggie, but to her utter amazement, Oliver paid special attention to her throughout the evening. She found herself chatting with him as though she'd known him forever. He regaled her with tales of his travels to India, Spain, and the West Indies.

At one point, he escorted her to the sitting room for a cup of hot spicy cider. Several of the young people were standing about in the sitting room talking as she and Oliver entered— Adelaide and Celia among them.

"Oh, there's Maggie," Celia said. "Adelaide's just learned about a Christmas gift she's getting. Tell her, Adelaide."

Maggie and Oliver stepped closer to the group gathered near the refreshment tables. "A gift from whom?" Maggie asked.

"My parents," Adelaide said. "They just took me into Father's study a few minutes ago to tell me about my Christmas gift from them." Adelaide's face beamed as she spoke. "They are getting me a girl of my very own!"

"A girl?" Maggie said. "Oh, you mean your own servant, like Hayley?"

"Silly." Adelaide took her fan from the cord on her wrist and fluttered it about her face. "I mean my own slave. She's on her way now from Trinidad. Her name's Melee, and she's just my age. She'll be perfect. I'm so excited; I can hardly wait till she arrives."

Maggie had heard none of the rest of Adelaide's words. "You don't mean you'd actually own another person?" she said. Suddenly, all the eyes of the group turned to her, and she felt her cheeks growing hot.

"Why, Maggie, whatever are you saying?" Adelaide said. "Nearly every family who is anyone in Boston owns slaves. You know that."

Maggie did know that, but she'd never thought of a young girl being a slave before. In fact, she'd never given much thought to slaves at all. She couldn't explain why this announcement gave her such a feeling of grief deep inside her.

"She's from a very poor country," Adelaide explained. "She'll probably receive better food and clothing here than ever before in her life."

"Come, Maggie," Oliver was saying, "they're announcing the final dance. Let's not miss out."

Woodenly, she followed him back to the ballroom.

"You certainly speak your mind," Oliver said as he spun her about the floor. "I take it you don't believe in slavery."

"It seems rather base and cruel," she said, struggling to sort out her thoughts.

"Father never would have owned slaves in England," Oliver told her, "but we had such well-trained servants there. Good servants are hard to come by in New England. Mother plans to begin to purchase slaves and to train them herself. I'm not all that keen on the idea of slaves, either, but then I'm not home much anymore."

Whether Oliver approved or disapproved would make little difference to the young girl now sailing toward Massachusetts to become a slave in the Chilton household.

The magical night was over, and Oliver and other of the young men thanked Maggie for her charming company. The flattery was exhilarating, unlike anything she'd ever experienced.

However, on the way home, thoughts of the ball faded, and her mind was filled with thoughts of a girl from Trinidad named Melee. Maggie wondered how she would feel if someone took her from home and family and forced her to live in a strange land. How terrible that would be.

The Embarrassing Accident

The cloaks for Sarah and Ann were finished the week before Christmas. They were of fawn-colored, tightly woven wool with soft flannel linings.

"Father can deliver these on his next visit to Mrs. Cradock," Maggie said as they folded each cloak neatly. Dr. Baldwin had reported that Sarah Cradock was slowly regaining strength.

"Why, Maggie Baldwin," Hannah protested, "this was all your idea. You should be the one to deliver them. It's not your father's place to do so."

The thought of going back to the dirty room had never occurred to Maggie. She wanted to help in some way, but going back there had not been part of her plan. "We could send Evan in the sleigh," she ventured.

"Evan may very well drive the sleigh, but you should be in it."

Hannah was right, of course, as she always was, and in the end Maggie reluctantly agreed.

"We can take a loaf of bread, a piece of salt pork, and a few vegetables from the root cellar," Hannah suggested. "What do you think?"

"That's a fine idea," Maggie agreed, getting a bit excited. "A little food would be a great blessing to the two of them. I'll go to the cellar if you'll prepare the hamper."

In the end, it was Father who took them to the Cradocks'. "I have a call to make near there," he told them. "I'll drop you off."

The air was cold enough to form little clouds of vapor as they talked while loading the sleigh in the dooryard. Gray clouds hung low in the sky, threatening more snow.

"I want you to know I think this is a commendable thing you're doing, Maggie," her father told her after they were on their way. "The Lord will bless you for reaching out to another."

"It's not much," she said, still wondering if it had been all that good of an idea.

"What a better world this would be if everyone did just a little," Hannah said.

Maggie hadn't thought of it like that before.

Father drove the sleigh down the crooked street and into the narrow alleyway. In the daylight and covered with layers of white powdery snow, the place didn't appear as threatening as the first time Maggie had seen it.

She carried the folded cloaks, and Hannah took the hamper. "I'll return for you in about half an hour," Father said as he drove off.

Ann answered their knock at the door with a look of surprise on her face. "You came back," she said to Maggie.

"Yes, I. . .I mean, we—this is Hannah Pierce, Ann. We've brought you some—"

"Christmas gifts," Hannah finished the sentence.

"That's right," Maggie agreed. "Christmas gifts."

Ann gave a little squeal. "Mother, did you hear that? Christmas gifts!" Ann opened the door wide to let them in and closed it behind them. The room was dim and close. The low fire in the small fireplace was doing little to ward off the cold.

"You may light the candle for our guests, Ann," Mrs. Cradock said from her bed. With some effort, she was able to sit up.

Ann ran to get the candle and lit it with a spark from the fire. Meanwhile, Maggie introduced Hannah to Mrs. Cradock. The little candle was set on the table, chasing away the late afternoon darkness. It was then that Maggie unfolded the cloaks to show them. She was overwhelmed at the expression of pure joy on Ann's face at the sight of her new cloak.

"For me?" she whispered.

"For you," Maggie said, "with God's blessings." She draped the cloak around the girl's small shoulders, giving her a gentle pat as she did so.

Ann pulled the cloak close about her. She put up the hood, then took it down again, put it up and took it down again. "It's lovely," she whispered. "Thank you so much. I shall never be so cold ever again. Mother, try yours. Please stand up and try on your cloak."

"I believe I'll do just that, Ann." Mrs. Cradock struggled to stand and allowed Hannah to place her new cloak about her. Reverently, she caressed the deep folds. "I can't remember when I've ever had anything so nice," she said to them. "It's been many, many years." Tears brimmed in her red-rimmed eyes. "I don't know what to say except a simple thank-you."

"We have brought bread, as well," Maggie said, emptying out the hamper and placing the foodstuffs on the table. "And a few vegetables."

"We can have a stew for Christmas!" Mrs. Cradock said, taking halting steps from the cot to the table. A new brightness glowed in her eyes.

A tapping on the door signaled Father's return. Ann ran to let him in. "Just look, Dr. Baldwin!" She whirled about. "Maggie gave me a new cloak."

"That she did, Ann. Merry Christmas! And Mrs. Cradock, how good to see you on your feet."

"The gifts from your household are so appreciated, sir," Mrs. Cradock said.

"The gifts appear to be better medicine than anything I could do as a doctor," Maggie's father said.

As they were preparing to leave, Ann ran to Maggie and gave her a hug. "Thank you, thank you, Maggie." To Maggie's own surprise, she returned the little girl's hug.

As they rode home with sleigh bells ringing, the snow sifted down thickly about them. Maggie settled back in the sleigh, weighted down beneath the heavy lap blankets, content to listen to the swishing of the runners through the snow. She didn't want to talk. Somehow she longed to capture this deep, contented sensation and hold it forever.

Maggie and Hannah attempted to decorate their dining room as beautifully as the Chiltons' home had been for the ball. It was the day before Christmas, and Father was still out on calls. Colder weather always meant more illnesses, and that kept him away from home more.

"We may not have money for yards and yards of ribbon,"

Hannah was saying, "but we have bits and pieces."

"And plenty of greenery," Maggie added.

Even Caleb and Evan joined in the fun. Since Evan was taller, he could stand on a chair or the sideboard and reach higher. Caleb cut the boughs and tied them together. The fragrance of pine and cedar floated through the dining room as they worked. Hannah had cleaned the parlor, and on Christmas morning all the guests would gather there to exchange gifts.

When the decorating was finished, Hannah rewarded them with a piece of her wonderful Marlborough-pudding pie. Maggie decided that Hannah must be in a rare mood, since she never allowed this most special pie to be cut until Christmas Day. Maggie savored the tart lemon flavor as they ate together.

Thankfully, Father arrived home in time to eat a piece of the pie, as well. They spent the evening in Father's cozy study, reading scriptures until time for bed.

Christmas morning pulsated with excitement. There were still the usual chores to do and more fires to lay since the parlor and dining room were to be heated. The snow had stopped falling, and bright sunshine sparkled on the fresh white drifts.

Uncle Reuben and Aunt Lucille came loaded with special gifts for everyone. They even brought gifts for the Pierce boys. Soon, the house was filled with laughter, happy conversation, and the shouts and giggles of the children.

Although Hannah didn't cook nearly as much on Christmas as she did on Thanksgiving, there was still much to eat. *It's more food than the Cradocks will have*, Maggie thought as she surveyed the table.

During the scramble of the gift exchanges, Maggie found

herself studying Aunt Lucille. Somehow her aunt appeared less sad. Perhaps it was the cheerful color of her new dress that brought a glow to her cheeks.

Later as they ate, Aunt Lucille joined in the conversation. Even her eyes appeared to be brighter, as though life had come back. Although Maggie was curious, she kept quiet. To ask questions might stir up memories that had finally been settled.

At one point, Aunt Lucille cuddled baby Henry on her lap, talking and cooing to him and smiling. Maggie tried to catch Hannah's eye to judge her reaction to this change, but Hannah was much too busy tending to the dinner. What with all the other excitement, the matter was soon put out of Maggie's mind.

Jacob announced to the younger boys that they would all go sledding after dinner—an announcement that brought forth noisy cheers.

"Marvelous idea, Jacob," Uncle Reuben said. "Take them out and let them burn off all their uproarious noise. Why, they sound like a bunch of revivalists at a barn meeting."

Suddenly a quiet hush fell on the table. Maggie wondered if her uncle knew that the Pierces not only believed in the new revivals but had attended a few of those "barn meetings," as well. Even Father was speechless and looked extremely uncomfortable.

But good old Ben was never at a loss for words. "I must say, Reuben, I have to agree with you. The cries of joy in a revivalist meeting are every bit as spontaneous and genuine as the joy of a little child. And often just as exuberant."

At that point, Hannah jumped up to ask who needed what,

and the conversation went on from there as though nothing had ever happened.

Maggie felt badly that Uncle Reuben could have been so insensitive, but Ben and Judith didn't seem to care what had been said.

"You're going sledding with us, aren't you, Maggie?" Jacob had cornered her in the kitchen as she was helping Hannah with the cleanup.

"I can't, Jacob, really. . ."

Caleb, who was standing nearby, echoed the invitation. "Oh yes, Maggie, please do come with us. It would be ever so much more fun with you along."

Ever since the Christmas ball, Maggie had felt years older, as though the evening had been her graduation into womanhood. Now they were asking her to come and play as a child. She just couldn't.

"Go with them, Maggie girl," Hannah encouraged. "Your childhood is fast slipping away. Run off and have fun while you can. Christmas comes but once a year. Enjoy yourself."

Evan appeared at the kitchen door red-cheeked. He'd been fetching the wooden sleds out of the carriage house. "Come on, gang, what are you waiting for?" Looking at Maggie, he said, "Put your hoops away, Maggie. Let's go have fun!"

What could she say? It did sound like fun. Tripping to her room, she changed into her day dress and left off her hoops. Wrapping her cloak around her and fastening her clogs to her feet, she ran out to join the boys.

"Let's go to the far side of Copp's Hill," Jacob said. "The best hills are there."

Evan and Jacob each pulled a sled, with Adam and Burke on one and Caleb on the other. Maggie squinted from the sun's glare off the snow. Together the little band trudged through the deep snow, laughing and talking until they reached the best hill. Squeals and shouts sounded through the cold, still day as one after another they took turns sliding down the hill, coming to a stop at Commercial Street near the ferry.

Evan and Jacob raced one another, lying on their stomachs and trying to catch the legs of the one in front. Then the younger boys tried it, upsetting one another and rolling in the snow, squealing with laughter.

Maggie's rides down the hill were tamer than the boys'. She skillfully guided the sled as Evan had taught her to do when they were younger. She was quite out of breath as she pulled the sled back up the hill after her turn.

"Ride with me," Jacob dared her. "I'll show you how fast a sled can truly fly."

"And I'll give you a push off," Evan said.

Against her better judgment, she sat on the long, wooden sled and let Jacob climb on behind. With a great thrust, Evan pushed them to the brink of the hill and let them go.

Maggie had never gone so fast. Her hood was down, and the air was whistling past her ears. If they didn't stop at Commercial Street, she was sure they would fly right out over the Charles River—perhaps landing on the other side!

Just as they came sailing down toward the road, a horse-drawn sleigh appeared out of nowhere.

"Look out!" Maggie screamed.

Instantly, Jacob turned the runners, and the sled veered

sharply away from the danger, landing both of them in a deep snowbank.

Maggie had a mouthful of snow, and her cloak was thrown over her head. As she slowly sat up and shook the snow from her face and eyes, who did she see in the sleigh but the elegant Adelaide Chilton with both Clark and Oliver out for an afternoon ride. With a little gasp, Adelaide exclaimed, "Why, Maggie Baldwin! Whatever are you doing? And who is this boy?"

CHAPTER 11

Consequences

Maggie was completely mortified. How she longed for the ground to open and swallow her up. Thankfully, Evan had seen the approaching danger, jumped on the other sled, and come down after them.

"Hello, Adelaide," Maggie sputtered as Jacob helped her to her feet. Clumsily, she attempted to pull her cloak around her plain, soaking-wet day dress.

In the nick of time, Evan, leaping from his sled, came over to the Chilton sleigh and jumped up on the running board. "Merry Christmas to you," he said, diverting their attention from Maggie. "Adelaide, Clark, Oliver."

"Why, hello, Evan," Adelaide answered, her voice going softer. She pulled one hand from her sable muff and adjusted the hood of her elegant cloak, also trimmed in sable. "Your sister very nearly got run over. Whatever are you doing out here?"

"You know how brothers can be," he explained. "I insisted she come along to help Jacob and me with the younger boys. They are quite a handful, you know. And she's such a regular sport, always ready to help. You've not met Jacob, I suppose. Jacob, let me introduce you to the Chiltons."

Maggie had never heard her brother say so much or say it so fast. He introduced Jacob to them, explaining that Jacob's father was editor of the *News Letter*. Of course they recognized the name.

"Father does quite a lot of business with that paper," Clark commented. "I say, Oliver, we'd best be on our way. Our guests will think we got lost."

"You're so right." Oliver gave the reins a little shake, and the horses stepped out.

"Bye, Maggie." Adelaide gave a little wave, then tucked her hand back into the sable muff. "See you on Sunday."

Maggie made an effort to wave back. By now she was shivering and soaked through to the skin.

After the sleigh had pulled away, Maggie turned to Jacob. "How could you? How could you put me in such an embarrassing situation? I've never been so humiliated in my life. Whatever will they think of me now?" She spun around and took off down the road.

"Where are you going?" Evan asked.

"Home," she answered. "To get warm."

"Does it matter so much what the Chiltons think of you?" Jacob called out.

Maggie couldn't answer. It mattered much more than she dared admit.

Late that afternoon, a drier, warmer Maggie said an awkward good-bye to Jacob when the Pierces left. She couldn't bring herself to forgive him for causing her such horrid embarrassment. He did apologize, of course, and she mouthed words of acceptance, but inside she was still angry.

Since Christmas fell on Wednesday, there was to be no dance instruction that week. Then on Sunday, the Chilton family left immediately after church to entertain their out-of-town company. Maggie had to wait a full week before she faced Adelaide. She prayed that her sledding misadventure would be forgotten in that time. Almost daily, she chided herself for getting talked into doing anything so childish.

Privately, Evan scolded her for taking her anger out on Jacob. "He had no way of knowing the Chiltons would drive along at that moment, Maggie. He felt badly about the whole episode, and you only succeeded in making him feel worse. It's hardly fair."

Maggie knew that. She also knew that Evan had boldly stepped in to talk to Adelaide, which he would never have done under other circumstances. Still, the hurt wouldn't go away.

The new year of 1741 arrived with little fanfare. On New Year's Day, Father gathered everyone into his study to pray for the forthcoming year and to give specific thanks for all that the Lord had done for them in 1740.

The next day, as Maggie stepped up to the Chiltons' front entrance for dance instruction, tight knots formed in her midsection. She tapped the door knocker, and there was Adelaide.

"Maggie," she said excitedly, "I knew it would be you, so I told the butler to let me answer. Come in. Come in. It's going to be ever so much fun today. Oliver is still here!"

This was an unexpected development. Maggie had assumed

the Chilton boys had returned to school and that she wouldn't have to face Oliver until spring. As the dour-faced butler took her wraps in the front entryway, Maggie could see Oliver coming down the hall toward her.

"Ah, Maggie, there you are. A pleasant turn of events that I should be here to dance with you once again. Clark is tending to business, but I had the afternoon free."

Maggie murmured her thanks as they moved into the parlor, where Celia, Pert, and Mr. Helver were waiting. No one had said anything about the sledding upset or her despicable appearance on Christmas Day. Then Maggie realized that the Chiltons were too well trained and polite to even mention it. Part of her was thankful; the other part wished they would refer to the event just so she could defend herself.

Dance instruction hour had never been so merry. Oliver's blue eyes twinkled with gaiety as he spun her about to the lilting melodies coming from the spinet. Mr. Helver presented new dances, which they walked through slowly before stepping out to the music. If Maggie was confused about other things, she knew one thing for sure—she loved to dance.

At half past the hour, they stopped to rest. As they sat about the parlor enjoying cool glasses of water, Oliver came over to where she was seated on the sofa.

"I didn't know before that you were friends with the Pierces, Maggie," he said.

So now the conversation would come back to the awful incident. Maggie braced herself for the worst. "My father and Benjamin Pierce grew up together," she explained. "They're as close as brothers."

"But are you aware that the Pierces attend the Brattle Street Church?"

"Not all the Pierces," she replied.

Oliver paused. "Not all?"

"Hannah Pierce lives with us—that's Benjamin Pierce's older sister—she attends North Church with us. You've seen her there."

"I wasn't aware of who she was. At any rate, Benjamin himself is quite outspoken in support of the revivalists."

"So he is." Maggie couldn't imagine what this subject had to do with her. She knew Ben was not only vocal about the revivals sweeping New England, but he also had written a few editorials about them in his paper.

Reaching over to a small table, Oliver picked up a book and handed it to her. "Since Mr. Pierce is so persuasive and since you happen to be in his company and that of his son's, you may want to read this book by the Reverend Chauncy."

She took the small bound book in her hands, still puzzled.

"This book explains in great detail," Oliver went on, "the evil dangers of the revivalists. They are all charlatans, you see, causing disorder. Quite simply, they are itinerant preachers who jump up and talk with no prepared sermons. It's a frightfully lazy manner of preaching."

Maggie had heard most of this before, and she was amazed at Oliver's concern for her beliefs. "Thank you, Oliver. I appreciate the gift and your thoughtfulness very much. I shall read this from cover to cover." Perhaps this book would answer some of the questions about the revivalists that had plagued her for so long.

"Enough of all this serious talk," Celia said, jumping to her feet. "Let's get back to dancing."

Following the instruction, Oliver politely excused himself with a low bow. "I've a horse to see about in the stables, so I'll leave you ladies to your teatime."

After Mr. Helver fetched his greatcoat and left and the girls prepared to retire to the nursery, Pert came up to them. "Maggie," she said, "I'd like a few words with you before you go up to tea, if you don't mind."

"Why, I don't mind at all," Maggie answered. She followed Pert back into the parlor, where the woman spread her satin skirts out on the sofa and motioned for Maggie to pull up one of the Windsor chairs.

"Maggie, I've been given to understand you met with an unfortunate mishap on Christmas afternoon. Am I correct?"

So here it was! Maggie could hardly bear to look at Pert's lovely face. Adelaide's mother was as perfectly put together as a delicately painted china doll. "Yes, ma'am, that is correct." She toyed with the small book Oliver had given her.

"I know you have no mother, Maggie," Pert said softly, with no condemnation in her voice, "and perhaps you've not received all the good training you've needed. You're thirteen now, is that right?"

Maggie nodded.

"In two or three years, you will be of marriageable age, and it would behoove you to think now of preparing to be a lady of refinement. The best way to prevent unfortunate instances such as that which occurred on Christmas is to think as a lady rather than as a child. Do you understand?"

"I think so."

Pert tapped her fan to her forehead. "The mind, Maggie. Become a lady first in your mind. Train yourself to think as a lady would in all circumstances."

"Yes, ma'am. I'll try."

Pert reached out to pat Maggie's hand. "I feel certain you will, my dear." She stood and drew Maggie to her feet. "After all," she said, smiling and spreading her fan, "who knows but what someday you may become part of the Chilton family."

An unwelcome blush crept into Maggie's cheeks, and she found she had no words. Pert laughed aloud at Maggie's embarrassment. The laughter tinkled through the air like notes from the spinet. "Go along now. Join the girls and have a delightful tea."

"Yes, ma'am. Thank you, ma'am."

As Maggie turned to go, Pert added, "And please read the book Oliver gave you."

"Oh, yes, ma'am, I will."

The girls were all abuzz by the time she entered the nursery.

"There you are, Maggie—at long last," Celia said. "I thought you would never come. Hurry and sit down. Adelaide has a secret to tell, but she refused to tell it before you got here."

Maggie stepped quickly to her chair to sit down, still amazed at the conversation she'd just had with Pert. Her tea had already been poured, and she took a sip, grateful for the uplift it gave her.

Adelaide passed the cake basket and waited till Maggie chose a dainty piece with sugary icing. "My secret is that I'm to travel to Salem by stagecoach to visit our friends, the Drurys.

I'm leaving as soon as the snow thaws enough for the coaches to travel again."

"Why, that's a wonderful secret," Celia said. "I'm so happy for you."

"But that's not the best part." Adelaide leaned forward. "The best part is that the two of you are invited to come along."

Maggie nearly choked on her cake.

"Oh, my!" Celia said with a little gasp. "I've always wanted to go to Salem. What a wonderful surprise to share, Adelaide. Thank you. My mother will be overjoyed."

"What about you, Maggie?" Adelaide asked. "Will you be able to come with us?"

The thought of expensive coach fare ran through Maggie's mind. "You're so very kind to ask. I would dearly love to go. But I will have to discuss it with Father."

"What do you think he will say?"

"I think he will be very pleased," she answered, but she wasn't at all sure what he would say.

"Be sure to explain that your coach fare will be paid," Adelaide said, passing the cakes around one more time.

Maggie gave an inward sigh. Her way would be paid. If that was true, there should be no objection from her father. What an exciting day this had been. "I can tell you his answer Sunday morning at church," she said.

Just then the door opened, and in walked the most beautiful dark-skinned girl Maggie had ever seen. She was dressed in a simple printed linen frock covered with a flowing white apron. Over her rich black curls, she wore a white ruffled mobcap.

"Melee!" Adelaide said sharply, "How many times have I

told you not to enter unless you knock?" *Tap, tap, tap!* Adelaide knocked on the table. "Knock! Knock at the door first. Or wait until I summon you." Turning to Maggie, she said, "Maggie, this is Melee, my slave girl. My Christmas gift."

The lovely girl gave a little curtsy. "Melee sorry."

Under her breath, Adelaide said, "She's really rather addle-pated. I'd hoped for a girl with more intelligence. She knows a little English, but not much. My work is certainly cut out for me."

Maggie looked at the girl again. Her skin was the color of polished mahogany, and her high cheekbones gave her face a look of chiseled distinction. Her slender frame was rather thin, as though she had not eaten well. She stood straight and unbowed, even after the harsh scolding, but her black eyes were filled with great sadness.

Maggie felt sorry for Melee and gave her a sympathetic smile. How terrible it must be to be taken from your family and forced to work for someone else! She couldn't believe that slavery was a good thing, no matter what others might think.

∽ CHAPTER 12 ∽

The Journey

The apprehension Maggie felt as she asked permission to go to Salem was as much in fear that Father might say yes as fear that he would say no. In spite of the times she'd spent with the Chiltons and with Celia, she continued to feel like an interloper, as though she didn't really belong.

The sensation wasn't due to the other girls. On the contrary, Adelaide and Celia had gone out of their way to be kind and thoughtful. And Oliver—well, Oliver had been more than kind. Visions of his blue eyes and kind smile would pop into her mind at the most inopportune times.

To her surprise, her father was agreeable to the trip to Salem and gave his permission for her to go. "I believe it would be a maturing experience for you to travel and meet new people," he said.

"But my clothes," Maggie started to protest. She was sure Celia and Adelaide would take a trunkful of dresses.

"And I don't believe a couple of new dresses would be out of the question," he went on to say. "More of my patients have paid in money this year," he told her. "It's been a good winter."

Maggie wasn't sure what to say. His willingness was a nice surprise. Even Hannah took on some of the air of excitement. Caleb didn't think it was fair at all since he'd always wanted to ride in a stagecoach. Evan was somewhat noncommittal about the entire thing but did ask if Oliver would be going along.

"Well, of course not," Maggie said quickly. "Oliver is back at school and will be there until the term is over in the spring."

Her brother seemed relieved at this bit of news.

Maggie spent several hours each day reading the book Oliver gave her. The arguments set down in the book seemed sound enough, but, strangely, it did nothing to quiet the confusion churning about inside her.

When she finished reading it, she offered the book to Evan to read. "I shouldn't wonder that Oliver would give you such a book," he commented.

"What do you mean?" she asked.

"He's a Harvard man. As I understand it, all the Harvard professors are up in arms about the matter. Frankly, I'm weary of the controversy. I wish it would all die down. Even Uncle Reuben is cynical about the 'awakening' as they call it. If it's all right with you, I'd just as soon not read the book."

The little outburst was quite unlike Evan, who was usually reserved. But Maggie agreed with him. She wished all the arguments and bickering would just go away.

In the days following, Hannah and Maggie were kept busy sewing the gowns for Maggie's upcoming trip. With every passing day, she grew more excited. The subject was on the girls' lips every Thursday afternoon as they enjoyed their grand tea party after instruction time.

Melee's skills at serving were becoming more polished as Adelaide worked hard to train her. To Maggie, she appeared quite graceful, but Adelaide continued to call her "clumsy oaf" and "fumblefingers." Whether or not Melee could understand the words, there was no mistaking Adelaide's tone of voice and expression of displeasure. Maggie believed that a touch of kindness would be more effective, but then what did she know about training slaves?

"You should have seen Melee's amazement at the snow," Adelaide said with a giggle. "She looked up into the sky, crying 'Magic! Magic!' She thought the snowfall was magic. Isn't that a fright?"

"Perhaps if we'd never seen snow before, we might also think it was magic," Maggie said.

"Perhaps," Adelaide said, "but with the intelligence we have, I doubt it. The worst is that she can never get warm. She wants to go about with a blanket wrapped around her. She seems to be cold all the time."

"After living in Trinidad, I don't wonder," Celia said. "My father says it's balmy there and just like a mild summer all the time, with brilliant-colored flowers everywhere. Too bad she couldn't have come in summer to give her time to grow accustomed to the weather change."

"But she was my Christmas gift, you ninny," countered Adelaide. "Christmas doesn't come in the summer"—a comment that set them to giggling again.

Maggie would have liked to have asked Melee about her home in Trinidad, but Adelaide had instructed her friends that they were only to speak to Melee when they had an order to give.

❧

Throughout the frigid days of January, Maggie and Hannah paid periodic visits to the Cradock home to check on them. With each visit, they took a few things with them—a blanket or a bit of food—for which Mrs. Cradock and Ann were always extremely grateful. Maggie couldn't explain the wonderful feeling she received from seeing Mrs. Cradock slowly regain her strength. She also couldn't explain why it was one thing she never shared with Celia and Adelaide, even though they had become her close friends.

The trip to Salem was planned for late February. The week before departure, Maggie suggested to Hannah that they pay a visit to the Cradocks before she left on her trip. Hannah never had to be asked twice.

When Ann answered their tapping on the door of the small alleyway room, Maggie received a stunning shock. There was a smiling, beaming Mrs. Cradock, hard at work scrubbing and cleaning the tiny room. One of the wooden shutters was thrown open, and fresh air filtered in along with the soft winter sunlight.

The straw tick had been emptied and aired and lay waiting for clean straw to be stuffed back inside. Clutter had been picked up, and the wooden floor was scrubbed.

Mrs. Cradock's face was wreathed in a warm smile as she came to the door with her hand outstretched. "Welcome, welcome, ladies. Please come in."

"You're so much better," Maggie managed to say. She looked over at Hannah. She, too, was speechless, but she smiled at the sight.

"I am better than you will ever know," Mrs. Cradock said. "Please sit down. She pulled out the crudely made wooden chairs from the small table. Hannah set the hamper on the table and sat down.

"Something's happened to you!" Hannah smiled as though she had been let in on a big secret.

"My brother took Ann and me to a revival meeting last week. And now I know God loves me and that Jesus died to take away my sins."

There was no denying the change in this lady's countenance, and her voice fairly bubbled over with joy and excitement. Maggie had never seen anything like it.

"We gathered together in a large barn near Roxbury. A barn! Can you imagine? But then, I'm not welcome inside a real church." She touched her hands to her cheeks and laughed aloud. "The place was so crowded there was barely room to stand."

"Who preached the sermon?" Hannah asked.

"The Reverend Jonathan Edwards."

"Yes, yes, the Reverend Edwards is one of the best," Hannah said. Maggie wondered how Hannah would know.

"He made the plan of salvation so clear and simple, even a child. . ." Mrs. Cradock stopped and looked at Ann. "Even my little Ann understood. Didn't you, Ann?"

Ann ducked her head as she nodded. Mrs. Cradock stepped to her daughter's side and put her arms around her. "Knowing that God loves us, truly loves us, has changed everything. I feel so clean on the inside, I wanted my place to be clean, as well."

"God's love can surely do that," Hannah agreed.

Mrs. Cradock went on to tell them that she'd been out inquiring for a place of employment and had been hired by the grocer on the next street. "I want to make a better life for Ann and me."

Throughout the visit, Maggie barely uttered a word. She was too astonished. How could this sinner have favor with God? It made no sense and certainly was different from anything she'd ever heard preached. Later, as she and Hannah walked to her father's shop, she asked Hannah about it.

"The scriptures are quite clear, Maggie, that salvation is a gift, free to anyone who believes."

"But Mrs. Cradock has never done anything for the Lord's work. She doesn't even attend church, and she has lived a life of sin."

"We're not born into God's kingdom according to our works, Maggie. One cannot work for a free gift."

Maggie had been in church all her life, and she'd never before thought of salvation as a gift from God. "But what about this Jonathan Edwards—how do you know about him?"

"I've attended his meetings with Ben and the family," Hannah replied.

This calm announcement surprised Maggie. Her own nanny. Of course, her family never asked what Hannah did on her days off, but she could at least have told about such a radical thing as following the revivalists.

❧

The next week was a flurry of excitement as Hannah helped Maggie pack her trunk for the trip. The lovely new dresses were folded and laid in the trunk with great care, along with her embroidered bodices and quilted petticoats.

The late February thaw served to open the roads to Salem, and the stagecoach had been running for a week or more. The night before she was to leave, Maggie could hardly sleep. Father was out late on calls, and Maggie never liked to fall asleep before he got home. When she heard the carriage drive into the back dooryard, she hurried downstairs to be in the kitchen waiting.

After putting the horses away, Dr. Baldwin came through the door. "You're up awfully late. Shouldn't you be getting your rest for the long trip?"

"I'm too excited to sleep."

"I'm afraid I have a bit of bad news for you," her father said as he hung up his greatcoat. "I've been at the Winthrops' this evening, and Celia has the grippe. She'll not be able to make the trip."

Maggie felt her heart sink. What a disappointment for Celia. "Does the Chilton family know?" She poured two mugs of cider, and she offered him one.

He nodded. "I drove by to inform them before coming home." He took a deep drink of the cider. "It looks as though it will just be you and Adelaide and her footman as your chaperone."

"And the girl, Melee."

"Oh yes," Dr. Baldwin said dryly, "the little slave girl."

Maggie could tell her father didn't think much more of the situation than she did. But there was nothing anyone could do.

She finished her cider, kissed her father good night, and went back to her bed. But sleep was awhile in coming. She'd never been away from home before. This would be a true adventure.

The Chiltons came for Maggie the next morning in their large carriage, which served to hold the girls' large trunks on the top. Maggie nervously bid farewell to her family, fighting to keep back tears. She didn't want Adelaide to think she was reluctant to leave. From there they took the ferry to the Pine Tree Tavern in Charlestown, where the girls would board the stagecoach to Salem.

If Maggie was nervous, Melee was even more so. Maggie could sense the girl's fear at yet another change. Melee's cheeks were more sunken than before, causing Maggie to wonder if the girl was being fed properly. The New England winter had obviously been harsh for one who was accustomed to tropical breezes.

A roaring fire blazed in the fireplace of the large common room inside the inn. The tall mahogany clock in the corner chimed seven o'clock. The agent informed them that the coach had arrived and fresh horses were being harnessed. While Adelaide and Melee sat down before the fire and Lucas went to the agent's desk to pay the fares, Pert took Maggie aside.

"Don't forget what I told you," Pert said softly. "Remember to think like a lady at all times."

"Yes, ma'am, I will," Maggie promised.

"Keep in mind these are our dear friends up there in Salem, and you'll want to make the best impression possible."

"Yes, ma'am," Maggie repeated. She certainly didn't want to disappoint Pert Chilton.

Just then the agent called out, "The Lightning Stage Line now departing for Salem. All passengers assemble!"

There were only the four of them boarding, for which Maggie was thankful. As Johnson helped her up, the coachman had already mounted his box and was blowing the long brass coach horn. With a loud crack of his leather whip, they were under way. Maggie could hardly contain her excitement!

CHAPTER 13

The Never-Ending Party

Unlike the smooth ride in the Chilton carriage, the stagecoach bounced and lurched about over the deeply rutted roadway. The coachman shouted at the team and snapped his whip continually until even Johnson, who was seated beside Maggie, was forced to hang on for dear life. Adelaide, with Melee by her side, sat across from Maggie.

In spite of the cold air, Maggie was determined to peek out around the rolled-down leather curtains to see everything she could. She enjoyed watching the farmlands and the villages whizzing by. The speed at which they were moving would certainly impress both her brothers.

Adelaide, on the other hand, had seen these sights many times, and she wanted to talk. She told Maggie about the Drury family at whose home they would lodge.

"Nelda is the older sister," Adelaide explained. "She's almost fifteen, but don't expect to talk much to Nelda. Her nose is continually in a book. She's read nearly every book in her father's library. Her mother scolds her to make her come out and enjoy fun and laughter with Julia and me. Julia's thirteen," she said, taking a breath.

"Sometimes we hide her book to get her to dance with us. Of course, she can always go find a new one again, but it's great fun to watch her searching high and low for the one we've hidden." Adelaide laughed at the happy memories, making Maggie eager to meet these two sisters.

"Melee!" Adelaide said sharply. "Sit up, girl!"

Melee, with her cloak wrapped tightly around her, had laid her head back on the leather cushion of the seat. The girl jumped.

"You should be paying attention to all that I say, Melee, so you'll know what is expected of you in Salem. This girl," Adelaide said to Maggie, "is turning out to be no bargain at all. For the high price my father paid, you would think I would get more response out of her."

"But she looks ill," Maggie said. "Melee, do you feel all right?" Maggie started to reach out and feel the girl's forehead, but Adelaide grabbed at her wrist.

"Never pamper a slave, Maggie. If you do, they become like spoiled children. If that happens, I will be doing everything for her rather than the other way around."

Adelaide's comment made little sense. How could the girl do anything if she were ill all the time? But Maggie kept still. After all, she'd promised Pert she'd not be an embarrassment to them.

Presently, the clear notes sounded from the coachman's brass horn, announcing their arrival at the upcoming stop. Maggie rolled up the leather curtain so she could see better. This tavern was much larger than any she'd seen before, with a wide front porch, an overhanging second story, and large stables out back. The swinging sign hanging from a porch post read BOGART'S INN. As they drew to a stop, the stable boys ran toward the coach to change out the team of horses.

"Right on time," the coachman boasted as he pulled his gold watch from his vest pocket. "Step smartly now. Lunch will be only fifteen minutes."

Inside the common room, the large table was set with several places. A wooden sign on the wall listed the selections. Johnson took Melee to sit at the far end of the table. They all ordered beef stew and ate quickly, knowing their stay was short. Maggie noticed that Melee barely ate at all.

When they were under way again, Melee stared vacantly out the window. As the coach continued to lurch about, she looked more and more ill. Suddenly Melee gave a little cry, and holding her handkerchief to her face, she threw up right there in the coach.

Johnson fumbled about, attempting to bring a bottle of water from the small hamper Pert had packed for them. Adelaide was furious and spouted angry words at Melee.

"Getting angry won't help," Maggie said to Adelaide. She took the water from Johnson and wet her own handkerchief to lay on the girl's hot brow.

Johnson willingly scooted over and let Maggie sit across from Melee. "I'm not much good at nursing," he said.

The smells made Maggie's stomach do strange things, but she knew the girl needed help. Melee gave another little groan as Maggie patted the cool cloth on her face. "Sick. Melee be awful sick. Like on ship."

"Pour a little water in one of the cups," Maggie told Johnson. As carefully as she could in the bouncing coach, she was able to give Melee little sips. "You were sick on the ship coming to Boston?" Maggie asked.

"Terrible sick," Melee answered.

"Wouldn't you know it?" Adelaide said in disgust. "I have to have a slave who gets seasick on a little coach ride. Such terrible luck I have."

Toward afternoon, the coach pulled to a stop at yet another tavern for a change of horses. Finally, Melee could rest a bit and get cleaned up. The smell, however, permeated the coach, and Adelaide continued to complain about it. Throughout the remainder of the journey, Melee seemed to rally some.

They arrived in Salem after dark, but the Brazen Head Inn was alive with lights, carriages, and people milling about. To Maggie's surprise, this entourage was a welcome party for them!

They were met with a noisy volley of greetings and clusters of people crowding about. Maggie had never seen such a jovial group. Laughter and shouts rang out as the trunks were transferred from the stagecoach to the waiting carriages. Introductions were made, and Maggie met Julia, Nelda, their parents, and dozens of other people whose names she would never remember.

The four girls were escorted to the same carriage, and, after giving them a hand up, Johnson climbed up to sit with the driver. Melee was escorted to another carriage by one of the Drurys' black slaves.

In answer to the sisters' questions, Adelaide explained about Celia falling ill and being unable to come along. Julia and Nelda expressed their sympathy toward Celia, even though they'd never met her.

Had there been no introductions, Maggie could have told the Drury sisters apart. Although they favored one another with their fair complexion and blue eyes, Julia's eyes were full of mischief, and Nelda's expression was gentler and quieter. They both sported curled, powdered wigs piled high with dainty curls.

"Adelaide writes to us that your father is a doctor in Boston," Nelda was saying. "I've read a great deal about medicine and find it quite fascinating."

"Since Maggie's around medicine all the time," Julia put in, "she probably doesn't find it fascinating at all."

"Her father has taught her Latin," Adelaide told them.

"How interesting," Nelda said, tapping her fan against her cheek. "How I wish my father thought my mind was worth cultivating."

"Oh, Nelda," Julia said, laughing, "Father has opened his entire library to you—of course he values your mind." Turning back to Maggie, she said, "Adelaide has told us you have a very handsome older brother. Does he have red hair like yours?"

"Evan is not a redhead," Adelaide answered for Maggie, "and shame on you for telling on me. Evan's hair is a rich, dark chestnut color."

"If my hair were as pretty a color as yours," Julia said to Maggie, "I would never cover it with a wig!"

And so it went all the way to the Drury home. The girls chattered continually, seeming to accept Maggie, yet never letting her get in a single word.

Maggie had often heard that Salem could boast of many more wealthy ship merchants than Boston. The sight of so many ornate carriages was testimony to that fact. And if the carriages weren't enough, the grand Drury house bore further evidence. This house was every bit as large and grand as the governor's province house in Boston. But in Salem, all along Chestnut Street, rows of houses just as grand as the Drurys' lined both sides of the street.

A party was in progress when they arrived, and the house was vibrant with lights and music. Maggie noticed elaborate carvings of eagles and anchors decorating the door lintel as they were escorted through the wide front entryway.

Once they were inside, Nelda turned to Julia. "You go on back and rejoin the party, and I'll show our guests to their rooms."

"Oh, thank you, Nelda," Julia said, appearing quite eager to return to the fun. To Adelaide and Maggie, Julia said, "You'll hurry down, won't you? It shouldn't take you but a few minutes to freshen up and change."

Come back down? Maggie could hardly believe it. All she wanted was to crawl into bed. But she was soon to learn that the society of Salem held parties late and slept till noon. As they followed Nelda up the stairs, Maggie asked Adelaide about Melee's whereabouts.

"Now, Maggie, don't you worry about that girl. Johnson has taken her to the slaves' quarters down in the basement. She'll be fine."

"You have your own slave girl now, Adelaide?" At the top of the stairs, Nelda turned to lead them down a long hallway.

"She's a Christmas gift from my parents."

"Don't you find it is a great deal of work to train them? Mother spends hours trying to train our slaves properly. Sometimes I wonder if it's worth it all." She stopped and opened the door of a large bedchamber, where a good fire had been laid in the fireplace. It looked cozy and inviting.

"We gave you this room, Maggie, and Adelaide will be right across the hall. I hope you'll be comfortable. If you need anything, simply use the bellpull there by the draperies."

Maggie's trunk had arrived ahead of her and sat open at the foot of the tall cherrywood bed.

"Thank you very much. I know I shall be very comfortable."

"Put on one of your party dresses," Adelaide told her. "I'll see you in a few minutes."

The party lasted until the wee hours of the morning. Every time Maggie tried to sit out a dance, either Julia or Adelaide pulled her back in again. Never could she have imagined not wanting to dance, but she'd slept very little the night before and was exhausted. By the time she did climb the stairs to her room, she could barely hold her eyes open long enough to get out of her dress and into her nightgown.

As she settled into the high, soft bed, her thoughts turned to Melee. No matter what Adelaide said, Maggie's heart went out to the girl. *Why,* she wondered, *does there have to be such a terrible thing as slavery?*

When Maggie awakened the next morning, it was broad daylight. The last time she'd slept this late, it was because she was ill. Having no idea what she should do, she arose and dressed. No one told her when breakfast would be served. She looked at the bellpull. At least she could ask one of the servants. Cautiously, she tugged at the tasseled pull.

Presently a tap sounded at the door. She opened to see one of the uniformed slaves neatly dressed in a dark bodice and skirt, with a starched white collar and apron. A ribboned mobcap with long ruffles in back covered her dark hair.

"Morning, m'lady," she said. "My name's Bessie. You is up mighty early."

"Early?" She glanced at the sun streaming in the windows. "Why, it must be nearly noon."

"Most folks in this house don't get up 'fore noon, m'lady. Less it's them menfolk going on a hunt. But that don't happen till weather warms. Shall I bring breakfast?"

"Is breakfast being served downstairs?" Maggie would much rather eat with someone.

The girl shook her head. "They take breakfast in they rooms, then come down for lunch," Bessie explained.

"Very well, Bessie." Maggie was too hungry to object. "Please bring my breakfast." She felt silly ordering this girl about, and she'd never been called "my lady" in her life.

When the tray arrived, she ate at a small table by the window overlooking the formal gardens. There were fountains, stone benches, and tall, well-manicured shrubs. The outlines of flowerbeds showed promise of an explosion of color when spring fully arrived.

She quickly devoured the light milk biscuits and pieces of salty ham, washing it down with cups of hot tea. But when she'd finished eating, she had nothing to do. Another full hour dragged by before Adelaide knocked at her door, urging her to come down for lunch.

Many of those who had been at the dance the night before were overnight guests, as well, so the lunch table was large and spread with a fare as fine as Hannah's Thanksgiving dinner.

That afternoon Mrs. Drury accompanied the girls in the carriage to the shops in Salem. Maggie had never in her life seen so many pretty and expensive things. The number of fine shops far outnumbered those in Boston, and the women seemed intent on taking in every one.

Adelaide, of course, had money with her and made several purchases. Maggie had just a little money her father had given her, but she'd planned to purchase gifts for her family members. So while the others were buying for themselves, she searched for the needed gift items.

On their return home, the ladies were served a light tea and then encouraged to rest in their rooms before the frolic that was scheduled for that evening.

In Maggie's world, a frolic referred to quilting bees or apple-paring time, when groups of people gathered to work together. In the world of the Drury family, a frolic simply meant traveling from one home to the next or sometimes to a large tavern, where the young people gathered for games, dancing, and refreshments.

Maggie soon learned that activities had been planned for nearly every evening of their two-week stay. The afternoons were filled with needlework and reading, but occasionally there were activities in the afternoon, as well. Maggie asked Nelda for permission to borrow books from the library, because she continually awakened before the others of the household.

Kindly, Nelda led her to the library and allowed her to make her own choices.

Before the first week was out, Maggie was plagued with an intense case of homesickness. Everything here seemed frivolous and meaningless. Even the Sabbath was taken less seriously than in Boston. Other than snippets of men's conversation regarding business, most of the conversation was empty and hollow. She recalled how she could talk to Evan about almost anything—especially things of a serious nature. She missed him terribly. She even missed the Latin assignments she'd been so happy to end after her birthday.

Her hands ached for something substantial to do. If she'd seen the servants doing laundry, she would have pushed them aside and started wringing clothes out herself! But, of course, she never saw them doing any work. The house was so large, all the laundry was done in the basement, and the kitchens were at the far end of the lower floor.

She caught quick glimpses of Melee as the slave girl went in and out of Adelaide's room, waiting on her mistress. In spite of the girl's dark skin coloring, she appeared sallow and ashen. Maggie was more concerned for her than ever.

Two nights before they were to leave, Maggie was in her room preparing for bed. The Drury home was like a wayside inn, with guests coming and going continually. That afternoon they had ridden in carriages to Crowinshield's Wharf to meet a new set of friends arriving from London. That evening there was yet another party held in Adelaide and Maggie's honor.

Maggie was thoroughly exhausted. Sitting on the chair by the windows, she pulled off her dance pumps and studied them, fully expecting to see holes worn in the soles from so much dancing. Suddenly, movement in the garden below caught her attention. She pushed open the window to get a better look. There on one of the stone benches sat a small, hunched form. In the dim, soft moonlight, Maggie could barely see, but she was certain the form was Melee!

CHAPTER 14

Maggie Dares to Help

There was only one way for Maggie to find out for sure who was huddled all alone in the garden. She pulled her wrapper about her, grabbed her cloak, and ran down the stairs. Winding through a maze of hallways, she searched for the back entrance. When she found it, it took a few minutes for her to get her bearings from where she saw the figure. While the March night air wasn't as frigid as winter, it was still very cold. Weaving in and out through the tall shrubberies, she drew her cloak more tightly around her.

At last, she followed around a curving path, and there on the bench sat the weeping, trembling Melee.

"Melee, whatever are you doing out here? You'll freeze."

Melee looked up and drew back with fear in her eyes. "Sorry. Melee sorry."

"Sorry for what? You haven't done anything." Maggie sat down on the cold bench beside her. "Why are you out here? Don't you have a room and a bed?"

"They laugh at Melee."

"Who laughs?"

"House people."

"The servants?"

Melee nodded. "Other slaves laugh."

"Sometimes people make fun of what they don't understand, Melee." She remembered how Hannah had said that to her once. Since most of the Drury slaves were from Africa, could they have made fun of her speech? Perhaps her appearance? Who knew?

"Don't listen to them, Melee." Not sure how much Melee actually understood, Maggie put her hands over her ears. "Ignore them. Pretend you don't hear. Now you need to get back inside and get to bed."

Melee's thin body convulsed in a hard shiver. "Lock door," she said.

"Who locked the door? What door?"

Melee shrugged.

"The room where you sleep? Is that the door that is locked?" She nodded.

"Poor girl," Maggie said, gently putting her arm around her. It was then she realized Melee was not shivering from cold. She had a fever and was shaking from chills. That settled it! She helped Melee to her feet. "You're coming with me," Maggie told her.

Not bothering to attempt to find the servants' entrance, she led Melee along the paths. Making her way slowly to the door, she helped Melee inside and then up to her room, where the fire was still banked and warm. With a bit of effort, Maggie assisted the girl up the steps into the high bed and tucked her in.

She dampened a cloth in the water pitcher and laid it across Melee's forehead. "I'm sure Massachusetts is nothing like Trinidad," she said softly. "How difficult all this must be for you."

"Trinidad." Melee's eyes fluttered open in response to the word. "Flowers," she said weakly. "Pretty flowers. Much sunshine. Mama, Papa."

"Poor girl," Maggie said, patting her shoulder. Nourishment was what she needed, and soon. Maggie stepped to the window and tugged at the tasseled bellpull. Within minutes, Bessie was at the door, sleepy-eyed and dressed in a white wrapper.

"Bessie, I need your help." Maggie drew her inside and waved to the bed. "This girl is very sick. I need warm milk, a bowl of gruel, and perhaps a few stewed quince. Can you do that for me?"

"What girl be sick?" Bessie asked. "Mrs. Drury should be told."

"No, no, don't tell anyone. I have Melee here."

Suddenly Bessie's eyes flew open. "You have the slave girl in your bed? Oh my! Oh my!"

With that, she was out the door and across the hall banging on the door and shouting, "Miss Adelaide, Miss Adelaide, come quick. Come see. Miss Margaret done put a slave in her bed! In her *bed*!"

One door opened in the hallway, then another and another. Questions were whispered. Slippered feet shuffled. Presently, Adelaide was standing incredulous in the room, followed quickly by Nelda, Julia, and their parents.

"Maggie," Adelaide demanded, "what's the meaning of this? Why is this girl in your own bed?"

Maggie's fear of what Adelaide might think had vanished. "She's sick. She was locked out of her room by the others in the basement quarters. She has a fever, and she would have died in the night air. I had no choice but to bring her in."

"You had no right. She's my slave. You should have brought her to me."

"Perhaps I should have. But I didn't."

"Please," Mrs. Drury interrupted, "let there be no anger." Turning to Adelaide, she said, "Didn't you tell me Maggie has no servants or slaves? So how could she possibly know the right way to handle the situation?"

The condescending tone infuriated Maggie further. "I would never own a slave," she snapped. "But if I did, I'd know enough to extend help when one is suffering."

Mrs. Drury smiled and ignored the outburst as though Maggie were a child throwing a tantrum. "Bessie."

"Yes, m'lady?"

"Fetch Adelaide's footman. Have him come and take this girl back to her quarters. Then you stay with her tonight."

Bessie rolled her eyes. "Yes, m'lady."

The crowd in the hallway was still buzzing when Mr. Drury ordered everyone back to bed. "Just a simple mistake," he told them. "Nothing to get upset about."

As Adelaide turned to go, she whispered to Maggie, "Wait till Mother learns how terribly you behaved and how you embarrassed me before all my friends."

"I was not thinking of you," Maggie stated flatly, "but of the girl."

After Melee had been carried away by Johnson, Mrs. Drury

ordered the linens to be completely stripped from the bed and fresh ones put on before Maggie could retire for the night. By the time all the commotion had quieted down, Maggie was still fuming. The copper kettle was definitely steamed up.

The remaining two days in Salem were rather awkward. Guests looked at Maggie with mirthful eyes and twittered behind spread silk fans. The Drurys now spoke to her in patronizing tones, but Maggie had ceased to care. She no longer ached to please Adelaide or to "think like a lady," according to Pert's orders.

Her attempts to learn of Melee's condition were ignored. Had there been more than two days before departure, she would have searched for the servants' quarters and banged on every door until she found the sick slave girl.

As the carriages were being loaded before dawn on Saturday morning, Johnson came from the rear of the house, carrying Melee. Maggie was relieved to see that the girl's dark eyes were brighter, but she was still too weak to walk.

The journey home was punctuated by Adelaide's complaints about having a sick slave girl. At last, Maggie could bear no more. "If you were to take care of her properly," she said, "Melee would not only be well and healthy, she would be more pleased to serve you."

"You know nothing about owning a slave," Adelaide retorted with a little sniff.

"Owning another person is wrong," Maggie stated. She was surprised at her own brashness, but once the words were out, she felt good. For once she'd spoken what she truly believed.

"I didn't *make* Melee a slave," Adelaide shot back. "She was already a slave. We simply made a purchase. If you're so against slaves, why don't you talk to your uncle Reuben? Melee came in on one of his ships."

Maggie didn't answer because she knew Adelaide was right. But her comment gave Maggie an idea.

That evening they were met in Cambridge by Pert and several footmen in one of the Chiltons' carriages. Adelaide wasted no time in relating the incident with Melee in vivid detail. Pert reacted to the incident exactly as Mrs. Drury had—attributing Maggie's action to simple ignorance.

"Maggie still has a great deal to learn," Pert said to Adelaide as though Maggie were not sitting right there in the carriage with them.

Maggie gave a polite smile and let the comment pass. How relieved she was when they drove up to the Baldwin house and all her family was there to greet her. Caleb bounced around everywhere, excited to see if Maggie brought him a gift. Even Evan gave her a warm hug of welcome.

Once her things were unloaded and the Chiltons were gone, she was treated to some of Hannah's wonderful plain cooking. How she'd missed it in the endless array of rich dainties at the Drurys'!

As they gathered about to hear all her stories, she told them of Melee's illness—carefully omitting the part about Melee in her bed. "Can you attend to her, Father? She needs help desperately."

"I understand your concern, Maggie, but I can't go unless they call me."

Maggie shook her head. "I'm not sure they will."

"But we can pray for her," Hannah said.

"Of course," Maggie agreed. Why hadn't she thought of prayer?

They bowed their heads, and Father led the prayer, asking for Melee's safety and well-being.

As they ate, Maggie surprised her father by asking him to reinstate her Latin lessons. When he asked her what prompted the decision, she simply said, "I now appreciate the fact that you think my mind is worth cultivating."

When their meal was finished, Maggie turned to her brother and said, "Evan, let's go for a ride."

Evan jumped up from the table. "I was hoping you'd say that."

"Father, may we ride over and see Uncle Reuben? I've something to ask him."

"Why, of course. There's no need to ask permission to see your own uncle."

"I may not be invited back to the Chiltons for dance instruction," Maggie told Evan as they trotted out over the pastures toward the Souder home.

"You don't sound too upset. A few months ago, you were captivated by the Chiltons. Did something happen on your trip?"

"Many things happened. But most of it happened on the inside of me. I see things differently now. On Christmas Day, I told Jacob that it mattered to me what the Chiltons thought of me, but that's not true anymore." When she told him of finding the sick Melee and putting her in her own bed, Evan laughed right out loud.

"How I wish I'd been there," he said. "What a sight to see the shock on their faces. I'm proud of you, Maggie. Very proud of you."

Maggie hadn't thought of Evan being proud of her actions. She only wanted to help Melee. But it was nice to have his approval. Later, she would tell Father and Hannah, as well.

"I must warn you about something before we get to Uncle Reuben's," Evan said, changing the subject.

Maggie turned to look at his face. "Aunt Lucille's not taken a turn for the worse, has she? She looked so much better on Christmas Day."

"Quite the opposite. She's totally changed."

"Changed how?" she asked as they rode into the Souders' back dooryard.

"You'll have to see for yourself. I'll only tell you that she calls it a conversion."

"Conversion?"

"She went to one of the meetings that Jacob is always talking about and she says. . ." He dismounted and came around to help her down. "I'll not say anymore. I'll let her tell you."

Evan was right—not only was there a change in Aunt Lucille but in the entire house.

The dark heavy draperies were gone. The house was bright and airy. Freegrace was beaming, and Aunt Lucille looked years younger. The change in Aunt Lucille was similar to what Maggie had seen in Mrs. Cradock. Perhaps Jacob and Ben Pierce were right—perhaps there was something to this "awakening" after all.

Evan and Maggie were ushered into the parlor, and Aunt Lucille asked several questions about Maggie's trip. Maggie politely answered them all, then said, "I'd like to talk to Uncle Reuben about something that occurred on my trip; but first, Aunt Lucille, please tell me what's happened to you."

By now Uncle Reuben had come in from his study. Quietly, he removed his spectacles, folded them into their case, and sat down on the sofa beside his wife and took her hand.

"I'm not sure how to explain it, Maggie," Aunt Lucille began. "I thought I was a Christian because I attended church, but as I attended the revivalist meetings, my heart was softened and touched. I wept for hours. Not tears of grief like for our babies, but of repentance. Tears of genuine sorrow for my sins."

As Aunt Lucille talked, Freegrace served tea, smiling and nodding as she listened.

"But you're not a sinner," Maggie protested. "You have never done anything wrong. You have always done good things for others."

"The scriptures tell us that all of us have fallen and come short of the glory of God, Maggie. That's why Jesus died for us—to pay for our sins. It's not according to our works but rather by His gift."

Maggie recalled the day Hannah had told her that very same thing, that salvation was a gift for all.

"I simply made the decision to open my heart and let Him in," Aunt Lucille continued. "When I did, He cleansed away all the pain and grief, and I was flooded with peace and joy."

Maggie looked at Evan and could tell he was touched by their aunt's words.

"She could go on and on," Uncle Reuben interrupted, "and sometimes she does. But I heard you say you wanted to talk to me about a matter. What is it?"

Maggie knew they must get home before dark, so she needed to get to the point. Quickly, she explained about Melee and her mistreatment by Adelaide.

"I've come to ask you to purchase Melee, set her free, and send her back home. I know it would cost a great deal, but the girl is quite ill and extremely homesick. Why, just being away from my family for a fortnight was almost unbearable for me. What a nightmare it would be to be sent away from them forever!"

Uncle Reuben had listened closely. Now he leaned back in the sofa and shook his head. "I'm sorry, Maggie. I understand your feelings, and I admire your mercy. Would that all persons had your measure of love and compassion. But Lucas Chilton would never sell that girl to me."

"But she came to Boston on your ship," Maggie said, hoping to persuade him further.

"I'm not personally involved in any slave trade, Maggie. I admit that I have transported slaves on my ships, but I've always done it for others who are involved in the market."

"Perhaps we should consider putting a stop to our limited involvement, Reuben," Aunt Lucille said softly. "Maggie is making me rethink my feelings about this matter of buying and selling another person."

"You may be right," Uncle Reuben said to her. To Maggie, he said, "I wish I could grant your request, but Lucas Chilton is a hardheaded competitor of mine and a tough-minded businessman. That girl is his property, and he would never agree to sell her."

"You can ask the Lord to take care of her, Maggie," Aunt Lucille suggested.

"Hannah suggested that very thing," Maggie said, "and we all prayed together as a family."

"Then you must rest in the fact that God will hear and answer your prayer."

Maggie wasn't sure. The best thing for Melee was to be able to go home. And Maggie wanted desperately to help her get there.

CHAPTER 15

Free at Last

The remainder of March turned blustery and sharply colder. Gray day followed upon gray day, and spring appeared to be delayed indefinitely.

To Maggie's surprise, she was invited to return to Thursday dance instruction, but the joy had gone out of it. When she learned that Melee was bedfast and Adelaide continued to complain about having a sick slave, Maggie found she could no longer bear to be there. How could she laugh and dance when Melee lay ill? Even Celia seemed somewhat subdued.

Late one night, Maggie had been in bed only a short time when she heard a commotion at the back door. She thought little of it since people often sent messengers at all hours to fetch her doctor father.

Presently, however, her father was knocking at the door of her bedchamber. "Maggie," he said, "I've been summoned to go tend the Chiltons' slave girl."

Maggie flew out of her bed, pulling her wrapper about her. Opening the door, she said, "Oh, Father, thank heaven. God has surely answered our prayers."

"Knowing your deep concern for her, I've come to ask you to accompany me."

"Me go with you?" She was stunned. Her father had never asked such a thing. "Why yes, I would like that. Thank you."

"I'll harness the horses. Come as soon as you can."

Maggie was dressed and outside in no time. As they rode to the Chilton home in silence, Maggie continued to pray for Melee.

Lucas Chilton was the one who directed them to the rear of the house where the servants' quarters were located. Maggie wasn't sure if Adelaide or Pert was even aware that Dr. Baldwin had been called. Neither of them came out.

They found Melee lying on a small cot in a corner of the servants' kitchen. It was warm and clean there, but she was so alone. The girl's dark eyes brightened at the sight of Maggie.

"Maggie," she whispered. "Maggie is friend."

Tears burned in Maggie's eyes. This girl desperately needed a friend, and Maggie had been fortunate to be that friend. She waited as her father examined Melee. A solemn Lucas Chilton stood nearby. Presently, Father approached Mr. Chilton.

"She's very ill," Maggie's father said. "I would ask your permission to allow us to take Melee to our home where I can give her closer attention."

Maggie couldn't have been more shocked! In all her days, she'd never heard her father ask to take a patient to their home. A few had slept over in the upstairs rooms at his apothecary shop but never in their home. Maggie held her breath, waiting for Mr. Chilton's answer.

"Do you think you can save her life?" Lucas asked. "She's worth a great deal of money."

"If she's in my total care, perhaps. Without it, she may not live to see another week."

"As you think best. Your carriage is open, is it not?"

Father nodded. "It is."

"Then I shall order one of our carriages to transport her immediately."

"Very good," Father replied. "Maggie, you ride with Melee."

And so it was that before the night was out, Melee was bedded down safely in the Baldwin nursery, where she was surrounded by love and attention. Hannah doted on the girl as though she were one of the family, and even Caleb wanted to help by fetching whatever was needed.

Maggie was never sure how the Pierces got word of the situation, but the next evening, Jacob came riding up to their house. Maggie had not seen him since her return from Salem. Somehow he seemed much older than before.

"We heard about the sick girl," he said after he'd been invited to sit at their kitchen table. Caleb ran to the study to call Father to join them.

"Father wants to know. . . ," Jacob began. "Well, I mean, actually, it was me who suggested it."

"Well, what is it, Jacob?" Evan said. "Can't you talk?"

The Baldwins had never seen a Pierce at a loss for words.

"May we— May I invite the Reverend Colman to come and pray with the girl?"

Maggie felt it was a strange request. No wonder he was tongue-tied. After all, they had Pastor Gee at North Church, who was perfectly able to pray for folk. Why would they need the pastor of the Brattle Street Church to come?

Her father once again surprised her by agreeing to the idea. "Please, Jacob," he said, "do ask your pastor to come. And thank you for your kind consideration."

Hannah was starting to set out mugs for cider, but Jacob jumped up. "None for me, please, Aunt Hannah. I must go. I told Father I would be gone only a short time." He moved toward the door. "I'll get the message to the pastor right away, Dr. Baldwin. Thank you."

After he was outside, Maggie turned to her father. "May I have permission to talk to Jacob alone for a moment?"

Father smiled. "You have my permission."

Running out the door into the cool night air, Maggie called out to Jacob, who was now astride his horse. "Jacob? I've something to tell you."

Deftly, he swung out of the saddle and jumped down. "What is it, Maggie?"

"I have never apologized to you for my terrible behavior on Christmas afternoon. I was rude to you, and I'm sorry. Do you forgive me?"

"I never meant to cause you harm or embarrassment, Maggie. You had every right to be angry." In the soft moonlight, she could see him smiling. "But I do accept your apology and thank you for wanting to do so. I must hurry now." Quickly, he remounted and was gone.

When the Reverend Colman arrived the next evening, he was

not alone. Accompanying him was a tall, slender gentleman with the kindest eyes Maggie had ever seen. The Reverend Colman introduced him as the Reverend Jonathan Edwards.

The infamous revivalist, Jonathan Edwards! Right in their house! Maggie could hardly believe it. But he was nothing like all the wild stories she'd heard. He was dressed in plain clothing with his brown hair tied back at the neck.

Maggie glanced at Hannah, who was smiling at her surprised expression. It was obvious Hannah knew exactly who he was. Hannah led the way to the nursery, where Melee lay. "You go in first," Hannah said to Maggie. "Make her understand these men are friends. We don't want her frightened all over again."

Because of Melee's trust in Maggie, no fear showed in her eyes as the men were allowed inside the room. Maggie listened as the soft-spoken Edwards explained in simple terms about Jesus' love and how He came from heaven to die for her sins.

Never had Maggie heard the plan of salvation explained in such a clear fashion. If this was what Mrs. Cradock and Aunt Lucille had heard preached, it was no wonder their lives were changed.

"Would you like to pray to become a child of God, Melee?" the Reverend Edwards was saying.

Melee was smiling and crying all at the same time. She placed her hands over her heart. "Loves Melee. Jesus loves Melee."

In halting broken English, Melee prayed a prayer of repentance with the Reverend Edwards. By the time they finished, everyone in the room was teary-eyed.

"You are now free in Jesus," the Reverend Edwards pronounced. "On the outside you may still be a slave, but on the inside you are free."

"Melee free," the girl repeated in awe. "Melee free."

In the following days, Hannah moved a feather tick into the nursery so she could sleep on the floor next to Melee. Hannah read scriptures to Melee and recited Bible stories. Maggie worked doubly hard to keep the chores done in order to free Hannah to be with Melee.

A few days following the pastor's visit, just before dawn, a knock sounded on Maggie's door. "Maggie, come quick," Hannah said. "It's Melee. She's asking for you."

Maggie's heart pounded as she jumped down from her bed and ran down the hall toward the nursery.

Hannah's face was somber. "Our young friend has taken a turn for the worse," she said.

"No! She can't." Maggie felt the breath go out of her. "She was getting better."

"Go to her," Hannah said softly.

Maggie stepped nearer the bed to hear her name being called very softly. "Maggie, Maggie. Thank Maggie."

"I'm here, Melee. It's me, Maggie. I've come to be with you."

The dark eyes fluttered open, and a soft smile made Melee's face relax. She reached out her slender hand. Maggie took the hand, feeling its coolness.

"Maggie is friend." Maggie felt a slight squeeze on her hand. "No slave. Melee is free."

"Yes, Melee, you're free now." Maggie turned to look at Hannah, who was weeping. "Get Father, Hannah. Melee needs him."

"Right now, she needs you," Hannah whispered. "Just you."

Maggie continued holding the hand and talking, just talking—not knowing what to say but talking anyway. Behind her, Hannah prayed. Presently, the little hand went limp. When she felt it go, Maggie slumped across the bed, sobbing.

She lay there till the crying was all spent; then she felt Hannah's strong arms lift her up. She stood and allowed Hannah to gather her into her arms and hold her as though she were a little girl again.

"Oh Hannah, Melee was so alone. I so wanted to help her go home."

"You did, my dear Maggie. You did. Melee's gone home. To her real home."

Spring arrived and worked its miracles on the countryside. Shade trees leafed out, flower gardens bloomed, the pastures were full of wildflowers; even the air smelled differently. Long-legged colts and frisky white lambs leaped and played in the meadows. Maggie took in a long breath as though she were trying to drink fresh air deep into her lungs.

Jacob laughed at her. "Don't breathe it all up," he said. "Save some for me."

Jacob had invited her and Evan to go horseback riding with him, and they'd taken turns racing without really caring who won. Now they were south of Boston Common, and the horses clopped along at a slower gait.

Three weeks had passed since they'd buried little Melee, and Maggie was only now beginning to feel like herself again. "I'm going to start a social work in the city," she was telling them.

"If anyone can do it, you can," Jacob told her.

"What made you decide this?" Evan asked.

"It was the first time I saw Ann Cradock on the dock last fall—when the other girls told me not to touch her. My heart ached, but I felt helpless."

She pulled her hood down off her head. Her red hair was loose and blowing, and it felt wonderful. "At first," she went on, "I shared my plan with Adelaide, and she discouraged me."

"But you asked the wrong person," Jacob offered.

"Exactly. Since then, I've talked to Hannah, and she suggested I begin with people like Aunt Lucille and like. . ." She looked over at Jacob, who was smiling at her. "Like your mother."

"And what about Mrs. Cradock?" Evan suggested. "I'd wager she knows the needs of the common people."

"Why, you're right, of course, Evan. What a marvelous idea."

Jacob seemed to be leading the ride as they traveled on southward crossing through the Neck, the narrow strip of land that connected Boston to the mainland. This area, referred to by old-timers as "cow common," was full of rolling hills. As they came up over the brink of one of those hills, there before them lay a sight that made Maggie gasp. Thousands of people had gathered in carts, buggies, carriages, and on horseback—it could be only one thing.

"Jacob, you've brought us to a revival meeting!" Maggie exclaimed. "You planned this all along."

"Very crafty," Evan added.

"Your father is coming with Caleb and Hannah in the carriage later on," Jacob said, smiling. "They're bringing along a lunch for us."

Maggie's defenses against the revivals had crumbled. After seeing the changes in Mrs. Cradock and Aunt Lucille and after meeting the kindly Jonathan Edwards, she was eager to hear the preaching. Soon her father arrived with Hannah and Caleb. They spread out blankets on the grassy hillside and shared a lunch. As the afternoon sun warmed the countryside, the outdoor congregation joined together in singing psalms. The glorious music ringing across the hillside sounded to Maggie like a choir of angels.

Soon the Reverend Jonathan Edwards came to the raised platform at the foot of the hill and began to preach. Many people around Maggie were crying openly, but there were none of the wild gyrations she'd heard about.

With a hungry heart, Maggie listened to the words that clearly explained God's love and mercy. The truth was clear to her now. She was responsible for her own decision to make Jesus her Lord.

Later, as the rosy dusk marked the closing of the momentous day, the crowds began to break up. As Maggie helped to fold the blankets, she heard a voice calling her name. She turned about to see Celia running toward her.

"Oh Maggie, you're here, too." Celia ran up and gave Maggie a hug. "It's nothing like we thought, is it? I'm so ashamed of all our senseless scoffing."

"We spoke in our ignorance, Celia, but now we know the truth." The look of peace in Celia's eyes told Maggie that she, indeed, knew the Truth, as well.

"Mother and Father have brought me out for nearly every

meeting. I've invited Adelaide to come, but she only laughs at me."

"We can pray for her," Maggie said. "God is faithful to answer our prayers."

"I know that now."

"Celia," Maggie said, "I am thinking of starting a work in Boston to assist those less fortunate. I don't know exactly how to begin, but I'm trusting the Lord to guide me. Would you consider becoming a part of the work?"

"Oh Maggie, what an unselfish plan. We laughed at you when you spoke of helping the girl named Ann. I am sorry now that I laughed. I'm sure Mother would like to be a part, as well," she added. "I must go now. They're waiting for me. Good-bye, Maggie." She ran a ways down the hill and then called back, "I'm so glad we're sisters in the Lord."

A cool breeze had come up, softly ruffling the leaves in the trees. One of the first stars winked overhead. As she walked along with her family. Maggie felt warm and content to the very depths of her soul.

"Let me take that," Jacob said, lifting the heavy blanket from her arms. Then he boldly grasped her hand as they strolled to the carriage together.

Lizzie and the Redcoat

Susan Martins Miller

A Note to Readers

While Lizzie Murray and her family and friends are fictional, what happens in Boston in this story is not. It is twelve years before the Revolutionary War, but Boston's streets are already filled with violence. Angry because of increasing taxes, mobs are attacking British agents and soldiers. They burn homes and destroy property. Even people who are forced to house British soldiers are not safe from the mob's fury.

While it is easy for us to look back now and see where these events would lead, things were not so clear to King George III, Sam Adams, James Otis, or the thousands of colonists who were trying to decide the right thing to do. As we will see in this story, even individual families were not safe from the conflicts that raged through the colonies.

Contents

CHAPTER 1

The Attack!

Lizzie loved winter.

Perched in a wing chair scooted up to the window, she pressed her face against the cold glass. The wind had blown a gentle curve of white powder against the clear pane. She studied the icy shapes that had formed on both sides of the glass. With her eyes squinted nearly shut, she tilted her head from side to side. Lizzie tried to imagine what the intricate patterns of the snowflakes might look like if they could only be larger. They might be like the spiderwebs she knocked down from the ceiling of her room, or they might be like the tatted lace her aunt Charlotte loved to make.

Lizzie had tried to learn to tat. Aunt Charlotte had been a patient teacher, but Lizzie's fingers simply would not go where they were supposed to go, and her projects always ended up being a tangled knot. She was almost twelve now. Perhaps she should try again. She would love to make a roomful of holiday lace—maybe even a whole Christmas tablecloth as a gift for her mother. A white lace tablecloth would look so festive on the long walnut table with the imported china dishes set just right.

Lizzie pushed her thick coppery hair away from her face and turned her cheek to the glass. The draft came in around the edges of the window and stirred up the fire in the front room of the Murray family home. Mama always said that the inside of the house was nearly as cold as the outside. The fire gave an especially loud snap, and Lizzie glanced at it. She loved the comfort of a roaring fire on a cold day.

Still, it was cold in the room, and Lizzie had been sitting in that chair near the window for almost an hour. She pulled her shawl snug around her shoulders and reluctantly crossed the room to warm her hands over the fire. The woodpile was getting low. At this time of year, it took so much wood to warm just the kitchen and front room of the family's home. Upstairs, in her unheated bedroom, Lizzie had learned to change clothes quickly and leap into bed.

Christmas was only a few days away. Lizzie could hardly believe that 1764 was almost over already. Mama had tried to tell her that when the years passed quickly, it meant you were growing up. Sometimes Lizzie wanted to be grown-up. She could choose her own clothes and perhaps drive her own carriage. But most of the time, growing up frightened Lizzie. Life in the colonies was changing, and if she were a grown-up, Lizzie would have to decide what she thought about everything. When it came to King George and the English Parliament, she was far too confused to know what she thought was right and what she thought was wrong.

Putting unsettling thoughts aside, Lizzie pictured the front room on Christmas Day. Soon the house would be filled with relatives and decorations and simple gifts of love. Her mother's brothers would come with their families. Uncle Blake and Aunt Charlotte would close down their carriage shop for the day and bundle up Isaac and Christopher. Uncle Philip would put a note on the door of his medical clinic telling people where he was in case of an emergency. He and Aunt Johanna and young Charity would descend enthusiastically on the Murray home.

A fire would burn in every room on Christmas. Her younger cousins would romp joyously through the house. They would all go to church together and come home for the biggest dinner of the year. Of course, this year holiday food would be harder to find than in the past. Boston was not the same as it had been a few years ago.

"Oh, there you are."

Lizzie turned toward the voice. "Were you looking for me, Mama?" Her mother had entered from the dining room.

"I thought you might like to see the quilt squares before I give them to Charlotte." Constance Murray spread two dozen carefully pieced quilt squares on and around the large chair next to the fire. A blue-and-white floral pattern emerged.

"They're beautiful, Mama," Lizzie said sincerely. "Your corners are perfect. I wish I could learn to quilt like that."

Her mother smiled. "You will. It takes years of practice."

"Aunt Johanna will love the quilt." Lizzie fingered the edge of one square and smiled faintly at the thought of her gentle aunt, married to her mother's younger brother, Philip. Lizzie was glad to have Aunt Johanna to confide in.

"I only wish Charlotte and I could have finished it in time for Christmas," Mama said.

"But Aunt Johanna's birthday is only a few weeks away," Lizzie said. "She'll have it soon enough." She looked up at her mother with a sly smile. "Do you think she suspects anything?"

"I certainly hope not." Mama started to gather up the quilt squares and stack them neatly again. "After all the hours Charlotte and I have spent on this project, I want it to be a complete surprise."

Lizzie chuckled. "I love the way Aunt Johanna holds her breath when she is surprised and doesn't know what to say."

Mama laughed, too. "Maybe that's why I like to surprise her." She offered the quilt squares to Lizzie. "Here. Why don't you take these down to your aunt Charlotte? I think she's at the carriage shop this afternoon. She's anxious to start putting the quilt together."

Lizzie looked toward the window. "But, Mama, it's cold out, and it will be dark soon."

"You have plenty of time if you just go and come directly back. Besides, I know you love the snow."

"Please, Mama, can't Joshua go?"

"Your brother is down at the print shop helping Papa. And I have to stay here with Emmett and Olivia. Don't be so contrary. It is not becoming to a young lady."

Lizzie heard the firmness in her mother's voice and knew she would have to go out whether she liked it or not. She did love the snow—her mother was right about that. And the walk to Wallace Coach and Carriage Company, owned by Uncle Blake and Aunt Charlotte, was not a long one. A crisp, bright winter day was Lizzie's favorite kind of weather, and Mama knew that. But it was no longer fun to walk around the streets of Boston. Lizzie much preferred to stay indoors and imagine that all was well.

"Wear your warmest cloak, and you should be fine," Mama said. "Tuck the quilt squares underneath to keep them dry."

"Yes, Mama," Lizzie said softly and went to fetch her cloak.

Outside, she took a deep breath and looked around. The street where the Murrays lived was a quiet one. The families who lived there were proud of their homes. They had worked hard to build their houses and make them every bit as comfortable as the homes newcomers spoke of having left in England. Goods came into the colonies from everywhere, but mostly from England. Business had been good for many years.

That was changing now. Some people were so angry with King George and the Parliament in England that they refused to buy anything that came from England. And Parliament disapproved of the colonies bringing in too many goods from anywhere else.

Lizzie turned a corner and started walking in the direction of Boston Harbor. Wallace Coach and Carriage was near the harbor. Lizzie knew that many people thought Aunt Charlotte had no business working at the carriage shop. But Charlotte was independent enough to do as she pleased, and Uncle Blake seemed to appreciate the help. Lizzie admired Aunt Charlotte's fire as much as she admired Aunt Johanna's gentleness.

Around the next corner, Lizzie's heart quickened at the sight of the British soldiers. They were standing guard outside the Customs House, the brick building where the king's treasury in Boston was kept. There were two guards, one on either side of the doorway. They stood silently still, with their red coats properly buttoned and their muskets always ready. Their white collars were so stiff they could hardly move their heads. Lizzie kept her eyes fixed on the street ahead of her and focused on putting one foot in front of the other just to keep moving. If she had gone the long way around, she might have avoided the soldiers. But it was too late now. Beneath her cloak, her fingers gripped the quilt squares that had brought her out on this day.

Lizzie hated the feeling she got in her stomach whenever she saw British soldiers on duty. British soldiers had been in Boston her whole life, but they had always been small in number with pleasant responsibilities. They had worked alongside the colonists for the good of both England and the colonies. Now, it seemed that they were everywhere, and they were here to do what King George wanted them to do, not what the Bostonians wanted.

Even the townspeople could not agree about what was best for the colonies. In the past, no one had seemed to mind the soldiers. Now, everyone argued about whether the soldiers should stay in Boston or be packed up and sent home on the next boat to England. Lizzie had heard her uncles dispute that question many times.

Not so long ago, Boston had been bubbling with energy. The harbor had been filled with boats, and everyone in town had been curious to see the new items they brought in. Books, fine furniture, and clothing had come from Europe, and the colonists had felt they were as much a part of life in England as if they still lived there.

At the same time, Boston had become a real city. Schools and newspapers—including Papa's print shop—had flourished. Carpenters were kept busy filling orders for furniture and equipment for the outlying farms. Craftsmen had worked on jewelry, dishes, and decorations for the homes of Boston's upper class. Blacksmiths kept shoes on hundreds of horses. Women from the other colonies traveled to Boston to see what the new fashions were. Church bells rang to remind the people to worship the God who had blessed them. The streets had been filled with horses and carriages as people came into town to shop and visit and exchange information.

Lizzie had loved living in Boston when so much was going on. She could go into Mr. Osgood's shop for a sweet treat or to the dressmaker's shop to see sketches of the new clothes from Europe. But those shops were closed now. The molasses that Mr. Osgood used in many of his sweets had gotten too expensive because of new taxes, and the dressmaker had taken an independent spirit and refused to follow the fashions from England.

Lizzie did not understand very much about the Seven Years' War. She knew that the colonies had fought alongside England against the French. At the end of the war, some of the land they had been fighting over was given to France.

From reading the small newspaper that her father published, Lizzie also knew that King George in England was not happy with the colonies. He thought that they did not help enough during the Seven Years' War and that they should have done much more to help the British troops. More of the men should have fought, the king thought, and those who did not could have given food and supplies more willingly. The Seven Years' War—which had lasted for most of Lizzie's life—had drained the treasury of England. The relationship between the colonies and their mother country was changed forever. Now King George seemed determined to control the colonies with an iron hand. So the soldiers were everywhere. Boston was still full of energy, but it was an angry energy, filled with dread of things to come.

Lizzie was past the soldiers now and could breathe more easily. Her brother Joshua, who was two years older than she, teased her about how nervous the soldiers made her. He liked to remind her that their own family had come from England and Ireland. "Maybe those boys outside the Customs House are our distant cousins," Joshua would say. "I think the red jackets are a bit odd, but I'm not afraid of the men who wear them."

Lizzie shuddered. The wind blew through her cloak. Now that she was down the street a few yards, she glanced back over her shoulder at the soldiers. They had not changed position. They seemed not to even notice the biting wind. No matter what Joshua said, the British soldiers made Lizzie nervous. Their presence meant that things were not going well in Boston. With Christmas just around the corner, Lizzie yearned to feel free of the foreboding presence that followed her everywhere she went.

Suddenly Lizzie was pulled off balance from behind! She tried to scream, but a firm hand on her mouth stifled the sound.

CHAPTER 2

The Customs Agent

Lizzie lost her balance and fell backward, straight into the chest of her attacker. He swung her around and lifted her feet off the ground, spinning her around three times. Her arms and feet flailed against the empty air. When she landed, she kicked backward as hard as she could until she struck something solid—a shin.

"Ouch!" With a grunt that revealed his pain, he released Lizzie immediately.

Once free, she started to run up the street—until she looked over her shoulder and saw the identity of her attacker.

"Joshua Murray! You frightened me half to death." She charged at her fourteen-year-old brother, who merely grinned back at her. He was amused by her anger. "Why in the world would you do such a thing?"

Joshua caught her wrists before she could strike him. "I'm sorry. I couldn't help myself. I saw you walking past the sentries and thought it would be a shame to let all that fear go to waste. You could not even look at their faces."

"What does that matter?" Lizzie asked indignantly. "I did not come out in the cold to visit with soldiers." She turned and began walking again.

"They wouldn't hurt you, you know." Joshua fell into step beside her.

"I don't want to talk about it."

"You're just a girl. You're not a soldier or a militiaman. You are no threat to them."

"I said I didn't want to talk about it." Lizzie speeded up her steps.

"Where are you going?"

"To the carriage shop. Mama has finished her quilt squares for Aunt Johanna, and Aunt Charlotte is going to put them together."

"I'll come along," Joshua said. "I always like visiting the carriage business."

"Doesn't Papa need you?" Lizzie asked.

"I'm finished for today at the print shop."

"Well, if you must, you may come along." Lizzie gave her brother a harsh look. Inwardly, however, she was glad to have Joshua with her. Not only was he bigger and stronger than she was, but he was not afraid. Nothing that had happened in Boston in recent months made him avoid being outside. When she was with Joshua, Lizzie felt less afraid herself.

Soon Boston Harbor came into view. The sun glinted off the water as the waves lapped into the protection of the half-frozen harbor.

"I love coming down here," Joshua said. He slowed his steps to gaze at the mass of boats and docks before them. He braced himself against a railing and looked directly out over the water. "Don't you ever wonder about all the places those boats have been, all the things that the crews have seen?"

Lizzie shrugged. "It's enough for me just to see the things they bring back. Except they don't bring much anymore."

Ships lined the docks, but the mighty masts were down on many of them. Only three ships were being unloaded. December was a difficult time to sail the ocean, and some of the shippers and other business owners had lost a lot of business because people in the colonies were refusing to contribute to the king's well-being by purchasing goods from England.

"Uncle Blake seems to be keeping busy enough at the shop. He has more business all the time. Just last week, seven more coaches were brought to him for repair, not to mention the orders he already had for new carts and carriages."

Lizzie nodded. "I think I heard Aunt Charlotte say something about that."

"When I'm sixteen, I'm going to ask Papa to let me work with Uncle Blake," Joshua said. "At least for a little while."

"I thought you were going to work at the print shop with Papa when you finish school."

"There is plenty of time for both." Joshua's eyes brightened. "I wonder what the cargo is on the ships that just arrived—and whether Uncle Blake is paying taxes on the goods he receives."

"Uncle Blake runs an honest business," Lizzie said with certainty. She gestured that they should resume their walk.

"I'm not sure anyone is completely honest anymore," Joshua said. He let his fingers trail lightly along the rail as he walked. "I've heard a lot of rumors about smuggling lately. Papa even has a story about it in the newspaper."

"Smuggling?" Lizzie asked. "What does the story say? Does Papa think it's true?"

"You know Papa. He likes to report the facts and let people make up their own minds."

"What about you?"

Joshua shrugged. "Who knows? Parliament is enforcing the Sugar Act, and the customs agents are watching all the ships carefully. I know Uncle Blake does not agree with the Sugar Act. He says it will cost everyone a lot of money in taxes."

Will I never escape danger? Lizzie wondered. She was on a simple errand to take quilt squares to her aunt, and she found herself suspecting her uncle of breaking the laws of England.

They approached the big wooden door to Wallace Coach and Carriage. Joshua and Lizzie had grown up visiting this office. Blake Wallace had inherited Wallace Coach from his uncle, Randolph Wallace, after an apprenticeship and a time of learning to run the business. Blake had expanded the company—and the name—after several years, adding newer models of carriages like the phaeton and the landau. Wallace Coach and Carriage had flourished under his direction and was quite the modern business now.

Joshua pushed open the door, and they went in. A man in a long gray coat stood across from Uncle Blake's desk, talking intently.

"He looks angry," Lizzie whispered.

"Don't mind him," Joshua said. "He's just the customs agent."

Lizzie's eyes widened. "The customs agent? Is Uncle Blake already in trouble?"

Joshua put a finger to his lips to hush Lizzie and steered her toward the back of the office. Aunt Charlotte stood in the doorway to the back room. She wiggled her finger to say they should join her. Her two small sons, six and eight years old, poked their heads around her billowing skirts to try to see what was happening in the outer office. Charlotte gently pushed their heads back.

"What's going on?" Lizzie whispered as Aunt Charlotte herded them into the back room.

"The customs agent thinks Blake is evading the required taxes on goods for the business."

Lizzie caught her breath. *Is Joshua right? Is Uncle Blake defying the king?*

"I knew it!" Joshua said victoriously. "Uncle Blake is not going to let the British push him around."

"You know no such thing," Aunt Charlotte said sternly. "What your uncle does with his business is no concern of yours, and I'll thank you not to spread rumors that you know nothing about."

"Yes, ma'am," Joshua said. He said no more, but Lizzie could see in Joshua's eyes that he still believed Uncle Blake was deliberately disobeying the king's laws.

"I'm sure you did not come to watch this little show," Aunt Charlotte said. "Has your mother sent you?"

"Oh! I completely forgot!" Lizzie reached under her cloak and brought out the quilt squares. "Mama sent me with these. I'm afraid I've wrinkled them a bit." She glared at Joshua. "I got a little nervous walking over here."

Aunt Charlotte set the squares on a table and began

smoothing them out. "These will do just fine. Your mother is one of the best quilters I know." She began moving the squares around in different arrangements. Without looking up, she spoke. "Isaac Wallace, you mind me. Stay in this room."

Little Isaac moaned and stepped back from the doorway. Lizzie smiled to herself. Like her own mother, Aunt Charlotte knew what her children were doing even when she could not see them.

The sounds from the outer office grew louder.

"I assure you, Mr. Wallace," the customs agent said, nearly shouting by now, "you will face consequences for your actions!"

"With all due respect, sir," Uncle Blake replied calmly, "you have not specified any actions worthy of consequences."

"See," Lizzie whispered to Joshua, "Uncle Blake is not doing anything illegal."

"That is not what he said," Joshua responded. "Maybe the customs agent hasn't figured it all out yet. He needs more information to charge Uncle Blake with wrongdoing."

Lizzie pressed her lips together and looked through the doorway at her uncle. Could Joshua be right?

Joshua quietly stepped into the outer office and leaned casually against the wall.

"Joshua! What are you doing?" Lizzie used the loudest whisper she could without drawing attention to herself.

"Just standing here," he answered. But he slid along the wall a few steps at a time.

"Boys, get back," Aunt Charlotte said to her sons.

"But Joshua is out there," the older one protested.

"Pay no attention to Joshua."

But Aunt Charlotte did pay attention to Joshua. Her eyes followed his movement around the outer office. Lizzie and her little cousins peeked out to watch, too. Slowly and silently, Joshua inched his way around the room until he was squarely behind the customs agent. Lizzie and Aunt Charlotte looked at each other and chuckled as quietly as they could. They knew what was coming next.

The customs agent's white powdered wig jiggled humorously as he shook his head at Uncle Blake. Behind him, Joshua scowled and shook his head from side to side in a comically exaggerated motion.

"It would behoove you to be honest with me, Mr. Wallace," the agent said. "I have the full authority of the king behind me. Do not try to deceive me."

Joshua mouthed an echo of everything the angry man said.

"I assure you, Mr. Byles," Uncle Blake said, "it is not necessary for you to be so curious about my activities. Wallace Coach and Carriage is a family business that has been operating for decades in full cooperation of British law. We did not organize ourselves simply to frustrate the king."

"Don't make fun of me!" Mr. Byles shouted, shaking a finger at Uncle Blake.

Joshua shook his finger in a stern gesture.

"I can assure you that if I find any evidence to support my suspicions, you will find yourself in serious trouble." Mr. Byles set his hands on his hips and glared at Uncle Blake.

Joshua did the same.

"Look at Joshua!" one of the boys exclaimed. "He's funny!"

"Hush!" Aunt Charlotte said. "Pay him no mind." But her

eyes caught Lizzie's and twinkled.

"I am fully aware of the consequences of evading taxes, Mr. Byles," Uncle Blake said. The slightest of smiles formed on his lips as he caught Joshua's eye. Joshua grinned back at his uncle.

"I would suggest you take that smirk off your face, Mr. Wallace. I do not take kindly to being ridiculed."

Joshua stuck out his lower lip and shook his head seriously.

Blake resumed a sober expression. "Of course not, Mr. Byles. I would not think of ridiculing you."

Mr. Byles huffed in disgust. "I can think of no reason why I should believe you," he said, "but I do have other business to attend to this afternoon."

"I am a fair man, Mr. Byles, and I understand the needs of government. I make no effort to avoid a reasonable tax."

"I can assure you that you have not seen the last of me." The agent thrust one arm up in the air to emphasize his point.

Joshua did the same.

"You are welcome to visit Wallace Coach and Carriage at any time, Mr. Byles. I trust the remainder of your day will pass pleasantly."

The customs agent turned around abruptly. Joshua immediately brought his hands down to his sides and smiled politely.

"What are you doing here?" Mr. Byles demanded.

"I have come to visit my uncle, sir," Joshua replied respectfully.

"Why did you not speak up?"

"I did not wish to disturb your conversation, sir."

"Your mother has brought you up well," Mr. Byles declared. Then he pushed past Joshua and left the shop.

"Joshua, you were wonderful," Uncle Blake said, grabbing

his nephew by the shoulders. "I don't know how you can do that without bursting out in laughter."

Aunt Charlotte came out of the back room and collapsed into a wooden desk chair, laughing. Lizzie and the boys followed her out.

"Cousin Joshua, you are so funny!" Both of the boys started making faces and shaking their fingers at each other.

"Some might think you are a disrespectful boy," Aunt Charlotte cautioned, "but it was an amusing sight."

Lizzie was laughing, too. The whole family loved to watch Joshua's impressions—even when he made fun of some of *them*.

But as she laughed, Lizzie remembered some of her uncle's words. He had not come right out and denied that he was cheating the king out of any taxes he owed. Obviously Mr. Byles was convinced he had good reason to suspect Uncle Blake. Lizzie wanted to believe her uncle was doing the right thing, but she was not sure what to think. *Does Uncle Blake feel that taxes are wrong?* Lizzie wondered. *Is he in danger?*

❦ CHAPTER 3 ❧

The Argument on Christmas Day

Carefully, precisely, Lizzie set the china plate perfectly between the fork and knife. Then she adjusted the crystal goblet ever so slightly until she was satisfied that the place setting was exactly right. She wanted the table to be perfect for Christmas dinner. Satisfied with the first place setting, she moved on to the next. Before she was finished, she would make her way around the long walnut table covered with a white damask tablecloth until all fifteen place settings were perfectly lined up. As she surveyed the table, she imagined the family gathered around it. There would be her parents, with Joshua and Olivia and Emmett. Uncle Blake and Aunt Charlotte would be there also, with Isaac and Christopher. And Uncle Philip, Aunt Johanna, and cousin Charity would complete the gathering.

Lizzie straightened a narrow ladder-back chair until it was perfectly lined up with the place setting before it. She paused to pick up a plate and admire it. She had always loved the delicate pink-and-green flower pattern. Seeing it and holding the plate made Lizzie feel a mysterious connection to her great-grandmother, who had received these dishes as a wedding present. Two of the plates had slight nicks, but none of the pieces had been broken. Lizzie likened the dishes to her family—they were not perfect people, but they were a family, bound together by love passed down for generations.

"Can I help you?" The request came from six-year-old Olivia, Lizzie's sister. Olivia was not exactly known for her gentle touch. She was a rambunctious child, fearful of nothing and always ready to try something new. Lizzie winced inwardly at the thought of Olivia touching their great-grandmother's china. Yet she did not want to hurt Olivia's feelings. She remembered how proud she had felt the first time she was allowed to help set the table.

"How about if we do it together?" Lizzie proposed.

Happily, Olivia agreed, and with one of Lizzie's hands on Olivia's shoulder and the other firmly holding the plate, they laid the next place setting.

"I helped, I helped!" Olivia cried and scampered off to the front room to brag to her cousins.

Lizzie smiled and turned back to her task. But she was soon interrupted again.

"I want to help!" announced her cousin Isaac.

"Me, too!" said his brother Christopher.

"I'll help," said five-year-old Charity, Uncle Philip and Aunt Johanna's daughter.

Lizzie's youngest brother, five-year-old Emmett, said nothing but looked up at her with his wide dark eyes. Lizzie could never resist Emmett when he looked like that. She was faced with three little boys and a girl who all wanted to help set the table with china and crystal.

Isaac reached for the stack of plates, and Lizzie stopped him just in time.

"I'll tell you what," she said. "You can all help, but you have to take turns."

"Me first! Me first!" Isaac and Christopher said, almost together.

Lizzie looked at Emmett. She knew he would never insist on having the first turn. Emmett and Lizzie understood each other. Despite almost seven years' difference in their ages, they were more like each other than anyone else in the Wallace or Murray families.

"Let's start with the youngest," Lizzie said as she took Emmett's hand. Systematically, she helped them all set a plate on the table in the proper spot: first Emmett, then Charity, then Isaac, and finally Christopher.

Satisfied, the little ones scurried away to return to their play. As Lizzie watched them go, she wondered what was going on in their minds. Although the older boys wore the long breeches of adult men, they were only children. Did they feel the sense of danger and fear that she felt? Did they know that the unrest in the streets of Boston was not normal? Lizzie comforted herself with the thought that they were young enough to fill their days and thoughts only with playing harder and learning the letters of the alphabet.

Lizzie had worked her way from one end of the table to the other. The voices of her father and her uncles, sitting near the fireplace in the next room, filled her ears.

"...has got to realize that it is unreasonable to expect that the people of the colonies will not want to move west," said Uncle Blake. "I cannot imagine what madness the king has fallen into to make him declare it illegal to settle any farther west than the Appalachian divide."

"I'm sure that is only for the time being," said Uncle Philip, the soft-spoken doctor.

"I should think so," said Lizzie's father, Duncan Murray. "There is an entire continent awaiting settlement—land for farms and towns. The people will not wait long."

"They are not waiting even now," said Uncle Blake. "Settlers had already started pushing west before this crazy rule came from London."

"But there are no real towns," said Papa, "no schools, no shops."

"You are right about that," Uncle Blake responded, "but those things will come. When enough people have settled and begun farming, they will organize themselves into communities and resist Parliament and the king."

"I'm afraid you are right," Papa agreed. "It would take a great many soldiers to stop the westward flow." He looked down into the mug of hot tea he held in his hand while he pondered the issue.

Through the doorway, Lizzie looked from her father to Uncle Blake to Uncle Philip, who had not said very much. Uncle Philip usually said little. He did not always agree with his older brother Blake, but it seemed to Lizzie that he would rather remain silent than cause conflict.

"Joshua tells me you had a visit from a customs agent," Papa said to Uncle Blake.

Uncle Blake chuckled. "It was nothing serious, I assure you. Ezra Byles is making regular rounds at all the shops and businesses near the harbor. He never comes right out and says what he thinks. I don't believe he has any real evidence of anything that he suspects."

"No doubt he is simply trying to frighten people into obeying the regulations from Parliament."

"Well, he does not frighten me, and I daresay he does not frighten Joshua either. You should have seen him. He was magnificent!"

Papa smiled. "Someday those imitations are going to get him into trouble."

Uncle Blake returned to the subject of Parliament. "The colonies have always contributed to the needs of the empire. We have been a hardworking lot, and the Crown has reaped the benefit of our efforts. We've educated our children right from the start. We have our own newspapers and colleges. We've governed ourselves peaceably with our own houses of assembly. We have no need for the interference of Parliament in our affairs."

"The colonies still belong to the Crown," Uncle Philip reminded his brother. "If Isaac or Christopher told you that they did not need you any longer, I'm sure you would set them straight. They are still your sons."

"Ah yes, but when they have grown, they may do as they please. The colonies have matured. We are not the frail, fledgling group that landed at Plymouth."

Lizzie sighed as she turned back toward the table and picked up another goblet. When Uncle Blake spoke, what he said made sense. But when Uncle Philip spoke, what he said made sense, too. The two brothers did not agree with each other, yet Lizzie was drawn to both sides of the question. She thought of herself as English, yet she had never seen London and probably never would. Her mother's family had landed in Plymouth almost 150 years before, and they didn't have any contact with the distant relatives who still lived there. Her life in the colonies was busy and full. Lizzie loved living in Boston and did not feel that she lacked anything because she had not been to London.

"Perhaps," Uncle Philip said, "the problem is not so much what Parliament is doing as it is how they are going about it."

"What do you mean?" her father asked.

"Even independent-minded colonists consider themselves loyal subjects of the king," Uncle Philip explained. "We can understand that the Seven Years' War took a heavy toll on the Crown's treasury. Perhaps if Parliament had not been so heavy-handed in the way it announced the Sugar Act, people would not disagree with it."

Uncle Blake shook his head vigorously. "No, Philip, I don't think so. We did our best to come to the aid of England during the war, and Parliament has all but ignored the contribution we made in winning the war. Parliament is treating us like we have been naughty children."

Lizzie smoothed a napkin that she had already smoothed a dozen times. It was impossible for her to judge who was right.

"I don't know what to make of it all, but I do know one thing," her father said thoughtfully. "Parliament and the colonies cannot continue this bickering for much longer without consequences. Men like Sam Adams have nearly reached their limits."

"Adams is a man of vision," Uncle Blake said.

"Adams is a man itching to stir up trouble," Uncle Philip said, disagreeing. "He's been in my clinic, spinning his stories about what is to become of the colonies."

"No matter what you think of him," Papa said, "he is a man to be reckoned with."

With a lump in her throat, Lizzie balanced herself against the ladder-back chair.

"The table looks lovely!"

At the sound of Aunt Johanna's gentle voice, Lizzie turned her attention away from the conversation in the next room and focused once more on the table.

Aunt Johanna laid one hand on Lizzie's shoulder. "No one lays a table as nicely as you do, Lizzie."

"I had some help," Lizzie said.

"So Charity told me. You are so patient with the little ones. Everything is beautiful."

"Thank you. The tablecloth needs mending. I think Mama would like a new one, but. . ."

"Yes, I know," Johanna said softly. "It's hard to find anything in the shops now."

"Mama said she had to make all sorts of substitutions for Christmas dinner. She couldn't find anything she wanted, and she wouldn't buy any of the things that came from England."

"I know. We tried shops all over Boston."

"I'm so glad Mama has kept this china," Lizzie said. "It helps me remember what Christmas was like when I was little, before all of this started." She turned her head back toward the men.

"Have you been listening?"

Lizzie nodded.

Aunt Johanna sighed. "I would love to tell you not to be concerned about anything you have heard and that everything is going to be all right. I would love to promise that by next Christmas everything will be the way you want it to be. But I can't."

"I know," Lizzie murmured.

"Many of the things that people are angry about started a long time ago. But you were too young to be concerned with politics and loyalties. Now you're growing up. You understand more."

"I'm not sure I like it," Lizzie said as she pushed a chair in neatly under the table. "Aunt Johanna, can I tell you a secret?"

"I hope you will."

"It's not really a secret. Joshua already knows."

"What does he know?"

Lizzie looked down at her hands. "That I'm frightened. All the time."

"What are you frightened of?"

"I'm not sure. . . . Everything, I guess. I'm afraid something bad is going to happen. Something bad will happen to somebody in the family. I hate thinking about it, but it's always in my mind."

"Do you think you can stop something bad from happening?"

Lizzie shook her head. "That's the problem. I want to stop it, but how can I? I don't even know what it is."

"Who could stop it?" Aunt Johanna probed.

Lizzie shrugged. "God, I guess. But I don't know if He will. He has already let a lot of bad things happen."

Aunt Johanna sighed. "These are not easy questions, Lizzie, so I will not give you easy answers. But remember who truly is in charge."

"What do you mean?"

"Is King George in charge?"

"Well, he thinks he is, but a lot of people don't agree."

"Is Sam Adams in charge?"

"He might like to be, but he's not."

"Think about who is in charge, Lizzie, and find your peace there."

Before Lizzie could press Aunt Johanna further, they both jumped at the sound of a crash above them.

Aunt Johanna rolled her eyes. "That would be Emmett and Charity jumping off the bed again. I've told them a hundred times not to do that." She gathered her billowing skirts and turned to go inspect the damage.

CHAPTER 4

The Mob

The temperatures rose, and the ice on the pond where Lizzie had taken Olivia and Emmett to slide around during the harsh winter months melted. The heavy snows of January and February gave way to the rains of March and April. The grass, brown and brittle during the winter, once again sprang up thick and green.

As much as Lizzie loved the winter, she loved the spring even more. She dropped her satchel of books in the grass and threw herself down beside it. She had had a hard time paying attention in school that day. Every time she glanced out the window and saw the clouds pushed along by the breeze, she wanted to be outside watching them. At last the clock had struck three, and the teacher had dismissed the class. Lizzie would have to work on her arithmetic after supper, but for now, she wanted to gaze at the sky and imagine.

What did she imagine? People always wanted to know. Anything and everything. That was her answer. She would imagine the clouds were exotic animals she had never seen or mansions she would never live in. And sometimes, lately, she would imagine that the clouds were British soldiers sailing across the ocean, back to their homeland. And she would imagine that there was peace in the colonies.

Lizzie lingered in the grass outside the school as long as she dared. Papa was expecting her at the print shop to help with errands. She did not want to be scolded. So reluctantly, she pulled herself to her feet, picked up her satchel, and began the walk. By now the other children were far ahead of her, and she could at least be alone with her thoughts.

When she came to the town square though, something was not right. Far too many people were gathered for the middle of the afternoon. Merchants who should have been busy in their shops were standing in little groups discussing something intently. The blacksmiths had left their fires, the carpenters had left their hammers, and the tailor had left his cloth. What could possibly have brought everyone out on a spring afternoon in the middle of the week? With a knot in her stomach, Lizzie quickened her steps and hurried to the print shop.

She could hardly get in the door. Inside the print shop were nearly as many people as she had seen on the square.

"Papa?" she called, but she knew he could not possibly hear her over the din of voices that filled the room.

She raised her eyes to the top of the printing press that rose from the floor and was bolted to the ceiling. Usually the huge beams of the press were the first thing she saw when she entered the shop. It was an enormous structure, and when she was six she had insisted that her father explain to her how it worked. She wanted to know everything about the iron workings inside the wooden frame, the metal that was cast into molds and pressed onto the paper that her father printed.

Today though, she could hardly see the press—only the top where it rose above the heads of the tallest people in the room. But Lizzie could see enough to know that the press was not moving. This was the busiest time of day for the print shop. The afternoon newspaper should be stacking up on the tray, and the smell of fresh ink should be filling the room. Yet the press was still. People liked to read the newspaper, but very few ever visited the shop where it was printed. Something was very strange.

"Papa!" Lizzie called out again, louder.

"Over here, Lizzie!" The voice that spoke her name cut through the din of the crowd, and she turned her head toward it. Joshua was gesturing that she should come stand beside him along one wall.

Getting through the crowd was not easy. Lizzie had to squeeze past elbows in motion and brush against swishing full skirts. No one seemed to notice her. Along the way she caught snatches of conversation.

"This is illegal!"

"Parliament has gone too far this time!"

"The colonies should act now! We can't let them steal from us like this!"

Finally Lizzie managed to reach her older brother. "What has happened?" she asked breathlessly. "What is going on?"

"The Stamp Act," Joshua answered.

"You mean the Sugar Act," Lizzie corrected. "But that's not new."

"No, I mean the Stamp Act. Parliament passed it in March. Only now has the message reached the colonies."

Lizzie leaned against the wall and let her shoulders sag.

"What does it mean?" she asked.

"I'm not sure about all the details yet," Joshua said. He almost had to shout to be heard over the crowd. "But I think it means that people have to pay for a stamp to put on papers."

"What kind of papers?"

"Any kind of paper. Legal documents, newspapers, almanacs. Just about everything."

"So why are all these people here? What does Papa have to do with it?"

"They want to know if he is going to charge more for the newspaper and the other things he prints. But most of all, they want to know if he is going to print a story against the Stamp Act."

"Papa always tries to be fair in the stories he prints." Lizzie had always admired her father's sense of fairness, but she was beginning to wonder if it would get him in trouble.

"These people are not concerned with what is fair," Joshua said. "They are angry."

"I can see that!" Lizzie said, her voice rising to be heard above the crowd. "Were all these people in the shop when you got here after school?"

Joshua nodded. "Most of them. I don't think Papa knows I'm here yet."

The crowd pushed forward toward the printing press. The door opened, and still more people entered.

Lizzie and Joshua squeezed themselves up against the wall and listened.

"Duncan, do you understand what this means?" one man shouted, shaking his fist.

"Of course I do. This will impact my business more than you know." Duncan Murray stood on a stool trying to calm the crowd. He shook his head. "Imagine, every paper I print with a stamp on it means I have to collect more money from all of you. I don't like it any more than the rest of you."

"Then what are you going to do about it?"

"I'm going to report the facts," Lizzie's father said solidly, "so that everyone will know exactly what the law is and what it means for them."

"We already know what it means, Duncan," another man called out. "It means that Parliament is trying to squeeze more money out of us."

"Yes," said another, "and this time they are taking money that ought to stay in the colonies. Take your business, for example, Duncan. You own and operate this business completely within Massachusetts. Why should a penny of your earnings leave the colonies to go into the treasury of the king?"

Papa held up his hand and shook his head. "I didn't say I agreed with the law. I simply said I was going to report the facts."

"Make sure you report all the facts!" Ezra Byles, the customs agent, shoved his way through the crowd and stood before Duncan Murray. "Make sure that you report the true condition of the king's treasury. The Seven Years' War was fought at a dear price, and the colonies were greedy, stingy, and uncooperative. Be sure to report that fact!"

"Stick to your job, Byles." The voice sounded aggravated.

"Don't you bother enough people down at the harbor?"

"Who let that redcoat in here?" demanded a gruff voice.

The crowd began to murmur the question over and over again.

Lizzie nudged her brother. "Why would Mr. Byles come into a shop full of people angry at Parliament? Doesn't he know these people don't like him?"

Joshua laughed. "Ezra Byles thinks that just because he says, 'The king said so,' everyone will be happy to obey. Maybe his job is going to include collecting the stamp taxes now, too."

Lizzie saw her father raise his hands above the crowd.

"Mr. Byles is free to come and go as he pleases," Papa said. "He has a right to his opinion just like the rest of us."

"Is that so? If he can come and go freely, then why cannot we do the same? Why should we pay a tax that we have not chosen?"

"We are still subjects of the king," another voice said. "We have a duty to obey this law, regardless of whether we agree with it."

"Balderdash!"

"Nonsense!"

"Another redcoat!"

"I never suspected Duncan Murray of being a redcoat!"

Lizzie gasped and looked at Joshua. Her father was being called a redcoat, one of the meanest terms anyone in Boston ever used. *How can anyone question his loyalty to the colonies?*

"Silence!" Duncan Murray shouted above the crowd. "I realize many of you disagree with this law. But it is the law of England, and we are part of England. If you want to change the law, you must take the right steps. Shouting at Mr. Byles is not going to change the law."

Lizzie's back tensed. She knew that tone in her father's voice well. He was reaching the limit of his patience.

"I want to know one more thing, Duncan," said the man who had started the whole discussion. "If an agent of the king comes to your shop and asks you to print stamps to put on legal documents, will you print the stamps?"

The room hushed. Everyone wanted to know the answer to that question. Lizzie froze, her mouth half open.

"I will not answer that question one way or another right now," Lizzie's father said. "I have not been asked to print stamps, and I may never be asked to print stamps. Now, please, I have a newspaper to print, and it is late already. Please let me get back to work." He hopped off the stool, turned his back to the crowd, and began loading paper into the press.

"I think we have some more issues to talk about," someone said.

"Not here, you don't," Papa said, wiping his hands on his leather apron. "This is a private print shop, not a public assembly hall." He lifted another stack of paper and fit the corners squarely in the metal tray. He did not look up at the crowd again.

Gradually the crowd broke up. At first they simply backed away from the press so it could be operated. Glancing at him every few seconds, they talked among themselves in low tones. But then Ezra Byles left. When they realized that the object of their opposition was gone and that Duncan Murray truly was not going to discuss the issue further, others started to drift out the door.

In a few minutes, Joshua and Lizzie were alone with their father. They looked at each other, unsure whether or not they should speak to him. Slowly they walked toward the press.

"Let me help you, Papa," Joshua said.

"I'll get the ink ready," Lizzie offered.

Papa opened his arms to his children, and they accepted his embrace. "I'm sorry if I seemed angry. I did not know you were here."

"We saw everything, Papa," Joshua said.

Papa handed Joshua a paper. "Here is a copy of the Stamp Act. You can read it for yourself."

"Are you frightened, Papa?" Lizzie asked.

Her father gave her a squeeze before answering. "Not frightened, exactly. But I am uncertain about what will happen now. Parliament has pushed the people too far this time." He turned to his son. "Joshua, from now on I want you to walk with Lizzie after school. Take her straight home or bring her here. I don't want her out on the street alone."

"Then you are afraid, Papa!" Lizzie cried.

"I'm just being careful," he replied.

"Papa?"

"Yes, Lizzie?"

"Will there be another war?"

Papa shook his head. "I can't believe anyone wants a war, Lizzie. We just have to straighten out a few wrinkles in the relationship between England and the colonies."

"So, no war?"

"No war."

CHAPTER 5

Sam Adams's Speech

B ut are you absolutely sure of that?"

Lizzie listened carefully to see how her classmate would answer the teacher's question.

"Yes, sir." Sixteen-year-old Daniel Taylor answered quite confidently. He stood next to his seat as he spoke, and his eyes blazed with conviction. "I have no doubt that England needs the colonies more than the colonies need England. The king recognizes this fact, and that is why he is so eager to make the colonies submit to his will, even when his actions make no sense."

"And you think the Stamp Act makes no sense?" the teacher challenged.

"None whatsoever," Daniel said. Voices around the classroom murmured in agreement. Only a few days had passed since news of the Stamp Act had reached Boston. Already the city was polarized. Loyalists supported the king and Parliament. Patriots found that their loyalties to the colonies ran deeper than their loyalties to England. It seemed that people talked of little besides the Stamp Act. Every newspaper or flier Lizzie's father printed was sold almost immediately. People could not seem to get enough information. And most people Lizzie overheard agreed with Daniel Taylor that the stamp tax made no sense.

"Let's suppose," the teacher said thoughtfully, "that your father suddenly became ill and could no longer work at his blacksmith's shop. Suppose that any money your parents had saved was used up by keeping the household running and seeking medical care. While the shop is still open, your father's hired hand is not able to keep up with all the work and makes very little profit. Are you following me, Mr. Taylor?"

"I'm not sure what you are getting at, sir."

"Under the circumstances that I have described, would you not consider it a reasonable request if your father were to ask you to contribute to the family finances, even if it meant a personal sacrifice on your part?"

"Well, I suppose, if my family needed money to pay for necessary goods, then, yes, I would try to earn some money and give it to my father."

"Think of all of England as your family, and the king as the father who can no longer take care of the family."

"I see what you are saying now," Daniel said. "Massachusetts and the other colonies are the children who need to help support the family."

The teacher raised his eyebrows above his glasses. "I see you understand my point."

"Yes, sir, I understand the comparison. But I believe it is flawed. With all respect, sir, may I explain further?"

"Go right ahead."

"If my father were to ask for my contribution and I were given the opportunity to give it gladly, there would be harmony in the family and all would be well. But suppose my father were to sneak into my bedroom at night and forcibly remove the earnings I have saved without my consent. Justice would suffer greatly, and the family might never be happy again."

"And you believe this is what King George has done— forcibly taken what you have saved, without consent?"

"Yes, sir, I do. Parliament has passed a law forcing us to make payments to the king without having asked us first if we would be willing to do so. This is taxation without representation. And it is a moral wrong."

The teacher reached into his pocket for his watch and examined it.

"Perhaps we can probe this further another day, Mr. Taylor. While such political debate doubtless is better for the mind than what you will engage in once class is dismissed, I am compelled by the statutes of Boston to release you now. Class dismissed."

As Lizzie gathered her books and slate, she glanced over at Joshua. He had wasted no time in seeking out Daniel Taylor, no doubt to hear more of Daniel's opinions about the Stamp Act.

Lizzie did not want to hear more political talk. She had come to believe her father was right. No one wanted a war. The Patriots simply wanted justice, and they would try to achieve it peacefully. In the meantime though, tension was growing in Boston. Remembering her father's warnings not to walk alone after school, Lizzie quickly collected her light spring shawl and waited on the steps for Joshua.

Spring rains had finally given way to the promise of summer.

The day was clear and bright. But Lizzie could not enjoy it. Inside, she was twisted up and confused. If everyone wanted justice and no one wanted a war, why was there so much anger and bitterness in Boston?

When Joshua arrived a few minutes later, he poked her from behind, making her jump.

"Joshua!" She slapped at his hand. "Must you make a joke of absolutely everything?"

"Isn't that Daniel Taylor something?" Joshua said, ignoring Lizzie's irritation. "He really understands the political issues. You should listen to him talk."

"I did listen to him talk, silly."

"No, I don't mean in class. You should have heard the things he said afterward. I believe someday he will be elected to the Massachusetts legislature, maybe even become governor."

"Yes, I suppose he's bright enough." Lizzie did not want to encourage further conversation on politics.

But Joshua had a one-track mind, and on that day the track was politics. "I wonder what his father thinks about all this. He's a blacksmith, after all. He talks to people all day long."

"He talks about shoeing their horses," Lizzie said flatly.

"Ah yes, but what do they talk about while he is putting the shoes on? He's in a perfect spot to find out what people are thinking."

"Most people just leave the horse and come back when the job is done."

"But not everyone leaves. Some people stay and talk. I've seen them. He could probably write an article for Papa about what people are saying."

Lizzie did not answer. Perhaps her silence would make Joshua find another subject to talk about.

They came around a corner and found themselves at the back of a large group. About twenty people had stopped to watch what was happening across the street, where a bigger crowd was circling a tree.

"What's going on?" Joshua asked, craning his neck to find the focus of attention.

"Over there," someone said. "Under that tree, across the street. Sam Adams is giving a speech."

"Really? Sam Adams?" Joshua asked. Lizzie could hear the excitement in her brother's voice. "What is he talking about?"

"What he always talks about," said a woman. "Freedom. Liberty. How the colonies are in bondage to England and it's time to break free."

"I've never heard him before," Joshua said.

"He's an earful, that's for sure." The woman moved along, having lost interest.

"We should keep going," Lizzie said, nudging Joshua. "Papa will be waiting."

"Just a few minutes," Joshua said, fixing his gaze on Sam Adams across the street. "Look at the way he stands, as if he were the preacher in the finest church in England, instead of standing under a tree that barely has its spring blossoms."

Joshua struck a pose that looked remarkably like Sam Adams. He stood with his feet solidly apart and his hands in the air, elbows up.

"How's this?" he said, grinning at Lizzie.

She smiled. She had to admit his imitation was accurate.

"That is really good, Joshua. Now you just need a tattered black coat. Can we go?"

Joshua did not answer. He was busy capturing the gestures of the outdoor speaker. He mimicked the way Sam Adams emphasized his points by thrusting his fists through the air and then pushing his arm straight up over his shoulder with only one finger raised.

"You're quite amusing, young man," said a mother struggling to keep a toddler under control.

"Where did you learn how to do that?" asked someone else.

Lizzie put her head back and rolled her eyes. Joshua had an audience. Now they would be there until suppertime. "Joshua!" she hissed.

But he paid no attention to her. He put his fists on his hips, threw out his chest, and surveyed the crowd, just as Adams was doing across the street.

"You're very good, Joshua," Lizzie said. "Quite convincing. Now can we go?"

"The only problem is that I can't hear him. I don't know what his voice sounds like."

"I'm sure it's just an ordinary voice."

"No, the voice of a man who gives speeches has a certain quality."

"He's just a man."

"Let's go across the street and get closer."

"Joshua, no, we can't do that!"

"Why on earth not? The man is just giving a simple political speech. This is Boston. People give political speeches all the time." He started to cross the street. Given her father's instructions to stay with Joshua, Lizzie had no choice but to follow. Joshua barely glanced over his shoulder to see if she was there as he worked his way up to the front of the crowd.

"We are not children," Sam Adams was saying when they got close enough to hear his words. "We are mature, educated men of sound minds." He punctuated his sentence with another thrust in the air.

Joshua did the same as he silently echoed Adams's words.

"Joshua, this isn't funny anymore," Lizzie pleaded. "Please, let's go."

Adams continued to talk. "What is one letter from the Massachusetts Assembly to the king of England? Neither New York, nor Pennsylvania, nor Maryland has seen this letter. If the assemblies in these colonies have also sent letters to the king, what does that matter? We have not seen their letters. We may plead one argument while they plead another. In such division there is weakness. The king is right not to be concerned with such disorganization."

Joshua looked at Lizzie. His expression had sobered, and his arms hung motionless at his sides. "You're right; this isn't funny anymore. But we can't go, not yet."

"Joshua, please," Lizzie whispered.

"I think what he says makes a lot of sense, and I want to hear it."

"You know as well as I do that Papa thinks Sam Adams goes too far," Lizzie warned. "He won't like it when he finds out we were late because you wanted to listen to Sam Adams talk under a tree."

"Lizzie, you're only twelve. But I'm nearly fifteen. I have to make up my own mind about these things."

"Suppose, however," Adams said, "that we were to unite in our objections to the king." He seemed to be looking directly at Joshua. "Suppose that instead of receiving a half-dozen different arguments, each of them weak in itself, King George were to receive one forceful document laying out all of the claims of the colonies. In such a circumstance, he would not dare to treat us as ignorant children."

"One letter to the king!" Joshua exclaimed. "Remind me to ask Papa if that has ever been done before."

"It hasn't," Lizzie said flatly.

"How do you know?" Joshua seemed to doubt that a twelve-year-old girl could know much of anything.

Lizzie shrugged. "I'm not as idle as you think. I listen to what is going on. I heard Uncle Blake and Papa talking about the same thing. It would be something called a *congress*."

"A Continental Congress!" Sam Adams said emphatically. "We must take the first step toward giving the colonies the freedom they deserve and the liberty they have earned."

Lizzie pulled as hard as she could on Joshua's elbow. "Joshua, you're keeping me in bondage. Now let's go."

"All right," he finally agreed, "but only because I have some questions for Papa."

CHAPTER 6

The Shooting

The pile of newspapers landed in the back of the cart with a *thwack*. Joshua pushed them to the corner and checked to make sure the string around them was tight.

"How many more?" Lizzie asked. The glare of the summer afternoon sun made her squint.

"Two more trips." Joshua disappeared back into the print shop to tie up more copies of the afternoon paper.

Lizzie inspected the hitch that linked the cart to the horse. Satisfied that Joshua had hitched the cart properly, she turned her attention to the horse.

"Well Merry," she said, stroking the side of the mare's head, "another round of deliveries. I'm not sure you really need Joshua and me. You've been doing this so long that you know exactly where to go."

Merry neighed softly and moved her head about, nuzzling Lizzie's hand.

Lizzie laughed. "You're looking for sugar, aren't you, girl? I'm sorry, but sugar is hard to come by these days. Mama says sugar is getting too expensive for people, much less for a horse. I do have an apple."

Lizzie produced the fruit, and Merry accepted it enthusiastically.

Joshua appeared with another stack of newspapers. He scowled at Lizzie.

"I don't think playing with the horse counts as part of helping with the route," he said sternly.

Lizzie made a face. "I'm making sure Merry is ready."

"Merry has been doing this since we were babies. Believe me, she's ready."

"Let me drive today," Lizzie said.

"Aw Lizzie!"

"Come on, Joshua. Merry is gentle. She knows the route. Nothing will happen."

"I could do this without you, you know," Joshua said.

"And I could do it without you. But Papa said to stay together."

Joshua surrendered. "Turn the cart around while I get the last stack."

Gleefully, Lizzie hiked up her skirts and climbed into the seat of the carriage. Twelve was a strange age, she had decided. She was old enough to know how adults behaved, and her parents expected her to behave like an adult. Yet she was young enough to enjoy the simple pleasure of riding in a cart and making the horse go where she wanted it to go. This was the first summer that Papa had let her drive the cart for more than a few yards, and she had been practicing for weeks. The sense of responsibility made her feel even more grown-up. She maneuvered the cart around so that she was facing the street and waited. A moment later, Joshua appeared with the last stack of papers. He threw it into the cart, then climbed in the back and sat on top of the stack.

"Ready?" Lizzie asked brightly.

"I'm never ready when you're driving," Joshua muttered.

Lizzie ignored him and nudged Merry with the reins. The old mare needed little encouragement to begin her trot down the main streets of Boston. They would stop periodically to drop papers off for agents to sell or sometimes stand on a corner and sell papers themselves.

"Good day, Mr. Kearney," Joshua said as he tossed a small pile off the cart.

"G'day to ye both," Mr. Kearney answered. "And how be the wee ones at home?"

Lizzie smiled. "Olivia and Emmett are just fine. Thank you for asking."

They trotted on.

"I'm going to give Uncle Philip a double stack today," Joshua said. "He told Papa that more and more people who come by the clinic want to read the paper."

Lizzie narrowed her eyes and looked straight ahead. "Joshua?" she said softly.

"Did you hear what I said about Uncle Philip?" Joshua persisted.

"Yes, he's the next stop. But, Joshua, look." Lizzie pulled on the reins slightly, and Merry broke her rhythm and stopped.

Joshua clambered over the piles of newspapers to look out the front of the cart. Two British soldiers stood poised on the street corner, squaring off against a dozen or more young colonists.

"What's going on, Joshua?" Lizzie's stomach churned.

Joshua shook his head. "I can't tell from here. Get closer."

"I don't think we should."

"Lizzie," Joshua said impatiently, "you said you wanted to drive. Now drive!"

Reluctantly, she got Merry started again, and they drew up closer to the encounter.

"Why don't you redcoats leave us alone and go home?" a man shouted.

"We did not come to stir up trouble," one of the soldiers said. "We simply want to pass this way to go to the docks."

"Why do you need to go to the docks?" another voice challenged.

Lizzie nudged Joshua. "Isn't that Daniel Taylor?"

Joshua nodded silently.

"With all due respect, we have jobs at the docks, and we are late already. Please let us pass."

"You don't need to work at the docks!" Daniel Taylor shouted. "You already have a job. The king pays you to do his bidding."

"The pay is not enough, and if you people in the colonies would recognize that, we would have no quarrel between us." The British soldier was clearly losing his patience.

"Let's all take pity on the redcoats," Daniel said in an exaggerated tone of voice. "They have only one set of clothes, after all." Daniel turned to his friends for encouragement, and they began shouting at the soldiers.

"Go home to England to get a real job!"

"If you leave us alone, we'll leave you alone!"

"Go home to your precious king and tell him your troubles. We don't want to hear them."

The soldiers glanced at each other, then started to force their way through the roadblock the young men had set up.

"Don't you shove me!" one of the young men shouted. And then he swung his fist at the nearest soldier.

"Joshua!" Lizzie cried. "Do something!"

"I'll try to talk to Daniel and get him to call off his friends." Joshua looked sternly at Lizzie. "You stay right here. Do you hear me? Don't move."

Lizzie nodded. She was too frightened to move. Where did he think she would go?

Joshua jumped down from the cart and dashed toward the group on the corner. He pushed past several young men until he found Daniel Taylor.

"Daniel," Joshua started. "Daniel, please, what are you doing?"

"This is none of your business, Joshua," Daniel said.

"I just don't want anyone to get hurt," Joshua said. "Please, tell your friends to go home. There is no need for a fight."

"Is that what you think?" one of the other young men said. "If you get in our way, that means you are siding with the redcoats."

"I'm not siding with anyone!" Joshua exclaimed. "I just don't think there is any need for a fight."

The man pushed his fist up under Joshua's chin.

Lizzie gasped, and as she did so, she let go of the reins. Merry started moving again.

"No, Merry, no!" Lizzie cried, scrambling to pick up the reins.

The old mare paid no attention to Lizzie's pleas. She continued her trot and walked right past the corner where Joshua stood. Desperately, Lizzie looked back over her shoulder at the fracas on the corner. Joshua ducked just in time to avoid being punched in the eye.

"Joshua!" Lizzie screamed. "Merry, stop! Stop!" Leaning as far forward out of her seat as she dared, she grasped for the loose reins. Finally, she had hold of them again. Immediately, she pulled Merry to a stop, jumped down, and tied the reins around a post. Then she scrambled back to the corner where she had left Joshua.

To her surprise and relief, Uncle Philip had just come out of his clinic and was trying to break up the fight. Fists and foul names were flying everywhere. Lizzie could hardly keep track of which arms belonged to which bodies.

"Joshua!" she called out as she ran toward him.

Uncle Philip heard her scream and turned toward her. Just at that moment, one of the strongest young men in the bunch swung a board. The side of Uncle Philip's face and the board collided. When she heard the *crack*, Lizzie could not tell if it was the board or Uncle Philip's skull that had broken. He slumped to the ground.

"Uncle Philip!" she screamed. "Joshua, help him!"

"Lizzie, stay out of this!" Somehow Joshua's voice rose to the top of the chaos. But Lizzie could not keep out. She ran toward her uncle. Just as she reached him, Uncle Philip sat up groggily. He held his head in his hands.

"Uncle Philip, are you all right?" Lizzie knelt beside him and gently touched his face.

Uncle Philip groaned. "I'm all right, Lizzie. You should do what Joshua says and get away."

"I can't leave you here like this."

"I'm all right, Lizzie. You must be careful for your own safety."

Helping Uncle Philip to his feet, Lizzie gasped again. One of Daniel Taylor's friends wielded a gun. Uncle Philip gripped Lizzie's shoulders and prevented her from moving.

"Daniel, stop this madness," Joshua pleaded. "Tell him to put the gun away."

"A man with a gun does what he pleases." The man spoke before Daniel could say anything.

"Just let the soldiers pass," Joshua said.

The man pivoted and pointed the gun at Joshua. Lizzie stifled a scream.

"Nobody will get hurt who doesn't deserve to get hurt," the man said. "You decide which side you're on, once and for all."

Lizzie held her breath, not knowing what Joshua would do or say. He said nothing. He did nothing.

In the scuffle that came next, it was hard to tell who did what. All Lizzie knew was that the man with the musket was pounced on by several of his cohorts. Apparently others in the gang had the good sense to know that their friend should not be trusted with a loaded musket. Lizzie saw the tip of the muzzle arching upward when it went off.

"Joshua!" But it was not Joshua who dropped to the cobblestone. It was one of the British soldiers, shot through the shoulder.

Uncle Philip released Lizzie and rushed past her to the fallen soldier. "Let me help," he called out. "I'm a doctor."

"We know who you are," sneered one of the men. "We heard the tailor was fitting you for a redcoat all your own."

Uncle Philip put his ear to the soldier's chest. "This man is badly wounded, but he's alive. Let me help him."

"Leave him be," said the man who had fired the musket. "Nature will finish my interrupted work."

"Have you gone mad?" said one of the others. "Take your musket and get out of here before the authorities arrive." Two others scurried away, taking with them the man who had shot the soldier.

"Joshua! Lizzie! Help me." Putting his hand behind the soldier's back, Uncle Philip propped up the wounded redcoat. The soldier's head rolled from side to side like a loose ball.

"Daniel," Joshua pleaded, "stop this insanity."

Daniel's face had gone white. He put his hands up. "It is out of my hands now. You decide for yourself what you are going to do."

Where she found the courage, Lizzie did not know. But she knew that she had to respond to her uncle's pleas for help. She squatted in the street with Uncle Philip and tried to lift the unconscious soldier to his feet. Blood flowed from his wound onto her dress and hands.

"We have to get him to the clinic," Uncle Philip said, "away from these brutes."

"They'll never let us in," Lizzie said.

"Only a redcoat would help another redcoat!" a voice shouted.

"You had better think carefully about your next step, Wallace."

"Ignore them, Lizzie," Uncle Philip said. "Start walking. Look straight at the clinic door, nothing else."

Lizzie nodded, squelching the sob that welled up in her throat.

"Clear the way!" Joshua shouted. He started pushing his way through the gang.

Uncle Philip grunted. "I know he's heavy, Lizzie, but go as quickly as you can."

A spray of stones splattered Lizzie's face.

"Girls can be redcoats, too, you know."

The angry words stung almost as much as the stones themselves.

"The clinic door, Lizzie," came Uncle Philip's steady voice. "Nothing else."

CHAPTER 7

The Wounded Soldier

Lizzie lurched across the threshold, catching herself just in time to keep from stumbling. Her thin shoulders bore the weight of the unconscious soldier. His lanky form was draped haphazardly between Lizzie and Uncle Philip. Her knees nearly buckled with every step, and her stomach churned violently.

Uncle Philip tugged her through the doorway and pointed at a cot along one wall. The mob was at their heels, screaming disapproval.

"Lobsterback!"

"Traitor!"

"Even doctors have to pay taxes!"

Lizzie craned her neck for a glance at the men outside. Instead, she saw the back of Joshua's head as he crashed the wooden door shut behind them.

"Secure the latch!" Uncle Philip shouted. "And get away from the window. Now!"

Joshua obediently pulled down the latch and stepped toward the center of the room, but he turned his head to look out the window.

"We need your help, Joshua," Uncle Philip said sharply. "Pay attention in here, please."

"What do you want us to do?" Lizzie asked, certain that she could bear the soldier's weight no longer.

"Joshua, help me lay him on the cot," Uncle Philip directed, taking the weight of the soldier from Lizzie. "Lizzie, get a bucket of water. You'll find some clean rags in the cupboard."

Lizzie surrendered her responsibility for the soldier to Joshua and turned toward the cupboards on the facing wall. Her lungs burst with the realization that she had not taken a deep breath in a long while. She gulped some new air and forced herself to move toward the cupboard. Uncle Philip's voice sounded distant, somewhere beyond the pounding of her own heart. Bleary with sweat and tears she had not known she was shedding, Lizzie's eyes refused to focus. She wiped her eyes with the back of her grimy hands and only then saw that her sleeve was drenched with the soldier's blood.

"Quickly, Lizzie," Uncle Philip urged as he straightened the soldier's form on the cot.

Lizzie blinked her eyes into focus, yanked open the cupboard door, and grabbed an armful of clean rags. The water barrel stood in the corner. She nervously filled a bucket and carried it to Uncle Philip.

"Good." Uncle Philip had unfastened the red jacket, the symbol hated by so many Bostonians, and was trying to pull the man's shirt away from his chest. Blood matted the white cotton cloth, causing the cloth to stick to the soldier's skin. "Joshua, stoke the fire. I don't want him to get cold."

Joshua started to protest. "But it's warm in—"

"Do as I say!" Uncle Philip cut him off, and Joshua picked up the iron to stir up the coals Uncle Philip always kept ready for service. "There is wood in the back room. Get what you need."

Joshua scurried into action, knowing better than to argue further.

"We'll have to expose the wound, Lizzie. I'll need a knife. There is one on the sideboard. We'll have to cut through his shirt and jacket to get at the wound in his shoulder."

Lizzie handed her uncle the knife and grimaced as he first slit the cloth of the man's jacket, then the shirt. Gently he pried the blood-soaked garment away from the skin. Lizzie clenched her stomach as she watched Uncle Philip work. The hole in the soldier's shoulder gaped up at her, still spurting dark purple liquid. Her hand moved to her mouth to stifle a scream.

"Stay with me, Lizzie," Uncle Philip said, his voice more gentle than before. "I need your help."

She swallowed hard and took a deep breath. "What do you need?" She grasped the back of a chair to keep from quaking. Her voice sounded braver than she felt.

"A wet cloth. Lots of water."

Lizzie dipped a rag in the bucket and handed it, still dripping, to Uncle Philip. In a few seconds, Uncle Philip had the area cleansed. Still the blood came.

"Should I get Aunt Johanna?" Lizzie asked hopefully. She knew her aunt was experienced at assisting Uncle Philip in emergency situations, as well as in the routine care of patients.

"There's no time. He's bleeding too much. Besides, you would never get out the door. Lizzie, you can do this. I know you can."

"I'm trying, Uncle Philip. It's just. . .the blood."

"You're doing fine. Just follow my instructions."

Lizzie nodded.

"Put your hand here," Uncle Philip said, pointing to the wound. He laid a fresh cloth over it and guided Lizzie's hand. "Now press down, and keep pressure on the wound."

A clatter of wood behind her made Lizzie jump.

"Keep pressing," came Uncle Philip's steady voice.

Lizzie threw a frightened glance toward the window. But the sound had come from Joshua returning from the back room with an armload of wood.

"How is he?" Joshua asked, arranging three logs on the fire and stirring up the coals once again. The dry wood immediately began to crackle. Bright flames spurted upward and threw shadows on the walls. Lizzie pressed harder.

Uncle Philip sighed. "He'll be all right if we can get the bleeding to stop. But he's still unconscious."

"Why?"

"Probably from the pain. We have to keep him warm." Uncle Philip unfolded a wool blanket on the end of the cot and spread it over the soldier's legs.

Joshua drew closer and studied the patient's face. Knotted light brown hair framed his pale face. "He's so young," Joshua said softly, thoughtfully.

"Just a boy," Uncle Philip agreed. "Hardly more than sixteen, I'd say."

"Two years older than I am," Joshua murmured, his eyes wide with the realization of his coming manhood.

"Did you see his boots?" Lizzie asked. "I could see newspaper wrapped around his feet showing right through the bottom of one of them, and the other is not much better. He probably hasn't been to the cobbler in two years."

"Keep pressing, Lizzie," Uncle Philip said as he felt for the young man's pulse. "A lot of the British soldiers are in the same condition. That's part of why Parliament has ordered the stamp tax—to provide for the soldiers on duty in the colonies."

"But, Uncle Philip," Joshua started, "there must be another way. Taxing us when we have no part in Parliament's decisions simply is not fair."

"But we do receive protection from the Crown."

"Why can't we pay the soldiers ourselves, like we always have?" Joshua persisted in his argument.

Uncle Philip shook his head. "There are no easy answers. But sending boys like this—or you—into dangerous situations is not fair either."

Joshua had no response. He knew his uncle was right.

Lizzie tried to imagine Joshua across the ocean, thousands of miles away from his home, following orders whether he agreed with them or not. Then she imagined how their parents would feel—how the soldier's parents must be feeling right at that moment—not knowing the fate of their son.

Outside, the mob throbbed against the clinic walls. Lizzie could hear their rocks striking the door. Uncle Philip casually glanced out the window, but Lizzie saw his concern. Joshua, too, studied his uncle's expression. Lizzie reached for a fresh rag and eyed her brother.

"Do you wish you were out there with them, Joshua?"

Joshua's eyes met hers briefly and then shifted away. "Don't be foolish."

"This could have been you!" Lizzie cried. "You could be lying in the street with no one to take care of you. Boston is dangerous enough these days. You're getting mixed up with Sam Adams, and that will only make things worse."

"You worry too much," Joshua replied.

Lizzie glared at him.

Uncle Philip checked on the wound. Lizzie looked down at her hands, covered in blood, and remembered the injury her uncle had taken in the fracas. "Uncle Philip, is your head all right?"

He touched his forehead, which was swollen and blue. "I will confess that I have a blinding headache, but I am certain it will subside in a few minutes."

"I felt so helpless when I saw that board aimed at your head. I don't know what I would have done if you had been hurt badly."

Uncle Philip smiled at her. "You would have done what you are doing now—taking care of the wounded."

Lizzie shook her head. "No, I wouldn't have known what to do without your help."

"You're doing a wonderful job, Lizzie."

His words made her calmer. Then she saw a face in the window, and her heart lurched. "Won't they ever stop?" she cried.

"Philip Wallace!" came the voice from outside, muffled by the glass. "You'll have to answer for giving refuge to a lobsterback." A spray of pebbles tinkled against the pane.

"Pay them no mind, Lizzie," her uncle said, wiping his own face with a cool cloth.

"But they might break the door down."

Philip shook his head. "If they were going to do that, they would have done it by now." He stepped over to the window. "Most of them have dispersed. The ones who are left are just agitating to make a name for themselves."

"The Sons of Liberty, no doubt!" Lizzie said scornfully.

"The Sons of Liberty are not agitators," Joshua said in defense of the friendships he had formed during the summer months. "They want to do what's best for the colonies."

"Rioting in the streets is good for the colonies?" Lizzie gave voice to her skepticism.

"Now stay calm, you two," Uncle Philip warned. "We don't need a civil war in the family as well as out in the streets."

A moan brought them all back to the reason they were in the clinic together. The soldier moved his head stiffly from side to side, and his eyes fluttered open.

Uncle Philip put a hand on Lizzie's shoulder. "I think the bleeding has stopped." He tried to nudge her away, but she was frozen in her spot. Her green eyes locked onto the gaze of the clear gray eyes of the soldier, and she saw in him the same fear that was in her own heart.

"It's all right, son," Uncle Philip said, gently prying Lizzie's hand off the soldier's chest. "I'm a doctor. I want to help you."

The young man moaned once again.

"I'm sure you are in a great deal of pain," Uncle Philip said, "and I will do what I can to make you comfortable. You'll have to stay for a few days until your wound is sufficiently healed."

The soldier's eyes followed Uncle Philip's movements as he examined him more fully.

"I'll arrange everything with your captain," Uncle Philip said. "Do you think you could manage to sit up a bit so we can take off your shirt and coat?"

The young man slowly turned his head toward his wound and spoke for the first time. "You cut my coat."

"We had to," Uncle Philip said calmly. "It was the only way to get to the wound and stop the bleeding."

"You cut my coat," the soldier repeated, his voice cracking. "It's my only coat."

"I'm sorry about that, truly I am, but surely you can understand the need."

The soldier turned his eyes away. "You cut my coat," he said again, softly, with defeat in his voice.

"Lizzie," Uncle Philip said quietly, motioning for her to help strip off the mutilated clothing. Gently, he supported the young man from the back, while Lizzie slowly worked the shirt and jacket off. She saw the soldier's thin chest and the bumps his ribs made. *When did he last have a good meal?* she wondered. Even in the midst of a boycott, her family managed to eat. None of them were as thin as this soldier.

Joshua moved restlessly back and forth across the room, stirring the fire and checking the window. Uncle Philip and Lizzie did not speak as they finished cleaning the grime off the soldier and bandaging his wound. The soldier grimaced in pain, but he did not moan again. When the job was done, he breathed heavily and fell asleep once more.

Lizzie joined Joshua at the window. Only two boys remained outside, and they were simply amusing themselves kicking rocks. Joshua turned once again toward the soldier.

"He's so young," Joshua said. "So young."

❦ CHAPTER 8 ❧

Aunt Johanna's Visit

Lizzie jumped out of her chair. Her book slid down the folds of her skirts to the floor. Sudden pounding on the front door had broken into her afternoon reading on a hot August day. She had been looking for an excuse to put aside the reading her mother had assigned her, but she had hoped for a more pleasant interruption.

"Coming!" she called out. She clutched her skirts and ran as quickly as she could across the front room toward the door.

At the same time, she heard her mother's footsteps rushing from the kitchen and Joshua thundering down the stairs. The pounding continued—this time even more insistently. The three of them converged on the front door, competing to be the one to pull it open and reveal the source of the ruckus.

"Aunt Johanna!" Lizzie said, shocked when the door was ally open.

"ohanna, get inside this instant," Constance Murray d her sister-in-law by the forearm and pulled her into . Before closing the door again, she scanned the street outside the house. Looking over her mother's shoulder, Lizzie could see nothing.

With Aunt Johanna was young Charity, who looked confused but secure in her mother's arms. She smiled at Lizzie and curled her fingers in a wave.

"Aunt Johanna, what's happened?" Lizzie questioned. "You look as white as a ghost."

Before answering, Aunt Johanna set her young daughter down securely on the floor and straightened her dress. "Charity, run upstairs and look for Emmett, please. It's playtime."

"Playtime!" squealed Charity. And before anyone said another word, she was gone.

Aunt Johanna let out a heavy sigh and smoothed her frazzled hair.

"Come in the kitchen, Johanna, and I'll fix you some tea," Mama said. She nodded at her daughter. "Lizzie, get the cups out."

"Yes, Mama." Lizzie obeyed her mother with her hands, but her ears, eyes, and mind were all fixed on her aunt.

Mama stoked the fire under the pot to boil the water. Aunt Johanna sank into a chair. Joshua glanced out the window.

"Now tell us what happened," Mama said.

"I'm so sorry to barge in on you in such a rude manner," Aunt Johanna said. "I suddenly felt that I must get off the street, and yours was the nearest house of someone I could trust."

"But what happened?" Joshua pressed his aunt.

"Yes, Aunt Johanna," Lizzie said. "Something must have happened to make you feel that way."

"I'm almost embarrassed to say that nothing exactly

happened. At least not yet. It's just that the street gangs make me so nervous. I especially hate to go out when I have Charity with me, but Philip was too busy at the clinic to watch her, and I couldn't avoid going out any longer."

Joshua moved to the window and peered outside. "Street gangs, you say?"

"Yes. This time it was Douglas Taylor's son and his rowdies."

"Daniel?"

"Yes, that's his name." Aunt Johanna gratefully accepted the tea that Mama poured.

"Are they out there now?" Joshua asked.

"They were a few minutes ago. Down the street a bit. They had no clear purpose that I could see."

Scenes from her own encounter with Daniel Taylor's gang flashed through Lizzie's mind. "You did the right thing to come here," she said, "especially when you had Charity with you."

"You mustn't take any chances," Mama said as she offered her sister-in-law some precious sugar for her tea.

"This is all the fault of Sam Adams!" Aunt Johanna exclaimed.

Joshua wheeled around. "What do you mean? Sam Adams is not part of that gang."

"No, but he has his own gang, and their presence in Boston grows stronger every day. Other people start gangs to be like him."

"Daniel and his friends just like to push people around. Sam Adams is trying to get something done."

"Their activities look very much alike to me," Aunt Johanna insisted.

Joshua was not satisfied. "I've never heard Sam say anything about terrorizing women and children in the street."

Aunt Johanna sipped the tea. "He doesn't have to say that in so many words. If he would stop standing under that silly Liberty Tree giving speeches, Boston might settle down."

Joshua looked away and said nothing.

Mama lowered herself into a chair next to Aunt Johanna. "I heard that the Shreves were forced to house two British soldiers against their will."

"Have you seen those soldiers, Constance?" Aunt Johanna asked. "They are nothing but boys who are too far from home. If it were Joshua, you would be glad to have someone take him in and give him a decent meal."

"But the Shreves have five children of their own, and they can hardly keep them fed as it is. Now they have two more full-grown men to feed. I can't imagine how they are going to do it—especially since Levi Shreve is one of the most outspoken Patriots in Boston."

"Oh Mama, you haven't heard, have you?" Lizzie said. Instantly she wished she could take back her words.

"Haven't heard what, Lizzie?"

Lizzie's fingers twisted around the ties of her apron. "The Shreves don't have to house the soldiers anymore. One of the gangs—"

"Don't tell me!" Mama exclaimed. "One of those crazy gangs broke into the Shreve house and threw the furniture around."

Lizzie nodded mutely. "There isn't much left. I saw Mr. Shreve's daughter Alyce outside the print shop yesterday. She won't be able to come back to school. They have to move away."

"But the house, the furniture—none of that belongs to the British soldiers. What is the point in destroying personal property needlessly?"

Aunt Johanna shook her head. "Do you see what I mean now?"

"You don't know for sure that Sam Adams is behind those activities," Joshua said. "Sam is trying to unite the colonies in an organized protest against Parliament. That's the only reason he goes around town talking."

"Sam Adams is doing far more than talking," Aunt Johanna said. "Talking doesn't hurt people. But families are being destroyed. People are losing homes that they have worked hard for—homes their parents built. I am on my knees every night asking God to bring an end to this madness."

Lizzie needed to keep herself busy while she sorted out what she was hearing. She stood up abruptly and started straightening the chairs around the table. Aunt Johanna had always been the person Lizzie could turn to when she was most confused. But right now, Aunt Johanna sounded just as confused as Lizzie was herself.

"I'm going to check on the children," Mama said.

"I'll just take a look down the street," Joshua said casually.

Aunt Johanna and Lizzie were alone. Lizzie's mind burst with questions she wanted to ask. She hardly knew where to begin.

"Aunt Johanna?" Lizzie stopped her fidgeting and stood with her hands on the back of a chair.

"Yes, Lizzie, what is it?"

"Do you think Sam Adams is in charge of Boston?"

Aunt Johanna smiled and sighed. "You remember what we talked about at Christmas, don't you?"

Lizzie nodded. "But you seem different now." She dropped into the chair beside her aunt. "Back then you seemed to know that nothing bad was really going to happen because God was in control. But now. . .now you seem as angry as everyone else in Boston."

"You may be right, Lizzie. These last eight months have been such a strain. Why, look at what happened to you and Joshua only a few days ago."

"And Uncle Philip."

"I thank God you were not hurt and that Philip suffered only a bad headache. But I can't promise you that no one in our family is ever going to be hurt. So yes, sometimes I am frightened and angry." She laughed. "I guess I must sound quite ridiculous going on about Sam Adams, as if he were mightier than God Himself. No, Lizzie, I do not think Sam Adams is in charge of Boston. God is still in charge."

"Then why is everyone angry all the time?"

Aunt Johanna sighed slowly. "That is a question I cannot answer. But God will work this out. I am sure of that."

Mama reappeared in the kitchen doorway. "Lizzie," she said, "perhaps you could take the children out in the garden for a little while. It's such a beautiful day. I'm sure if you stayed in the back, near the house, you would be quite safe."

Lizzie looked from her mother to Aunt Johanna. Her aunt nodded. "Go on, Lizzie. I would like it if Charity could play in the fresh air."

"Yes, ma'am," Lizzie said, and stood up. She pushed her

chair in neatly under the table.

At moments like this, she hated being twelve. Mama and Aunt Johanna were going to have a discussion that would no doubt be more interesting than playing with three small children. But she would not be allowed even to overhear it from the next room.

Olivia, Emmett, and Charity charged past her and out the back door into the yard. Lizzie reluctantly followed. Outside, she sat on a tree stump and surveyed her surroundings.

The yard was quite pleasant, actually. The children could play in a large square of grass, hidden from the street. And beyond the play yard were the flower gardens. Her mother had worked hard all summer to make the flowers grow, and they were in full bloom. Their colors melted from one shade into another and cascaded across the property. Behind the flower gardens was the vegetable patch. Soon it would be time to pick the beans and squash and store them for the winter. Lizzie had been helping with that process for as long as she could remember. At the back of the lot, the ground sloped up, forming a stubby hill for winter sledding.

Lizzie shook her head. How could she be thinking about flowers and vegetables, knowing that her mother and her aunt were sitting in the kitchen discussing the hazards of life in Boston? Her uncle was still tending a wounded British soldier and being criticized because of his decision to care for the man. Her father was under pressure to use his newspaper and printing press in a revolt against the Stamp Act. Yet she was longing for fresh vegetables and white, smooth snow.

She looked up at the frolicking children, who were chasing

each other around the enclosed yard. Olivia had recently graduated out of the clothes of toddlers and into the dresses of older girls and women. But she was unconcerned with ladylike behavior at that moment. She tackled Emmett, and they tumbled to the ground, squealing.

Lizzie sincerely hoped that all the children thought about was flowers and vegetables and when they would next be able to play together. Olivia was boisterous, and it was not always easy to tell what she was feeling. Emmett had a sensitive spirit; he probably understood more than he talked about. Charity was full of common sense. If she were a few years older, she would no doubt have her own opinions about how to solve Boston's problems in the way that made the most sense.

"Where is Joshua going?" Emmett's fragile voice broke into Lizzie's musings.

"What do you mean?"

Emmett pointed. Joshua was closing the door carefully behind him, making sure it would not slam. He carried a small leather pack. Lizzie jumped off her stump.

"Joshua?" she said loudly.

He put a finger to his lips to hush her. She gathered up her skirts and ran over to him before he could get away.

"Where are you going?" she said in a half whisper.

"It's better if you don't know."

"That's ridiculous, Joshua." She stamped her foot. "Tell me where you are going."

"Lizzie, this is not your business."

"You're my brother. Of course it is my business."

Joshua looked toward the kitchen window. They could see

their aunt and mother still engrossed in conversation.

"Aunt Johanna is wrong," Joshua said. "Sam Adams is not responsible for what happened to us the other day."

"Oh Joshua, she was just letting out her frustration. She was frightened. Can you blame her?"

"No. I don't blame her for being frightened. But she's wrong about Sam Adams."

"Where are you going?" Lizzie asked again.

Joshua shook his head. He was not going to tell her.

"Why are you taking your pack?" Lizzie persisted.

Again, Joshua only shook his head.

"Something is happening tonight, isn't it, Joshua?" Lizzie said. "Aunt Johanna is frightened for a good reason, isn't she?"

"Lizzie, please, I'm not going to say anything more. Please let me be!" He turned to go.

"Joshua?" Lizzie said softly.

With a groan of frustration, Joshua turned to face her again.

"Take care of yourself."

CHAPTER 9

What Joshua Saw

Punching her pillow, Lizzie wondered what time it was—again. Then she answered her own question. It was ten minutes later than the last time she had punched her pillow and wondered what time it was. Her bedding was a tangled mess. Across the room, Olivia slept serenely. Lizzie could hardly believe that anyone, even an exhausted child, could sleep through the night that had just passed. Lizzie herself had not slept a minute all night.

When Joshua had not arrived for supper, her mother and father had turned their attention to Lizzie. They were convinced that she would know where to find him. Since Lizzie and Joshua had been instructed to stay together when they were walking around town, her parents reasoned that she had been everywhere that Joshua had been in recent days. Lizzie reminded them that although she had been forbidden to go out alone, Joshua was still free to come and go as he pleased. Surely he had had many opportunities for conversations or activities that Lizzie knew nothing about.

Mama had burned the supper, and no one ate much. The silence at the table was broken only by Mama's occasional coaxing to get Olivia and Emmett to eat a few bites. Lizzie had cleared the table and washed the dishes without being asked. Hardly noticing her efforts, her parents went out looking for Joshua. By then he had been missing for several hours. Lizzie tucked Olivia and Emmett into bed—over their protests about the absence of their parents—and sat alone in the front room. She tried to focus her thoughts on the usual sounds of a summer evening: crickets in the grass, horses clip-clopping on the cobblestone, boys playing with sticks and rocks in front of the house next door. But she did not hear those sounds. Carriages rumbled past the house, one after the other. Their tumult drowned out the crickets' song, and the boys were shouting patriotic slogans instead of keeping score on their game.

Something was going on in the street that night. Every few minutes, Lizzie got out of her chair to part the drapes and peek outside. People ought to be finishing supper and settling in for the night. Why were so many people running around the streets? Even if she could muster the courage to investigate, she dared not leave Olivia and Emmett alone in the house to go find out.

And what did Joshua know about all this? For surely he had known before this all began. His steadfast refusal that afternoon to tell her where he was going had been the beginning of her suspicion.

When the light grew dim, Lizzie did not bother to light a lamp. She simply sat wondering where Joshua was and what he was doing, and worrying about what her parents might find.

As best she could, she prayed that Mama and Papa would find Joshua and bring him home safely. She wanted to believe, as Aunt Johanna did, that they were all in God's hands, whether what happened was good or bad. Lizzie sat in the dark, listening to her heart pound and wondering if she could ever believe that.

Mama and Papa came home at last. They were alone. They had covered a dozen square miles in their search, and Joshua was nowhere to be found. Once again they questioned Lizzie, and once again she could tell them nothing.

"What is happening out there?" she asked them. "Why are so many people moving about the streets at such a late hour?"

Mama and Papa looked at each other. Mama put her hands to her temples and closed her eyes. Papa put one arm around his wife's shoulders and met his daughter's questioning face.

"We're not sure what is happening, Lizzie. The streets are in chaos. We were concerned only with finding Joshua. But everywhere we went, we heard people talking about Sam Adams."

"Joshua is with Sam Adams, isn't he?"

Papa nodded. "That's what we think. We couldn't find him. We'll pray he comes home safely in the morning when all this is over."

"But what if he doesn't?" Lizzie cried.

"We'll pray that he will."

Mama had ordered Lizzie to bed at eleven o'clock. She had heard the town clock strike every hour since then. Twice she had gotten up to check on Emmett in the room next door. Both times she had seen that her parents still had a lamp burning downstairs. They did not come upstairs all night. Between concern for Joshua and the commotion in the street, sleep was impossible for Lizzie and her parents.

At long last, light filtered through the curtains of Lizzie's bedroom. She judged the time to be about five o'clock in the morning, still too early to get out of bed without being sent back to her room as soon as her mother saw her.

Then the front door creaked open. Lizzie heard the muffled voices of her parents greeting Joshua with both relief and anger. When they moved through the hall and into the kitchen, she could not hear anything. She lay still and waited, wondering if they would send Joshua straight up to his room. Finally, she could stand it no longer. Lizzie got out of bed, wrapped a light shawl around her shoulders, and crept down the stairs.

Downstairs, she pressed herself against the wall of the dining room so she could see Joshua through the doorway without being seen by her parents. He sat in a chair pulled back from the kitchen table. He was covered in soot, his breeches were torn, and he was so tired he could hardly hold his head up. But Lizzie barely noticed all that. What she saw was the fire in his eyes, the excitement, the passion. Wherever he had been, whatever he had done, he had been changed by the experience.

"You can come in, Lizzie," her mother said.

Lizzie stepped into full view. "I'm sorry, Mama. I couldn't sleep. I've been worried all night."

"I know. Come and have some tea."

Lizzie sat across from Joshua and let her mother set a teacup in front of her.

"Joshua," Papa began, "you have to know we disapprove of these street riots. I cannot imagine what possessed your mind to think you should be involved in one."

"Please let me explain, Papa," Joshua said. "Let me tell you what happened."

Mama pressed her lips together and then said, "All right, tell us what you saw."

"It's true that I knew something was going to happen," Joshua said, "but I didn't know when. I had heard rumors for several days. Then, when Aunt Johanna said she had seen Daniel Taylor and his gang just down the street, I knew that the day had come."

"The day for what?" Mama asked. "Street riots have been common in Boston since the Stamp Act was announced. Why was this day different?"

Joshua turned to his father. "Papa, did you see the effigies hanging from the Liberty Tree yesterday?"

"Effigies?" Lizzie asked. "What are effigies?"

"Effigies are like full-sized puppets," Papa explained. "Dummies of real people."

"Right," Joshua said. "Did you see them?"

"Yes, I did. One looked like Andrew Oliver, who is supposed to distribute the stamps."

"And the other was Lord Bute, the king's adviser," Joshua explained. "Sam Adams has been talking about those effigies for a while now. But I didn't see them until I went out in the afternoon."

"They burned them, didn't they?" Mama said. "I saw the smoke last night when we were looking for you."

"Do you approve of this, Joshua?" Papa asked.

"Papa, I don't think burning a bunch of paper made up to

look like a person hurts anyone. I don't think the stamp tax is a fair one, and the people have a right to protest." He sighed and looked down at his hands. "If only it had stopped there."

"But it didn't, did it?" Papa said sharply. "It never does."

"Daniel was in the middle of it, Papa, suggesting all sorts of terrible things—tearing up people's houses, burning ships, things like that. I thought if I could talk to him, make him see that he was accomplishing nothing, perhaps he would go home and leave well enough alone for the night."

"And did he?" Lizzie asked.

Joshua nodded. "Yes, after they burned the effigies, he told his boys to go home. But they were just a bunch of boys, Papa! There were so many men out there—real men—that it hardly mattered that Daniel went home."

"We heard the racket for half the night, Joshua," Mama said, "but you might as well tell us everything that happened."

"They went to Andrew Oliver's private dock in the harbor."

"To the stamp building?" Papa asked.

Joshua nodded. "They tore it apart, board by board. It wasn't even finished being built yet, but they tore it down. Just because it was supposed to store the stamps. I stood there feeling completely helpless! I don't agree with the Stamp Act any more than any of the other people down there, but it was a mob. They tore down a building. I couldn't get anyone to listen to me. Tearing down a building is not going to stop the stamps from coming. They'll build another building or rent one from a Loyalist."

Papa put his hand on his son's shoulder. Joshua put his elbows on the table and lowered his head into his hands.

"After that," he continued, "they went to Oliver's house and started tearing up his garden. A lot of the men wanted to break into the house, but Lieutenant Governor Hutchinson arrived with the sheriff, and that slowed things down a bit. Some of the people went home then. But a lot of others just stood there yelling and making threats. Finally Oliver came out."

"He came out into that mob?" Lizzie could not believe what she heard.

"Well, not right out into the mob. There's a balcony on his house. He stood on the balcony and promised to resign as stamp distributor."

Mama sighed. "That won't stop anything either. The authorities in England will appoint another stamp distributor."

"Yes," said Lizzie, "somebody like Ezra Byles, who doesn't care what anyone thinks about him."

"Things settled down after that," Joshua said, winding down his story. "I heard people saying that they might go after Lieutenant Governor Hutchinson next."

Mama shook her head. "When will this madness stop?"

"When the British leave," Joshua said resolutely.

"Oh Joshua, that's an extreme opinion," said his mother. "We're British, after all."

"No, Mama, I don't think so. Not anymore. We're Americans, and it's time that the British treated us as equals."

"You may very well be right, Joshua," his father said. "I have heard some of the wisest men in the colonies make such a suggestion."

"You're a man of sound thinking, Papa," challenged Joshua. "Don't you agree?"

Duncan Murray looked from his son to his wife to his daughter. Then he sighed heavily. "Yes, I believe I do agree."

"What does that mean, Papa?" Lizzie asked.

"It means that Sam Adams is right—about some things. He is right that taxation without representation is unjust, and the colonists have good reason to resist. And it means that if the king continues with this course of action, the British Empire itself will be torn apart."

"You are right about that, Papa," Joshua said. "I don't want a war. I don't even want any more street riots. But I do want the colonies to have the freedom they deserve. I believe Sam Adams is the man who will make that happen. I want to be with him when it does."

And the fire in his eyes burned bright and vigorous.

❦ CHAPTER 10 ❦

Mischief at the Print Shop

"Mama, I'm hungry."

Mama, Papa, Lizzie, and Joshua all turned to see five-year-old Emmett standing in the doorway.

"Can I have some breakfast?" Emmett asked, twisting the hem of his nightshirt.

"Of course you can," Mama said. "I'll warm some bread for you. I'll just be a few minutes." She turned to the others. "How about the rest of you? Are you hungry?"

Lizzie shrugged, and Joshua shook his head. Neither of them felt like eating yet.

"I'd better eat something before going in to the shop," Papa said. "I'm sure today will be busy."

"Joshua?" Emmett asked as he climbed into a chair next to his brother. "What happened to you?" His brown eyes were wide with questions.

Joshua touched his hand to his face and smeared a streak through the soot. He glanced at his mother, who met his glance with raised eyebrows. "Well, Emmett, I had a very long night.

I was trying to stop a fire."

"Did you?"

"No," Joshua said sadly. "I didn't. A building down at the harbor burned last night."

"Mama and Papa were angry when you didn't come home for supper."

"I know. I've told them I'm sorry for worrying them. Everything is going to be fine." He stroked Emmett's head gently.

"Ooh, you're dirty! Don't touch me!"

Everyone laughed.

"Why didn't anyone wake me up?" Olivia burst through the door, rubbing her eyes with one hand.

"It's still early," Lizzie said.

"But everyone else is up. I don't like to be asleep when everyone else is awake." She blinked and looked at her oldest brother. "Joshua, did you fall into the cinder box?" She stuck a finger in his cheek and inspected the soot that rubbed off.

Lizzie and Joshua laughed.

"He was putting out a fire," Emmett said proudly.

"Really?" Olivia's eyes grew wide with excitement. "Are you a hero, Joshua?"

"Hardly. I was just trying to help take care of Boston."

"Heroes do that. Like Sam Adams. You always tell me that Sam Adams is a hero."

Lizzie watched as her father and her brother looked at each other.

"How about some breakfast, Olivia?" Papa said, changing the subject. He swooped her up and set her in a chair. "Constance, let's slice some more bread. We should all have something to eat."

The bread was soon on the table along with a pot of steaming tea and a chunk of butter. Mama produced some honey and rationed it carefully.

"Mmm. I love bread and honey," Olivia said emphatically, licking her sticky fingers.

"I should probably get to the shop early today," Papa said. "After last night, there will be a lot of activity to report on."

"Like the fire?" Emmett asked.

"Yes, like the fire."

"Are you going to write that Joshua was a hero?" Olivia asked. Her sense of adventure was in full swing.

"I think your hero needs to go clean up," Mama said, giving Joshua a motherly look. "You're getting cinders all over the table."

"Sorry, Mama."

"You should get some rest," Mama said as she looked from Joshua to Lizzie. "Both of you."

Joshua nodded. "I'm exhausted. I'll clean up and go to bed. But don't let me sleep all day. I have some things I need to do this afternoon."

Lizzie wondered what business Joshua had that was so urgent. But to her surprise, neither of her parents pressed Joshua on the point. Lizzie sighed as she watched Joshua leave the room. No doubt Sam Adams was going to hold a meeting of the Sons of Liberty to discuss their activities of the night before, and Joshua planned to be there.

"You should go back to bed, too, Lizzie," Mama urged.

Lizzie shook her head emphatically. "I just know I wouldn't be able to sleep. I want to go to work with Papa."

"I'm not sure that's a good idea today," Mama said. "He'll be very busy."

"That's why I should go. I can help."

"Duncan?" Mama turned to Papa.

He nodded. "It's all right. She'll rest when she's ready. In the meantime, I could use another hand around the shop. She's pretty good with the typesetting." Papa winked at Lizzie.

They did not speak as they rode the carriage from the house to the shop. Merry trotted along cooperatively. She showed no sign that she sensed anything was different about this day. But Lizzie knew that the day was different. Joshua had made a decision from which he would not turn back. Even her parents seemed to recognize that his actions had not been a boyish impulse, but a decision of manhood.

With only two years between their ages, Lizzie and Joshua had played together as small children and watched out for one another as they grew up. They had been inseparable, the way that Olivia and Emmett were constantly together now. But today Joshua had taken a step ahead of Lizzie. He was going to a place where she was not ready to go. And she felt strangely lost without the comfort of his presence.

When they arrived at the print shop, several of the people who wrote stories for Papa were already out front, eager to give firsthand accounts of the night before. Lizzie could tell just by looking at them that they had been up all night. Although they had cleaned up a bit, they were haggard, and their clothing was not on quite straight. Most of all, they had the same fire in their eyes that she had seen in Joshua's.

Papa unlocked the shop and let the eager writers in. He

left Lizzie to get Merry settled until they would need the mare again. Lizzie looped the reins around the post in front of the shop, then stroked Merry's head.

"Did you hear anything last night, girl?" Lizzie asked. "Were you frightened?" Merry nuzzled her hand. Lizzie fished in her pocket and came up with a sugar cube.

"Mama doesn't know I have this. I've been saving it for you." She laughed as the horse took the cube and licked her hand, looking for more. "I have to go inside now. I said I would help, so I'd better get to work."

Lizzie and her father worked peacefully side by side for several hours. Lizzie tried to guess what Papa would need before he needed it—more paper, more ink, a tray of brass molds for setting the type, even a drink of water every now and then. They worked hard, and by lunchtime the day's edition was ready to print. Mama had packed some bread and ham and apples for them, and they allowed themselves a few minutes to relax and enjoy their food.

"Let's get the press going," Papa said, wrapping the remains of their lunch in some old paper.

Lizzie knew what to do next. She reached for the jar of thick black ink and started smearing it on the rows of metal type. Her father dampened some paper, laid it on the inked type, and got ready to bring the weight of the press down on it. He pulled down on the iron bar, and the ink on the rows of type was pressed onto the paper. Lizzie lifted the sample page and held it up for inspection. She ignored the fact that the lead story was about the burning of the effigies the night before. Instead, she simply took pride in the work she had done.

"Perfect!" she said.

Papa nodded. "It looks pretty good. Let's do the rest."

A spray of pebbles hit the window, startling them both. Outside, Merry neighed loudly.

"What's wrong with Merry?" Lizzie asked, losing interest in the sample sheet.

Papa nodded toward the door. "Go check on her."

Lizzie pulled open the shop door and gasped. A group of little boys, not more than nine or ten years old, were gathered around Merry. The horse was obviously distressed by their actions.

"Leave her alone!" Lizzie cried.

"Redcoat!"

"Lobsterback!"

The boys ignored Lizzie and formed a circle around Merry. One threw a rock that bounced off Merry's hoof. The boys laughed as the horse lifted her foot and neighed again.

"Get away!" Lizzie shouted.

"We'll show you that we are not idiots! You cannot treat us like children."

"We have a right to govern ourselves."

"Light the torch!" one of the boys commanded.

"Stop!" Lizzie screamed. This time she forced her way into the circle of boys, pushing two of them off balance. Around Merry's neck hung a paper cutout that was crudely shaped like a man and suspended by clothing lines.

"What do you think you are doing to my horse?" Lizzie demanded.

"Didn't you hear about last night?" one of the boys said. His excitement was obvious. "They burned the stamp distributor."

"They burned something made to look like him," Lizzie corrected. "Mr. Oliver is quite well this morning." In one emphatic motion, she ripped the paper cutout from around Merry's neck and threw it at the boy.

"He deserves to be burned in the flesh," the boy retorted.

"Why would you say such a thing? That's cruel." Lizzie soothed the restless horse with a stroking hand.

"It's what my father says. He was there last night and saw the whole thing. He even got to carry the effigy for part of the time."

Even Lizzie was surprised when a big hand reached into the group of boys and grabbed the shirt of the boy who was speaking.

"Do you think that is something to be proud of?" Papa asked.

Lizzie had not heard her father come out of the shop, but she was glad he was there. She leaned her face against Merry's, receiving as much comfort as she gave. Her eyes darted nervously from boy to boy.

"Sure it is," the boy asserted. "My father is no coward. He is not going to stand around and let King George do whatever he wants with the men in the colonies."

"Young man," Papa said, "I know your father. It is true that he is a free thinker and makes up his own mind about what he believes. No one tells him what to think."

"That's right!" the boy said proudly.

"I suggest that you learn something from your father. You have your own mind, too. Use it to decide what you think. Standing around the street pestering an innocent animal is no act of courage."

The boys looked at him, stunned. Papa looked them in the eyes, one by one.

"Now go on about your business and leave the horse alone," Papa said. The boys scampered away in several directions. Merry calmed down. But Lizzie was still nervous. What if Papa had not come out when he did?

"Thank you, Papa," Lizzie said as they went back into the shop.

"You were doing just fine, Lizzie. You stuck to the facts, and you remembered that cruelty is no virtue."

"It's stupid for a bunch of boys to act like a horse is a tree!" Lizzie cried. She hated to think what could have happened to Merry if the boys had tried to light the effigy they'd hung around her neck.

"They're just children," Papa reminded her. "They were only imitating what they see and hear adults doing."

Joshua's breakfast account of the night before was still vivid in Lizzie's mind. If those boys had heard their fathers and brothers tell the story, too, then they knew enough details to spend the whole day imitating what they had heard.

"Papa, last night. . .what does all this mean for Boston—for the colonies?"

Papa guided Lizzie to sit in a chair and took one of her hands in his.

"Lizzie, you're growing up, trying to understand things for yourself. That's good."

"But I don't understand," she insisted. "Joshua seems to know everything, but I don't understand why this has to happen."

Papa shook his head. "Sometimes I don't understand either,"

he said. "Things are changing. We cannot deny that. Joshua reminds us of that every day. But I can tell you this. Boston will settle down again. The people of this city are proud of what they have accomplished, and they want a good life for their families."

"I'm afraid Joshua will get hurt like that soldier that Uncle Philip took care of."

Papa nodded his understanding. "I worry about that, too. People are doing things that you and I think are crazy. In his heart, I believe Joshua thinks their actions are crazy, too. But he believes in their purpose. And I respect him for acting on what he believes."

Papa pulled Lizzie to his chest for a long hug. She nestled her face against her father's shoulder, and suddenly her head felt as heavy as a stone.

"Papa?"

"Yes, Lizzie?"

"I'm tired."

Papa chuckled. "You can sleep on the cot in the back room."

Lizzie stumbled into the back room, laid down up on the cot, and immediately gave in to the blackness of her exhaustion.

CHAPTER 11

Rooms for Redcoats

I always thought you were a fair man, Papa!"

Joshua slumped into a wooden chair and tried to control his frustration. His jaw was set tightly, and he glared at his father through narrowed eyes.

"You may think what you like about me, Joshua, but I have made up my mind." Duncan Murray could be every bit as stubborn as his son. He could remain calm and even-tempered no matter how much Joshua ranted and stormed about the print shop.

Lizzie sat on a stool, listening. She was setting the headline type for that afternoon's edition of the newspaper. Her father and brother seemed to have the same discussion every few days. Lizzie continued working as she listened.

Boston had settled down for a few days after the riot Joshua had witnessed. But there had been other riots. Some of the mobs were more organized than others, but they had all tried to draw attention to their cause by actions that the public could not ignore. Lizzie had seen Daniel Taylor hanging around the street corners with his followers. Daniel had not returned to school when classes resumed in the fall. Apparently, he had decided to devote all of his time to being patriotic.

Joshua went to school and, in the afternoons, helped in the shop, but from time to time he mysteriously disappeared. He never again worried his parents by staying out all night, and he insisted that he thought the violence was wrong. But Lizzie knew that he would often take a detour when he was delivering papers in the afternoon. He wanted to spend a few minutes under the elm tree in the center of town—Sam Adams's Liberty Tree.

Lieutenant Governor Hutchinson's home was invaded, as Joshua had predicted. His furniture had been thrown out the window and the house itself nearly destroyed. He and his family had escaped with only the clothes they wore and what little they could hurriedly gather and carry. While Joshua continued to agree with his parents that the violent actions were wrong, he also continued his friendship with Sam Adams. He believed in the changes Sam wanted to bring to Boston and all the colonies.

"Sam Adams only wants what is fair," Joshua said as he continued his dispute with his father. "Surely you can appreciate that."

"Of course I can," Papa said calmly. "But do you think what the Sons of Liberty did to the Hutchinson house was fair?"

Joshua had no answer.

"Hutchinson publicly opposed the Stamp Act," Papa continued, "but the mob attacked his home and family simply because he is an agent of the government in England. That, I assure you, is not fair."

"The Sons of Liberty were not the only ones involved in that," Joshua argued. "The mob got out of control."

"But who stirred up the mob? It was Adams, I tell you. Hutchinson is chief justice of the superior court, and that mob took away everything he owned. He was right when he said that simple indignation could touch off an uncontrolled emotional frenzy. The indignation may be just; the frenzy is not. The Sons of Liberty are only hurting their own cause by such behavior."

Joshua stood up again and folded his arms across his chest. "But you agree that taxation without representation is not fair, don't you?" he pressed.

"You know that I agree. We have discussed this many times before. The Stamp Act will draw resources out of the colonies. We are being taxed without having a say in the decision for how to use the taxes. That is not fair."

"Then why won't you print this?" Joshua thrust a paper toward his father.

Papa did not take the paper. He had already looked at it closely enough. He turned to the tray of metal letters on the counter next to Lizzie. She watched him expertly pick the letters he needed. "What is written on that paper is inflammatory and lacking in facts. I will not print it." He began setting the letters in the tray he was working on.

"Papa, be reasonable."

"That is exactly what I am trying to do."

Lizzie watched her father work with admiration. She wondered if she would ever be able to set type as fast as he could. Even Joshua's nagging did not distract him.

"What is written on this paper is important to the cause of the colonies. Papa, you have a printing press. Surely you realize what a great help that is to the cause. You can make an important contribution without ever leaving your shop."

"I will not print that article, Joshua." Papa spoke without turning around.

"Then let me do it," Joshua said. "I know how to work the press. I've been helping you for years."

"I will not contribute to the violence, Joshua, even indirectly. I will not stir up the anger of the people so that they go out and destroy property. I do not wish to endanger lives without just cause."

"I'm not asking you to do any of that. I just want to print a few papers."

"Rewrite the article. Then come to me again."

"I can't change the article, Papa. Sam Adams wrote this himself."

"Then ask him to rewrite it."

"I can't do that."

Papa finally turned from his tray of type. "You can do anything you choose to do, Joshua," he said as he looked his son in the eye. "You have already proven that."

Joshua sighed and stuffed the paper into his pocket.

The first time Lizzie had overheard such a discussion, she had been shocked that Joshua would use such a tone with their father. When they were younger, talking back to their parents had been strictly forbidden. She herself would never question her father's authority.

However, after several of these discussions, she knew just

how both Joshua and her father would sound. Joshua would plead for his father to be more involved with the cause of the Patriots. Specifically, he thought Papa should use his press to print only literature in favor of the Patriots. He argued that the Loyalists had more than enough support coming from England. But the Patriots had to organize themselves from nothing and make the most with what little aid they could find. Duncan Murray's press could be a precious resource.

Lizzie's father, on the other hand, reserved the right to examine and approve anything that his press was used to print. In the newspaper, he was concerned about being fair. He gave the facts on both sides of any controversy. When everyone else in Boston seemed free with their opinions, Duncan Murray held up the facts and held back his tongue. In fliers and pamphlets, he steadfastly refused to print anything he thought would cause further violence, no matter who had written it.

This infuriated Joshua. If Sam Adams was seeking what was fair for all the colonies, why shouldn't Duncan Murray help?

"It's important that people understand what the Stamp Act Congress is, Papa," Joshua pleaded. "The colonies have to work together to oppose the Stamp Act, and this congress is the way to do that. Will you at least print Sam's article on the congress?"

"I have already printed several articles informing people the congress is taking place," Papa answered.

"I know, Papa, and Sam appreciates that. But the people need more than information about when the congress will happen. They need to understand why it is needed. This will be the first time that all the colonies stand united in one protest against Parliament. This is a new strategy, for the good of the colonies."

"All right." Papa turned back to his typesetting. "Sam Adams may write a piece, and if it is not inflammatory, I will print it."

"Thank you, Papa."

"But," Papa continued, shaking a finger at Joshua, "if someone else chooses to write an article opposing the congress who presents reasonable arguments, I will print that, too."

Joshua sighed. "I suppose that is only fair."

"Good. You see my point at last."

Lizzie was relieved that this one battle seemed to be over.

The shop door opened, and the bell tinkled. Lizzie swung around on her stool to see her uncle Blake enter. He was red in the face and angrier than Lizzie had ever seen him.

"Blake!" Papa exclaimed. "What's going on?"

Uncle Blake waved a paper. "They want Charlotte and me to take in two British soldiers; that's what's going on."

Lizzie hopped off her stool to greet her uncle and pay closer attention to the conversation.

"The Quartering Act," Papa stated flatly.

"Yes, the Quartering Act. Is it my problem that the king's army cannot provide enough barracks for its own troops? They have brought that upon themselves, if you ask me."

"Let me see the paper," Papa said, reaching for it. He read it closely. "They leave you no option, Blake. You could face severe penalties if you refuse to do this."

Uncle Blake pounded the edge of the printing press. "Charlotte and I are barely finding enough food for the boys and ourselves as it is. How can we possibly stretch our meager rations to feed two more full-grown men?"

"We'll help all we can," Papa assured him.

Lizzie pictured her mother trying to make her precious staples extend to another household.

"You already have six mouths to feed at your house," Uncle Blake retorted. "You haven't got a morsel to spare, and you know it."

"Especially not for a British soldier," Joshua blurted out. "I'll not have my brother's and sisters' food cut back so that a lobsterback can eat well."

"And I would not take a crumb out of their mouths," Uncle Blake assured Joshua. He sighed. "Duncan, I don't know how you keep going. If things do not get better soon, Wallace Coach and Carriage will face serious problems. I hate the thought of closing up the business. I want to give my boys the same legacy my uncle gave me when he left me Wallace Coach."

"And you will, Blake, you will."

"Do you see why we need the congress, Papa?" Joshua said. "Forcing residents of Boston to feed and house British soldiers is just another form of taxation without representation. We have to stop this before it goes any further."

"Listen to the boy, Duncan," Uncle Blake said. "He's absolutely right about this."

"You are in favor of the congress, then?" Joshua asked hopefully.

"Certainly, I am." Uncle Blake was emphatic.

"And you think Sam Adams is right?"

"Sam Adams—and a lot of other people. I know Sam has drummed up a lot of support. He gives talks under the Liberty

Tree and organizes the Sons of Liberty. But he is not the only man in Boston thinking this way. The idea of the congress really came from James Otis. It makes a lot of sense to me."

"It's against the law," Papa said. "Any governor who sends representatives will be openly defying the king. The men who attend could be arrested as soon as they return."

"It will be worth that price if the congress accomplishes what James Otis hopes it will," Uncle Blake said.

"That's right!" Joshua exclaimed.

"Not everyone agrees," Papa pointed out. "The governors of Virginia, Maryland, North Carolina, and Georgia have forbidden their representatives to attend."

"That still leaves nine colonies," Uncle Blake said, "a large enough majority to make an impression on the king. And the other governors will no doubt send their own letters of protest. We are all suffering because we are boycotting British goods. Eventually the boycott will hurt England more than it does us. Then the progress we make will be worth the price we are paying now."

"I am concerned that the Stamp Act Congress will bring more violence to the streets," Papa said.

"The violence will come with or without the congress," Uncle Blake insisted. "When the Stamp Act goes into law in November, madness will follow. But if the people believe in the Stamp Act Congress, if they commit to a reasonable course of action, then perhaps less damage will be done."

"I think Uncle Blake is right," Joshua said. "And what you print can influence people to support the congress and help stop the riots."

Papa smiled faintly as he looked from his son to his brother-in-law. "The two of you are sure thinking alike." Papa handed Uncle Blake the quartering orders. "But none of that changes this command, Blake. It will be unpleasant, but for the sake of your family's safety, you must obey."

Blake shook his head. "If I refuse, I am in danger with the government. If I obey, I am at risk with the mobs. I am not worried about myself or even Charlotte. But I do not want the boys to be caught in the middle of all this."

"Send the boys to stay with us," Lizzie suggested.

"That's a great idea," Papa agreed. "Olivia and Emmett would love it. Just until things settle down."

Lizzie was glad she had made the suggestion. Like her uncle Blake, she hated to think that anything might happen to Isaac or Christopher. Her little cousins would be safer at her house. But would things ever settle down enough for Isaac and Christopher to go home?

CHAPTER 12

Just One Soldier

"They're back!" came the cry.

And suddenly the cobblestone street was filled with activity. Merchants left their shops. Women grabbed their babies and left their homes. Horses and carriages and people on foot gathered in the town square to greet the Boston representatives of the Massachusetts Assembly. They had returned safely from the Stamp Act Congress in New York City, and the whole city of Boston was curious to hear their report.

"Whoa." Lizzie tugged on the reins and pulled Merry to a stop. The afternoon deliveries would be delayed for a few minutes. Without waiting for the cart to stop, Joshua abandoned his newspapers and leaped down from the seat. He ran toward the returning delegation and became part of a crowd clamoring for information. Lizzie did not even try to persuade Joshua to stay with the cart. He had been waiting for this moment so eagerly. For the past few days, he had talked about little but the Stamp Act Congress and how Parliament would respond.

Lizzie decided to stay with Merry, lest any harm come to the old mare in the middle of a crowd. She held the reins tightly in case a sudden movement spooked the horse into action. She could not hear much, but because of the height of the cart, Lizzie could see most of what was happening.

The representatives were tired, dusty, and eager for a hot meal. They would make a complete report later, but the townspeople would not wait for formalities. They wanted their news firsthand and immediately. Those closest to the mounted representatives asked the questions on everyone's mind.

"Did you tell the king to forget about his taxes?"

"Do all the colonies agree?"

"What's next?"

The report was organized soon enough, and word filtered back through the crowd. Nine colonies had sent representatives, and the other four had agreed to abide by the outcome of the congress. The result of the meetings had been a letter to the king declaring certain American rights and listing the complaints of the colonies about the British government's recent actions.

Joshua came whooping out of the crowd. Thrashing with excitement, he pushed his way past a line of human obstacles and hurled himself up into the carriage next to Lizzie.

"Did you hear all that, Lizzie?" he asked.

The fire in his eyes was burning brightly, and he grinned as he had not grinned for weeks. She nodded.

"And do you know what it means?"

Again, Lizzie nodded. Then she said, "But, Joshua, the letter will not reach King George for weeks. The Stamp Act will be in effect before that."

Joshua took the reins and nudged Merry forward ever so slightly. "That's true. But the congress is about more than just the Stamp Act."

"What do you mean? It's called the Stamp Act Congress."

"But it goes beyond that." Joshua paused to reach back and throw a small bundle of papers to a waiting merchant. He continued. "We're Americans, and we have rights. That's what it is about. The king has to see that we will not stand for the Stamp Act or anything else that does not respect our rights and independence. You see, we aren't simply trying to change the stamp tax. We're trying to change the way the British government looks at the colonies."

"That sounds like an awfully big job to me."

"It is. But the Stamp Act Congress is an important first step."

"And in the meantime?" Lizzie asked, dreading the day the Stamp Act would take effect.

Joshua shrugged. "We live one day at a time and see what each day brings."

Lizzie reached over and pulled on the reins. "You missed a stop. We're still delivering papers, remember?"

"Right." Joshua jumped down. "Help me with these. We leave two stacks at this stop."

Lizzie got down. She could not lift the bound stacks as easily as Joshua could. She often pleaded with him to tie smaller bundles, but he just told her to grow bigger muscles. He was already gone with the first stack. Huffing, she tugged the second stack off the back of the cart and strained to carry it to the shop's door.

"Here, let me help you with that."

Lizzie looked up into the face of a British soldier. Her heart leaped in her throat. Never had a soldier spoken to her before. But this was not just any British soldier. She recognized the clear gray eyes and soft brown hair. This was the young man she had helped care for in Uncle Philip's clinic.

After that day when the soldier had been injured, Lizzie had stopped by the clinic to check on his recovery several times. But she had always spoken with her uncle, never directly with the soldier. She had not seen him at all in the six months since Uncle Philip had declared him fit and sent him back to his regiment.

"I can manage," she muttered, adjusting her load. Her heart pounded. Any second she was sure to drop the newspapers on her foot.

"I insist," he said, and he took the stack from her. "Where do they go?"

She gestured. "Just over there, by the door." Her voice was hardly more than a whisper.

Joshua came out of the shop.

"Hey, what are you doing?" He snatched the papers from the soldier.

"I was just helping your sister." The soldier's response was calm. "I wanted to repay her kindness of some time ago." He looked down at Lizzie with steady gray eyes. She had looked into those eyes six months ago and seen fear. Now she saw emptiness. Her heart softened as she returned his gaze.

"I appreciated the way you cared for me," the soldier said. "You could have left me to bleed to death."

"I would never have done that." Lizzie did not know how she found the strength to speak. "Besides, it was my uncle who knew what to do."

"All the same, I've been wanting to thank you. But I did not know how to find you."

Joshua finally realized who the young man was. "You're . . .you're better." He let the stack of newspapers drop to the ground several feet off target.

"Yes, I am fully recovered." The soldier turned to look at Joshua. "And I extend my thanks to you as well."

Lizzie looked at his jacket and saw the crude stitching on one shoulder. Someone inexperienced with a needle and thread had tried to repair the uniform where Uncle Philip had cut it. The soldier looked even more thin and ragged than he had six months ago, if that was possible. Lizzie's heart tightened.

"Are you on duty?" Lizzie asked. He carried no musket.

The soldier glanced around. "I am looking for work."

"Around here?" Lizzie asked. She knew that the merchants in this neighborhood were not likely to be able to pay a hired hand—even if they would agree to hire a British soldier, which was doubtful.

"The jobs at the docks are all taken," the soldier explained. "I thought it could not hurt to look elsewhere."

"But you have a job. You're a soldier." Joshua spoke with an edge to his voice. Lizzie glared at him. If Joshua would only look at the pitiful state this soldier was in, he would not say such cruel things.

The soldier's voice was low. "I have not been paid in months," he said. "The barracks are crowded. There is not enough food."

His voice drifted away.

Lizzie glanced down at the soldier's boots, wondering if he had gotten new ones or if he still filled the holes with layers of newspaper.

"Perhaps we can help you," Lizzie said impulsively.

"Lizzie!" Joshua said in a harsh whisper. "May I speak with you?" Without waiting for an answer, he grabbed her wrist and jerked her back over toward their cart. Merry neighed and swished her tail.

"Have you gone mad? Lizzie, why would you offer to help a British soldier? Have you listened to nothing that I have said in the last few months?"

Lizzie twisted out of her brother's grip. "Of course I've heard you. Every word. You never stop talking about your cause. But have you looked at him, Joshua? Really looked at him?"

Lizzie put a hand on the mare's neck, both to steady herself and to give herself something familiar to concentrate on.

Joshua kept his eyes on Lizzie. "I realize he is having a difficult time. But we all are."

"Don't be silly, Joshua. You must weigh twenty pounds more than he does. Mama makes sure that you eat properly, even in hard times."

"Suppose he were one of the soldiers living in Uncle Blake and Aunt Charlotte's house?" Joshua argued. "Suppose he were one of the ones taking food away from Isaac and Christopher?"

"But he's not!" Lizzie retorted. "And he's hungry and cold just like any human being would be. Look at him, Joshua! Look at him!"

She punched his shoulder until he gave in and turned

around. The soldier, not believing that Lizzie would return to help him, was leaning up against the side of the building. In his dejection, all he could do was trace shapes in the dirt with his ragged boots.

"We have to help him, Joshua."

"You're helping the enemy, Lizzie."

"He's not the enemy, Joshua. He's just one soldier. That could be you in a couple of years."

Joshua was silent and swallowed hard. "I don't know, Lizzie, I don't know."

"Why is it so hard for you to see he needs help? He needs us now just as much as that day in Uncle Philip's clinic."

"This is not the same thing."

"Yes, it is. You're always preaching about doing what is fair. Something that is truly fair is fair to everyone, not just to people you agree with. It's not fair that you should have enough to eat, and he does not."

Joshua did not answer.

"If I want to help him, you can't stop me," Lizzie insisted.

"Well, if it isn't Joshua and Lizzie Murray."

A gruff voice from behind surprised them both. Lizzie wheeled around to face Daniel Taylor. Behind him were three of his gang, casually thumping sticks against the palms of their hands.

"I saw you talking to that soldier, Lizzie."

Lizzie tossed her hair back proudly. "So what if I did? It's not any of your business."

"I'll make it my business if I see you talking to him again."

"Don't threaten my sister," Joshua growled.

Daniel turned haughtily to Joshua. "Don't tell me you're turning into a lobsterback, Joshua. I would have thought better of you than that."

Joshua put up his fists. "You mind your own business, Daniel Taylor."

The boys behind Daniel stood poised with their sticks in the air.

Lizzie lurched between Daniel and Joshua and grabbed Joshua's wrists. "What are you doing, Joshua? Fighting won't solve anything."

Daniel laughed. "Ha! Now I know why you say that to me all the time, Joshua. You're taking orders from your little sister."

"I'm not taking orders from anyone!"

"Just don't talk to that soldier again," Daniel said, staring at Lizzie. She stared back at him, her chin in the air and her stomach churning violently.

When Daniel moved on down the street, Lizzie searched for the soldier. He was gone.

CHAPTER 13

Night of Terror

Crash!

Lizzie ran to the front window. Joshua was close behind.

"What was it?" she asked as they leaned against the glass and peered into the street.

"I can't see anything from in here," moaned Joshua. "If Mama and Papa would just let me go out for a few minutes, I could find out what is going on."

Their father spoke behind them. He made no move to get any closer to the window. "Joshua, we discussed this already, and you agreed to stay in."

"But, Papa, I just want to find out what is happening. Aren't you curious?"

Papa shook his head. "This is November 1. The Stamp Act took effect today. We all knew what would happen when this day came."

"You are going to have to report on this in the paper tomorrow. I could write a story for you."

"I have other sources. I see no need to put my son at risk."

Constance Murray came down the stairs. She had been upstairs for more than an hour with Emmett, Olivia, Isaac, and Christopher, trying to settle them down and coax them to sleep.

"I think they've settled at last," she said.

"I don't see how they can sleep with all this noise," Lizzie remarked. There was far too much activity in the street to be able to relax and sleep. She knew she would not sleep a moment all night.

"They are exhausted," her mother said. "I made sure that they played very hard today. I knew the night would be like this." Mama ran her fingers through Lizzie's red curls. "You should try to get some rest, too."

Lizzie shook her head vigorously. "No, I'm sure I couldn't sleep."

"Are you going to stay up all night, Papa?" Joshua asked.

Papa nodded somberly. "A rock thrown off course might break a window. A stray spark would do far more damage."

"I'm a member of the Sons of Liberty now, Papa. I should be with them on a night like this."

"For what purpose?" Papa raised his voice slightly, startling Lizzie. "You are one person, Joshua. You cannot stop the rampage, especially when your fellow Sons of Liberty are very likely at the center of it. Most likely, Sam Adams and his gang have spent the evening in their favorite tavern. Now they are so full of ale they have lost their common sense."

"Papa!" Joshua protested. "You can't possibly know that for sure."

"You and I both know that it has happened before. People have gotten hurt because of a gang's drunken street brawl."

"That is not Sam's purpose."

"No, but it has happened. I have no doubt that the taverns of Boston have seen a lot of business tonight."

"It's a protest, Papa, against an unfair law," Joshua insisted.

"It's madness, Joshua, plain and simple. The king is across the ocean, no doubt enjoying a fine breakfast right now. These riots mean nothing to him."

"Oh Papa!"

"Joshua," Papa warned. "I don't want to hear another word about it. You are forbidden to go out tonight."

Joshua flung himself into a chair to sulk. Papa picked up an iron poke and stirred the fire. The flames danced and cast an orange glow on the room. Mama stood behind Papa and rubbed his shoulders.

"Mama!" came a cry from upstairs.

Mama sighed. "That's Olivia. I guess she's still awake after all."

"I'll go," Lizzie said and turned to the stairs. She welcomed a reason to escape the tension in the front room. The disagreements between her father and her brother were almost as difficult to listen to as the ruckus outside.

Upstairs, she crept into the room she shared with Olivia. "I'm here, Olivia," she said softly.

"I can't sleep," the little girl said as she rubbed her eyes with her fists.

Lizzie sat on the bed next to her sister. "I know. But you must try. I'll stay with you until you fall asleep."

Olivia pulled the bedding up under her chin and rolled toward the wall. *Our mother is right,* Lizzie thought. *Olivia is exhausted.*

Gently, she rubbed her little sister's back to soothe her.

The street noise was muffled on the second floor of the house. Lizzie could still sense that the neighborhood was active, but she could not make out the sounds. Nevertheless, she could not relax. Without a fire and her parents in the room with her, she felt even more on edge. She was isolated, alone. Even as she tried to bring comfort to Olivia, her own fear grew.

In the dim moonlight that filtered through the window, Lizzie studied Olivia's face. In her sleep, Olivia looked far less overwhelming than she was when awake. She was a boisterous child, always seeking adventure. She could hardly sit still for more than three minutes at a time. In many ways, Olivia was like Joshua. They were natural leaders, not afraid to say what they thought. People enjoyed being around them and paid attention to what they did.

If Olivia were older, she would probably have the same fire for the colonists' cause that Joshua had. Lizzie was glad Olivia was too young to get involved in the controversy between England and the colonies. Lizzie sincerely hoped that by the time Olivia was Joshua's age, the debate would be long over. Surely in ten years, life in Boston would once again be comfortable and peaceful.

At last Olivia's breathing was even and deep. Lizzie crept from the room and down the stairs. Joshua had scooted his chair closer to the window, and her parents had sat down together. No one was speaking.

Even though Joshua was grouchy and complained about having to stay in, Lizzie was glad their parents had forbidden him to go out. Joshua thought he was grown-up enough to make his own decisions, but Lizzie was glad to have someone looking out for him. At least she would not have to spend the night worrying about his safety.

Lizzie returned to her post beside Joshua at the window. Outside, a steady stream of people rushed through the streets, some with torches. *Are the torches to give light or to set fire to something?* Lizzie shuddered at the thought of more fires erupting in Boston.

Papa was right: This was more than a crowd protesting an unfair law. It was a mob determined to find revenge. People were running in every direction. Men swung their guns around in the air. Boys not much older than Joshua were out there, standing below the windows of Loyalists, shouting names and throwing rocks. The Stamp Act Congress had brought hope for a few weeks—hope that the law would be short-lived once King George received the protest of the colonies. But her father was right. They all had known that Boston would explode in fury on the day that the law took effect. Now they watched out the window to learn how vicious the fury was.

"Lizzie, come sit with us," her mother invited. "You've been feeling poorly. I don't want you to catch a chill standing by the window."

"Joshua can watch out the window for all of us," her father said.

Joshua raised his eyes to give his parents a dejected glance.

"Come, Lizzie." Mama raised one arm to welcome her daughter.

Lizzie snuggled in next to her mother. She shivered despite the roaring fire.

"You're safe here, Lizzie," her mother said in low, soothing tones.

As Lizzie leaned her head against her mother's shoulder, she felt the welcome weight of a quilt spread over her. The fire was the only light in the room. It snapped and crackled, mesmerizing Lizzie. Despite her earlier protests, Lizzie gave way to her exhaustion and slept.

The pounding on the door woke her up.

She threw off the quilt and sprang to her feet. "What is it?" she cried. *How long have I been asleep? Why am I in the front room and not in my bed?* The disorientation cleared, and she remembered the events of the evening. Blinking her eyes, she saw that it was still dark outside the window.

Mama pulled Lizzie back as Joshua and Papa went to the door. The pounding came again.

"Who is there?" Papa demanded. With one hand, he double-checked the bolt on the door.

"We need to see Joshua!" came the gruff reply.

"I demand that you tell me who you are," Papa insisted.

"Just open the door!"

"That's Daniel Taylor!" Lizzie exclaimed.

Papa looked at Joshua, who nodded. "She's right. I'm sure that's his voice." He looked out the window, then said, "There are seven or eight boys out there. They look mad."

"I know he used to be a friend of yours," Papa said to Joshua. "Have you had anything to do with him recently?"

"No, Papa! I have seen him in the streets, but he is not one of my friends any longer."

Papa turned back to the door. "What business do you have

here?" he shouted through the bolted door.

"My business is with Joshua—and Lizzie."

"Me?" Lizzie cried. "I have nothing to do with Daniel Taylor." Her mind flashed back to the scene in the street, when Daniel had thwarted her determination to help a hungry soldier.

A spray of rocks pelted the front door. Lizzie clutched her mother's arm.

"Please leave!" Papa shouted.

"No rocks!" Daniel screamed at his companions. He turned back to the door. "I promise you no harm will come to you, Mr. Murray. I simply want to speak with Joshua and Lizzie."

Father glared at Joshua. "What have you been up to, Joshua? Why does Daniel Taylor want to speak to you? And have you gotten Lizzie involved in your inflammatory behavior?"

"Papa, no!" Joshua said adamantly. "Daniel and his gang are on their own. I promise you I have had no dealings with them."

"Then why does he want to see you so badly?"

"I don't know. Truly, I don't know."

Papa turned back to the door. "Send your companions away, Daniel. You may speak to Joshua alone."

Lizzie held her breath. Her father was not about to unbolt the door and give entrance to a gang, but would he allow Daniel to come in?

Grunts and scuffles followed.

Joshua watched at the window and reported, "They're going. They've backed up into the street. Everybody but Daniel."

"Does he have a weapon?" Papa asked.

Joshua shook his head. "Not that I can see. He carries only a torch. . .and some sort of bundle."

"My friends have gone, Mr. Murray," Daniel shouted, "but if you do not open the door, I will call them back and we will break it down!"

"He means what he says, Papa," Joshua said.

Papa pointed at a spot on the floor about ten feet from the door. "Stand there, Joshua. This hooligan will not enter our home. He may speak to you from the doorway."

Then Papa wedged one foot against the door, unbolted it, and opened it about twelve inches. "You may speak."

Lizzie could see Daniel's face, darkened with the grime of the night's riot.

"I have something you may be interested in," Daniel said. His nostrils flared as he sneered at Joshua and threw his bundle into the house.

It landed at Joshua's feet and fell open.

"A redcoat's jacket?" Joshua asked.

Lizzie gasped. She could think of only one reason why Daniel Taylor would bring them a soldier's uniform. She broke from her mother and scrambled to get the jacket.

Daniel laughed outside the door. "I thought you would be interested in that!"

Ignoring him, Lizzie held the jacket up for inspection. On one shoulder were the crude stitches she was looking for. She knew who the jacket belonged to.

"Where did you get this?" she demanded.

"Where do you think?" Daniel answered. "I took it off the back of your friend."

"What is he talking about?" Mama demanded. "What have you to do with a British soldier?"

Lizzie barely glanced at her mother. She had no time to explain now.

"Why did you take his jacket?" Lizzie hissed at Daniel. She clutched the dirty jacket to her chest and determined to hold back the tears.

"He won't be needing it anymore." Daniel roared with laughter again.

At that moment, Lizzie loathed Daniel Taylor. She swallowed the lump in her throat, but she could not stop the tears any longer. "You killed him, didn't you?"

Daniel shrugged. "No, I didn't kill him. I just found him that way. So you see? All your tender care was for nothing. You should have let him bleed to death six months ago."

"That's enough!" Papa said, and he shoved the door closed and bolted it.

They could hear the whole gang laughing as Daniel rejoined them in the street.

Lizzie fell to her knees and sobbed.

✌ CHAPTER 14 ✌

The Accident

Christmas came that year just as it did every year. The riot that had broken out when the stamp tax took effect had subsided into a series of minor skirmishes. Sam Adams rallied the young men of Boston even more vigorously. Some people flatly refused to buy the little blue stamps for their legal documents. This made doing business very difficult.

Finally, in late December, Boston settled down to a peaceful observance of the Christmas holiday.

Lizzie set the table meticulously, as she did every year. Once again, Uncle Philip, Aunt Johanna, and Charity would share Christmas dinner with the Murrays, along with Uncle Blake and Aunt Charlotte and their two boys. But this year, even having the family together added to the tension.

Uncle Blake had become quite outspoken about his Patriot leanings. If Uncle Blake was doing something dangerous—well, Lizzie did not want to know about it. Many of the Patriots in Boston were disobeying British laws, especially if the law was about money. Joshua considered such defiance to be a patriotic act. He was still sure Uncle Blake was avoiding tax fees.

Uncle Philip was equally emphatic about his tendency to agree with the Loyalists. He still thought of himself as British, unlike Joshua, who considered himself an "American." Although Uncle Philip had never been to England and probably never would travel there, he trusted England to govern the colonies in a fair way. He argued that the colonies would not have developed as rapidly as they had without the aid of England. It was only right that the colonies should help the mother country when she needed them.

Lizzie's parents tried to continue their neutral stance, but they received constant pressure from both sides. And of course, Joshua's agitation grew every day. Lizzie's heart was heavy when it ought to have been full of joy.

She set the last goblet in its place.

"A beautiful table once again," Aunt Johanna said.

Lizzie smiled as earnestly as she could. "Thank you."

"You do such a lovely job. It's always wonderful to see these beautiful dishes."

"Especially when it's hard to have a real Christmas dinner right now," Lizzie said.

Aunt Johanna's smile faded. "Yes, it's difficult. The food will be simple this year, with no delicacies. But we are all together and all safe. That is what is most important."

Lizzie nodded. "I want to try to make this a nice holiday for Olivia and Emmett. I want them to have wonderful memories of family holidays, even without fancy food."

Aunt Johanna chuckled. "They don't like to eat fancy food anyway."

Lizzie smiled, this time sincerely. "You're right about that. But they do like to play in the snow." Her face brightened as she tucked a chair under the table. "I think I'll take all the children outside. We can throw snowballs and pull the sled around."

"That's a wonderful idea. I'll help you get them bundled up."

"*Ahh!*" Olivia stuck her tongue out to catch snow flurries. With her arms stretched out wide, she spun around in circles until she tripped over her own feet and collapsed in the snow. Her brother and her cousins followed her lead.

Lizzie laughed at the sight of the five children, from six to nine years old, sprawled in the powdery snow with their tongues hanging out. It felt good to laugh.

"This is fun!" Emmett, the youngest, exclaimed joyously.

"You said we could play on the sled," Olivia reminded Lizzie.

"We want the sled!" Christopher joined in.

Soon all five were repeating the refrain. "We want the sled. We want the sled."

"All right, all right, we'll get the sled." Lizzie happily gave in to the pressure. She trudged back toward the house and took the sled off its hook. Glancing through a window, she saw Joshua sitting with his uncles. Clearly he considered himself one of the adults. He had far too much on his mind to romp in the snow with children. Lizzie missed the old Joshua, the one who would have been outside acting sillier than all the other children put together.

Lizzie dropped the sled solidly in the snow.

"Me first! Me first!" the children all seemed to say.

One by one, Lizzie dragged the five children in a wide circle around the backyard. The other four clamored behind, throwing snowballs at each other. Seeing their faces and sensing their excitement, Lizzie felt better than she had while setting the table. These children had not taken up sides as either Patriots or Loyalists. They were just children, cousins who enjoyed playing together. She hoped that moments like this one would form their strongest memories.

But she was exhausted. After five trips around the yard, trudging through the snow as fast as she could, Lizzie pleaded for a chance to rest. Then she would give everyone a second turn.

"You play by yourselves," she said. "The older ones can pull the younger ones."

"And then you'll pull us again?" Olivia wanted to be sure the fun was not over.

"I promise. Just let me sit down for a few minutes." Lizzie collapsed on the back stoop outside the kitchen and watched as the children continued to streak through the snow with the sled. They squabbled about who would get to ride in front of the sled and which direction to go. But Lizzie welcomed these signs of normal childhood behavior and did not interfere. Perhaps by next Christmas the stamp tax controversy would be over. Boston would settle down again, and the children would indeed have normal childhoods.

Gradually the children drifted farther and farther back into the yard. Now only the highest pitches of their conversation reached Lizzie's ears. She had nearly regained her energy, and she thought that at the next sign of a quarrel, she would take over pulling the sled again.

Lizzie looked up to see Olivia pulling the sled up the hill at the back of the yard.

"Wait, Olivia!" she called. The hill that divided the Murray property from the neighbors' was not high, but it was steep. Olivia had never before gone down that hill by herself on a sled. Lizzie jumped to her feet and pushed her way through the snow. Instinct told Lizzie that she should ride down with Olivia.

But Olivia was too far ahead of Lizzie and had much more energy. Before Lizzie was halfway up the hill, Olivia had seated herself on the sled.

"Push me!" Olivia demanded. And her cousin Isaac obeyed.

"No, Olivia!" Lizzie shouted. "Stop!"

But she knew Olivia could not stop the sled once it was in motion. She held her breath and watched. Olivia squealed with delight as she whizzed past Lizzie on her way down.

Suddenly, the sled's left blade hit a rock hidden in the snow. Olivia tumbled off. Lizzie screamed as she saw her little sister land on her head while the sled bumped on down the hill.

"Olivia!"

The little girl did not move. Lizzie felt as if time had stopped. The snow felt like iron weights around her ankles. She could not make her feet move fast enough. The other children were scattered around the yard, and they stood still, too stunned to move.

"Olivia! Are you all right?" Lizzie called out. No answer came. Finally, she reached the girl. Olivia's eyes were closed, and she lay still. Her chubby face, usually rosy, looked pale against the snow.

Lizzie frantically looked around the yard to spot the child

nearest the house. "Christopher!" she shouted. "Go get Uncle Philip! Tell him to come quickly."

Fortunately, Christopher unfroze and ran into the house.

Lizzie laid her hand against Olivia's face and called her sister's name again. Olivia's arms and legs were sprawled in every direction. With all the thick clothing she was wearing, it was difficult to tell whether any of her bones might have been broken in the tumble. Lizzie was afraid to touch her or try to move her. Lizzie looked toward the back of the house. There was no sign of anyone coming to help.

"Uncle Philip!" she screamed. She turned to Emmett. "Emmett, go check and see if Christopher found Uncle Philip. Hurry!"

Obediently Emmett scrambled through the snow toward the house.

"Olivia," Lizzie pleaded, "wake up." Lizzie groped for Olivia's wrist and tried to find a pulse, as she had seen her uncle do with his patients. But she did not really know what she was doing, and when she could not find the pulse, her panic deepened.

A hand on her shoulder made her jump.

"It's all right, Lizzie, I'm here." Uncle Philip knelt in the snow and examined Olivia.

"She landed on her head, Uncle Philip," Lizzie explained. "She won't wake up. I think she broke her neck."

Uncle Philip shook his head. "No, her neck is fine. I don't think anything is broken. Her pulse is a little fast, but she's just been knocked unconscious by the fall."

"Are you sure?"

"Quite sure. I'll take her in the house. You bring the other children."

Uncle Philip gathered Olivia, unconscious, into his strong arms and carried her toward the house.

"Please, God," Lizzie said as the tears began to come, "please let Olivia be all right."

By the time Uncle Philip laid Olivia on a quilt in front of the fire, she was beginning to moan. The whole family was gathered around.

"What. . .happened?" Olivia asked weakly as her eyes fluttered open.

"You took a spill in the snow," Uncle Philip said.

Olivia smiled. "I went down the hill by myself."

"Yes, you did," her uncle said softly.

Constance Murray pushed past her brother to check on her daughter for herself. "We'll talk about that later, Olivia," she said sternly. But her voice also held relief.

Across the room, Lizzie leaned against the wall with her own relief. Olivia could have been seriously hurt, but all she cared about was that she had gone down the hill by herself. Yes, Olivia was all right.

"She'll be fine, Lizzie." Aunt Johanna had come to stand beside her.

Lizzie nodded. "I know." She sighed. "I should have been watching her more carefully."

"No one is blaming you for the accident."

"I should have known she would try something like this," Lizzie insisted. "She's been like this since she was a baby. She has no sense of what might be dangerous."

"Lizzie, you cannot watch everyone every minute of every day."

Lizzie choked back a sob. "I know—especially not Olivia. She gets into too many things."

"That's right." Aunt Johanna chuckled. "She's a very determined child. But you must realize that this was simply a childhood accident. It could have happened to any of the children."

Lizzie glanced at the other children gathered around Olivia. Charity and Christopher were teasing her. And Olivia was already planning her next attack on the hill.

"As I recall," Aunt Johanna said, "something like this happened to you when you were younger."

Lizzie smiled through her tears and nodded. "When I was five, I made wings out of paper from Papa's shop and thought I could fly. I nearly broke my arm when I jumped off a stack of papers in the back of the cart." She shivered. She had not even noticed that she was cold.

"That's right," Aunt Johanna said. "Now, why don't you take that wet cloak off? You're dripping all over the floor."

Lizzie surrendered to her aunt's attempt to remove the soaked clothing. "Aunt Johanna, in a way I'm glad this happened."

Her aunt raised her eyebrows.

"I've been so worried," Lizzie explained, "that Joshua would get hurt, or someone would get angry at Papa for what he prints, or that there would be a war. You kept telling me that God is in charge of all those things."

"That's right," Aunt Johanna said, not quite understanding what Lizzie was getting at.

"Olivia could have been badly hurt, and it had nothing to do with the stamp tax or Parliament or anything. It was just a sled ride. God is in charge of things like that, too."

Aunt Johanna smiled.

"This doesn't mean that we shouldn't be sensible," Lizzie went on seriously. "I shouldn't have jumped off that cart, and Olivia shouldn't have gone down that hill. And I still think that Joshua should stay away from the riots," Lizzie said emphatically. "But no matter what happens, God cares about us. And that's what matters most of all."

Lizzie shuddered and wrapped her arms around herself. "I guess I got wetter than I realized. I think I'll go change my clothes."

And she left her aunt standing in the hall with a satisfied smile on her face.

Victory!

Spring came sweetly in 1766. The rumblings of the Patriots and the retorts of the Loyalists did not interrupt nature's rhythm. The winds warmed, the rains came, the trees budded, and the hills and meadows around Boston were lush and thick once again.

Joshua and Lizzie sat next to each other on the seat in front of the cart on an afternoon in the middle of May. They did not talk. They had finished their rounds with the afternoon's papers, and they were hungry and tired. Their last stop would be back at the print shop to pick up their father and go home for supper.

Lizzie was thirteen now, almost fourteen, and Joshua had passed his sixteenth birthday. Brother and sister did not always agree with each other, but they understood each other well. Joshua respected his parents. He would never do something that he knew would hurt any of his relatives. Lizzie was certain of that. But his decisions were his own now. Somehow the stamp tax controversy had moved Joshua from boyhood to manhood.

Lizzie had watched the gulf between her and her brother widen and wondered if she and Joshua would ever find their way back to each other.

Lizzie no longer yearned for life to go back to the way it was before Parliament began imposing so many restrictions on the colonies. She felt better now than she had a year ago. She was still not sure that she agreed with Joshua's choice of friends. In the last two years, she had witnessed people doing many wild things. But she knew Joshua was right about one thing: Change was coming, and no one would be able to stop it—not even the king of England himself.

Merry trotted along steadily, just as she had for many years. Lizzie swayed with the rhythmic *clip-clop, clip-clop*. Merry was a good horse, a calm, gentle, reliable work partner. With sadness in her heart, Lizzie calculated the mare's age. Even Merry would not be with them much longer. Her father had already remarked several times that they ought to be looking around for another work animal and let Merry live out her old age in peace.

Joshua halted the cart. They were back at the shop. No doubt their father would be wiping down the counters one last time before locking up. The day's work was done for all of them. They would soon relish some rest and nourishment in the family home.

Lizzie pushed the door open and the bell tinkled.

"Papa? Are you ready?"

"I'll just be a minute. Did you have any trouble today?" Duncan Murray had asked his daughter that question every day for months—ever since her encounter with Daniel Taylor during the route so many months ago.

"No, Papa. Everything was fine."

The bell tinkled again and Lizzie turned, expecting to see Joshua impatient to go home. Instead it was her uncle Blake, with Joshua right behind him.

"We did it!" shouted Joshua gleefully. He pushed past his uncle and grabbed Lizzie's hands, pulling her off balance.

"Did what?" Lizzie asked. She broke from Joshua and steadied herself against the counter.

"What has happened?" Papa asked, tossing aside his rag.

Blake slapped the back of a chair happily. "I've just come from the harbor. A boat came in from England today. The word is that King George has repealed the Stamp Act. He did it on March 18, and Parliament voted to approve it. But the letter only came today."

Joshua clucked his tongue. "I wish there were a faster way to exchange information between England and America."

"Are you sure?" Papa pressed.

"Absolutely! I saw the letter myself."

"Isn't this incredible?" said Joshua, nearly dancing around the room. Lizzie stepped out of his way. "We've done it, we've done it. The congress worked!"

"Lizzie, quick!" Papa said. "We'll do a special announcement and get it out on the streets tonight. Get the letter trays out."

Lizzie flew into action. Her father had just finished cleaning up the day's work. Everything was neatly put away. A moment ago they were ready to go home for supper. But everything had changed in that moment.

"What will the headline be, Papa?" she asked as she pulled

out a tray of headline letters.

"King Repeals Stamp Act!" Papa answered.

"No," said Joshua. "Americans Defeat King!"

Papa laughed. "All right, Joshua, have it your way."

"What about supper?" Lizzie asked as she picked out the letters to spell *Americans*. "Mama is expecting us home any minute."

Papa turned to Uncle Blake and raised his eyebrows.

"Don't worry," Uncle Blake said, grinning. "I'll go by the house and tell her the news myself."

"Thank you, Blake. We may not be home for several more hours."

"Before I leave, I must tell you one more thing."

"What's that?"

"Along with the letter of repeal came a new act from Parliament."

Joshua groaned. "Have they learned nothing?"

Uncle Blake shook his head. "Apparently not. This one is called the Declaratory Act."

"What does it say?"

"It asserts Britain's ownership and control over the colonies. I can promise you that Sam Adams and James Otis are not going to like it."

"The work of the Sons of Liberty is not over," Joshua declared. "It's just beginning."

"Can you get us a copy of the act?" Papa asked Uncle Blake.

"I'm sure I can. After I see Constance, I'll run back over to the harbor."

"We greatly appreciate your help, Blake."

"I'll be back as soon as I can." And Uncle Blake was gone.

Papa rubbed his hands together energetically. "Let's get to work! Joshua, get the press ready. Use fresh ink. Lizzie, let's decide what this announcement should say."

"Papa, you relax. Let us do this," Joshua said. "We know what to do."

Lizzie watched the exchange between her father and her brother. Joshua was serious. He wanted the responsibility of getting out this special edition. Papa studied his son's expression for a moment, then nodded.

"All right. You write up the story and let me check it. Then I'll help Lizzie with the typesetting, and you can print it."

"Papa, thank you! You can trust me."

"I can see everything is in good hands," Papa said. "I believe I'll use this opportunity to catch up on some accounts in the back room."

When their father was gone, Joshua grinned at Lizzie.

"I'm glad you got what you wanted," she said.

"It's not just what I wanted," he corrected. "It's what is best for the colonies—for America."

"The way you say that, it sounds as if you think of the colonies as a separate country."

Joshua nodded. "There are some who think that way. But the Declaratory Act means that there is still a lot of work ahead of us if we are to make Parliament see things from our point of view." He picked up a quill and dipped it in ink. "Enough chatter. I must write my story."

Lizzie smiled at his seriousness as he began to scratch on the paper. He was not imitating anyone. This was Joshua being himself, working hard on something he believed in.

Joshua was probably right. Change was coming. The colonies and Britain would have to establish a new relationship. The change would affect even ordinary people on both sides of the Atlantic.

Lizzie found the last letter of her headline: AMERICANS DEFEAT KING! As she read the words, spelled out in front of her on the counter, she felt their impact. The Loyalists in Boston would not like this headline. But Lizzie did. It put words on the fire she had seen glowing in her brother's eyes.

Lizzie Murray was ready to face the change. And she and Joshua would find their bond once again.

American Dream
Bonus Educational Material

SARAH'S NEW WORLD:
THE MAYFLOWER ADVENTURE

VOCABULARY WORDS

bushel—a unit of measure for grain, fruit, and other food items
*"Well, we have most of the dried goods taken care of. There are thirty-two **bushels** of meal and eight **bushels** each of dried peas and oatmeal for the four of us."*

buccaneers, freebooters, and **sea rovers**—other names for pirates
*Names like **buccaneers, freebooters,** and **sea rovers** danced in John's head.*

calloused—being hardened and thickened
*Klaus reached out a **calloused** hand, as if to touch her hair, then snatched it back.*

cooper—a person who makes and repairs wooden barrels and tubs
*"I've been working here in Southampton as a **cooper**, making tubs and casks."*

culprit—someone accused of or guilty of a crime
*Loud wails soon showed that the **culprit** was being punished for the latest of his sins.*

currant—a type of small, seedless raisin
*"Fresh fruit won't last long," Mother continued to explain, "so we're packing dried prunes, raisins, and **currants**."*

horizon—the line where the earth and sky appear to meet
*"This is more like it," John told Sarah, watching the sun set in a fiery splash on the ocean **horizon**.*

landlubber—a person who is not familiar with the sea or sailing
*"I wish Klaus would stay with us, but he probably wouldn't make a very good **landlubber**."*

lanky—tall and thin
*John Robinson lifted his arm, and the **lanky** boy shot off faster than an arrow from a strong bow.*

loom—a frame for weaving thread or yarn into fabric
*She patted a low stool next to the **loom** where she sat weaving.*

lout—a rough or crude person
*"Unhand my son, you miserable **lout**!"*

persecute—to cause to suffer, especially because of religious or political beliefs
*"There are no kings to say we cannot take game from the forest. There are no kings to tax us and **persecute** us. Mother, we will be free."*

provisions—needed materials and supplies
*They found Sarah and Mother going over a stack of labeled **provisions**.*

scowl—a frown that makes a bad-tempered or threatening look on a person's face
*Klaus either ignored them or grunted. He continued to **scowl**.*

seize—to take control of suddenly or by force
*"If you join that treasonous, despised group, the king's tax collectors will surely **seize** your land."*

shallop—a small boat used in shallow waters
*A few slept in a small **shallop** that would be used to explore the rivers of the New World.*

talebearing—spreading gossip or rumors
*Mother frowned on **talebearing**. Unless something was absolutely true, their children were not to repeat it.*

treason—the betrayal of a trust, especially to a person's own country
*Such talk was **treason**, and some of the London Strangers loyally followed the king and the Church of England.*

voyage—a long journey, especially by water, air, or in space
*Preparations for the **voyage** went steadily forward, although the number of people who agreed to sail continued to drop.*

wharf—a structure built for ships to move alongside to load and unload cargo and passengers

One day, John was returning from the **wharf** *when he came upon a group of people surrounding William Bradford.*

IMPORTANT PEOPLE AND THINGS AROUND 1620

William Bradford

William Bradford was born in Yorkshire, England, in 1590. He joined the religious group called the Separatists, now known as the Pilgrims, when he was seventeen years old and fled with them to Leiden, Holland, to escape religious persecution in England. Later he helped lead the Pilgrims' journey to America on board the *Mayflower* in 1620, in search of true religious freedom. He survived the journey and helped set up the **Plymouth Colony**. William served as governor of Plymouth for thirty-five years after the first governor, John Carver, died in 1621. In the fall of 1621, William declared a celebration to honor the Pilgrim's first harvest in the New World of America. Their first winter had been hard, and they would not have survived if the Native American Wampanoags had not helped them. William invited the chief of the Wampanoags, Chief Massasoit, and his people to join the pilgrims in their feast, and this event is known as the first Thanksgiving Day celebration. Bradford died in 1657.

John Smith

John Smith, born around 1579, was an English colonizer who helped found the permanent English settlement in America at Jamestown, Virginia, in 1607. John was born in Willoughby, Lincolnshire, and worked there on his father's farm until he left home as a teenager to become a soldier. He traveled Europe and fought in Hungary against the Turks, who captured him and sold him into slavery until he later escaped. By 1604, he had returned to England and become a member of the London Colony Council, and by 1606, he set sail with a colonial expedition to America. The expedition founded the settlement of Jamestown, Virginia, in May 1607 and chose John as president in 1608. He organized trade with the Native Americans, helped build houses, and made river voyages that allowed him to make the first accurate maps of Virginia. On one of these voyages, Native Americans captured him and according to legend nearly put him to death, but he was saved by the chief's daughter, Pocahontas.

Sir Walter Raleigh and the Lost Colony

Sir Walter Raleigh, born in the early 1550s, was an English adventurer, writer, and explorer of the Americas. He became interested in the New World when he sailed to America in 1578. In 1585 and again in 1587, Raleigh tried to found the first English settlement in America on Roanoke Island, but the settlement failed. One colonist left Roanoke to get supplies in Europe, and when he returned, the colonists were gone and so were their houses. All he found were the letters *CRO* carved in a tree by the beach and the word *Croatan* carved on a post. No one knows exactly what happened to the "Lost Colony" at Roanoke Island—some say disease, Native Americans, or a hurricane killed the colonists, but no evidence that they actually died has ever been found. Many believe they left the colony with friendly Croatan Native Americans. Another theory is that the colonists suffered from severe food shortages because the study of growth rings from nearby cypress trees suggests that the colonists disappeared during one of the worst droughts in the last eight hundred years.

Plymouth Colony

The Pilgrims set sail on the *Mayflower* September 16, 1620, from the English port of Plymouth—for which they would later name their new settlement in America. Two months later, they made it to the coast of America, but farther north than they had hoped to land. The Pilgrims arrived at Cape Cod, where a small group of them landed to search for a good site for their settlement. They found the Plymouth area on December 21, and the rest of the Pilgrims who had stayed onboard the *Mayflower* came ashore at Plymouth Rock on December 26, 1620. Before they went ashore, the Pilgrims created the Mayflower Compact, a document in which they promised loyalty to each other and pledged to work together in the new colony. As the Pilgrims began to settle their new colony, they depended on the Native American Wampanoags, who showed them how to grow corn and hunt for food. After their first successful harvest in the Plymouth Colony, the Pilgrims' governor, William Bradford, organized the first Thanksgiving Day celebration and invited the Wampanoags to join them in thanking God for their success. The success of the Plymouth Colony encouraged more settlement in America, and in 1691, it united with other New England colonies to form the Massachusetts Bay Colony.

HISTORY IN PERSPECTIVE TIMELINE

May 14, 1607—Jamestown, Virginia, the first permanent English settlement, is founded.

1608—Dutch scientist Hans Lippershey is said to invent the first telescope.

1610—Henry Hudson discovers Hudson Bay.

September 16, 1620—The *Mayflower* sets sail from Plymouth, England.

December 26, 1620—The Pilgrims come ashore in America at Plymouth Rock.

Fall 1621—The Pilgrims and Native Americans celebrate the first Thanksgiving Day together.

1626—City of New Amsterdam, now New York City, is founded.

1636—Harvard College is founded in Cambridge, Massachusetts.

1638—The log cabin is introduced to America by Swedish colonists of Delaware.

1642—French inventor Blaise Pascal invents the first mechanical adding machine.

Rebekah in Danger:
Peril at Plymouth Colony

Vocabulary Words

ambassador—an official representative of one government to another government
*In desperation, two **ambassadors** were chosen to go see Massasoit and ask him to call a halt to the frequent visits.*

boatswain (pronounced BO-zun)—an officer on a boat who is in charge of hull maintenance
*"Remember the **boatswain** who never missed a chance to curse us and tell us how worthless we are?"*

cloak—a loose-fitting outer garment, similar to a cape
*Then she snuggled her wool **cloak** more tightly around her shoulders and wrapped her arms around her knees.*

cooper—someone who makes wooden casks or barrels
*John Alden continued his **cooper** business.*

foreboding—a feeling that something bad is about to happen
*She disappeared up the ladder to the upper deck. Rebekah waited, her blanket clutched around her against the morning chill, her heart pounding with a terrible **foreboding**.*

habitation—the act of living in a particular place
*"We saw no signs of **habitation**."*

heathen—someone who does not acknowledge God of the Bible
*"You sound like a **heathen**."*

maize—another name for corn, especially that grown by Native Americans
*"I asked Squanto how he knew the very best time to plant **maize** and the seed we brought with us," Will explained.*

musket—an early, large caliber, muzzle-loading gun
*"I know you're almost a man, but you don't know how to fire a **musket**."*

pagan—something or someone with no religious basis
*The Pilgrims considered Christmas a **pagan** holiday and did not celebrate it, but the others on ship had a small feast which they invited the Pilgrims to share.*

pallet—a small, hard bed
*Will, who had wearily dropped to a **pallet** on the floor, sat up straight.*

plague—a bacterial disease, often spread by rats, that causes severe illness and sometimes death
*"**Plague** took him, as it has taken many others and will take more."*

scurvy—a nutritional disease caused by a lack of vitamin C, characterized by loose teeth and spongy gums
*"When Mother and I aren't cooking and washing and mending clothing for our own family, we help those who are too sick from **scurvy** and pneumonia to take care of their families."*

sentry—a soldier who stands guard over something
*With hurried steps, she headed toward the **sentry**.*

Separatists—a group of people who broke away from the Church of England rather than attempt to change it
*Her parents and the other **Separatists** had come to Holland so they could worship God the way they wanted, without the king forcing them to meet secretly.*

shallop—a small, open rowboat that is used mostly in shallow water
*Meanwhile, carpenters examined pieces of the damaged **shallop**.*

stockade—an enclosure made with posts and stakes
*A sturdy **stockade** surrounded it.*

succotash—a dish made of beans and corn
*"If I never see a dish of **succotash** again it will be all right with me."*

treaty—an agreement, usually in writing, that ends a conflict
*At last, they made a **treaty**.*

tuberculosis—a serious lung disease
*"We don't intend to get your **tuberculosis** and pneumonia."*

whelp—a young dog, sometimes used as a term of disrespect for a human child
*"Quiet, **whelp**!" Standish roared.*

woebegone—expressing sorrow or misery
*"Here." Rebekah scrambled out from between the chicken coops and lifted her **woebegone** face to her brother.*

IMPORTANT PEOPLE AND THINGS AROUND 1624

Wampanoag Indians

The Wampanoags, sometimes called the Pokanokets after their primary village, were a confederation of tribes that stretched from Rhode Island into Massachusetts and up to New York. Two Wampanoags, Squanto and Samoset, were sent by tribal leader Massasoit to help the **Pilgrims** in Plymouth Colony, Massachusetts. They taught the Pilgrims how to grow the crops that would provide them with the food they would need. Although Massasoit was friendly to the colonists, his son, Metacom (Philip), was the central figure in the deadliest war the Wampanoags would have with the colonists. Conflicts over land sales and the murder of a Christian Native American informant by Wampanoags (of which Metacom was suspected of planning) led to King Philip's War in 1675. The English won, and the Wampanoags were almost wiped out. In 1990, however, there were more than two thousand Wampanoags in the United States, most living in Massachusetts.

Myles Standish

Myles Standish was born in 1584, but it is unclear exactly where. His family was very well known in England, and Myles began a distinguished career in the military after being disinherited. Standish began his career as a drummer, but he rose through the ranks of Queen Elizabeth I's army. The **Pilgrims** hired him to be their military advisor, and he led the first group of men to go ashore when the colonists reached New England. As the military leader, Standish defended Plymouth Colony when there were problems with the Native Americans. Standish served as the colony's representative in England and was the assistant governor and treasurer of the colony from 1644 until 1649. Myles Standish died October 3, 1656, in Duxbury, Massachusetts, a town he helped to establish.

William Bradford

William Bradford was born in Yorkshire, England, in 1590. Both of his parents died when William was a small child, and he was passed from family member to family member. By the age of seventeen, William was closely associated with the Separatist movement in England. When that group sailed for the Netherlands, William went with them. They stayed for twelve years, and he supported himself in the textile industry. When the **Pilgrims** made plans to leave the Netherlands and journey to America, William Bradford was instrumental in the organization of the trek. When the Separatists left the Netherlands, first for England and then for America in 1620, William Bradford was one of the 102 people on board the Mayflower. In 1621, he became the governor of the colony. He died at Plymouth Colony on May 9, 1657.

Pilgrims

The Pilgrims were a group of English Separatists who wanted to practice their religion freely and to live under their own laws. They did not want to break away from England, but neither did they want to be a part of the Church of England. When King James I began harassing the Separatists with threats of imprisonment, some of them fled to the Netherlands. They lived there peacefully for twelve years. When the Dutch government, pressured by England, began to make life difficult for the Separatists, about half of them sailed to Southampton, England, where they boarded the Mayflower and set sail for America on September 16, 1620. Their original landing site was in northern Virginia, where they had received the deed to land owned by members of **William Bradford's** family, but weather sent them off course and they landed in Cape Cod sixty-five days later. Eventually, the Pilgrims settled in present-day Provincetown, Massachusetts. Because they had no authority to be there, the Pilgrims drew up the Mayflower Compact, in which they agreed to be a self-governing colony. The Pilgrims were not as rigid as one may be led to believe from stories and pictures in modern books. Although they wanted to stamp out sin in their colony, they did allow drinking, although not to the point of drunkenness. Instead of the black and white outfits most pictures show, the Pilgrims often wore brightly colored clothing.

HISTORY IN PERSPECTIVE TIMELINE

October 12, 1609—"Three Blind Mice" is published in London by Thomas Ravenscroft, a teenage songwriter.

April 5, 1614—Native American Pocahontas marries English colonist John Rolfe in Virginia.

January 1, 1622—In the Gregorian calendar, the one used by most of the Western world, January 1 becomes the first day of the year, rather than March 25.

March 22, 1622—Algonquin Indians kill approximately 347 English settlers in the Jamestown Massacre.

1623—Wilhelm Schickard invents the "Counting Clock," an early mechanical calculator.

September 6, 1628—Puritans settle in Salem, which will become part of the Massachusetts Bay Colony.

February 22, 1630—The Native American Quadequine introduces popcorn to the English colonists.

September 8, 1636—Harvard College is established in the Massachusetts Bay Colony. It is the first colony founded in the Americas.

1639—The first printing press in North America is started in Cambridge, Massachusetts.

1640—The Bay Psalm Book is the first book printed in North America, in Cambridge, Massachusetts. It remained in use for more than one hundred years.

MAGGIE'S DARE: THE GREAT AWAKENING

VOCABULARY WORDS

alcove—a recess in the wall of a room
*They scurried down the long hall into an **alcove**, which opened into the spacious, sunny nursery.*

charlatans—people who falsely claim to be experts at something
*"They are all **charlatans**, you see, causing disorder."*

countenance—someone's face or facial expression
*There was no denying the change in this lady's **countenance**, and her voice fairly bubbled over with joy and excitement.*

decorum—the correctness that is socially expected
*But at age twelve, she was expected to use **decorum** befitting a lady.*

fervor—extreme level of emotion or belief
*"The **fervor** for God is there, and we see genuine conversions among common folk of the city."*

grippe—another term for influenza, flu
*"I've been at the Winthrops' this evening, and Celia has the **grippe**."*

heathenistic—an offensive term used to describe someone acting in a manner that does not acknowledge God or a major religion
*"I can tell you one thing," Adelaide said. "You'll never catch me going near one of their wild, **heathenistic** meetings."*

high tea—a late afternoon meal consisting of a cooked dish (usually hot) served with bread and butter, cakes, and tea
*Following the launch, she would be a guest for **high tea** at the Chilton home, and Celia would be there, as well.*

incredulous—unable or unwilling to believe something
*Presently, Adelaide was standing **incredulous** in the room, followed quickly by Nelda, Julia, and their parents.*

infamous—well-known for a bad reason
*The **infamous** revivalist, Jonathan Edwards! Right in their house!*

itinerant—someone who moves from place to place, especially to find work
*"They follow the **itinerant** preachers, Maggie."*

livery—a uniform
*When Hannah opened the door, there stood one of the Chiltons' footmen, arrayed in his bright green-and-gold **livery**.*

ominous—threatening
*"This must not be an **ominous** occasion," he said as he pulled a chair nearer to his writing desk and waved her toward it. "Your face is cheery, and all the freckles seem to be glowing at one time."*

paltry—an insignificant amount of something
*But even as she made her decision, she wondered how her **paltry** efforts could ever make a difference.*

psalters—books containing psalms, or the book of Psalms
*The congregation brought out their **psalters** as they sang psalms together in lovely harmony.*

quaint—having an old-fashioned quality
*When Maggie was a little girl, she'd loved all Hannah's **quaint** sayings.*

riled—made angry or irritated
*Judith gave the impression of being the perfect mother, never getting **riled** or speaking a cross word.*

sublime—awe-inspiringly beautiful
*Adelaide leaped to her feet and spun about. "How **sublime**. A ball!"*

sullen—showing a bad temper by a refusal to talk or to be sociable or cheerful
*"Yes, ma'am," she answered, her voice **sullen**.*

tricorn—a three-cornered hat
*The same gold braid was repeated on his cocked **tricorn** hat.*

vile—something extremely unpleasant to experience
*"Really, it's quite **vile**," Celia said, as she tried to catch her breath.*

IMPORTANT PEOPLE AND THINGS OF ~~1744~~ 1722

Jonathan Edwards

Jonathan Edwards was born on October 5, 1703 in East Windsor, Connecticut. His family was Puritan. As a student, Edwards learned about the latest trends in philosophy coming from Europe and the debates between the Puritanism of his childhood and the new ways of movements. In 1726, Edwards followed his grandfather, Solomon Stoddard, as the pastor of Northampton, Massachusetts, the largest church outside of Boston.

In 1750, the Northampton Church dismissed him when he tried to make it more difficult for congregants to receive the sacraments. From there he went to Stockbridge, Massachusetts, where he served a small church and was the missionary to some Mohawk families. In late 1757, he accepted the presidency of the College of New Jersey (now Princeton University). He died on March 22, 1758, of complications from a smallpox inoculation.

Edwards's religious beliefs emphasized the sovereignty of God, the immorality of humankind, the reality of hell, and the need for "New Birth" as a sign of acceptance of Jesus Christ. His writings on signs of sainthood and false beliefs were highly influential, including in the field of psychology. Some have called him the first American philosopher.

Joshua Gee

Joshua Gee was born in Boston, Massachusetts, on June 29, 1698. He graduated from Harvard in 1717. In 1723, he was ordained as the pastor of the Old North Church in Boston. He served with Cotton Mather until Mather's death in 1728. Gee served the Old North Church until his death on May 22, 1748.

On July 7, 1743, Gee attended a conference of clergymen to discuss the progress of religion in America. After the conference, he complained to the conference leader that most of the clergy who attended were wrong in their beliefs about salvation and faith.

Some scholars claim that, although Gee was well educated and had great reasoning ability, he was a lazy intellect, making no real effort to change things.

The Revivalist Movement

Also called the Great Awakening, the Revivalist Movement was a populist (rather than upper-class) religious movement of the early 1740s. It extended throughout all of the colonies, including Georgia. Historians consider it the first mass movement in American history.

Due to societal influences such as the Enlightenment, religious fervor had been in decline for many years. Although revivals had been held on the local level under the control of the local minister, the Revivalist Movement saw the birth of the traveling minister, going from place to place to preach for a short period of time. The Reverend Jonathan Edwards was the first to bring the colonial Protestants to a "reawakening" of God, with English preacher George Whitefield continuing the movement.

In these revivalist meetings, services were held outside, and music played a large part in the service. The sermons featured highly emotional language, and often the result was physical responses, such as weeping, shouting, and wild movements, among those in attendance. Many of the traditional clergy saw these services as the work of the devil.

The Revivalist Movement influenced more than religious services. The rhythm of the revivalists can be seen in the work of later poets such as Emily Dickinson, and the movement influenced the social consciousness of America as well. Preacher Henry Ward Beecher used the crowds at his revivals to support abolition, universal suffrage, and other social causes.

History in Perspective Timeline

1740–1748—War of Austrian Succession; some battles take place on the North American continent.

1741—William Browning invents mineral water.

December 25, 1741—Anders Celsius develops his own thermometer scale, Celsius. He dies on April 25, 1744.

April 8, 1742—The first performance of George Frideric Handel's oratorio *The Messiah* occurs in Dublin, Ireland.

April 13, 1743—Thomas Jefferson, the third U.S. president, is born.

September 13, 1743—The Treaty of Worms is signed between Great Britain, Austria, and Sardinia.

November 11, 1744—Abigail Smith, future wife of second U.S. president John Adams and mother of sixth president John Quincy Adams, is born in Massachusetts.

October 22, 1746—The College of New Jersey (now Princeton University) is founded.

1750—Joseph Hanway is the first Englishman to use an umbrella.

January 1, 1752—Betsy Ross is born.

February 11, 1752—Pennsylvania Hospital, the first hospital in the United States, opens.

June 15, 1752—Benjamin Franklin proves that lightning is electricity.

January 1, 1753—Britain and her colonies agree that January 1 should be New Year's Day to reflect the adoption of the Gregorian calendar in September 1752.

LIZZIE AND THE REDCOAT: STIRRINGS OF REVOLUTION IN THE AMERICAN COLONIES

VOCABULARY WORDS

bickering—fighting or arguing
*"Parliament and the colonies cannot continue this **bickering** for much longer without consequences."*

contrary—acting stubbornly or having a stubborn attitude against something
*"Don't be so **contrary**. It is not becoming to a young lady."*

controversy—a debate or fight over different opinions
*Lizzie was glad Olivia was too young to get involved in the **controversy** between England and the colonies.*

converge—to come together in the same place
*The three of them **converged** on the front door, competing to be the one to pull it open and reveal the source of the ruckus.*

effigy—an image or model, especially of a person and often used for making fun of the person
*"He was there last night and saw the whole thing. He even got to carry the **effigy** for part of the time."*

evading—getting out of doing something
*"The customs agent thinks Blake is **evading** the required taxes on goods for the business."*

formalities—the usual rules for being polite or following tradition
*They would make a complete report later, but the townspeople would not wait for **formalities**.*

frenzy—a fit of extreme, sometimes violent, excitement or activity
*"The indignation may be just; the **frenzy** is not."*

haggard—having an exhausted look
*Although they had cleaned up a bit, they were **haggard**, and their clothing was not on quite straight.*

indignation—anger that is caused by something that is unfair
*"He was right when he said that simple **indignation** could touch off an uncontrolled emotional frenzy."*

lobsterback—a disrespectful name that colonists called British soldiers because of the bright red coats of their uniforms
*"Especially not for a British soldier," Joshua blurted out. "I'll not have my brother's and sisters' food cut back so that a **lobsterback** can eat well."*

mesmerize—to fascinate and hold someone's attention
*It snapped and crackled, **mesmerizing** Lizzie.*

phaeton—a type of four-wheeled horse-drawn carriage
*Blake had expanded the company—and the name— after several years, adding newer models of carriages like the **phaeton** and the landau.*

landau—a four-wheeled carriage with a top in two sections that can be folded away or taken off and with a raised seat outside for the driver
*Blake had expanded the company—and the name—after several years, adding newer models of carriages like the phaeton and the **landau**.*

reckon—to deal with
"No matter what you think of him," Papa said, *"he is a man to be* **reckoned** *with."*

ridicule—to make fun of
"I would suggest you take that smirk off your face, Mr. Wallace. I do not take kindly to being **ridiculed.**"

ruckus—a noisy disturbance
The disagreements between her father and her brother were almost as difficult to listen to as the **ruckus** *outside.*

smirk—a know-it-all smile
"I would suggest you take that **smirk** *off your face, Mr. Wallace. I do not take kindly to being ridiculed."*

smuggling—bringing something into or out of a country without obeying the laws
"I've heard a lot of rumors about **smuggling** *lately. Papa even has a story about it in the newspaper."*

treasury—the money or wealth of a government
They were standing guard outside the Customs House, the brick building where the king's **treasury** *in Boston was kept.*

Samuel Adams

Samuel Adams was born September 27, 1722, in Boston, Massachusetts. After earning his Master of Arts degree from Harvard College in 1743, he entered private business as a clerk. He later joined his father's business, but eventually lost all the money his father had given him. When his business failed, he became a full-time politician, and was elected to the Massachusetts legislature in 1766. Adams was a vocal opponent of the Stamp Act and other taxes that the British government placed on the colonists. He helped organize the **Sons of Liberty** and was a participant in the Boston Tea Party. Adams was a member of the first and second **Continental Congress**es, and was governor of Massachusetts from 1793 until 1797. His cousin, John Adams, would become the second president of the United States. Samuel Adams died October 2, 1803.

James Otis

James Otis was a lawyer and important leader in the politics leading up to the Revolutionary War. He was born in 1725 in Massachusetts and graduated from Harvard College in 1743. His wife was Ruth and they had three children. In 1761 James Otis began challenging British authority by arguing boldly against the writs of assistance, which were search warrants that would allow British authorities to enter any colonist's home at any time without giving a reason. Soon after this, he was elected to the Massachusetts House of Representatives and wrote several important patriotic pamphlets during his life. James Otis is given credit for the phrase, "Taxation without representation is tyranny." He died in 1783 after being struck by lightning.

The Quartering Act of 1765

The Quartering Act of 1765 was passed by British Parliament and forced colonial authorities in America to give British soldiers stationed in their towns places to stay, food to eat, and transportation. It gave specific instructions about where to house soldiers if barracks were not available, such as in local inns, stables, and ale houses, and if those were filled then any empty houses, outhouses, barns or other buildings had to be fixed up for the soldiers. The

Quartering Act affected colonists in New York most of all, and after much rebellion against it, it was finally allowed to expire in 1770.

The Sugar Act
The Sugar Act was a law passed by British Parliament on April 5, 1764, to try to end the smuggling of sugar and molasses into the American colonies from the West Indies and to raise more money for the British government. It reduced the previous tax on molasses but it also created new taxes on foreign foods such as sugar and coffee and it regulated the export of lumber and iron. These new taxes and regulations increased the anger of many colonists under British rule and helped fuel the rebellion that led to the Revolutionary War.

History in Perspective Timeline

1760—A Belgian man named Joseph Merlin creates the first known roller skates.

January 1, 1764—Eight-year-old musician and composer Wolfgang Amadeus Mozart plays for the Royal Family at Versailles in France.

May 24, 1764—Boston lawyer James Otis denounces "taxation without representation" and calls for the colonies to join together in opposing Britain's new tax measures.

June 7, 1767—Daniel Boone begins exploring present-day Kentucky.

October 18, 1767—The famous Mason-Dixon line, the boundary between Maryland and Pennsylvania, is set.

August 26, 1768—Captain James Cook begins his first voyage on the *Endeavor* in the South Pacific Ocean to eventually find present day Australia and New Zealand.

June 17, 1775—The deadliest battle of the Revolutionary War, the Battle at Bunker Hill, is fought near Boston.

July 4, 1776—The Declaration of Independence is adopted by the Second Continental Congress in America, and on **September 9, 1776**, the nation is officially renamed the "Unites States of America" rather than the "United Colonies."

December 18, 1777—The United States celebrates its first national day of Thanksgiving.

1783—The fighting of the Revolutionary War ends early in the year, and the war officially ends with the signing of the Treaty of Paris on **September 3, 1783**.

If you enjoyed
American Dream
be sure to read

American Challenge

Girls are girls wherever they live—and the Sisters in Time series shows that girls are girls whenever they lived, too! This new collection brings together four historical fiction books for 8–12-year-old girls: Lydia the Patriot: The Boston Massacre (covering the year 1770), Kate and the Spies: The American Revolution (1775), Betsy's River Adventure: The Journey Westward (1808), and Grace and the Bully: Drought on the Frontier (1819), *American Challenge* will transport readers back to the formative years of our nation, teaching important lessons of history and Christian faith.